LO

'You're such *a baby* about love sometimes. Harry's a good man. They're hard to find.'

'Tell me about it,' Martha said, looking up from the sugar with a tight, uncomfortable smile. 'Anyway, what about me? I'm a good woman too. Good and ready for some fun.'

He gave her an odd look. 'It's a dangerous thing, fun.'

She wrinkled her nose thoughtfully, dropped a sugar lump into the remains of her coffee and crushed it viciously under her spoon. 'Yes, well, danger's a fun thing sometimes, too.' Suddenly her frown dissolved into a smile, wide, pink and voluptuous. 'If only I could bloody well find some.'

He did not return the smile but gazed at her thoughtfully for a moment. 'You will,' he said. 'You will.'

SALLY BRAMPTON

L♡vesick

Mandarin

A Mandarin Paperback
LOVESICK

First published in Great Britain 1995
by William Heinemann Ltd
and Mandarin Paperbacks
imprints of Reed Consumer Books Ltd
Michelin House, 81 Fulham Road, London SW3 6RB
and Auckland, Melbourne, Singapore and Toronto

Copyright © Sally Brampton 1995
The author has asserted her moral rights

A CIP catalogue record for this title
is available from the British Library
ISBN 0 7493 1898 8

Printed and bound in Great Britain
by Cox & Wyman, Reading, Berkshire

For J.P.

1

Something bad happened to Martha. What it was, Phil won't say.

And as for Harry, why, he never even mentions her name. He's never been much of a talker, he's slow to answer at the best of times, and he has these deep, sunken eyes with tremendously hooded lids which make him look half asleep even though he's wide awake. People who don't know him well have been known to walk out on him in mid-conversation, but if you're patient he does eventually answer.

Except when I ask him about Martha, and then his eyes droop so badly it's as if the effort of remembering exhausts him and the words are like weights in his mouth.

It used to drive me mad, even though Phil explained that it wasn't his fault. 'It's got nothing to do with you,' she said, rather shortly, when I complained about Harry's tendency to drop off on me. Then she sighed. 'Look, some people shout when they're upset, other people cry. Harry goes to sleep. That's all.'

One day, when I'd been pestering him too much with questions and his answers came slower and slower until I thought him asleep, he said, 'She's gone and now we must live as best we can.' I nearly jumped out of my skin, but it wasn't that which made my heart go cold. It was his voice, so slow and tired and cracked with misery. Even Harry's best, I thought, is nowhere near good enough.

That slow, painful weariness, though, is nowhere near as bad as one of Harry's smiles. 'The future's the thing,' he says, with a terrible, bright look. You can always tell when Harry's lying. He smiles that awful smile. Well, I *know* he's lying about not being able to remember because I've seen him late at night, after Phil's gone to bed, sitting in the old wooden rocking chair with the tapestry seat, the one which used to be in Martha's bedroom. He keeps a photograph of her wrapped in an old scrap of frayed pink silk in a drawer in his desk, refusing to let us frame it and put it on the piano or on one of the tables by the sofa where we could see her every day.

'Best not,' he said quite nicely when I asked him, but there was something in his voice which made me not want to argue. He lets me get it out, though, to look at, whenever I like. Which is almost every day.

The photograph was taken on a beach. You can tell because there are rocks and greeny yellow tufts of coarse grass in the background. There must have been a wind, strands of her hair have escaped from the checked green scarf knotted in a bow on the top of her head, and are stuck to her cheek. Her hair looks almost red, although I know it was a bright, golden blonde, so it must have been the sun shining on it that turned it that fiery colour. She's wearing a dress, dark green and printed with splashy red roses, which makes the photograph look as if it was taken a long time ago. Phil says it could only have been about twenty years, 1978 she thinks would be about right, and the reason that the dress looks old is because it was. Martha had a passion for second-hand clothes, and for roses.

Martha can't have known that Harry was going to take the photograph because she hasn't put on a camera face but is captured in some private thought. Perhaps she was worrying about something, the way she's chewing her bottom lip and squinting so her forehead's crumpled, and her eyes are half closed so you can't really make out the colour.

'Blue as the sky on a fine summer's morning,' Phil said when I asked her, but then she's part Irish and her father was a writer, which accounts for that poetic streak in her. 'Poetic?' she repeated, and laughed as if I'd said something funny. She stopped smiling and gave me a curious look, her eyes distant as if she was looking at something far, far away. 'Martha was the poetic one,' she said, her voice quiet. 'I was always the rational one. If ever I had poetry in me, it was because of her. You remind me so…' She turned away so that I couldn't hear but I knew what she was going to say. I remind her of Martha.

It's what they all say, the people who come to the flat. I know most of them but there's the odd person I've never met before. Phil says that I'm being silly or over-sensitive, that they come to see her and Harry, not me, but she doesn't see the way they look at me, probing with their curious eyes, their fingers stiff with the effort of not poking at me.

Phil says they're old friends of Martha's but I don't believe her, not since she told me, her voice bitter in a way that I've never heard it before or since, that nobody bothered to come and see Martha those last few months. They catch me looking at them and then they turn away, but not before I hear them murmur in high, unnatural voices, 'Such a tragedy…' or 'Poor Martha…' I want to shout at them, 'What *happened*?' but I don't. I pretend to be deaf because I don't want to hear it from them with their hard fingers and cold eyes.

I plague Phil with questions about her instead. How she looked, what she wore, how she spoke, the sound of her laugh. I must have driven her half mad with asking; it took a whole summer of mornings to get the exact right colour but one day, there it was, a sky as blue as Martha's eyes. 'That's it, that's it exactly,' Phil said, gazing up into it. It was a bit of a disappointment, paler than I'd expected.

She was really very pretty although she never believed it. A smile like strawberry ice cream, says Phil, pink and sweet and melting. The photograph doesn't do her justice; the camera is unkind to her, as it is to some people, making her mouth appear too big, reducing her nose to a shapeless blob and rubbing her deep-set eyes into smudges of shadow. I don't mind. It's all we have. Martha burned the rest.

I try not to pester Harry, really I do, because I think about him saying how he's living as best he can, but it's difficult because I want so much to know. All he tells me are facts, not *things*, like she was an artist and, he says – and he knows about these things – a much better artist than ever she was given credit for. She was too pretty to be thought really good; the brilliance of her face eclipsed the brightness of her art. We have a few paintings but not many. She gave most of them away or destroyed them if they displeased her, which they usually did. She earned money painting greetings cards, 'Insipid watercolours,' he says, with contempt, 'much loved by mothers and maiden aunts.'

But if ever I ask him what she was *like* he only smiles that sweet, sad smile of his. 'She was a good woman.' In all my growing years, that's all I ever got from him: a good woman.

After one particularly bad session when Harry's words coagulated to a formless mumble, I left him comatose in his chair and ran to find Phil. She was sitting at the table in the kitchen, her neat little body tucked up in a chair, happily chopping up onions for supper. I remember the bright warmth of the room and Phil's contained, humming energy; the smell of bread and herbs and garlic, the sound of music playing, and Phil's small, serious face breaking into a smile as she saw me and then her tender, worried frown as I stood over her, fists clenching and unclenching, shouting, 'I don't believe he loved her. I don't believe either of you ever loved her. If you had, you'd talk about her together, you'd tell me about her. Not what she looked like, or what she wore, but what *happened* to her.'

I stopped to draw breath and saw the tears gather in Phil's large, protuberant eyes and the shame of it nearly silenced me. I had known her since I was a baby, could remember no mother and no kindness except it came from Phil. But the rage to know was in me, filling me with an awful, righteous indignation. 'You have no right, no *right*,' I gasped, my voice strangled with tears, 'to keep her to yourselves.'

I blush now to think of it. Dear, kind Phil. She said nothing, only bent her head and chopped at the onions with clumsy, shaking hands. I stood there, my voice ringing hugely, shamefully in my ears as I stared at the vulnerable white skin at the nape of her neck and the way the dark hair, threaded with grey, curled into the lick of a duck's tail. The silence grew until it seemed monstrous and I thought that if the secret was so terrible then perhaps I didn't want to know. I wanted to hug Martha to me, her gold hair, blue eyes and strawberry smile; not have her stand before me, pale and cold, diminished by the truth.

I saw Phil's face, white and crumpled like an old tissue, laid my head wordlessly on her shoulder and felt the fragile bones against my ear as she stroked my hair with cold, onion scented hands.

She must have understood, I suppose, that my imaginings were more terrible than the truth could ever be, like that mother on the television the other day whose child was murdered and the man who did it refusing to

5

say what happened in the two hours between the boy disappearing and dying. Her white face on the screen, and her thin, rustling voice. 'It's all I can think of,' she whispered. 'Not the five years he lived, but the two hours before he died.' Awful. *Awful.*

Phil's thin arms tightened and she hugged me to her. 'She was a good woman. Never forget that.'

This, then, is Martha's story. It begins when she left Harry because Phil says that while Martha thought it was the end, it was really only the beginning.

2

Harry put down the menu and smiled at Martha. 'I think
this time I'll have the prawns.' It was what he always
said.

Martha returned his smile absently and stared
around at the familiar dim, cluttered restaurant; Le Tour
Eiffel, it was called. They sat on spindly legged gilt
chairs, crouched up against tattered burgundy flock
wallpaper on which posters of Paris were dustily
framed. Years ago, in a brief rush of enthusiasm, someone had put lamps on the tables in the shape of little
gilt Eiffel towers lit by a bulb, battery operated, that
went up and down like a lift. They were usually broken
but that evening the one on their table happened
to be working, so Martha sat and watched the little
light flicker aimlessly up and down on its journey to
nowhere.

Harry and Martha had been together for seven years,
since 1976, and met at the restaurant every Friday evening which, Martha had once calculated, amounted to
three hundred and fifty Fridays if you allowed twenty-
four days off for Christmas, New Year, bank holidays
and their annual summer holiday. She had been thinking a lot about her life recently, which was unusual for
her, but just lately the weeks had started to stretch into
a grey sameness which made her feel as if she'd had
somehow got on to a motorway which had no exit lanes.
That evening she calculated that, by her reckoning of

7

three hundred and fifty Fridays, she had sat for a whole year of her life and listened to Harry order prawns.

But then, she wanted the lamb again so she was in no position to criticise. So she started instead to talk about her day and tried to ignore the irritation that scratched away at the back of her mind, although it made her eyes water and caused a certain pinkness in her cheeks. But when the prawns arrived she discovered that the scratching had become an itch and the itch a sneeze about which she, like all of us, could do nothing at all.

She remembered those prawns for years afterwards, the little curls of coral pink dotted with bright green parsley lying on the striped blue and white plate, could see the blade of the knife suspended over an exposed pink neck, watch the faint whitening of his finger as he pressed down and hear herself saying, as if from far away, 'Harry, I'm leaving you.' Then the faint crunch of head leaving body, then nothing, only an astonished silence.

Harry's heavy-lidded eyes drooped, their colour barely discernible, glittering slightly in the flickering glow of the Eiffel Tower light. 'Why?' he said, at last.

She looked at him, taken aback. Only five minutes before, she had not known that she was leaving him. So it hardly seemed fair to say that it was because of the way he ate his prawns, topping and tailing them like runner beans, heads to the right of the plate, tails to the left, and then a deft incision down the belly and the pale pink bodies pulled out of the shells with a quick twist of the wrist, the shells placed in a neat pile between heads and tails before he ate even a single one.

The prawns made her think of sex. Perhaps it was because they looked so nakedly pink and vulnerable. She and Harry only made love once a week these days. Not that bad really, not after being together for so long, but, try as she might, she could not get the thought out of her head. She, who had never minded at all, found that she minded very much indeed. For seven years, she thought, she had watched Harry eat prawns on a Friday and fold his clothes on a Saturday.

'Why?' Harry asked, again.

Martha stared miserably at the decapitated prawn. 'I need some space,' she muttered, at the same time idly wondering why prawns turned pink when they were cooked and then, with greater attention, how to achieve the colour, bright but tender, with her paints.

Harry frowned. 'You know I hate it when you talk American.'

'Sorry,' said Martha automatically and then wondered how better to phrase it. Harry, you don't excite me any longer. Harry, there is too little passion in our relationship. Harry, I'm young, or young enough to want more than this, this – she searched for the word and, with a small sigh of regret, found it and it was just as Phil always said, her voice breaking on a little note of yearning, this *contentment*. They had a good life together. They loved each other. So why did she feel so empty? Try as she might, Martha could not say what she did want, only what she didn't, and then, on top of it all, Harry was Martha's best friend, not counting Phil who was not so much a friend as a part of her like an arm, a leg or a heart, which was why she found herself in the appalling position of not being able to tell her best friend her dearest wish, which was to be free of him.

'Well?'

She looked up in surprise. 'Well what?'

He picked up his knife and with a slow, lazy motion, snapped the head off another prawn. 'For God's sake, Martha, if you're going to leave me, you could at least explain why.'

It was a slight gesture, that beheading of the prawn, but it seemed in Harry's hands like an act of extreme violence. Martha gazed at the prawn's eyes, grains of black caviar on pink sticks, and shuddered. 'I can't,' she said quietly.

'That's not like you.'

Martha blushed. For years she had loved his careful, gentle nature; the way he had of thinking everything through before he spoke. But lately it had begun to irritate her and she found herself rudely shoving her way through his words. The first time she had done this he had merely looked at her curiously for a moment and then carefully retraced his words, repeating them and adding the ending he had intended. Which gave quite a different meaning to the sentence that Martha had so precipitously finished for him. That did not stop her. Or him. On the contrary, the more she interrupted, the more slowly his words emerged and the more frequently he smiled that slow, sweet smile until, finally, he smiled all the while he was speaking and she, feeling herself mocked, cried, 'Oh, why must you be so *slow*?'

Only the sharp jerk of his head showed her that she had hurt him. 'I prefer to think *before* I speak,' he had said eventually, in a slow slur of words.

They so rarely quarrelled. Knowing that she criticised him not for what he did, but for what he was, shamed her so that she became more, not less, impatient. 'Oh, think, think, *think*!' she'd cried, in a sudden passion. 'Why can't you just do, or even *be*? Why must everything be so –' she searched around for the word – 'so *cautious* with you?'

He was silent for a time and she knew that he was looking for the right words, tumbling them around in his mind, which once would have made her smile, for it was just the way Harry was, but seemed at that moment like the most deliberate provocation. In his eyes, had she cared to look closely, she would have seen the shifting of panic as he searched for words to heal the rift between them, but she did not look and nor did he speak because he could not find the words to say.

'Oh, you don't care!' she cried, which in turn provoked him for he did care, and very deeply.

'I'm sorry if I made you think that,' he said coldly, and turned away. She let him go regretfully, smiling unwillingly as she watched his familiar figure; tall, with a massive head and powerful chest but long, skinny legs and arms which looked, in motion, as if somebody had taken the parts from two quite separate people and stuck them together in a hurry.

Watching his curious, jangling walk, Martha was all at once filled with the old familiar love and longing and so she ran to catch up with him, taking him by his arm and pulling his face down to hers to cover it in kisses and tears, exclaiming, 'I'm sorry, I'm sorry, I love you. I didn't mean any of that, I don't know what's wrong with me at the moment.'

He let her kiss him, standing with his arms by his sides as she pulled frantically at his face and shoulders and then his arms came up to hold her and he hugged her to him. 'Those were careless words, Martha,' he said, and she heard the anger in his voice but she didn't care because she heard passion there too. And so she pulled him, half resisting, half laughing back towards his flat and by the time they got there he was kissing her too and teasing her about her flushed, pink cheeks and pulling her jumper off over her head so she stumbled, blinded, through the front door and into the bedroom. When they finished making love she got up to fetch some wine and smiled with delight. There, strewn across the floor, were Harry's clothes, and it was only Wednesday.

Within the month Martha was finishing his sentences.

Which is how they came to be sitting across the table

from one another in Le Tour Eiffel that night and why Harry, who had not changed but who still ate his prawns in exactly the same way he had eaten them all his life and formed slow, gentle sentences because that was the way he had always formed them; because he was the way he always had been which was a way that no longer pleased Martha but seemed, on the contrary, merely to irritate her, about which he could do nothing other than change his very nature, so Harry said the only thing which seemed to him to be true. 'You no longer love me.'

And Martha, because she knew that he was right, not about loving him (because she sincerely believed that she did), but about wanting him to be a different person but at the same time to be Harry; because that was, she knew, impossible and because the more she wanted him to change the more she hurt him and because the change she wanted was to do with her and not with him at all, so she replied, 'No, I don't suppose I do.'

3

The morning after the scene with Harry, Martha decided to wash the curtains in her flat. As a task it would be both useful, the curtains were in serious need of washing, and useless, the launderette beneath her would do the job better: a conflict which perfectly suited her frame of mind. She tugged the yards of shocking pink cotton down from their brass curtain poles, an easy enough task since they were simply draped over them, dumped them in the bath and emptied half a packet of soap powder on top of them. Turning on the taps, she climbed in and trod splashily up and down, crying noisily.

Phil, after ringing the doorbell, assumed that Martha was either out or asleep so let herself in using the spare key which was kept hidden on the ledge above the door. It was known as the spare key but was in truth the only key; Martha had lost its twin the week she moved in and had never got round to replacing it. Phil had done her best to persuade her to get a second cut and not to leave a key in a place where anybody who had even half a mind to break in would look, but Martha said that she'd rather they burgle her and leave the front door on its hinges than rob her, leaving her with the added expense of a new front door.

'Anyway,' she said, 'they'll let themselves in, see there's nothing worth taking, and piss off.'

It was, as she also pointed out, difficult for most

people even to find her flat, which was approached through a narrow gateway, sandwiched between the launderette and the all-night grocer's and easy to miss were you not looking for it, down a narrow passageway, up a metal fire escape, through a rusted metal door, down a narrow corridor piled high with old books and papers until finally a wooden door, and the entrance to Martha's flat. Her front door led directly into the kitchen, a long narrow room painted a pale powdery blue with high cream-coloured ceilings, lined all along one wall by a narrow wooden cupboard above which were rows of shelves reaching almost to the ceiling whose surfaces were covered by an assortment of jars of pickled vegetables, spices, herbs, jams, honeys, jumbled up with a random collection of books. Tacked along the bottom two shelves were assorted bunches of dried herbs, the skeletons of long dead roses and grasses and clumps of polished, dried gourds. An old splintered wooden desk stood at one end of the room, by a tall draughty sash window from which the sash cords had long since disappeared. To the side of it was the door which led through to the sitting room; at the other end stood an oven, a fridge, its door held on by strips of bright blue industrial tape, and an old cracked butler's sink. Above the sink hung, at a precarious angle, an Easy Maid from whose wooden poles dangled saucepans, ladles and cooking forks.

Phil banged the door shut behind her and took the flowers she was carrying over to the sink. It was, as usual, piled high with dirty plates and cups. Sighing slightly, she dumped the flowers on the floor and walked through to the sitting room.

Every surface in the room, this one painted a pale lilac and with the same high ceiling, was cluttered with objects, although not one of them, as far as Phil could see, was a vase. She headed across the expanse of wooden floor, once polished but now scarred and dusty, to the long table which stood under a triple row of sash windows. On it stood a cluster of glasses, all of different shapes, colours and sizes, some of them still holding dregs of ruby coloured wine; an assortment of bowls each filled with fruit and vegetables arranged according to colour, clementines with lemons, glossy orange and yellow peppers, deep purple aubergines with red cabbage, rosy sweet potatoes and russet apples; a litter of tubes of paint and sticks of charcoal; candlesticks each with a magnificent, brightly coloured stalagmite of wax; books, papers and out of date magazines.

Eventually, after finding a vase and depositing the flowers safely in fresh water, Phil went back into the kitchen, rolled up her sleeves, ran hot water and with slow, methodical movements tackled the pile of dirty cups and pans and glasses. As she washed, rinsed and dried, she listened to Martha crying, trying to gauge her mood.

Martha liked a good cry. She cried alone, among friends, in front of acquaintances, and even beside strangers in the aisle of her local Sainsbury's. Harry, at first horrified, had grown so used to it that he scarcely noticed her tears and was thus once astonished to find himself verbally assaulted by a woman in a bus queue who accused him, in shrill, passionate tones, of being a cold-hearted bastard, while Martha stood beside him sobbing with pleasure.

By the time Phil had finished the washing-up, Martha's sobs had quietened to an occasional deep shudder of breath and so she made two cups of coffee and carried them through to the sitting room, a corner of which had been reclaimed to make the bathroom. It had as its door an old double stable door with a metal drop latch which Phil clashed noisily to warn Martha of her presence.

She put Martha's mug on the side of the bath and leaned against the door frame, her small, neat body tidily packaged in a dark navy trouser suit. Martha, her face scarlet with heat and tears, gave her friend a grateful if distracted smile before continuing to stamp noisily over the curtains, wading up and down through the now blackened water.

Watching her, Phil smiled slightly. Martha was dressed in her habitual eclectic fashion; a crumpled white collarless man's shirt haphazardly buttoned under an antique patchwork velvet waistcoat and, just visible behind the flapping tails of the shirt, a pair of lace-trimmed red silk cami-knickers. Her thick, long hair was bundled inside a rust silk scarf patterned with blowsy pink and scarlet roses, from which errant curls had escaped and become plastered to her damp, flushed face or tangled with the massive silver and turquoise earrings dangling almost to her shoulders.

'Are you all right?' said Phil, when the splashing had quietened.

Martha hiccupped slightly. 'Perfectly all right. Well, perhaps not *perfectly* at this minute. But I suppose I will be eventually.' She smiled briefly. 'Sorry, I'm not at my best this morning.'

Phil considered this for a minute then tore off a piece of toilet paper, carefully wiped a faint smattering of white talcum powder off the black lid of the lavatory seat and sat down, arranging her legs in a tidy line. 'What happened?'

Martha blinked, distractedly pushing at a stray curl which bobbed over her hot, damp forehead. 'I told Harry I was leaving him.'

'Oh dear,' murmured Phil, a worried frown creeping across the pale, high dome of her forehead. 'I hadn't realised. I thought it was one of your therapeutic sessions.'

'I thought it might make me feel better,' Martha said pensively, her face crumpling as she sat down heavily on the edge of the bath. 'Oh, Phil, it's all such a muddle. He looked so *helpless* in that ghastly, heart-rending way that big men do.'

'He wasn't expecting it, then?' Martha pulled a face and shook her head. Phil looked at her thoughtfully. 'And nor,' she said slowly, 'were you?'

'Not really.' Martha poked fretfully at a frayed corner of curtain with her big toe. 'I mean, it *must* have been in the back of my mind but, really, I never meant to say anything. I've been feeling a bit – well, grey, recently, wondering if this is all there is to my life. You know, me and Harry, pottering along, having a perfectly nice time but…I was as shocked as he was when the words came blurting out. Then, when he asked me why, I simply didn't know.' She looked away, embarrassed. 'It sounds so silly now but it all started because he eats his prawns with a knife and fork.'

'It is,' Phil said, 'one way of eating them.' Phil was the most reasonable person Martha had ever known.

Martha sighed. 'I suppose so, but it seems unnatural, somehow. I wish, just once, that he'd pick them up in his fingers and suck them, get his lips and hands covered in oil and garlic and parsley.' She was flushed and her breath came in quick little blasts. Phil smiled at the sight of her hectic face, which made Martha blush a deeper pink. 'I know it sounds absurd but there's so little *passion* in the way he does it.'

Phil looked at her carefully, as if she was waiting for Martha to add something, but when she didn't Phil merely nodded and blinked shiny, slightly protruding brown eyes. 'Not much,' she agreed.

Martha twitched her shoulders in a sharp, irritated shrug. 'Oh, God, it's not about *that*, of course it's not. I'm the problem, not Harry. Everything seems so predictable.

17

I want –' She shook her head and buried her face in her hands. 'I don't know what I want. *That's* the real problem. Excitement? Passion? Christ, it sounds so adolescent.'

Phil smiled slightly. 'I don't think boredom's the preserve of adolescence.'

'Is that all it is?' Martha asked sharply, raising her head. 'Just boredom?'

'Sounds like it,' Phil said briskly. 'And maybe a bit of depression too. They generally go hand in hand. Being bored is depressing. Being depressed is boring.'

Martha looked interested. 'What about feeling restless? And irritable? And I'm not sleeping too well either. Are those all symptoms of boredom?'

'Yes. That or love.'

Martha laughed. 'Good old Phil. Ever the romantic.'

'And are you really going to? Leave him, I mean.'

'I think so. Well, I suppose I already have.'

Phil considered this in silence, her pale, smooth face thoughtful. 'Are you quite sure about all this?' she said tentatively after a while. 'It's just that he's such a –'

'Such a wonderful man,' Martha finished, on a note of exasperation. 'I *know* he's wonderful. He's decent and kind and honourable and true and he'll never let me down…' She sighed sharply. 'Christ, Phil, don't you think I know all that? Don't you think everybody tells me that all the time? You, Jane, my friends, even my mother, for God's sake.'

'I didn't mean –'

'I know you didn't. But it drives me completely bonkers, hearing all the time about the wonderfulness of Harry. Why do you think I'm sitting here racked with guilt and indecision? I *know* I've done the right thing, that we couldn't go on the way we were. Or maybe it was just that *I* couldn't go on the way we were. Harry thinks we're fine. Everybody thinks we're fine, for that matter.' She sighed heavily and looked at Phil. 'But they're not me, are they?' Phil shook her head and Martha slid her eyes away to stare up at the ceiling, as if a message might be printed above her head. 'What a bloody mess. Trouble is, I know I'll never find anyone as wonderful as Harry again. The fact that I can't stand another moment of his wonderfulness has nothing to do with what he's really like and everything to do with what's in my head.' She kicked moodily at the wet curtains. 'Decency has its irritations too, you know.'

'Yes,' Phil murmured. 'Yes, I can quite see that it must. Poor Martha.'

Martha kicked at the curtains again. 'Oh, for God's sake,' she exclaimed, 'I'm not a bloody basket case yet, you know.' They were silent for a while then Martha stood up and stamped so hard at the sodden fabric that water sprayed the room. 'Sorry. I didn't mean to snap. Guilt, I suppose. Christ, look at this water. It's disgusting. How can curtains get so filthy when all they do is just hang there?'

'Pollution,' Phil said absently.

'Look after him, will you?'

Phil glanced up, startled. 'Who?'

Martha rolled her eyes. 'Who do you think? Harry, of course. Find him a good woman or something. Mend his broken heart.'

'You'd hate that.'

'Maybe, but not as much as I hate myself.'

'Well, don't.' Phil's tone was sharp. 'It'll do neither of you any good.'

Martha sighed. 'I suppose you're right.' She stepped out of the bath, trailing water after her. 'Oh, for God's sake let's have a drink or something. And I need a cigarette.'

Phil stood up, carefully smoothing the wrinkles out of her trousers. 'Shouldn't we wring that lot out first?' she said, indicating the curtains.

'I can't face it. I'll do it later,' Martha called over her shoulder as she clashed open the door and wandered into the sitting room. 'Now, where the hell did I put them?'

'What?'

'My cigarettes, of course. Maybe they're in the kitchen.'

Phil watched a trail of damp footprints emerge sharply on the dusty wooden floor behind her. 'Martha,' she called, 'you're hopeless.'

'And you,' said Martha, walking back into the room clutching a bottle of wine and a packet of cigarettes, 'are an angel. You've done the washing up again.'

'Yes,' Phil said, a quick, rueful smile lighting her solemn face. 'I'm a creature of predictable habits.'

After they had poured the wine and settled in Martha's shabby but comfortable old wing chairs by the fire, they sat in companionable silence reflecting, each in their different way, on the flawed nature of life. It was like a glass, thought Martha, a beautiful, jewel-coloured Venetian glass which, from a distance, looks perfect. Only when you pick it up and study it in the light do you see the minute cracks fracturing its delicate stem and exploding in starbursts in the bowl. Phil's glass, she thought, glancing covertly at her friend through half-closed lowered eyes, is half full, whereas mine is always, somehow, half empty.

Phil, who had a pragmatic mind, thought of life as being like a car, inclined to cough and splutter or even stall on you for no apparent reason. While apparently safe, after all everyone had one, didn't they, it was liable to hurt or even kill you if not handled with proper care and attention. Martha's car, she thought, is covered with dents and scratches and the engine tired from being driven too fast but, still, it's painted a marvellous, sing-

20

ing pink and decorated with shiny chrome strips, whereas mine? Mine is grey and serviceable, with a perfectly good engine which I drive at a steady speed and is almost entirely free of dents because I indicate, almost half a mile before I need to, that I am turning left or right. And when I die, she thought, there my life will sit, right out in the front of the used car lot with a neat little sign pasted to its windscreen. 'Bargain. One cautious lady driver only.'

The morning stretched into the afternoon. Martha lay sprawled in her chair, legs dangling over one of the upholstered arms, a newspaper resting, opened but unread, on her chest. Phil had fallen asleep, bolt upright, her thin body arranged in a neat package; hands clasped in her lap, feet placed together on the floor. A slight frown dented her high brow, the only wrinkle marring the smooth, pale oval of her face. Martha watched her for a while, thinking how peaceful she looked. She has arranged and pressed and ironed her life, she thought, and a little sigh of envy escaped her lips, until it hangs smooth and comfortable around her. She thought of Harry and with another sigh lay back and closed her eyes, wondering how it was that even love, which is the messiest part of life, seemed in Phil's hands so neat and pretty, so perfectly *contained*.

Phil's lover of ten years was Peter Reed. Martha remembered with wry amusement the look of displeasure, pain almost, which had dented his brow when she, eager to assume an immediate intimacy with this man who caused Phil's solemn face to light up, had called him Pete. 'Peter,' he had said, correcting her in his dry, clear barrister's voice. He was married to Mary, they had been at Cambridge together and had married a week after finishing Finals, although they had both always understood that his career would take him to London whereas her inclination would take her to the country and a small but perfect Georgian house in Gloucestershire. They met at weekends (he drove down late every Friday evening returning on Sunday at about eight o'clock), and holidayed each summer, during the month of August, in France. They had two young children, Jamie, eight, and Emma, six, and shared what Peter described as a deep affection and understanding.

When Martha had said that their understanding couldn't be as deep as all that since it didn't extend to his telling Mary about Phil, Phil said, with a tiny frown of displeasure, that it was an arrangement that suited them both very well. After that, Phil talked to Martha about Peter very rarely, but then Phil was not much given to exchanging girlish confidences and there was probably not, Martha had decided, very much to tell. Peter and Phil seemed never to quarrel, about that or anything else, and the arrangement had suited them both admirably for over ten years. So well that Phil had over the years become more and more adamant that she did not want him to leave Mary. Not that she ever said as much; just hoped that it was understood.

When Phil got home late in the afternoon she found a note lying on the doormat in the hallway shared by all the flats. Stooping to pick it up she recognised Peter's precise, crabbed hand and the thick black ink which he habitually used. He was, unusually, spending the weekend in London rather than in the country with his family. 'Pressure of work,' he said. They had arranged to have dinner together that evening.

Frowning, Phil read the note. 'I called round to see if you were in. I thought tea at the Savoy might make a pleasant change from dinner. Actually, I'm afraid that's rather an excuse. I can't make it tonight. Something's come up. I know you'll understand.'

Damn, thought Phil, unlocking her front door and

stepping carefully over four cats who wound their way purring around her legs, I could have done with a bit of company tonight. She closed the door behind her, locked and bolted it then put her car keys carefully in the antique Chinese pot which stood on a little polished wood table, its surface bare save the pot, a clothes brush and an African violet which had never flowered. She stood for a while, looking around the dim, peaceful room. Everything was just as she had left it, everything was always just as she left it. The thought made her feel suddenly bleak.

4

David doodled absently on his note pad, trying to contain his impatience. If the meeting went on for much longer he would be late. He glanced furtively at his watch. Five-thirty. He'd never get a taxi now, not in the middle of the rush hour; he'd have to take the Metro. He groaned inwardly. That meant two changes and a ten minute walk at the other end, so he'd arrive feeling hot and disagreeable. And when the hell was he going to telephone Jane, to tell her he couldn't get home until tomorrow? He would have called earlier but this thing came up at the last minute, just as he was about to go into the meeting. Oh well, nothing else for it; he'd have to call her when he got to the flat. It wasn't the best way to start the evening but they'd get over it soon enough. He felt a worm of pleasure wriggle suddenly in his stomach and a faint dampness in the palms of his hands. He wiped them surreptitiously on his trousers. Jane would be upset of course; she always was. He imagined her shrill, anxious voice on the other end of the telephone. 'You are all right though, darling? Don't let them work you too hard.' Oh, Christ, she'd want to know which hotel he was staying at. She liked to call him in the morning, first thing. 'Just to make sure you're OK, darling.' He'd have to go and check in somewhere first, which would add another half hour to the journey. Maybe he could chance not taking a room, just this once? He could tell Jane he didn't know the hotel's telephone number, would call her with it later. No, that was no good, she'd get into a panic, 'What if something happened to one of the children?' and he'd never get her off the phone, not until he promised to call right back with the number. It was hardly the way to start a seductive evening, with his wife, hysterical, on the other end of the phone. Christ, his neck hurt. He could feel the muscles, tight as steel bands. What he needed was a large Scotch. He stared morosely at the bottle of Perrier in front of him and cautiously eased back his shoulders. Guilt always made him tense.

The sales director, Jean Villeneuf, caught the slight movement. 'Perhaps Mr Carrington does not agree?' His voice was silky, unctuous.

'Well, of course I do,' David said abruptly, trying to quell a note of dislike. 'It's an excellent product. As a matter of fact we've already tested it on a couple of focus groups in the north *and* the south. The response was –' he paused deliberately – '*overwhelming*.' A dim smile hovered palely on the chairman's face. David flipped a couple of heavy documents on to the table. 'It's all in there,' he said, prodding at them with an emphatic finger. 'And that's just a sample of the research we intend to do. On the basis of that alone, I'd say that the market is ripe for it right now.'

Jean Villeneuf smiled unpleasantly. 'Then it has recently changed,' he said. 'We've tested a few of our products over there in the past. In our experience British women are, how shall I put it, careless in their personal habits?'

Patronising fool, David thought, smiling benignly across the table at him. 'Perhaps that's because you've only tested for moisturisers; you've never hit them where it hurts,' he said, spreading his hands and indicating the lower half of his body.

A flicker of interest briefly illuminated the chairman's

lugubrious face. 'This makes a difference, you think? They worry about their thighs more than their faces?'

David shrugged. 'Sure. They're no different from women anywhere else in the world, even France. Cellulite is cellulite, no matter how you pronounce it.'

'Perhaps,' the chairman said slowly.

'Your marketing man, Joe Larusso, spent a lot of time in Britain and he seems pretty convinced.' David kept his tone light.

'Then it's a pity he's not here today. The rest of us feel that the British are notoriously…' Villeneuf shrugged eloquently. 'Our research shows that they don't even know that they *have* cellulite.' He cast a sly glance at the chairman. 'It would be an expensive mistake to make,' he murmured.

'They'll know about it by the time I'm through with them,' David said belligerently. The chairman's reptilian eyes flickered with distaste. Christ, David thought, bad move. Relax, don't blow it now. He smiled pleasantly. 'There's a growing awareness among a certain group of women,' he continued, careful to keep his voice even. 'With a careful strategy, a word or two in the right ears…the opinion formers in the top newspapers and magazines…' He spread his hands expansively.

Villeneuf shrugged dismissively. 'If it's so easy,' he said, 'then perhaps it should be handled from Paris.'

David leaned back in his chair, pretending indifference. 'By all means,' he said. 'If you have personal access to the right people then I don't see why that shouldn't work. It would take a little longer, of course. And your competitors…' He let the sentence trail away as he leaned forward to take a sip from his glass of Perrier.

'Our competitors are considering the British market?' The chairman gave Villeneuf a sharp look. 'Jean, is this true?'

Villeneuf flushed. 'There's been some talk,' he admitted.

The chairman turned away impatiently, looked at David and tapped the side of his prominent, red-veined nose. 'As Jean says, an expensive mistake…' He gave him a hard, assessing stare. 'Prove to me that British women know about cellulite and I'll give you exclusive rights to market my product in Great Britain. You have six months.'

David smiled. 'In six months, not only will every woman in Britain over the age of twelve know about cellulite, she'll have it, too.'

It took David another ten minutes of exchanging pleasantries before he could leave the meeting. He dashed along the corridor, struggling into his coat as he ran, and stood in an agony of impatience in front of the lift's blank steel doors. Christ, there were twenty floors in the building and how many people all leaving at the same time? He'd never get out of there. He stared feverishly at the panel above the doors. Both lifts seemed to be stuck on the floor above. He jabbed furiously at the call button. 'In a hurry?' Villeneuf said smoothly.

David threw him a harassed look. 'A plane to catch,' he said tersely, thrusting his wrist out of his coat sleeve and looking agitatedly at his watch. Six-thirty. Perhaps he should skip checking in to a hotel and go straight there, but he felt a sudden, keen urgency to phone Jane, to tell her about this afternoon's triumph. He knew she'd be genuinely pleased for him, could hear her voice, thin and high with excitement, crackling down the line from London: 'Darling, you're so clever. I knew you could do it, I just *knew* it.' Christ, where was the bloody lift? He jabbed impatiently at the call button again, conscious that Villeneuf was watching him, a small, amused smile on his smooth face. 'That won't do any good,' he said, with a startling high, yelping laugh. 'It obeys only electricity.'

27

David shot him a look of cold fury. Ha bloody ha. Christ, the French were cold fish. He hated Villeneuf, hated Paris, hated the whole bloody city and everybody in it. Jane's small, pointed face swam suddenly into his mind and he thought longingly of her and his house and his two fine sons. What am I doing here, he thought in despair. I could lose everything, and for what? It's not even pleasure, not real pleasure; more like an addiction, something I have to do in order to survive. He knew he ought to walk out of the building, hail a cab and go straight to Charles de Gaulle airport. He also knew that he wouldn't. He knew that he would spend the next two hours in a blind panic, running around Paris, paying for a hotel bed he would never sleep in, raising his blood pressure on the crowded, smelly Metro travelling to some god-forsaken suburb on the outskirts of the city where he would screw his brains out and drink too much, then have to get up too early, his mouth like a parrot's cage, his head like a lump of boiled mutton. Then he'd scramble across Paris to get back to the hotel room in time to call Jane and pretend that he'd had an early night, dinner in his room and ten hours' sleep. And for what? So he could feel the cold, slimy writhing of disgust and remorse in his belly when he saw Jane's smiling, excited face waiting for him at the airport. He felt the beginnings of an erection twitch at his thigh and banged impatiently at the call button with a clenched fist, furious with excitement and loathing. Just then the doors flew open, revealing a dozen pairs of startled eyes. David dropped his raised arm and, giving them a sheepish grin, stepped into the crowded lift.

5

Martha's flat seemed always to be full of people; old friends, new acquaintances or Mrs Hammond from the launderette below, just popped up for a cup of tea, wanting to take the weight off her troublesome legs. Then there were others, the drifting community of Ladbroke Grove who, on their way to the market wandered up Westbourne Park Road and loitered outside Martha's window. 'Martha, Martha, are you there?'

She always was, working she said, as she poked her head out of the window, hair still wet from the bath or tousled from sleep. 'Come on up,' she'd call. And they would, but only for a minute, mind. But there was always coffee to be made or glasses of wine to be poured and sometimes a good bit of cheese and bread or some strange new cake which Martha had discovered in one of the Portuguese shops up the road.

Phil often found them there, slumped on Martha's accommodating sofa; sometimes, even, lying in a tangle of sheets on her unmade bed, talking earnestly while the early evening sun flooded through the room. And Martha among them but always somehow apart, sitting alone at the long table over by the window fiddling with tubes of paint or charcoal, throwing them warm, distracted smiles as if they were stray dogs or cats come to warm themselves by her fire, or tossing them scraps of conversation. The telephone at her elbow seemed always to be ringing, and she would pick it up and engage in long, desultory conversations, the receiver cradled against her neck while she painted or drew in long, lazy strokes while they chattered like birds around her. Phil, arriving, would stand in the doorway, hovering uncertainly on the fringes of the colourful, dishevelled group in her neat navy suit until Martha looked up, her face breaking into a wide, sleepy smile as she yawned and stretched, lazily exclaiming, 'Good lord, is that the time?' Then the group would reluctantly disperse, stacking their dirty cups and glasses in the sink, trailing long bright streamers of conversations as they left, clattering down the metal stairway.

Phil knew she could never live like that but still she couldn't help a stab of envy when she thought of her large, peaceful flat to which nobody came, except by invitation. She felt sometimes, too often for it to be an entirely comfortable feeling, that her life was a play in which she had no real part other than that of a spectator who has paid her money and is thus entitled to sit in the audience laughing and weeping, never from the heart or even from the soul but from a detached, occasionally amused, sometimes ironic position; engaged but never connected; all the time longing, *longing*, to be up there, like Martha, taking part.

It amused people sometimes that the two of them were friends, they were so different, but they went back for ever, for as long as either of them could remember. They had met at nursery school where Martha, solitary but noisily gleeful amid a storm of Plasticine, papier-mâché and paint, could not help but notice the slight, dark, neat girl who never played or painted but stood alone, watching her with shining eyes. Martha watched her in return, throwing covert glances at the girl whose eyes grew bright with excited admiration as Martha formed splashy, colourful pictures and Plasticine puppets. She began to hold them up for her solemn, silent inspection at which the girl, whose name she knew was Sarah Phillis because that was what was called out in class each morning, blinked harder and out of the small, solemn oval of her face unfolded a smile, shy and rare and, to Martha, infinitely pleasing.

One day, Martha had just finished putting emerald eyes in a crimson Plasticine lion when she noticed a girl with green eyes and a spoiled mouth and a sudden blur of movement. Sarah Phillis did not flinch, only the slight watering of her eyes and a heightening of colour in her pale cheeks told Martha that the green-eyed girl had jabbed a stealthy, vicious blow to her stomach.

It was the passive resignation with which she received it that made Martha realise this was not the first time she had been hit, that it had been going on for days or even weeks, and so she got up, stepped over her paints and punched the girl in the face, bloodying her mouth.

The girl's mother had to be telephoned and Martha's, too, arriving to collect her from school with a face red with embarrassment and an anger which became a cold fury in the face of Martha's stubborn silence. Martha was marched through the cold, dark streets to a big, brightly lit house, hard fingers jabbing at her back. They stood on the door-step, Martha in the centre, while the girl, whose name was Mary Anne, stood safe behind the comfortable prison of her mother's legs and smirked at Martha with poisonous green eyes. Martha, staring back in stony silence, would not, could not form the simple word. Finally the girl's father, perhaps seeing the ugly spite in his daughter's pretty face, said that, well, girls would be girls and they'd be friends again soon as maybe, just see if they wouldn't. Still there was Martha's mother, face stiff with anger and disgrace, refusing to move until Martha said she was sorry, hissing, 'You're not going back there again until you do.'

Martha relented, not because she wanted to go back to the school, because she didn't, would have been happy anywhere so long as they gave her paint and Plasticine, but because she understood that the world was an unfair, even a treacherous place, and that Sarah Phillis would never let her down.

It was Martha who gave her the boyish nickname, Phil, when they were both ten. She looked like a boy with the shining cap of dark hair hugging her pale, serious face; dark, feathery eyebrows flying above large, protuberant brown eyes. Out of school uniform she dressed like a boy, too, in old, soft faded blue jeans and white aertex shirts with tidy little collars. She had a baseball jacket which she always wore, a real American one made of emerald green wool with brown leather patches on the elbows and big yellow fuzzy felt letters on the back. Her father had bought it for her when he was on a lecture tour in America. When she looked at that jacket, Martha thought she might die of envy.

The name Phil had started as a joke because the man in the corner shop where they bought their sweets after school always said, 'And what'll it be for you today, sonny?' It wasn't his fault, he never saw below the school blazer because the counter was so high and anyway, Phil never put him right, just smiled solemnly and chose the same thing she always had, a gob-stopper which protruded from her thin cheek, pushing out the pale skin in a shining mound which deflated slowly during the afternoon and was gone with a pop and a crunch just in time for tea.

Martha suspected, although she did not say so, that Phil was secretly pleased to be thought a boy. She never wore dresses or even a skirt other than the regulation bottle-green pleated affair they had to wear every day for school which was measured, three inches from the ground when you were kneeling down, at the beginning

32

of each new term. It was the mid Sixties and the girls at school, filled with passionate yearning to be teenagers, rolled their eyes in horror at the length of their skirts. Most of them rolled them over at the waistband, not in the least disconcerted by the lumpy folds which thickened their slim waists beneath thin wool jumpers; some were even daring enough to have them shortened after the ritual measuring. Not Phil, who wore the dowdy regulation length with contemptuous indifference, who did not even, as was fashionable among the other girls at that time, push up the sleeves of her jersey and pull down her white shirt to show three inches of snowy cuff.

Phil never bothered to rebel against things which she despised, saying that she thought it a waste of precious energy; a remark that Martha found thrilling in its weary sophistication. The other girls thought Phil dull. When they teased her, she responded with a courtesy they found unpardonable, for there was no pleasure in it. They found her stoic endurance disturbing, just as they disliked her large, dark intense eyes which were never trained on them, as they would have liked, but fixed on some inner, more interesting place. More than anything, they resented her air of self-containment, of not needing them. They wanted passionately, as all small girls do, to be needed.

Then, of course, there was Phil's father, who was sometimes written about in the newspapers and not just in the local *Messenger*, although as a local author of immense repute he was mentioned with shameless regularity, but in the proper national newspapers. It was bad enough to have a father who was famous, let alone a father famous for being clever. The girls at school reproached her for it, silently at first with raised eyebrows and rolling eyes whenever Phil raised her hand to give a correct answer in class, but more loudly when they discovered that her father was her Achilles heel,

33

the soft underbelly through which she could be pierced. When Joyce, a diminutive red-head with a large, bullying nature, hurried into the playground one day fresh with the excitement of a chance remark overheard at home, that Phil's father, Jim Phillis, was an immoral writer, it was all Martha could do to separate them. Phil launched herself at Joyce like a small dark cat, teeth and nails bared, arms and legs scrabbling for purchase on the red-head's body.

Summoned before the headmaster, who questioned her with gentle, perplexed concern, she turned her sullen face to the wall and would not speak. After that, every day in the playground brought some fresh hell, but Phil never again reacted, just murmured some vague politeness before retreating into her book or a conversation with Martha.

Jim Phillis died, suddenly and unexpectedly, when Phil was fifteen. When Martha heard the news she ran straight out of the classroom, through the school gates and all the way to Phil's house, so terrified by what she might find that she never once paused to draw breath. Phil opened the door, her solemn face paler than ever and her large eyes dimmed to an inscrutable black. The house was filled with people ministering to an hysterical Julia, Phil's mother, who lay on the chaise longue in the drawing room, a tear-drenched handkerchief pressed to her eyes, a glass of brandy to her lips, graciously receiving all those who had come to pay their respects.

Phil smiled politely in response to each of the profound inanities offered her that terrible afternoon but Martha never saw a tear escape her dark eyes, so clouded with grief it was as if she were blind. Nor did she ever see her cry over her father or outwardly regret his death, but she understood instinctively that the pain Phil suffered, then and for years afterwards, was so intense that it was literally unspeakable.

6

'I just don't understand you,' Jane said, efficiently separating a tangle of washing into piles of coloureds and whites. 'I mean, it's not as if you were unhappy or anything. In fact, you seemed perfectly content.' She flicked quickly through the pile of socks which she was carefully pairing, turning one inside the other, and sighed. 'There's one missing. I think this machine eats them.' Bending down, she scrabbled in the empty drum of the washing machine and emerged, flushed but triumphant, a small black sock held aloft. 'Here it is. Well, were you?' she added, her small, bright eyes narrowed in a sharp glance. 'Were you unhappy?'

Martha looked at her sister thoughtfully, noticing suddenly how thin she had become. She had always been small boned and slender, had inherited their father's slight stature, but what had seemed in her teens and twenties so fragile and appealing now seemed, as she neared forty, brittle, desiccated even. She wore a navy cashmere sweater, tightly belted with red suede around her thin waist and enlivened by a red and navy silk scarf tucked in at the neck, a plain navy skirt, navy tights and sensible low-heeled navy shoes. Her dark hair, fine as silk, which she had for years worn cut in a neat bob, was swept back off her face with a velvet Alice band, the childish style serving only to emphasise the sharp triangle of her face and its small, pointed chin. Even her face seemed fleshless, the smooth olive skin drawn tight across wide cheekbones and the soft pad of flesh above the pronounced bow of her upper lip diminished, revealing a glint of teeth. She looked, Martha decided, like a small but elegant brown mouse.

Martha, who had inherited her mother's height and large, fleshy frame, her big square hands and feet, thick white skin and unruly red-gold hair had, as a child, resented Jane's sharp prettiness and even sharper nature. But while the sisters had each inherited one parent's appearance, they were as unlike that parent emotionally as they were like them physically.

Poor Mum, thought Martha, surprised by a sudden sharp stab of sympathy as she remembered her mother peering at her with curious, hopeful eyes as if she sought, in the clear mirror of her daughter's face, some sympathy for her own uncomfortable nature but found only her husband's gentle, perplexed diffidence.

'Martha!' said Jane in exasperation, 'you're not listening. Just like Daddy. He never listened either. Mummy says it used to drive her mad. I know just what she means,' she added darkly, frowning.

'And you're just like Mum,' Martha said sharply, wondering why a lack of unhappiness should be thought necessarily to signify happiness. 'Anyway, Dad did listen. He just didn't want to hear. And I wasn't exactly unhappy,' she admitted, 'more sort of *muffled*.'

'Muffled?' Jane raised a dark, plucked eyebrow. 'What on earth does muffled mean?'

Martha lit a cigarette and blew a series of haphazard smoke rings as she considered the question. 'As if I was wrapped up in cotton wool,' she said, watching the blue circles tremble, flutter and dissolve. 'No pain, but no real pleasure either.'

Jane looked at her in exasperation. 'Honestly, Martha, you don't know when you're well off. Most people spend their lives looking for this – this muffler person, to keep them safe and warm. Pleasure's so *tiring*.' Her heels clicked efficiently across terracotta tiles as she moved to the fridge and pulled out an assortment of bowls. 'Coronation chicken or cold roast beef? *Must* you do that?' she added, flapping a hand in the direction of the smoke. 'It makes everything smell so disgusting. After you've left I feel as if I'm living in an old ashtray.'

Martha, who still found an absurd, childish pleasure in irritating her sister, smiled lazily. 'Chicken, please. And must I do what,' she said, 'smoke, or blow rings?'

Jane's mouth tightened as she briskly decanted Marks & Spencer bean salad into a bowl and set the table with silver knives and forks and white damask napkins. 'Please yourself. After all, you always have.' Martha, who was so used to her sister's sharpness that she scarcely registered it, went on smoking silently.

'There, that'll do for us,' Jane said. 'You don't want much, do you?' she added, staring doubtfully at her sister's large frame. Martha, stubbing out her cigarette, gazed at the cutlery on which not a water mark was visible, at the crisp, crackling surfaces of the starched damask napkins, and said nothing. What was there to say in the face of such certainties?

'Good.' Jane perched on the edge of a chair. 'Let's eat. I'm starving.' She took two tiny mouthfuls then hopped off her chair and scurried across the kitchen, sharp heels tapping, to load the separate piles of whites and col_oureds into grey plastic baskets.

'Was that lunch?' Martha said, staring in astonishment at her sister's untouched plate.

'I've never thought it necessary to eat two large meals a day,' Jane said, looking faintly disapproving. She picked up a blue felt-tip pen and wrote in a clear, rounded hand on the Don't Forget board which was stuck with magnets to the fridge, 'Mrs March, please remember to starch collars and cuffs.' The board already bore the cryptic reminders, 'Simon dentist 4.30 Thursday' and, 'David Paris Friday 7am'.

'Today's her afternoon,' she explained, catching Martha's quick, amused look, and adding irritably, 'just wait till you have a husband and kids, you'll be writing notes too.' She sighed, casting her sister a bemused, exasperated glance. 'Talking of which, I really thought that this time...' She paused, and cleared her throat delicately. 'Well, I thought that you and Harry... He seemed so *reliable*. Mummy and I were saying just the other day how *nice* Harry is and how he seemed such a good influence on you.' She frowned. 'It's a worry for Mummy, you know. I really don't think you realise. She does so want to see you settled before –' Her mouth tightened but she went on bravely. 'Daddy dying has been very difficult for her. I know you two have never really got on but...' She slid her gaze away and then looked back, her voice subdued. 'Oh, Martha, she's so *miserable*. Well, you haven't seen her so you wouldn't... She hardly goes out these days, doesn't even bother to get her hair done regularly. You can see the grey roots – I was shocked, although, of course, I didn't say anything.'

'It's about time,' said Martha drily, 'that she gave up trying to pretend she's a natural blonde.'

'That's typical of you!' exclaimed Jane. 'I know what all this is about, and don't think Mummy doesn't. So she had a little – a friendship, after Daddy was gone. What's wrong with that?'

'Friendship! She was dancing on his grave. Wearing new bloody high-heeled bloody shoes, too.'

'Oh, don't be such a sanctimonious prig. You should listen to yourself sometimes, babbling on about pain and pleasure. Really, Martha, that's teenage stuff. Mr Right and all that. I'd have thought you'd have grown out of that by now. Not that you ever will now, I suppose. Even in your twenties you were running after every man who even smiled at you. One kiss and there you were, "in love". Love!' Her voice rose in contempt. 'What do you know about love?'

'Considering my present situation,' Martha said, with a slight lift of her eyebrows, 'obviously not much.'

Jane looked at her with exasperation. 'The perfect relationship doesn't just happen, you know. You have to work at it. I know my marriage isn't perfect –' She paused, waiting for her sister to demur but, when she did not, added sharply, 'Well, at least I've stuck to it through thick and thin and haven't thrown up my hands and wandered off when things weren't going right.'

'It may have escaped your notice, but I've never been married.'

'Don't be stupid, stupid,' Jane said, reverting to an old childhood expression. 'I'm talking about *relationships*, which in your hands are like so many disposable tissues. Love! You call yourself a romantic but –'

'I'd never describe myself as anything so absurd,' interjected Martha.

Jane looked at her sharply but, deciding that the argument wasn't worth pursuing, veered off and returned to her previous point. 'Take Mummy and Daddy. They may not have had a perfect marriage either but at least she stuck by him.' Martha smiled slightly. She had always admired her sister's tenacity; her small, determined chin and pointed nose sniffing at a subject like a terrier, her little mouth biting into words and worrying at them until all the life and meaning had gone out of them. It was not Jane's imagination that made her a good interior decorator, although she owned a certain reliable good taste, but her determination to track down the exact shade of paint, the right fabric, the precise lamp to stand in a corner which made her so sought after by people who had neither the time nor the inclination.

'In a sense,' Jane went on, the words falling limply, spent, from her mouth, 'Mummy and Daddy were the perfect example of what love really is all about, staying together through the bad as well as the good times.'

'A fine example to us all,' Martha said acerbically, helping herself to more bean salad.

'Christ! You really don't care at all, do you?'

'Oh, come on, Jane.' Martha's tone was sharp. 'She loathed him. The poor man couldn't even read a newspaper without her sighing in irritation at the way he turned the pages.'

Jane's mouth tightened and she gave a quick sly look at her sister. 'I wasn't going to tell you this but Mummy said – She said that she thinks that somehow you blame her for Daddy's death.'

'Well, she would, wouldn't she?' Martha said shortly. 'It's called guilt. She made his life miserable and now she wants us to feel sorry for her. Silly bitch.'

'How unkind you are!'

Martha sighed. 'Am I?' She thought of her father, as silent and lonely in death as he had seemed to many people to be in life. Not that he had been, by nature, a silent man. The silence was a habit which grew on him over the years, a refuge from his wife's disappointed, querulous nature. When he was away from the house and working in the wooden outbuildings which housed his toy-making business and which had grown out of a shed in their back garden and spread, higgledy-piggledy, over the fence into the field behind, he was quite a different man; laughing, happy, talkative. Did her mother resent that, wondered Martha. Did she even know it as she sighed over the sink and gazed sourly out of the kitchen window at those ramshackle buildings into which she never ventured?

As a child Martha had sought him out every day, after she got home from school, racing across the back garden to find the warm, companionable man with his easy smile who was really her father; not the morose stranger she knew he would become, later that evening, at home.

When Martha left home they drifted apart. At first she missed him terribly and sent long, chatty letters about her new life at art school. She wrote every week for a year until he took her quietly to one side and asked her to stop. 'It's your mother,' he explained, with a sad, discomfited smile. 'She thinks we're keeping secrets from her.' Martha, outraged, had protested that she would do no such thing and had written another two or three letters, but the memory of his smile and the cold, unforgiving silences which she now knew must follow the arrival of each letter, finally stilled her pen. On the rare occasions when she went home to visit, the three of them sat in chilly uncomfortable silence over her mother's interminable meals. Once, when Martha suggested that she would like to go and see the new set of toys he was working on which were now, to her mother's grudging surprise, selling well, his face had momentarily been illuminated by that same warmth and joy she had once found in him. But her mother had snapped that Martha visited them rarely enough and couldn't they sit still just for a few, civilised hours, adding in a muttered undertone that Martha was far too old to want to dirty her feet walking over the fields to his grubby sheds. The joy had faded from his face and only a slight wistfulness lingered in his gaze as he bade Martha goodbye.

Martha had not mourned him when he died; had even, stupidly she now supposed, thought he would find a relief of sorts in the cool, dark earth. 'Cry for him,' her mother hissed out of the corner of her thin mouth as they stood side by side watching the pale wood inch slowly into the black earth. She turned to her daughter and stared accusingly at her chalky, tearless face. 'You should cry for him,' she said and then, perhaps seeing the shadow which darkened her eyes, added more kindly, 'It will help you.'

Martha, remembering a lonely day long ago when some brief storm of adolescent misery had driven her to seek out her father in the toy sheds and the misery of him not being there, and never being there again, felt the tears begin to dribble slowly down her face. As she remembered, the pain of losing him sharpened to a terrible grief and she sank to her knees over his grave.

'He's gone out to buy wood,' Joe had said that day, adding after a quick, kind glance at her tear-stained face, 'but you just go and make yourself comfortable in the back, pet. He won't be long. You'll see.' Then the unspeakable joy of her father finding her, huddled damply among the fragrant, crackling spirals of wood shavings at the back of his workroom, and the smell of him, wood and varnish and the sweet, fusty scent of the little hand-rolled cigarettes he smoked, the thin, spittled dog-ends abandoned in bent tin ashtrays in his workshop. He was never allowed to smoke in the house.

'What is it, titch?' he had asked, reverting to the old childhood name he had given his strapping daughter, his warm hand massaging her neck.

'Mummy says I'm hopeless and that I'll never make anything of myself because I'm just like you,' she had sobbed, hating her mother for the carelessness of her cruelty towards her father but still, somehow, half proud of the comparison. 'I hate her,' she said bravely, for she had never dared say it before but now she was almost grown… She watched his reaction with careful eyes. But he only smiled.

'You don't hate her, sweetie,' he said gently. 'She doesn't mean most of what she says. It's not you she's angry with. She's had a difficult life. She's not good at –'

He hesitated, and then his voice grew urgent as he stumbled over the few words, 'She loves you very much. She's just not much good at saying it.'

And then her mother, years later at the funeral, fumbling at her daughter's hunched body, pulling her gently to her feet and pressing her in a quick, awkward embrace. Then, later, her thin figure standing gracelessly on the railway platform as she waved goodbye, the tears coursing down her pale, angular face and rolling unchecked into the wisp of black chiffon tucked into the collar of her stiff black shirtwaister dress. And the guard slamming the door and her mother's strong, bony hand grabbing her quickly by the wrist and handing her a piece of paper, folded and turned and folded a hundred times so each fold was rimed in black. And the train pulling out and Martha slumped in the fetid air of a smoker's carriage, bitterly rebuking herself for never having sent those letters, haunted by the memory of his last wistful, lonely smile. A week spent sitting in bed, under the comforting tent of blankets, as tissues and tea cups accumulated around her and finally, feeling better, and remembering the note and opening it.

'Dearest child,

'I know how hard you must be grieving. Your father was the kindest man...' here the word man was crossed out and in its place she had carefully capitalled the word *person* and underlined it with three dense strokes... 'person I have ever known. You are very like him.

'Your loving, Mother.'

'Perhaps you're right,' said Martha slowly, remembering. 'Perhaps I am unkind.'

Jane stared at her in amazement. It was an old, childish point of principle never to admit that the other was right. 'Of course you're not unkind, not really,' she exclaimed, mollified, 'and I do know how difficult

Mummy can be. She does love you, you know. It's just she's not very good at saying it.'

'No,' said Martha slowly, gazing at her sister, wondering if their mother ever told her that she loved her.

'She doesn't even say it to me much,' Jane added, as if reading her thoughts, 'and you know how I bully her. I told her that if she doesn't express her emotions then she'll wither up like an old prune.' She laughed suddenly. 'Well, you know how vain she is. These days she tells me everything, she's totally unstoppable.'

Martha smiled and Jane, her manner suddenly awkward, said, 'Look, I didn't mean to preach. I'm sorry. It was a bit of a shock, hearing you'd split up with Harry after so long.' She turned away and started fiddling with the pen which was attached by a ribbon to the notice board. 'Actually, I was a bit hurt that you hadn't told me yourself, to tell you the truth.'

Martha, remembering how difficult Jane had always found it, even as a child, to admit that she was wrong, sidling up like a crab with a muttered, graceless apology and then busying herself with some small, unnecessary task, smiled at her thin shoulders and averted head and said, 'I'm sorry I didn't telephone you sooner.' And then, because she knew it would make Jane feel better, she added, 'It was just that I wasn't really feeling up to talking about it.'

Jane wheeled around, her smile bright with eager sympathy. 'Oh, Martha, now *I'm* sorry. Of course I should have realised that you were upset.' She paused, head cocked on one side, pert nose twitching slightly as she sniffed out more confidences. Jane was universally acknowledged to be sympathetic, which she herself knew to be true since she voluntarily gave up two hours of her busy life each week to work as a counsellor for a marriage guidance organisation. 'It really does do the world of good to talk, you know,' she said in a high, bright voice. 'So, if you ever feel like it, I'm here.'

'Thank you,' said Martha and then, finding herself unable to offer her sister assurances that she would do any such thing, groped around in her mind for some distraction. Finding it, she said fervently, 'Paris! Lucky old David.'

Jane, who loved conversations about relationships so long as they were not her own, looked slightly disappointed at the new tack the conversation was taking but rallied quickly. 'Yes, lucky David,' she said, carefully dropping the word old. 'I've been angling for an invitation. Imagine, a weekend in Paris! But he says he'll be busy the whole time so I'll just be bored. Never mind, it's a big project so I'm sure there'll be lots of chances later on.'

'If not there, then somewhere else.'

Jane looked at her sharply. David and Martha did not get on.

'What's that supposed to mean?'

Martha shrugged. 'Nothing. Sorry. Don't mind me. Early menopause or something.'

'You're not serious!'

'No, of course I'm not,' Martha rolled her eyes and lit another cigarette. 'So, go on, tell me. What's David up to in Paris?'

'Some French skin-care company who specialise in hips and bums. Oh, you know what I mean,' she said, seeing Martha's bemused expression. 'Cellulite. That dimply stuff you get on your bum. This stuff's supposed to work miracles. David met the marketing director at a trade fair and they're both convinced there's a huge market for the stuff in this country but the chairman's one of those old French men who think that the British don't even wash, let alone use beauty products. If David can convince him that he's right then he gets the account, which is worth a small fortune.'

'Well, good luck to him, but do you honestly think the

British care about their bottoms, except to make jokes about them?'

'Cellulite's no laughing matter,' Jane said. 'You should see the women queuing up at that new health club I go to on the Fulham Road. Thighs like curdled cottage cheese.'

'Enough,' laughed Martha, holding up her hands. 'I believe you.'

'Tell you what,' said Jane suddenly. 'This man David's been working with in Paris, the marketing guy. I met him briefly when he was over here. He's completely gorgeous, actually I think he even used to model for magazines and stuff, and I'm pretty sure he's not attached.'

Martha looked at her suspiciously. 'So?'

'So, he'd be perfect for you!'

'Hardly,' said Martha drily. 'I don't even know what cellulite looks like.'

'Don't boast. David says he used to be an artist or something but had to give it up because it paid so badly.' Her little eyes shone with excitement. 'Don't you see? It would be perfect. You can talk about art for hours. The next time he's in London I'll invite you both to dinner.'

Martha looked at her sister doubtfully. 'Dinner with a male model turned seller of bum creams,' she said. 'Are you quite sure?'

Jane laughed. 'You'll love him. He's not my type at all but he is very charming, if you like that sort of thing.'

'What sort of thing?' asked Martha suspiciously.

Jane giggled and two high spots of colour glowed in her cheeks. 'Sort of rough and smooth, all at the same time.'

'You make him sound like a pumice stone.'

'Well, if you don't like him,' Jane said, her thin cheeks pink with the prospect of match-making, 'you never have to see him again. Where's the harm in that?'

Phil went to the dry cleaners, as she did every Saturday, to deposit her weekly pile of clothes, then strolled on up the hill, tacking her way slowly through the quiet, peaceful roads of St John's Wood, admiring the neat, manicured front gardens, peering into windows, amused and startled anew each time by the idiosyncrasies of people at home with themselves; from there up to the High Street to Blooms to buy lunch for her and Martha and then any bits and pieces she thought she might fancy for herself, of which there were always quite a few and which she inevitable regretted during the slow trudge home.

The shopping and cleaning done, she wandered languidly around her cavernous flat, tending to the window boxes, tenderly amputating the odd dead leaf or dried flower head, watering and feeding the plants, polishing their already glossy leaves. The lack of a garden was her one regret, but it wasn't a very large one set against the astonishing good fortune of having been left the flat outright in the will of a spinster great-aunt. There was a condition, said the solicitor who rang the morning after her aunt's death. The bequest included the contents of the flat and the contents included four cats. 'Cats?' Phil repeated, still bemused from sleep. 'Did you say cats?'

'The condition of your taking on the flat is that you must agree to take on the cats as well. If you do not agree to these terms,' he explained in an unemotional voice, 'then the flat will be put immediately on to the open market and the proceeds of the sale donated to your aunt's favourite feline charity.'

Phil was silent. She did not much like cats. 'I see,' she said, eventually.

Impatience made his tone brisk. By the terms of the will, Phil must either move in that day or relinquish her right to the property. Although, he added, as Phil's silence lengthened and stretched down the telephone wires all the way to Lincoln's Inn Fields, he felt sure that in the circumstances the timing might be made a little more flexible; say a matter of a week? But a week, he cautioned, was really all he could allow her. Still Phil said nothing which eventually precipitated a small, dry explosion which she took to be an impatient cough and so she arranged to collect the keys from him at lunch-time.

The moment she put down the telephone, she regretted it. She already had a perfectly adequate flat in West Hampstead; it was comfortable, quiet, and suited her well. Why should she exchange it for one which was no doubt small, dark, and which must, inevitably, smell overpoweringly of cat? She was just about to pick up the telephone again to instruct the solicitor to dispose of the flat when she felt a sudden curiosity and decided that even if she had no intention of taking it, and those wretched cats, it couldn't do any harm to at least go and have a look.

As she left Maida Vale Tube station and walked down the broad leafy avenue in the direction of the flat, the low, grey blanket of cloud which had shrouded the sky all that afternoon lifted suddenly, the sun dappling the new green of the trees and suffusing the surrounding buildings with a rich, warm red. Phil looked around her with increasing pleasure. She was used to the narrow,

48

crowded streets of West Hampstead, had always accepted that oppression as a part of living in London, but in these broad avenues and wide pavements she felt a sudden sense of freedom. She hurried towards the flat, pausing now and then to stop and take stock of her surroundings, allowing herself a small, pleasurable thrill as she contemplated the peaceful streets and the solid, handsome red brick buildings, even allowing herself to imagine that she might in the future be walking this way home.

Reprimanding herself severely – she had learned as a small child never to anticipate too eagerly because her expectations had always been confounded – she reminded herself that the flat was bound to be pokey and dingy and that there were her future companions, the cats, still to be considered. Nonetheless, she could not quite quench the feeling of excitement when she turned the corner of an avenue and saw the sun gilding the buildings a fiery red, throwing into sharp relief the black wrought-iron railings which crested the curved cream painted balconies. It was with a sense of anticipation that she fitted the small, gold Yale key into the lock of an arched double front door and from there made her way down a vast, dim tiled hallway to stand outside a polished wooden door marked number ten.

She let herself in cautiously, worried about the cats escaping, and quickly slammed the door behind her. As her eyes became accustomed to the gloom she realised that the flat was not small. On the contrary, if the hallway was anything to go by, it was enormous. Although she was there by invitation, she felt like an intruder. Stepping carefully across the slippery, polished parquet floor towards a pair of huge wooden swing doors which stood directly opposite the front door, she tentatively pushed one open.

It swung inwards to reveal a large room; she

49

supposed it must be the kitchen for, while it was many times larger than the usual modern kitchen and contained, as far as she could see, no refrigerator or dishwasher, a couple of handsome porcelain butler's sinks were set against one wall. Light flickered through tall sash windows, filtered by the leafy branches of trees, illuminating walls lined with wooden cupboards painted an intense dark green; those and the elaborate Victorian green and cream tiled floor gave the whole room a submerged, subterranean quality. In the middle of the room and almost dwarfed by its surroundings stood a massive old pine refectory table. Phil walked towards it, feeling curiously as if she were swimming through the green half-light, her arms working in deep strokes as she felt her way across the room, coming to rest at last in front of the table. She suddenly experienced the uncomfortable sensation of being watched and, looking down, found herself confronted by four pairs of wide, unblinking eyes. On each corner of the table sat a cat.

'There you are,' she exclaimed, feeling as if she had lived in this flat all her life, had just stepped out for a minute and had come back into this room to find the cats exactly as she had left them. They, in turn, stared at her impassively, with neither curiosity nor hostility, as if she were already familiar to them.

'Hello,' she said, feeling slightly foolish, 'I'm Phil.' They blinked slowly, in unison, but did not move and eventually she became restless and began to prowl cautiously around the room. It was immaculately clean, the old scarred wooden work surfaces gleamed dully with years of polish, its lavender fragrance still faintly discernible. She opened a cupboard and peered in but, feeling the eyes on her, closed it quickly. Looking at the cats severely, she pretended an aloofness she did not feel and went to inspect the rest of the flat. At the doorway to each room, the cats lined up and watched her carefully. In this manner they conducted her around the flat, until she had inspected all four bedrooms and the dining room, at which they led the way into the sitting room where they settled, each on separate chairs, and regarded her unblinkingly. She sank into the only empty chair, feeling a sudden, tremendous sense of peace. The ginger tom arched his magnificent back in a languorous stretch, then, with a faint, contented hiss, like a tyre being slowly punctured, settled his chin on his front paws and closed his eyes.

It took her very little time to move, her previous flat had been rented so she owned no furniture, and she settled in quickly. The cats accepted her as if she had always been there. She found something curiously comforting in their indifferent familiarity, in the heavy, silken caress of their fur against her legs as they came, each in their turn, to bestow on her a casual greeting when she arrived home each evening. She continued to protest that she did not like cats but found, over the years, that somehow they each came to have a replacement as one by one they died.

Years later, Phil sat in that same chair hugging the precious, empty minutes to her as she waited for Martha who would be, as she always was, at least an hour late for lunch. She was thinking about Harry, remembering something he had said the last time she saw him; something about not giving up on the world altogether. His tone was teasing and she had smiled but even so she had been stung, turning his remark this way and that in her mind, worrying whether it meant that he found her boring. She was a little frightened of Harry; he seemed so *decided* about everything. She saw the way his grey eyes slowly flickered behind their lazy, protective lids, weighing people up and deciding whether they were worth his time. Harry, she thought, had a slow but dangerous brilliance, born out of an unquenchable certainty about life. It was not so much arrogance as an absolute sureness of being which drew people inexorably towards him. She knew herself to be a little bit in love with Harry. It did not surprise her. Most women were a bit in love with Harry. She wondered how he was, whether that certainty of his had been badly shaken by Martha's leaving, but did not worry much, knowing there would be plenty of women eager to pick up the pieces.

Peter, too, had begun to complain that she was becoming too solitary. 'You seem to prefer your own company to everyone's, even mine,' he had said, turning away with a smile, but not before she saw the wounded look in his eyes. She sighed. It was growing increasingly easy to hurt Peter. Whatever she did seemed to be wrong although what was really wrong, she knew, was that she did not love him as much as he wanted to be loved. Was she solitary? She preferred to think of herself as contained. Certainly, she had few friends and none who really *mattered*, except Martha, and she was not so much a friend as a part of her. She was not sentimental about Martha, just as she was not sentimental about any person, living or dead; there were certain characteristics in Martha's nature of which she did not completely approve. It was not that she judged them against her, she simply acknowledged that they existed just as she knew that there were things in her own nature of which she did not fully approve but accepted as a part of being herself.

She could not imagine life without Martha, but neither could she imagine life without something as familiar and dear to her as, say, her sight. Life without it would be quite a different sort of life, would lack an essential dimension of colour and light. It would be flatter, greyer, but it would also, she had no doubt about this, go on. She remembered a woman in the solicitors' offices in which she worked exclaiming, a few days previously, over a newspaper article about a woman who had lost her husband in some tragic accident and her saying how she could not *bear* to go on living if such a thing happened to her. She had looked at Phil's questioning frown and exclaimed again, 'Well, could you? Could you *bear* to go on living?' Phil had replied that while she did not have a husband and so could not answer the question with proper honesty, nonetheless she thought that, yes, she could bear to go on living for it was not so much a question of whether life could be borne but *how* it was borne.

The woman had raised a cool, offended eyebrow and turned away in silence but later, as Phil passed the little kitchenette in which they made their coffees and teas, she heard the same woman remark to a colleague that she had always suspected Sarah Phillis was a cold fish and now she knew that she was not simply cold, but frozen. 'Frigid, I dare say,' the colleague added knowingly. Phil was not much offended, for she took no offence from people whose opinion she did not respect, but it had given her a small, cold shock to hear herself speculated about. She did not much like being asked personal questions, found the increasingly popular habit of baring one's soul in public distasteful, but even that seemed to her preferable to being *thought* about. Thoughts seemed to her to be so much more impertinent than questions, for thoughts had no boundaries, were as invasive as weeds, while questions could be contained by the protective edging of answers.

The sudden jangling of the door-bell startled her into awareness and she looked around the room in confusion before she realised that it must be Martha. Walking quickly through to the hallway, she pressed hard on the intercom.

Martha tumbled in through the door of the flat, shaking her heavy hair like a dog, her face scarlet with exertion. 'Sorry,' she said breathlessly, 'it's pissing with rain and I've been running. I was painting and completely forgot the time. Am I *very* late?'

'Yes,' Phil said, with a smile. 'But what's new? Oh, thanks,' she added, taking the bottle and Martha's deep green velvet coat, which was sodden. She looked at it reprovingly. 'You can buy coats which are waterproof, you know,' she said, shaking the coat vigorously to remove the worst of the rain. 'They're called macs. And there's a marvellous new invention called an umbrella.'

'They're so ugly,' Martha complained. 'Oh, Phil, just dump it anywhere. That coat's been through worse than a bit of rain. Here, let me.' She took the coat and draped it over the corner of a door, almost tripping as she did so over a ginger tom who had come to wind his greeting around her legs.

Phil plucked the coat off the door, arranged it neatly on a hanger on the coat stand and nudged the cat gently out of the way with her foot. 'Do get out of the way, cat,' she grumbled. 'He's been waiting for you for at least half an hour,' she called over her shoulder as she led the way through to the kitchen. None of the cats had a name. Phil called them all cat. She said it was easier.

'He's got to get his affection somewhere,' said Martha.

'I'm perfectly nice to him,' Phil protested. 'I just don't drool over him in that idiotic way that people do with animals. Here's the welcome committee,' she said as she pushed open the heavy doors to the kitchen.

Three cats, sitting on different corners of the table, gave Martha a long, lazy blink of greeting but otherwise did not move. The fourth circled her legs, watching for the slightest indication that she might sit down. When she eventually did, he let out a small, urgent cry of pleasure and leaped on to her lap, settling there with a deep-throated purr.

'I wish you wouldn't encourage him,' Phil said mildly. 'After you've gone he follows me around, wailing, like a small child deprived of its favourite toy.'

'Don't pretend you don't like it. You're mad about those cats.'

Phil shrugged, went to a drawer and rummaged around for a corkscrew. 'How was your week? Is the painting going well?'

Martha sighed. 'It goes,' she said, 'but agonisingly slowly and I don't know about *well*. I keep getting distracted doing silly little bits and pieces to try and earn some money. I promised a whole pile of stuff to some new greetings card company thinking it would take me a day to knock out a few dozen and, of course, everything takes weeks longer than you imagine.' She took the glass of wine Phil held out to her. 'Thanks.' She held it up to the light, examining the pale yellow liquid thoughtfully. 'Then I do get quite lonely; it is lonely being by yourself for long stretches of time, particularly when things are going badly. I long for people to come and distract me, but when they do, I long for them to go away again.' She pushed a distracted hand through her hair, pulling at a curl which had become tangled in a dangling silver and turquoise earring. 'I can't seem to settle, somehow,' she went on, tugging viciously at the hair and in the process unsettling the cat from her lap. He shot her a reproachful look then stalked off to find less restless comfort.

'Here, let me,' Phil said, deftly unwinding the curl. 'There, that's it.'

Martha sipped moodily at her wine. 'Thanks. Harry was right,' she said. 'He always said that I was an expert at frittering away whatever small amount of talent I once had.' She sighed extravagantly then glanced slyly at Phil to assess the effect of her words.

'Don't misquote him,' Phil said severely. 'What he actually said was that you were in danger of wasting a real talent.'

'Whatever.'

'It's not the same thing.'

'If you say so.'

Phil looked at her sharply. Martha caught the look and grinned sheepishly. 'You're so stern,' she complained, starting to laugh. 'Can't I even wallow for a minute?'

'Not on my time, you can't.'

Martha smiled affectionately. 'What would I do without you? You and Harry are so alike. You make no allowances for weakness.' She sighed suddenly. 'I do miss him. At least he shamed me in to getting down to some work.' Phil said nothing, busied herself washing lettuce and preparing a dressing for the salad. 'Do you think I should call him?' Martha asked in a light, careless voice.

Phil shrugged. 'It depends why you're doing it,' she said, without turning round. 'If you mean, should you call Harry because you miss him and want to see him then, yes, by all means call him. But if you mean should you call him because you're feeling a bit lonely and fed up about your work then, frankly, I think it's a lousy idea.'

'So it's a lousy idea.'

Phil turned and looked at her severely. 'So don't do it.'

Martha sighed again. 'OK, I won't. It would be crazy anyway. What I really need is a mad, passionate affair, something to get the blood beating. Then I could paint, I know I could.' She stared moodily into her glass then looked up at Phil. 'Would you, though? Call him, I mean. Just to see if he's OK. He's not good at emotional stuff, goes into a kind of a stupor when he's made to talk about anything…oh, *difficult*, as he calls it. But not talking about it is even worse; he gets all tangled up inside.'

Phil looked doubtful. 'What would be the point?' she said. 'He'll only want to talk about you and I have nothing helpful to say to him. At least nothing,' she added with a grimace, 'that he'll want to hear.'

'Just call him,' said Martha. 'Please?'

'If you insist.' Phil shrugged. 'But I don't promise anything. Now let's eat this food I spent hours preparing.'

'You mean you walked all the way to Blooms,' Martha said, laughing. Phil's culinary skills, or lack of them, were famous.

'And back,' Phil reminded her with mock severity. 'Let's not forget the walking back.'

8

Jane let herself into the house, being careful not to bang the front door. Hearing a slight noise, she glanced nervously up the stairs, worried that she might have woken David. He had been so irritable of late; the last thing she wanted was another quarrel like the one they'd had at breakfast.

The morning had started well enough. He was on a diet, which always made him crabby, but otherwise everything had been fine until she'd reminded him that she was going out that night so she'd leave his dinner in the oven.

'You didn't say,' he said, his face tightening peevishly. Jane looked at him with exasperation. She *had* told him about the meeting, three or four times in fact, but David only remembered things which either affected or interested him. In a rare moment of mutiny she had once pointed out that she and the children appeared to do neither. He had said nothing; the expression in his eyes had been enough to silence her.

'You don't mind, do you?' She was irritated to hear the note of anxious pleading which crept in to her voice.

'Why should I?' He did not look up from the newspaper.

'It's just that I might be rather late, so please don't –'

'I won't.'

She glanced at him anxiously and, noticing that he was scrabbling around blindly for the pot of coffee, started forward to help him. A faint pink mottled his smooth cheeks, always a danger sign. Looking up, he snatched the pot from her with a resentful, faintly martyred look. 'I can manage, thank you.'

Jane applied herself to her bowl of All Bran and skimmed milk. The cereal had collapsed to a repulsive grey mush but she consoled herself with the thought that it was doing her good. She glanced warily at David and tried a little sigh. No response. She sighed louder. He flicked the newspaper but did not look up.

'Darling,' she said tentatively, 'you're not really pissed off about me going out, are you? I thought you might enjoy a chance to stretch out by yourself and relax. Be nice, for a change.'

David stared at her in baleful silence then poured himself another cup of coffee. As he banged the pot down on the table, a few drops spilled on the gleaming surface. 'And what exactly does "for a change" mean?'

Jane glanced anxiously at the spilled coffee, sure that she could already see a water mark on the wood's glossy patina. She longed to go and get a cloth and wipe it up but knew it would only irritate him. 'It's just that you've been working late quite a bit recently, darling. A quiet evening at home might be nice.'

'Oh, very nice,' he said in a tight voice. 'I love coming home after a long, hard day to a solitary supper of cold cuts.'

She looked at him in bewilderment. 'It's not cold cuts. I've made you a beef casserole.'

'Casserole, cold cuts, what's the difference? I'll still be eating it on my own.'

Her eyes slid over to the table again. There was definitely a mark. 'Sorry, darling,' she said absently, wondering how long she dared leave it before it left a permanent scar.

'Well, you really sound it,' he said belligerently,

picking up a knife and slashing at the butter in its pretty crystal dish.

'Diet,' she said automatically, as she watched him load butter on to his toast and take a large bite.

Looking baleful, he stared accusingly at the toast and slapped it petulantly down on his plate. 'Casseroles are fattening anyway, and you know perfectly well that if I eat on my own then I'm inclined to eat too much.'

'Well maybe you'd prefer something else. I could do you some cold meat and salad,' she said, in sweetly reasonable tones.

He scraped his chair away from the table and got up. 'What I'd prefer,' he said, his rounded, smooth-shaven cheeks livid with red blotches, 'is a wife who actually behaved like a wife. As far as I can see, you spend all your time counselling other people about their marriages and neglecting your own.'

Jane opened her mouth to protest, then closed it again. She wondered if he'd been up to something recently; he was always bad-tempered if he felt guilty. On the other hand, he might just be going through one of his occasional bouts of insecurity. She thought her husband was capable of being the nicest man in the world. But only if he felt he was the *only* man in the world. If she let him get upset now, he'd sulk for days. 'Darling,' she said, 'you know there's nowhere I'd rather be than at home with you but I *promised* to go this evening. We're interviewing for new counsellors and you know how important that is.'

'Oh, very important,' he said, getting up and snatching his jacket off the back of a chair where Jane had hung it. He thrust his arms clumsily into the sleeves then wrestled furiously with the collar which had turned neatly in on itself. 'Blast this thing. It's those bloody dry cleaners you go to. They've ruined this suit.'

Jane reached up and straightened his collar with a

deft flick of her wrist. 'There, it's fine, but your tie's a bit crooked.' As she reknotted the heavy silk, she gave a little sigh and murmured, 'I suppose they *could* manage without me.'

He stared over her head at his reflection in the mirror. 'Oh, go, for Christ's sake. I expect I can cope,' he grumbled, giving himself a small, admiring glance. Picking up his briefcase, he dropped a brief, grudging kiss on her cheek. 'Although I don't know why you bother. It's not as if it does any good. According to *The Times*, the divorce rate goes up monthly.' He stomped off down the hallway; she could hear him picking the letters up from the mat and slapping them down on the little table. 'More bloody bills. And a letter from Charles,' he shouted.

She rose from the table, started to hurry towards the kitchen door. She woke early every morning, hoping for one of those small, tear-blotched notes from her eldest son.

'Think I'll take it to read on the Tube,' he called. 'I'll bring it home this evening.'

'David,' she called, her voice desperate with pleading, but the only response was the banging of the front door. She ran into the hallway, threw open the door and stared after him, her eyes filling with tears. It was her punishment. He could not have chosen a better one. She stood, watching after him, until the street was empty.

When she went into the kitchen, she found the casserole sitting in the oven, untouched. Sighing, she grabbed an oven cloth and pulled it out, grimacing as she imagined the dried out meat sticking stiffly to the bottom of the heavy pan. She placed it carefully on the top of the cooker to cool and cleared away the silver knife and fork, white oval porcelain plate, silver salt and pepper cruet, crystal wine glass and damask napkin that she had laid earlier that evening. Then some instinct made her go and check the contents of the dishwasher. It was stacked to the brim with dirty dishes, the remnants of her lunch and Simon's tea. She had even filled the little white compartment with soap powder so all David had to do was load his plate and turn it on. As she was about to do so, she noticed his empty whisky glass dumped in the sink and retrieved it, resisting a momentary urge to smash it on the terracotta tiled floor. Instead, she rinsed it carefully and put it in the dishwasher.

Comforted by the machine's efficient, soothing hum, she made herself a cup of tea and picked up a navy blue sweater which hung lopsidedly on a chair. She stroked it absently. It was one of Charles's although he was too big for it these days so Simon wore it. She wondered how her eldest son was, tried to picture him in his lumpy iron bed, his striped pyjamas sewn firmly with a name tape so everybody, in that cold, unfamiliar house two hundred miles away, would know who he was. She wondered if he was happy, was getting enough to eat, whether he missed being kissed goodnight. His empty room squatted like a reproach at the top of the stairs and she suppressed a sigh as she thought of his teddy bears lying abandoned on the bed because the boys at school would think him a baby if he'd taken them with him. To her he was a baby, only seven years old; much too young to be away from his mother. She had begged David to let him stay at home until he was eleven and then join the senior school, but he'd said, with an unpleasant sneer, 'What, and have him turn into a Mummy's boy? He's bad enough already.'

He didn't see the fear in Charles's eyes each term when she loaded him and his trunk and tuck box on to the train at Victoria station. Nor did he feel the pain which tore at her insides as she watched the train pull slowly out of the station, feeling with every turn of the wheels, her stomach become more and more twisted until she thought that she could bear it no longer and fled, weeping, into the safety of the nearest taxi. How could David know all that? He was never there to see it.

It was not that David did not want the children but nor did he passionately *want* them, either. It was she who'd decided when they should have them, planning the births like military campaigns mapped out by calendars and thermometers, and while he'd played his part in all of it she knew that he wouldn't really have cared if they hadn't had them; not with that deep-down wrenching of the guts caring that happened each time her period arrived. Oh, he'd have *minded* because not to have children would be a reflection on his virility or some such other masculine vanity, and because he enjoyed the image of himself as a family man. He liked to sit behind his heavy oak desk and watch his clients' eyes widen, particularly women's, as they saw the silver-framed photographs of two perfect, tow-haired boys grinning out from behind the green marble pen holder. Then, of course, all his friends had them too.

He had taken very little notice of them for the first year of their lives but she did not blame him for that; they were still too attached to their mother, both literally and emotionally, to be of much interest to anyone else. But when Charles began to take his first steps and say a few words, the first of which, unfairly it seemed to her, was 'Dada', she had hoped that David would take a greater interest in him. In a way, he did; he liked to boast to friends and colleagues that his son had begun walking at ten months and talking when he was not many weeks past his first birthday. 'Of course,' she would hear him say at dinner parties, usually to an attractive woman, 'I knew he'd be bright but really,' a little self-deprecating laugh, 'we hadn't imagined he'd be quite so advanced.'

Occasionally, on a Sunday afternoon, he would insist on taking Charles out for a walk on the Common. 'You put your feet up or something, darling. No, really, I don't mind,' cheerfully waving to her as he strode manfully away from their front door, pushing the buggy ahead of him. At first she had been pleased to have a little selfish time to herself to collapse in a chair with the Sunday newspapers but when she offered to accompany them, thinking sentimentally of the picture they made, a little happy family strolling through the leafy suburban Common on a sunny Sunday afternoon, David wouldn't allow it. 'I'd like to spend some time alone with my son,' he insisted. 'I so rarely get to see him.'

When she saw how much it meant to him she felt guilty that she had ever imagined that he didn't like his child. Charles, though, would somehow always come home dirty and crying and more than once with a nasty graze to his knee or chin. She rarely rebuked David; it was bad enough seeing your child hurt without being forced to feel guilty about. Charles seemed none the worse for his scrapes and bruises; she supposed he enjoyed the rough and tumble with his father. She thought guiltily that she was too careful with him, exclaiming loudly at the slightest chance of danger, flapping furiously at bees and wasps and refusing to allow him to climb on the steel frame in the park. Perhaps it was her fault that he was such a nervous, fretful child, never rushing to join the other children at their games but clutching on to her skirts even though she encouraged him to go and play. David said she spoiled him, spoiled both of them when Simon finally made his appearance. She thought sometimes that that was the reason he was so determined to send them away from her.

Once, when she had been washing a particularly

64

nasty graze on Charles's knee, dabbing at it with cotton wool, he put a starfish hand over hers and patted it enthusiastically. 'Nice lady,' he said solemnly, 'nice lady.' 'Who's a nice lady, darling?' she asked, but he only smiled with delight, pointing at his knee and nodding vigorously, 'Nice lady, yah, nice lady.' When she asked David what Charles had meant he remarked casually that some woman had picked him up when he fell over in the park.

She thought no more about it until, some months later at a drinks party for David's work, David had had a few drinks too many and was boasting to one of his colleagues, a single man with no children. 'What you need, old boy,' he said genially, 'is a child. They're marvellous for attracting women.' The man, who wore thick pebble glasses and had a tide mark of acne receding from his chin down his neck, frowned, bewildered. 'You just take them off to the park, plonk yourself on a bench and look harassed. It's like bees around a honey pot. Women appear out of nowhere, especially if the child falls over and hurts itself. Nothing serious, mind,' he added, his glazed eyes registering his wife's disapproving frown, 'just a scratch to bring out the Florence Nightingale in them.'

'So our child is an accessory for pulling women, is he?' Jane said in a quiet voice as she drove them home later that night.

'Darling,' David protested, 'it was a joke. I thought I'd get old Peter wound up a bit, the poor bugger's always desperate to get off with women. Bit of a laugh, don't you think, to see him trying to pull a bird with a baby, a buggy and a bottle.'

'Ha ha,' said Jane.

'You don't really think I'd use our baby for that, do you darling?' he said, putting his hand across and stroking her thigh persuasively as she drove. She could tell from the pressure of his hand, slightly too urgent, that he was feeling guilty.

'Of course I don't,' she said, trying to keep her voice light, 'but I think, next time, I'll come with you and hide behind a tree. Just to see if there's anything in what you say.'

'You do that, darling,' he said, pushing his hand further up her thigh, squirming his warm, firm fingers between her legs.

'Please stop doing that,' she said through gritted teeth, 'or I'll crash the car.'

He sighed. 'What a lovely way to go. You're not cross with Big Bear, are you?' he pleaded in a whispery, growly voice, easing a finger under the elastic of her pants. 'Not really cross enough to say he can't have his honey tonight?'

'David,' she warned.

'Say you're not cross,' he whispered in the same voice. 'Say Baby Bear's not cross with Big Bear and I'll stop.'

'I'm not cross but I will be if you go on doing that.'

'Say Baby Bear isn't cross,' he pleaded. 'You know how Big Bear hates it when Baby Bear's upset.'

'Baby Bear's not cross,' she said reluctantly.

'You're not using Baby Bear's proper voice,' he complained. 'Say it properly and when we get home Big Bear will go upstairs and build a lovely cosy little den in our big comfortable bed and make it all soft and warm and when Baby Bear climbs in he'll spend hours and hours licking the honey from the honey pot.'

'Baby Bear's not cross,' Jane whispered in a tiny, breathless voice.

She sighed, remembering. To be honest, she didn't much like sex, not really *like* it, but she liked even less the feeling which had begun to niggle away at the back of her mind recently that David didn't like it either. At least, not with her. She told herself that she was being silly, he was just tired. He worked too hard. But then she remembered his flat defeated voice when he asked her if it had ever occurred to her that he might be tired of always being the one who made the running. She had been slightly startled by that; in her limited experience it was always men who made the approach. She thought uneasily that nice girls didn't push themselves but the thought, which had begun to make her feel even more uneasy lately, occurred to her again, that if she didn't make the first move then maybe...Gulping down the last of her tea, she hurried upstairs to find her husband.

She found him asleep on the bed, fully dressed, with all the lights on and the television blaring. She sat down gently so as not to wake him and watched him as he slept. He looked so vulnerable; his smooth pink skin and a slight plumpness to his cheeks gave him the look of a young boy. As she stared at him, admiring the contours of his full pink mouth, its petulance softened by sleep, he suddenly seemed to her quite without defences. She felt a faint flickering of desire.

She knew that he was spoilt, demanding and selfish but at least he was never boring. Nobody could accuse David Warrington of being dull. He was also, when he got his own way, expansive, generous, and irresistibly charming. His wife, anyway, had never found herself able to resist him or perhaps, she thought, watching him, it was simply that she found that life ran so much more smoothly when she didn't.

She noticed a faint bruising tracing the translucent skin below his eyes. He's exhausted, she thought, frowning with concern. He works too hard. Mind you, he had always worked hard, at first labouring to get his company established, building it up all through the long, difficult years of the Seventies and lately, now that it was proving to be a success beyond even his wildest

67

dreams, he worked just as hard keeping it there. It meant long hours, particularly in the evenings. There seemed to be endless business dinners which he had to attend, but that, she supposed, was the nature of his job. Sometimes she went with him; she quite enjoyed those occasions, being Mrs David Warrington, but more often than not he went alone, saying that they were going to talk business all evening and she'd be bored. She didn't mind. She knew he did it for them, for her and Charles and Simon. 'In four or five years' time,' he promised, 'if everything goes according to plan, we can go public and I can sell. Then we'll be rich, rich, rich.' He laughed and threw his arms around her in a suffocating embrace. 'And I'll retire and you'll be so bored by the sight of me you'll long for the days when I was out all the time.'

'I'll never be bored with you,' she said.

Now she bent forward and kissed his mouth then fluttered her eyelashes against his cheek. He loved butterfly kisses, said that they were her speciality. He felt the slight movement and, opening his eyes, blinked in momentary confusion. 'What?' Then his eyes came into focus and he smiled sleepily. 'Sorry, darling, must have fallen asleep. What time is it?'

'Ten-thirty.'

He grunted, rolled over and sat up. 'You're late, aren't you?'

'Yes,' she said. 'The meeting went on for hours. We were interviewing for new counsellors and you know how careful you have to be about that. We can't hurry it,' she smiled affectionately, her voice rising to a playful, breathless whisper, 'however much we might want to hurry home to our loved ones.'

A slight frown flickered across his smooth face and was gone. 'Sorry I didn't eat the casserole, darling. It was either food or sleep and I'm afraid sleep won.'

She leaned forward and rumpled his fine, silky hair.

'Never mind,' she said lightly. 'Would you like me to go and boil you an egg or something?'

He shook his head abruptly, dislodging her hand. 'No, I'm fine. Think I'll get undressed and turn in.'

'All right, darling,' she said, reluctantly getting up from the bed and moving over to her dressing table. She began to cream her face. 'I know what I wanted to ask you. Is Joe in town over the next couple of weeks?'

'Joe?' he repeated, his voice casual.

'You know. Joe. The man who's taking you away from me.'

He looked discomfited. 'What do you mean? Taking me away?'

'You know perfectly well what I mean,' she said teasingly. 'You spend more time with him than you do with me these days.'

He smiled awkwardly then shrugged. 'That's probably because you're not worth a quarter of a million pounds to me.'

She looked at him, startled. 'That much?'

He could not help a small, self-satisfied smile. 'Near enough.'

She turned back to the mirror, began to tissue cream off her cheeks. 'Anyway, I've got an idea. Is he in town in the next two weeks?'

He shrugged. 'He might be. Why?'

'Well, weeks ago I promised Martha I'd organise a dinner party so they could meet. I thought they'd get on splendidly, both being artists of sorts. And Martha's quite lonely, I think.' She frowned as she caught sight of his face, reflected in her dressing-table mirror. 'I can see that you don't think it's a good idea,' she added, her voice flat. 'So forget I even mentioned it.'

A smile began to dawn on his face. 'You mean Joe and Martha, together?' He laughed suddenly. 'I think it's the most splendid idea.' He laughed again, uproariously.

'It's the best idea you've ever had. Why didn't I think of it?'

'Steady on, darling,' said Jane, frowning slightly. 'Don't let's get carried away. They might not like each other. In fact they might loathe each other on sight. But then again –' She smiled, pleased that he thought an idea of hers so amusing. 'He's not married or anything, is he?'

'No,' said David. 'Definitely not.'

'And he's OK?' asked Jane. 'Not got some ghastly secret?'

'I should think,' said David slowly, 'that he's almost definitely got some awful secret. He's the type, don't you think?'

Jane turned and looked at him solemnly, then smiled. 'Oh, well.' Her voice was light. 'Martha does keep saying she wants some excitement.'

He swung his legs off the bed and walked over to her with a light, jubilant step. 'What a clever little thing you are,' he said admiringly.

She caught his hand, held it fast. 'How clever?' she asked, in a playful, growly whisper. He frowned, confused. 'Very, very clever?' she murmured, looking up at him from beneath her sparse eyelashes.

He looked down at her, his smile uncomfortable, then extricated his hand from her grasp and patted her gently on the shoulder. 'Not now, darling,' he said, dropping a kiss on her greasy forehead.

9

'You're late,' Paul said without looking up from his magazine. 'I've ordered you coffee and some of that marvellous strawberry tart.'

'Goody.' Martha dropped a kiss on the top of his bent head, noticing a glimmer of skin shining palely through his dark curling hair. The faint scent of tea rose from him. 'I love tarts,' she said, sniffing voluptuously.

He glanced up, twitched his large, bony nose, and gave her his peculiarly sweet, lop-sided grin. 'Don't be vulgar.'

She smiled serenely, shrugged off an antique brocade coat with a deep velvet collar and tossed it carelessly on to the chair next to him. He gave a quick, disapproving lift of an eyebrow then rearranged it deftly, scooping the trailing hem off the dirty floor, smoothing its lustrous folds with fastidious hands.

'Something of yours?' she asked, catching sight of an illustration in the magazine.

'Yes. Well, it used to be, before they got their hands on it,' he said, staring at it gloomily. 'Frankly, I don't know why I bother, the reproduction's so filthy.'

'You always say that.' She leaned across the table and examined the page carefully. 'It's not that bad. Anyway, it's *Vogue*, so who cares?'

'I do,' he said haughtily, plucking up the magazine with long, elegant fingers and putting it carefully away in a black leather rucksack. 'I have a reputation to consider.'

Martha looked at him fondly. Paul treated his reputation as tenderly as he did the thick cashmere sweaters he habitually wore, so carefully preserved that they always bore freshly pressed creases along the sleeves. He owned several of them, all exactly the same, big and luxuriant with a plain round neck, which he wore with black track pants, white socks and black plimsolls. In the summer, he simply exchanged the sweaters for white T-shirts. Over the past ten years, she had never seen him dressed in any other way. 'How is your reputation these days?'

He smiled suddenly, an expression which lit his long, cadaverous face and mournful eyes with mischief. 'Not nearly as wicked as I would like.'

Martha laughed. 'That's easily remedied.' She glanced around quickly. 'Anybody in today?'

'Nobody who matters, if that's what you mean,' Paul said, his expression settling back into its usual morose lines. 'Only the usual pack of children.' The tea room was occasionally frequented by artists' agents and critics, although not nearly as often as its reputation implied; the usual crowd came from the art school nearby so the place was always packed with students, idling away the morning, stretching a cup of coffee to last for two hours. Paul glared contemptuously at a group at the adjacent table. 'How I loathe their nauseatingly fresh faces.'

'Envy them, you mean,' Martha said, leaning back in her chair and watching them. 'That was us, fifteen years ago.' She laughed suddenly. 'Don't you remember how we used to order a cup of coffee and two spoons because we never had enough money to buy one each?'

'Plus ça change,' Paul said with a shrug, waving an impatient hand at the waitress. 'Elsie, is that coffee coming?'

Elsie rolled her eyes, flapping her frilled white apron at him as she passed. 'At the double, your highness.' She reappeared carrying a tray filled with Martha's coffee, a slice of strawberry tart and a pot of Earl Grey tea. 'Here's the milk for the coffee, love, hot like you like it.' She smiled at Martha and fixed Paul with a challenging eye. 'Lemon's off, you'll have to make do with milk.'

Paul raised an imperious eyebrow. 'How can lemon be off, as you so charmingly phrase it? There's a fruit and veg market at the end of the road.'

'Well, be a love and run up there and grab some,' Elsie said calmly, winking at Martha as she left.

'I might just do that,' Paul said, lifting the lid off the teapot and peering at the contents. He wrinkled his bony nose approvingly. 'Well, at least they haven't resorted to teabags. Not yet, anyway.'

Martha smiled. 'Ah well, there's hope for civilisation yet,' she said, lazily lifting her hands to bundle her tangle of hair into an untidy knot at the nape of her neck. 'How's Stevie?'

Paul blinked mournful eyes, their colour a clear, delicate amber, fringed with absurdly long eyelashes. 'Still weak, but nearly back to normal, thank you. He sends his love.'

'Send it back. I mean, send him mine back. Have they said what it was?'

'They're not sure. Some weird new strain of pneumonia. Anyway he's –' He shrugged dismissively, flashed her an abrupt, nervous smile. 'Well, he's better. What about you? Have you seen Harry?'

Martha flushed slightly, fiddled with a long, dangling earring. 'No, and I don't intend to.'

Paul regarded her thoughtfully, his eyes unblinking.

Martha's flush deepened. 'But I *have* got a date.'

'A date?'

'Don't sound so surprised. I'm still of marriageable

73

age. Well, just about. Jane's discovered some man David works with. Says I'll love him.' She took a large forkful of strawberry tart. 'This is delicious. Do you want some?'

Paul shook his head. 'And where's this splendid event to take place?'

Martha grimaced. 'She's giving a dinner party at her house next week. I'm dreading it,' she added, wiping a smear of cream from her mouth. 'I haven't a clue what to wear. You know how proper she is. Everything I own is completely unsuitable and I can't afford to buy anything new.' She shrugged slightly. 'Not the way things are at the moment, anyway.'

'Don't be ridiculous. You'll look marvellous. You always do.'

She looked at him gratefully. 'Do I really? How good you are for a girl's ego.' She hesitated. 'Talking of which, I don't suppose... You wouldn't come and do my make-up for me, would you? I'd feel so much better if I was properly armoured.'

Paul inclined his head graciously. 'Of course.'

'Actually, it's moral support I'm after more than cosmetic, although I don't suppose that would go amiss either,' she said with a nervous laugh. 'Phil did offer but she's so hopeless about that sort of thing. She'll tell me to dab on a bit of lipstick, take a deep breath and get on with it.'

'How is she?'

'Oh, you know, she's Phil.' Martha pulled a face. 'She's quieter than ever, if that's possible. One day I think she'll disappear altogether and all that'll be left is a neatly folded white T-shirt and a navy trouser suit.' She frowned suddenly. 'To be honest, I think there's something bugging her but I can't work out what it is.'

'Maybe you should ask her.'

'Don't be daft. You don't ask Phil questions like that. Far too personal. I think she's in love with somebody –

74

and it's not Peter,' she added quickly, shaking her head. 'From the look of her, it's going very badly, if it's going at all.' She sighed. 'She gets these hopeless crushes on completely unsuitable people, not that she ever tells them, just sort of hopes they'll get the message by telepathy or something.'

'And what about you? Are you hopelessly crushed on anybody at the moment?'

Martha grimaced. 'Just the milkman. No, really, I'm serious. He's gorgeous. I get up early every morning just so I can look at him. I stand in the window combing my hair like Rapunzel and he never even notices me.'

Paul looked at her affectionately. 'Absurd woman. And I suppose you still let those idiots hang out in your flat all day, distracting you from working.'

'They're not idiots,' she protested. 'Anyway, they like me and you know how much I need to be appreciated.'

Paul sighed. 'Don't we all?'

Martha smiled sympathetically as she lit a cigarette and inhaled a large gulp of smoke. Paul looked at her reproachfully. 'Are you still doing that? I thought you were giving up.'

Martha flapped a hand at him. 'Next week. How's the work going?'

'Well, the most extraordinary thing,' Paul said, looking vaguely perplexed, 'is that it's going marvellously well.'

Martha balanced her burning cigarette on the edge of her plate of half-eaten tart and took a large mouthful. 'That's nice. Are you sure you don't want any of this? It's very good.'

'You know I never eat sugar. Do listen to me, I'm being perfectly serious. It's all rather disconcerting. Some new art magazine in New York published one of my illustrations last week and the phone hasn't stopped ringing since. They're over me like a rash.'

'But that's wonderful,' Martha exclaimed, picking up her cigarette and taking a large drag before extinguishing it in the middle of the remains of her tart. 'Isn't that what you've always wanted?'

'I'm not entirely sure.'

Martha rolled large, expressive blue eyes. 'Are you serious?'

'Probably not,' Paul said, with a brief smile. 'It's just that since Stevie got sick…' He shook his head abruptly. 'Maybe there are more important things to worry about.'

Martha laughed, her voluptuous pink upper lip spreading to reveal strong, square white teeth. 'Why, Paul, how very unfashionable of you.'

'No doubt,' he said absently, his concentration distracted by something in her face. He squinted at her thoughtfully. 'You do have the most marvellous smile,' he murmured. 'I wonder if you'd mind coming to pose for me? I've been wrestling with an illustration for a new toothpaste commercial and I can't seem to get it right.'

'You're not really serious?' she exclaimed.

'Yes, really you do. It's the way your top lip –'

'No, not *that*. About not wanting to be rich and famous.'

He frowned at her. 'I don't recall ever mentioning anything about not wanting to be rich.'

'You can't have one with the other. Not these days. No fame, no fortune.'

Paul sighed. 'No infamy, no fortune more like.'

'Well, I'm sure we could think up a really ghastly story about you. There must be something sinister in your past.' She flashed him a cautious look. 'Like drugs, for example.'

'There was nothing of the sort,' he said sharply. 'I merely… experimented a little.'

Martha shrugged. 'Once dabbled in recreational

substances, so you're dangerous but reformed which always goes down well, and then there's the mysterious foreign parentage.'

'Oh, very mysterious. Spanish immigrants living in north London,' he said wryly.

'Yes, I suppose that's hopelessly unglamorous,' she said teasingly, then shot him a curious look. 'How is your mum? Still hoping for the big day?'

'Don't be a bitch,' he said, without rancour.

'I'm not,' she protested. 'I'm thinking of her best interests. She's going to have to know some day.'

'I don't see why. She merely thinks I'm a confirmed bachelor.'

'But it's not true and it's not fair on Stevie. You're as firmly married as any man I've ever met.'

'Don't be such a sanctimonious little cow,' he said, arching a haughty eyebrow. 'Stevie doesn't need your misplaced liberalism, however well intentioned it may be, and nor does she. What she doesn't know won't hurt her.'

Martha pulled a face. 'If I was a mother, I'm sure I'd prefer to know.'

Paul lifted a supercilious eyebrow and stared at her unblinkingly. 'Well, you're not. And while we're on the subject of facing up to the truth, I want to talk to you about Harry.'

She shifted uneasily in her chair. 'What about him?' she asked, her eyes sliding away.

'I think you should go back to him.' Martha flicked her head in an impatient, dismissive gesture but said nothing. He looked at her thoughtfully. 'I think that in a few months' time, you might find that you've thrown happiness away in favour of some adolescent dream.'

'Now who's being sanctimonious?' she muttered, cheeks flaming.

He watched her frowning face regretfully. 'I'm sorry,

I don't mean to be, and I know it's not what you want to hear. But I really do think you should go back to him.'

She stared silently into her cup then, after a quick uneasy glance at him, looked away and concentrated on balancing sugar lumps one on top of the other in a teetering pile. 'Well, fuck you,' she said eventually.

'Martha, Martha,' he said gently. 'Don't be like that.' He smiled at her flushed, sullen face, leaned forward and plucked at a stray curl, tucking it behind her ear. 'You're such a *baby* about love sometimes. Harry's a good man. They're hard to find.'

'Tell me about it,' Martha said, looking up from the sugar with a tight, uncomfortable smile. 'Anyway, what about me? I'm a good woman too. Good and ready for some fun.'

He gave her an odd look. 'It's a dangerous thing, fun.'

She wrinkled her nose thoughtfully, dropped a sugar lump into the remains of her coffee and crushed it viciously under her spoon. 'Yes, well, danger's a fun thing sometimes, too.' Suddenly her frown dissolved into a smile, wide, pink and voluptuous. 'If only I could bloody well find some.'

He did not return the smile but gazed at her thoughtfully for a moment. 'You will,' he said. 'You will.'

10

Scarcely had Phil got through the front door of the tall, thin house in north London than Emma wrestled her out of her coat, thrust a glass of warm white wine in her hand and propelled her towards a stout man who was standing disconsolately by the rack of coats. 'Thank God you're here,' she said through gritted teeth. 'The place is stuffed with Mike's theatre types. All charming but not a brain to rub between them. I'm desperate for a clever woman to talk to Barnaby. He's something important in the government think-tank. At least, I think that's what Mike said.'

Phil, who loathed parties and became intensely polite when confronted by anything or anyone she disliked, smiled obediently at Emma, promised to at least try to look clever and fixed an attentive gaze on Barnaby, to whom she had taken a passionate and instant dislike.

It did not help that he had misheard her name and kept calling her Philippa, with infuriating insistence. She wondered if he had been on one of those American management courses which seemed to be becoming so popular; he was fond of concepts and ratification and streamlining and for a while she amused herself with counting the Americanisms which peppered his conversation like grit.

Eventually she grew bored and began to look around, searching for less self-absorbed company. She wondered if Harry would turn up and allowed herself a small, pleasurable thrill of excitement. She had not called him, despite her promise to Martha, and knew that it was because she was frightened to. Suddenly she saw a familiar head and looked away, overcome with shyness. When she looked back it took her a minute to locate the dark head of thick hair among the crowd, then she found it again, its familiar, tender sprinkling of grey and the slight kink of a wave as it curled, too long as usual, over the collar of an old leather jacket. Phil composed her face, was about to call out to attract his attention when she saw a small, white-ringed hand sneak possessively up his shoulder and tangle playfully in those dark curls. She averted her gaze, feeling her face flush under a hot, painful wave of jealousy. Barnaby's reptilian eyes flickered with sudden interest, slid towards the door and back to her face, but the flow of words did not falter. Of course Harry would be with somebody, Phil thought miserably. A man like Harry did not stay alone for long.

She pasted on her face a bland smile of welcome and, raising her gaze, came face to face with the owner of the hand. She smiled warmly into the woman's startled face then raised her eyes to meet Harry and found herself confronting a perfect stranger. He gave a brief, puzzled nod and turned away. Her warm smile faded to a foolish grin and she flushed with humiliation. This really will not do, she told herself severely, startled by the sudden, intense rush of jealousy. She was used to feeling for Harry a vague, distant emotion which she had not civilised with a name; but now he had left Martha she understood that what she felt for him was neither distant nor vague but a yearning that threatened to engulf her.

'Are you?' Barnaby said, watching the conflicting emotions on her pale, solemn face with interest. Phil started with surprised confusion. She had forgotten that he was there.

'Are you interested in the theatre?' he shouted.

She nodded, guilt causing her smile to widen eagerly, yet at the same time she blushed at her own cowardice, vehemently wishing that she had said that frankly, no, she wasn't. Irritable at being recalled from her thoughts by a question of such inanity, she found herself wondering what sort of a fool would think that anybody would come to a party like this and say that they loathed the theatre and everybody in it?

'Sorry?' he said. 'Didn't quite catch that.'

Phil cursed the politeness which froze her senses and forced her to nod like those absurd animals which grin at motorists from the back seats of cars. 'Yes,' she shouted, her voice cracking with the strain of making herself heard.

Barnaby smiled briefly, nodding with satisfaction before launching back into his monologue which was by this time rising to such a pitch of enthusiasm and evident self-congratulation that Phil realised, to her intense relief, that no further contribution was required from her. She watched him with distaste. Barnaby was one of those men and, she thought, there are many like him, who do not seem to mind to whom they are speaking so long as they have a body placed before them. Wondering idly why men enjoy a captive audience while women prefer a captured one, she leaned against the rack of coats and waited to be rescued.

It was a long wait. The awful thought that Barnaby knew nobody at the party or, worse, that they knew him and were intent on avoiding him began to dawn on her and she regretted, again, the creeping paralysis of politeness which had marooned her, over the years, in countless draughty hallways, cramped kitchens and cold bedrooms.

81

The trouble with politeness as opposed to mere shyness, she thought, is that it is so *receptive*. Even to men like Barnaby, with dandruff settling like late frost in their eyebrows and vol au vent crumbs decorating their wet, shining lips, morsels of which occasionally became dislodged to cling, pale and glistening, to the satin lapel of her suit.

'Don't you think, Philippa?' said Barnaby, gazing at her intently.

Phil, who had not heard a word, muttered, 'Yes. Oh, yes I do. Absolutely.'

Barnaby looked at her with renewed interest. 'You do? Marvellous. Yes, splendid.' A fine spray of saliva showered her face as he dropped his voice to a more confidential note. 'It's just that *most* people think that a proposal to end subsidies for the arts is an absolute heresy. Particularly this lot,' he said glancing around, 'who talk about the arts in almost the same breath as they speak of God. A bad analogy, no doubt,' he added, raking the room with a contemptuous glare, 'in as much as they wouldn't speak of God at all, it being unfashionable in such circles to manifest any enthusiasm, let alone a religious one.'

'Ah,' said Phil, a rictus of panic stretching her face into an idiotic smile as her eyes searched furtively for her hostess. So that's what Emma had meant by needing a clever woman. Why the hell didn't she say so? No doubt Mike, who was a prominent theatre director, had invited Barnaby to the party so he could be talked out of his ideas and here she was quietly allowing him to be talked into them. Oh, well done, Phil, she thought, staring gloomily at Barnaby's purple veined nose. Now I'll get merry hell when Barnaby calls Mike tomorrow to say he met such a charming, such a sympathetic woman at the party.

'Although to be fair they do have their one enthusiasm,' said Barnaby, curving his pendulous lips into a smile of chilling intimacy. 'Themselves. There they are, elevated above the rest of us on their wooden boards with halos of light shining around their heads, strutting around and declaiming at the masses who, frankly, don't give a damn about them. But try telling them that. Dare to even whisper it…'

Phil interrupted him with a little nervous laugh. 'Good Lord,' she said, immediately regretting the phrase, 'for a minute you almost sounded as though you despised them.'

Barnaby smiled grimly. 'I do.'

Phil, wondering desperately how to extricate herself from the situation or, more urgently, from Barnaby, gestured weakly at her empty glass. He went on talking. 'I said I'd love another drink,' she shouted above the noise.

He frowned, vaguely affronted. 'You'd like a drink, you say? Now? Oh, well, I suppose I could go and find a bottle,' he said ungraciously. 'But let me finish this point first. It's rather a complex one and I feel sure you'd like to grasp it properly.'

I'd like to grasp you, thought Phil crossly, somewhere where it hurts. She was still considering the various forms of torture to which she could subject Barnaby when she saw, over his shoulder, Harry's head disappearing through the doorway opposite and into the crush of bodies in the sitting room. 'Harry,' she shouted, into Barnaby's startled face, 'Harry, I'm over here.'

To her intense relief he heard her and, turning, elbowed his way through the crowd of people to her side, enveloping her in a warm, wordless embrace. He was wearing an old corduroy jacket, softened with years of wear and smelling of turpentine and the small cigars he smoked. She breathed in the smell appreciatively, nuzzling her head against his shoulder until, suddenly aware of what she was doing, she stepped abruptly out of the circle of his arms and stared up at him in confusion. Harry, blessedly, had not noticed, was too busy manoeuvring her out of the tangle of coats and around the bulk of Barnaby's heavy body. He kept his arm lightly around her as he bent down to shout above the din of the party, 'I was hoping you'd be here. I've been boring everyone rotten, asking if they'd seen you.' He grinned down at her then looked over at Barnaby. 'Sorry to take her away, but I simply must get her views on the new exhibition at the Tate.'

'By all means,' called Barnaby, gazing sorrowfully after Phil.

'Thank you,' she said gratefully when they were out of earshot and installed in a quiet corner of the sitting room. She still felt a warmth across her back where Harry's arm had held her and wished suddenly that he had left it there.

'I'm not sure he would,' said Harry with a brief smile. 'He'll be after Emma for your number before the night's out.'

'Oh dear,' Phil said, looking worriedly towards the door. 'I do hope not. Unfortunately I think I've rather gone and put my foot in it. He's the man from the Ministry who thinks subsidies should be withdrawn from the arts and whom, I think, we were all supposed to beat into submission with charm and brilliance. Thing is,' she glanced miserably at Harry, 'I think I agreed with him.'

'I shouldn't worry too much about it,' he said. 'I'm sorry to say that it would make little difference to him either way.'

'Oh, you're probably right but I do wish I wasn't quite so hopeless at parties. I go completely deaf and then my voice is so quiet that nobody can ever hear me so I always end up nodding and smiling like a lunatic at some dreadful man who thinks I'm madly interested in him. Martha always says –' her voice tailed off and she shot a quick, worried glance at him.

'It's all right,' he said gently, 'you can mention her name.'

'Yes, I know. Of course I can. It's not as if you...I mean, you're both – I've been meaning to ring you. I should have done. Sorry.' She looked at him regretfully. 'There you are, I've gone and put my foot in it again. Martha always says that I'm hopeless at...Oh God, now I'm making it worse, aren't I?'

His eyelids drooped heavily but his mouth twitched in a slight smile. 'Now that you mention it, yes.' He stepped back suddenly as a woman pushed between them, elbowing her way through the crowd, her cigarette held like a lethal weapon in front of her. In her wake trickled a slow stream of bodies, flowing into the spaces around them.

Harry peered over the heads and, seeing Phil's pale, anxious face, shouted, 'I didn't mean that. Don't worry, I'm fine. And we may as well get Martha out of the way now or it's going to ruin whatever chance of a conversation we might have had.' He elbowed his way to her side. 'As much of a conversation as you can have in this lot, anyway. Is she coming?'

'No,' said Phil at which Harry, looking both relieved and disappointed, muttered, 'Fine, fine.' Then, casting a sidelong glance at Phil, he added, his voice casual, 'Is she well?'

'I think so.' Phil looked at him doubtfully, thinking of the febrile light in Martha's eyes and her nervous, agitated manner during the past six months. 'Well, she says she's fine. She's working hard,' she ended lamely.

'Is she painting?'

'Yes,' said Phil slowly, wondering whether producing watercolours for the fronts of greetings cards could truthfully be called painting. 'It's Mother's Day soon. Well, not soon, but you know how many months ahead these things have to be done.' She smiled suddenly. 'They're very keen on baskets of dried flowers this year so you can imagine what the flat looks like. She's even got them hanging from the chandelier.'

Harry returned her smile. 'At least she's earning some money. She's managing, is she?' he asked, a note of anxiety creeping into his voice.

Phil shrugged. 'Oh, Martha always *manages*. And she is doing some of her own work. She mentioned that a gallery in the East End is interested in giving her an exhibition some time next year, so she's hard at it.'

'She's not – she's not distracted, then?'

'Distracted?' repeated Phil, confused, and then saw the flicker of hope in Harry's face and said quickly, 'Oh, no. No, she's not at all *distracted*, although I think she's partying a bit too hard for her own good.' She paused and laughed quickly, 'But you know Martha, she always was fond of a party.'

'Yes,' said Harry ruefully, 'I know Martha. I think –' he shook his head – 'oh, what does it matter what I think? Everyone seems to think it was inevitable.' A trace of bitterness edged into his voice.

Phil looked at him regretfully. 'You mustn't mind about other people.' She believed passionately that people's emotional affairs were their own business and to meddle in them was unwise and, more often than not, unhelpful. She knew what people were saying, had heard the same sentiments expressed often enough, that Martha and Harry were the original odd couple, him being so dark and Martha so golden, he so slow, she so quick, he loved silence, she loved noise, he liked method, she liked chaos and so on and so forth. Phil believed that it was in his very oppositeness to Martha that the strength of their relationship lay. He treated her like some rare, strange creature whose habits he did not entirely understand but had the great good wisdom to respect. That very thing in Martha which her lovers wanted to possess, her glittering, carefree vitality turned to fool's gold when they held it fast in their hands.

Nothing would make Phil say as much to anyone, certainly not to Harry who sensed in her, she suspected, a dangerous sympathy. At least, it was dangerous to him, for hope seemed to Phil as fragile as a spider's web but with the enduring strength of spun gold. Sympathy, she thought, gilds hope.

'No, I suppose you're right,' Harry said. 'One shouldn't mind about other people. It's just…' He stared into his drink for a minute as if he might find the answer in his glass. 'Well, I suppose it's just that they all say the same thing, that we were entirely unsuited.'

'It's easy to comment after the event,' Phil said. 'And I daresay they only say it to be comforting.'

Harry shrugged. 'Maybe,' he said slowly. 'But sometimes I think that I –' he gazed at her intently for a minute then shrugged lightly. 'I think that I should have ended up with you instead of Martha. No, don't look like that, I don't mean to offend you. I'm really not putting this very well. All I mean to say is that, in many ways, we're so much better suited.' He looked at her with a little, regretful shake of his head and she turned away, sure that her eyes must reveal something of what she felt. He, mistaking her abruptness for embarrassment, said, 'Forget I even mentioned it,' and gave a short, forced laugh. 'I don't know why I'm bothering you with all this. That's what comes of being alone so much. You start talking to yourself, speaking your thoughts out loud.'

Phil forced herself to speak lightly. 'I shall take it as a compliment then.'

He smiled. 'I hope so.'

'But you're all right?' she asked, wanting to distract them both from thoughts of Martha. How can I, she thought miserably. How can I feel like this about a man with whom Martha says she's still in love?

'I get by,' he said in a low voice, and then his face contorted slightly. 'God, Phil, I miss her. Sometimes I don't think that I can bear the way that I miss her.'

Damn Martha, thought Phil fiercely. Damn her for making him suffer like this. 'She –' Phil began, and then thought better of it. What was there to say? She missed him? So she said. She loved him? She said that as well. But what use was any of that to Harry?

'I miss him terribly,' Martha had said. 'But I can't ring him. I just can't. I know what would happen. We'd have dinner and get on well, because we always do, then perhaps we'd fall into bed and everything would be fine until I began to get restless again. It just wouldn't be fair to him. I've got to get this – this *feeling*, whatever it is, out of my system.' She had shrugged. 'Maybe then…'

'Maybe then he won't be around,' Phil had said warningly.

Martha had sighed and smiled ruefully. 'I know. But you do see?' She'd looked urgently at Phil. 'You do see that it's hopeless like this?'

Phil had agreed. 'Yes. Yes, I suppose I do.'

Harry, recovering his composure, smiled reassuringly. 'Sorry,' he said. 'It was just seeing you again, you remind me –' He shrugged and looked around. 'What the hell. As we're here I suppose we may as well get drunk.'

'More like poisoned,' said Phil, gazing into the contents of her glass.

Harry laughed. 'Yes, it's filthy, isn't it?'

'Did I hear you mention the word filthy, darling?' A woman with blood-red hair and lips to match insinuated her full-hipped body between them. She gave Phil a cold little smile and took Harry by the arm. 'I heard you were on your own again, darling,' she said, pale fingers with lacquered nails digging possessively into the faded corduroy of his jacket. 'Good news travels fast.'

Phil stepped back to avoid being forcibly pushed out of the way. 'How do you do?' she said politely. The woman turned her face back towards Phil, the pencilled line of her eyebrows raised in comic surprise. 'Why, I do very well, thank you. Just ask Harry.' Wriggling her body against his, she tilted her head to stare up into his face.

He looked down at her and to her amazement Phil saw a gentle, almost tender smile illuminate his face. 'Hello, Tania,' he said, hugging her affectionately. 'This is Phil. Also known as Sarah Phillis.' He paused, hesitating slightly. 'A close friend of Martha's.'

Now why did he say that, Phil wondered, watching his sudden, discomfited smile. Is it purely for my benefit, to let me know something that Tania has already made perfectly apparent, that he once had, or indeed is still having, an affair with her? She felt a sudden stab of jealousy and, flushing miserably, muttered something about needing a drink. As she turned away she felt Tania's hand curl around her arm.

'Me too,' she said lazily, waving her empty glass in the air with her free hand. Her grip tightened on Phil's arm. 'Be a darling, Harry. I want to have a little girls' talk with Phil here.'

Harry looked startled. 'Yes, of course,' he said, with a quick anxious look at Phil.

She jerked her arm away abruptly. 'I'll go. I know where they keep the drink. I saw a whole pile of bottles earlier, in a bath full of ice.'

Tania watched her with a small, contemptuous smile.

'Don't be silly, darling,' she said. 'Send the men. It's what they were put on this earth for.'

Harry gave Phil an apologetic smile but, as he went to take the glass out of her hand, he realised that it was still full. 'I won't bother with the glasses,' he said with a quick, startled glance, 'a bottle would do us better anyway. Won't be a minute.' He hurried off, a worried frown deepening the already pronounced lines on his forehead.

'Handsome bastard, isn't he?' Tania said, 'in an ugly sort of way. Odd, isn't it, how imperfection in a man is so attractive, but in a woman...' She gave Phil a hard, assessing stare then shrugged expressively and glanced away towards the mirror which hung above the fireplace in front of which they were standing. Smiling provocatively at her own reflection, she smoothed the front of her dress with her long, pale hands, further exposing the milky smoothness of her breasts. 'Although I don't suppose you think of him like that, do you?' she said, giving Phil a sly sideways glance. 'Him being part of the family and all that.' Her smile widened voluptuously. 'I'll tell you something, though. He's great in the sack. One of the best.'

Phil flushed and turned away from the smile. 'How very interesting,' she said coldly.

Tania raised a thin, pencilled eyebrow. 'You don't mind me mentioning it, do you, my sweet?' She gave a high little laugh. 'Oh, you *do* mind. I am sorry. I was sure that darling Martha must have told you every little detail.'

Phil took a sip of wine. 'We never discuss such matters.'

Tania registered the full glass with a slight sardonic smile. 'No, of course you don't. Women like you never do. At least not out loud.' Her smile sharpened maliciously and she watched Phil with interest. 'Have I hit a nerve, my sweet? Don't tell me you're lusting after Martha's man?' Phil gazed stonily at her glass so Tania shrugged elaborately and sighed. 'Well, it's all the same to me, my sweet. Frankly, I wouldn't care if you'd fucked the Pope. They're all the same to me. Men, I mean. Had one and you've had them all.'

'No doubt,' Phil said, glancing at her with distaste.

Tania smiled languidly. In the full curve of her mouth and the lazy tilt of her heavy-lidded slate grey eyes there lingered the ghost of a formidable beauty. 'So, you're a friend of the famous Martha? Did she tell you about me?'

Phil's glance flickered over her briefly. 'She's never even mentioned your name.'

Tania's smile dimmed and she shrugged lightly. 'No, I don't suppose she would have,' she said, swaying slightly on high heels. She looked consideringly at Phil, her green eyes narrowed. 'And have you told her about you and Harry?'

'There's nothing to say.'

Tania gave a sharp, unpleasant laugh. 'If you say so, my sweet. I believe you, but then I'm a trusting sort of girl.' Phil said nothing. 'God, you're a bundle of laughs. Can't think what he sees in you, frankly.'

'Sees?'

'Harry, sweet. Who'd you think we were talking about?'

'We are friends,' Phil said firmly. 'Nothing more.'

Tania threw back her head and laughed, exposing a magnificent white throat. 'Yes, sweet, and I'm Liz Taylor.' Her laughter stopped abruptly. 'You can drop the innocent act with me.' Her voice was suddenly malevolent. 'He's susceptible all right and we all know what a girl can do when she's got her eye on the main chance, even a plain little thing like you. You'll be in his bed before the month's out.'

To her horror, Phil felt herself blushing furiously. 'I've just remembered that I promised to meet somebody,' she said quickly. 'Tell Harry I had to go.'

Tania's eyebrows quivered in surprise and she smiled wolfishly, revealing sharp white teeth. 'Don't tell me you're still at the panting stage, hot with guilt and frenzied with loyalty to poor darling Martha? How perfectly quaint.' Her eyes narrowed. 'Well, don't bother, my sweet. She won't thank you. They never do.'

'I must go,' Phil said, stumbling in her hurry to get away. She heard Tania's high, mocking laughter following her and pushed roughly past somebody, clumsy in her urgency to get out of the room. Feeling her arm being grabbed, she looked up to see Harry's startled face. 'What's the matter?' he asked anxiously. 'Are you all right?' She nodded dumbly, aware of her flaming cheeks and quick, nervous breathing. He bent to look at her face more clearly. 'Has Tania said something to upset you?'

'No.' Her tone was so sharp that Harry jerked his head back in surprise, then stared at her in bewilderment. She smiled weakly. 'Sorry, I didn't mean to snap. I'm feeling a bit faint, that's all. I need some air.' She turned away from him, heading blindly for the door.

'I'll come with you. I could do with some air myself.'

She stopped, shaking her head. 'Please don't. I'd much rather be on my own.'

He let go of her arm reluctantly. 'Very well. If you're quite sure.'

Phil felt dangerously close to tears. 'Yes.' She gave him a quick, grateful smile. 'You'd better go. Tania's waiting for that wine you promised.'

'You will come back?' he said, searching her face anxiously. 'You won't leave without telling me?'

She nodded, desperate to be gone. 'Soon as I can.' The crowd in the hallway had thinned out considerably but

Barnaby was still there, his considerable bulk bent over a wispy blonde in faded violet silk. Her pretty face wore an expression of sullen defeat, as if the simple act of walking away from her tormentor was beyond her power or strength. With one outstretched arm, she hung grimly on to a hook on the coat rack, perhaps to take the weight off her feet, while the rest of her body was propped against the wall. In her faded silk she looked pathetic; a sad, broken butterfly.

As she leaned past Barnaby to pluck her coat from the rack, Phil flashed her a sympathetic smile. The woman returned it wearily, her face closing in patient despair as she realised that Phil had not come to rescue her. Struggling into her coat, watched unhelpfully by Barnaby, Phil felt an irresistible urge to puncture his complacent arrogance. She knew that it was not Barnaby she was angry with, but Tania, or perhaps herself, but in that brief moment she didn't care.

'She's dead,' she whispered into Barnaby's ear.

He looked startled. 'Philippa?' he said uncertainly. 'It is Philippa, isn't it?'

'My name is Sarah,' Phil said, fixing him with a glittering smile. 'And this poor woman died of boredom. About an hour ago, I should say.'

She did not wait for his reaction but, turning on her heel, hurried towards the front door. As she opened it she glanced over her shoulder to see that Barnaby had disappeared and the blonde woman was standing alone, her smile dazed but grateful.

11

'Tania and I had dinner together last night.'

Phil took the receiver away from her ear and pulled a face at it but then she put it back again and composed her voice to sound sweetly reasonable. 'How nice for you.'

'It wasn't, actually,' Harry said. When Phil said nothing his voice grew louder, as if he was faintly exasperated. 'Tania said she'd been a bit of a bitch. That's why I'm calling, I thought she might have upset you. Her tongue gets a bit sharp after a few drinks.'

'Does it? I didn't notice.'

'Well, good. I'm glad.' Again, he waited for her to say something but when she didn't he broke the silence abruptly. 'You didn't come back.'

'I'm sorry.'

'Was it something I did?'

'No,' she exclaimed, adding in a more moderate tone, 'No, it was nothing like that. I was tired, that's all.' Harry said nothing and Phil wondered if he was annoyed. She gave a small sigh. 'Look, I'm sorry. I know I promised to tell you I was leaving but I couldn't face struggling through all those people. I went home.'

It was true, she *had* gone home, although not to bed, instead she'd sat on the floor of her sitting room, watched with astonished interest by the cats, and drunk the better part of a bottle of wine. As she drank, she thought about Harry, and as she got drunk, she thought about him more. The more she thought, the less she understood until eventually she gave up and went to bed.

When she woke the next morning, she realised that she must have fallen straight into a deep, dreamless sleep. This made her feel strangely guilty. Perhaps, after all, she felt nothing for Harry; all that messy emotion had been a brief, hysterical delusion. As she sat at her kitchen table drinking hot, strong tea, he seemed diminished by the routine ordinariness of the morning. It was a lovely day, the sky crisp and blue, hung with stiff curls of white cloud; outside her kitchen window she could see the starched, springing petals of crocuses, violet, yellow and white, standing jauntily to attention. She sipped her tea, feeling peaceful; Harry seemed no more to her than a friend.

His voice, abrupt and resentful, brought her back to the present. 'I waited for you.'

'I'm sorry,' she said quickly, feeling vaguely irritated. He couldn't have waited all that long. She herself had left fairly late so he and Tania must have gone soon after, hurrying to find a restaurant before they all closed for the night.

'You said you felt faint. I thought you might have been taken ill, or something.'

'Well, I wasn't,' she said sharply.

'So I gather. Although you did look pretty strange before you left.'

Phil, remembering her graceless exit from the party, felt a brief flush of embarrassment and said quickly, 'Yes, I was feeling a bit odd. I'm sorry. Did you wait very long?'

'Long enough for Barnaby to start snooping around looking for you,' he said heavily. 'Once I realised you'd gone, I dragged Tania off to some dreadful all-night café in King's Cross to get some food in her.' He hesitated and then said, his voice curious, 'What *did* she say to you? She was very remorseful once she'd sobered up a bit. Kept saying she'd been a terrible bitch.'

'She wasn't that bad,' Phil said carefully. 'Did she – er, did she say anything else?'

'Just that, that she'd been a cow.'

'Oh, well,' Phil murmured, relieved. 'She was probably just upset about something. A man, I would think.'

Harry laughed. 'What else?'

Phil felt a sudden flash of irritation. 'What do you mean, what else? A man like you, for example?'

'She told you about our magnificent affair, then,' Harry sounded faintly amused. 'Is that what she meant by being a bitch?'

'No, it isn't. And she didn't need to tell me. You told me yourself, by the way you looked at her.'

There was silence for a moment. 'Did you mind?' Harry said, his tone thoughtful.

Phil, who found that she minded very much, said quickly, 'No, of course not. But I expect Martha did.'

'I doubt it. It ended as soon as I met Martha.'

'Then perhaps Tania does have a reason to feel angry?'

'Well, actually she doesn't.' His voice was sharp. 'And nor do you. Unless,' he added slowly, 'you're angry with me because of Martha, for some reason?'

'Of course I'm not,' she said, realising suddenly that she *was* angry with him. She was angry because he made her feel vulnerable and guilty. 'Why should you think that?'

'Well, you're certainly pissed off with me about something.'

'No I'm not.'

Harry was silent, as if he was thinking something over. Eventually he said, with a heavy sigh, 'Look, Phil, you're making me feel as if I've done something to upset you. And if I have, then I do wish you'd tell me what it is. Last night, when you just disappeared like that, I thought…'

'What?'

'Oh, never mind. It's not important.'

But it is important, she thought wildly, it *is*. 'Harry, you've done nothing to upset me,' she said quickly. 'Nothing at all. I left last night because I was feeling rotten and Tania… well, she looked as if nothing was going to stand between you and her, especially not me.'

'Some friend you are,' he said ruefully. 'I could have done with a bit of protection.'

Phil pretended a lightness she did not feel. 'Have you seen her fingernails? I'd be dead by now.'

'Impressive, aren't they?'

'Lethally.'

'Oh, Tania's all right. She's just a bit lonely.'

'Aren't we all?' Phil said, and blushed.

'Yes.'

There was a sudden awkward silence.

'Phil, er, you don't… you don't feel like going for a walk this afternoon, do you?'

'A walk?' she repeated, startled.

'Oh, never mind. Another time, perhaps.'

'No! Yes, I mean I would. Like to, I mean.'

'Good. Well, that's settled, then.'

'Where?'

'What? Oh, I see. Hampstead Heath all right? About two.'

'Two would be fine.'

'Let's meet at the car park then. Do you know the one on the south side?'

'Intimately.'

Harry laughed. 'Good. Well, I'll see you there, then. At two o'clock.'

'At two o'clock,' Phil repeated gravely.

'Goodbye, then.'

Phil smiled. 'Goodbye, Harry.'

97

12

'I think the black silk is better.'

'Not too ageing?'

Paul stared at her imperiously over the bony beak of his nose. 'My, my, we are in a state tonight.'

'Piss off.'

'Well, excuse me for breathing.'

'Sorry.'

He shrugged, and cast her a sly glance of amusement. 'I thought you said you weren't interested in meeting this man.'

'I'm not.' Martha stripped off an antique black lace dress and, naked apart from a pair of crumpled black silk knickers, went on picking up and discarding clothes. Paul, his long, thin body draped over the mantelpiece by the fire, watched her with detached interest. She felt no self-consciousness; the lines and curves of her body were to him simply a series of curling charcoal strokes on paper.

He made a sudden, impatient gesture. 'Keep still a minute. Stand with your arms out,' he raised his hands, 'like so.'

She raised her arms obediently and held the pose limply, while he studied her. 'I'm working on a swim-suit series for *Vogue*,' he murmured, watching her carefully. 'No, that's not right. Turn slightly. Put your chin up, keep it in line with your shoulder and arm. There – that's it.' He smiled slightly at Martha's expression of pained but patient resignation. 'You can stop now.' She dropped her arms and turned back to the wardrobe, riffling through hangers. 'I'm so out of practice,' she complained. 'The idea of a date with somebody frightens the life out of me, let alone a blind date with somebody my *sister*'s picked out for me. I don't even know his bloody name.'

'You'll find out soon enough.'

'You're enjoying this,' Martha said, staring balefully at him. 'You're as bad as she is. Why either of you think I might be interested in some French creep who sells beauty products, and bum creams at that, is beyond me.' Tugging viciously at a hanger which had become caught in another, she pulled most of the contents of the wardrobe on to the floor. She stared glumly at the mess. 'Jane says he's handsome, which means he's bound to be insufferable. I loathe beautiful men. They're so self regarding.'

'Not all of them.' Paul extended a bony, elegant hand and carefully plucked a slip of scarlet antique lace and satin from the pile. 'Some of them are perfectly charming. Try this on.'

Martha frowned thoughtfully at the dress. 'Do you really think *red*, for a blind date?'

Paul flicked the shining fabric impatiently. 'Go on. Do at least try it on.'

'Oh, all right,' Martha said, squirming her body into the dress, 'but I warn you, it's not a pretty sight.' She bent to check her reflection in the mirror. 'Oh, perfect,' she said disgustedly, staring at herself. 'It matches my eyes.' She ripped it off, tossed it on to the bed, where it joined a growing pile of rejected clothes, and then threw herself on top of them. 'I hate dinner parties. Especially my sister's dinner parties. They're full of people who are really *interesting*. You know; like they've climbed Everest, written a fashionable new novel or met Diana.

99

Either that or they're terribly nice people from Putney and Barnes whose only source of conversation is the price of property or the criminal cost of private education.' She draped a hand across her forehead in an attitude of despair. 'They'd all *much* rather send their kids to state schools, but you know, sweetie, one just can't trust the system these days, and what's a social conscience in comparison to your child's future?' She let her arm flop back on the bed. 'All they talk about is mortgages and school fees. I'm not sure which lot is the more tiresome. And none of them ever smoke.' She rolled over and lowered her head and arms over the side of the bed to scrabble around under it for a pack of cigarettes.

'The black,' Paul said firmly.

Martha sighed and stood up, drooping pathetically, a cigarette dangling from her lips. 'The spectre at the feast.'

'Well, we can at least do something to make that face less spectral,' he said, handing her a faded olive paisley silk dressing gown. 'Put this on.' She slipped her arms into it, flounced over to a chair by the window and sat down with an irritable sigh. 'Let's see what we can do with you,' he muttered, squinting at her through narrowed eyes. 'Yes, I think a pale base with a touch of rouge. Dark eyes, a defined brow, red lips.'

'Go easy,' warned Martha, 'this is a dinner party in Barnes, not a wild night down the Café de Paris.'

Paul raised an eyebrow. 'No need to look provincial just because you're dining in the suburbs. And we'll have to do something about this,' he said, lifting a handful of hair and letting it fall down her back. 'Nothing elaborate; a few simple curls, that sort of thing.'

'I *told* you,' Martha said irritably, 'I'm not interested.'

'Yes, I know you did, my dear,' he said imperiously, 'but you're not the one who has to look at you. It's only polite to look one's best if one is going to sit for four hours at a dinner table. I'll just pop into the kitchen and get my Carmens. I put them in my bag earlier, just in case.'

She made a face at herself in the mirror, screwing up her eyes and poking out her tongue, then relaxed, smiling affectionately at his reflection. 'What would I do without you,' she sighed.

Paul wrinkled his large nose. 'Fade away, my dear. Simply fade away,' he murmured.

Martha closed her eyes and leaned back in the chair as Paul, armed with a battery of brushes and sponges and little pots of colour, set to work on her face. 'How's Stevie, anyway?'

A flicker of emotion briefly disturbed the calm surface of Paul's thin face but then he shrugged and said evenly, 'He's OK.' He began to dab blobs of foundation on to her face with long, bony fingers, gradually smoothing it into the skin with a small, damp sponge. Martha murmured appreciatively. 'Too many late nights,' he admonished as he massaged the area around her eyes, his elegant fingers fastidiously gentle on the delicate skin. 'There,' he said, 'that should make you look a bit brighter, just for the evening. But it's only temporary, mind.' He peered into her face, his eyes thoughtful. 'What you need, my girl, is a bit of steadiness in your life.'

'Ah, yes, Harry,' Martha said, rolling her eyes at his reflection in the mirror. 'I wondered how long it would take to get round to him again.'

'You could do worse.'

'I could do better.'

'He's a good man.'

'So you said.' Martha looked at him impatiently. 'Oh, do stop lecturing me.'

Paul frowned, concentrating on drawing in the arch

of an eyebrow. 'Very well,' he said eventually, with a barely perceptible sigh.

'Look, I just want to have a bit of fun before I die, is that so very much to ask?'

Paul stared at her curiously for a time and then his eyelashes drooped, shuttering his clear, mournful eyes, and the shadows deepened in his morose face. He flexed his fingers, examined them minutely. 'Perhaps not,' he said eventually.

Martha, watching him, frowned suddenly. 'Paul, are you all right?'

He smiled lop-sidedly, with brief sweetness. 'Yes,' he sighed, 'quite all right.' Giving her a searching stare, he opened his mouth as if to say something, changed his mind and closed it again.

Martha touched him on the arm. 'Sure?'

Nodding, he looked away, his long fingers searching carefully for the right brush. Finding it, he picked it up and began brushing it across a block of deep brown powder. 'I worry that you'll regret leaving him,' he said, without looking up. 'That's all. Sometimes we forget what we have until it's too late.'

'We?'

He shrugged. 'None of us is safe from complacency,' he said, advancing towards her with a brush loaded with colour. 'Now, close your eyes and don't move.'

Martha leaned her head back obediently. 'Not even you?'

'Certainly not. Just hold still while I do this bit.'

'But I'm *bored* with Harry,' Martha complained, her voice muffled by trying to speak without moving a muscle in her face.

'No, you're not,' Paul said sharply. 'You're bored with yourself. Don't confuse the two. Harry gives you what you need and if you don't understand that, then you're a daft cow. There, I'm done.'

Martha opened her eyes and stared at him belligerently. 'And you're an interfering old bag.' Paul raised an affronted eyebrow but said nothing, and after a sharp glance Martha turned and squinted at herself anxiously in the mirror. 'You don't think that perhaps the eyeshadow's a bit over the top?'

'No, it's fine.' Martha pulled a face at her reflection in the mirror. 'Oh, come on, if it's bothering you I'll tone it down a bit. Close your eyes for a minute, there's a good girl.' He dabbed gently at her eyelids with a big, soft brush. 'This is a bit delicate, keep absolutely still. I said *absolutely* still,' he insisted as she squirmed with impatience. His lips twitched slightly, and he smiled his peculiar smile. 'Poor old Martha,' he murmured, 'I suppose everyone's trying to run your life for you.'

'You said it,' Martha muttered through stiff lips, not daring to move.

'Well, I suppose it's better than nobody caring.' Paul frowned in concentration. 'Don't move.' He drew a fine brush along the contours of her mouth. 'OK, you can talk now. There, what do you think?'

Martha gazed at herself in the mirror, her eyes widening in gratitude. 'You're a genius.'

He sat back and admired his handiwork. 'Not bad,' he said, with a small satisfied smile.

Martha slipped her feet into a pair of strappy black satin sandals and bent down to do up the fiddly buckles. Looking up eventually, her face flushed with effort, she said, 'You don't really disapprove, do you?'

'Only of your unhappiness.' He smiled his sweet smile, and held out a long, elegant arm to help her to her feet. 'And if this date of yours turns out to be unsuitable, don't think I shall keep quiet on the subject. Now, come along, off you go.' He collected her cigarettes and lighter and tucked them neatly into a satin evening bag as he escorted her to the door, wrapping a black stole around her bare shoulders. 'You look marvellous. Now go and give them hell. No,' he warned, raising a bony finger, 'don't kiss me. You'll smudge your lips.'

When Martha arrived at her sister's house, Jane opened the door wearing a blue and white butcher's-stripe apron with the words, 'I Wear The Trousers' emblazoned in bold yellow letters on the front, which was so large it almost entirely obscured her thin frame. 'Very nice,' said Martha, kissing her. 'Jean Paul Gaultier? French designer,' she added in answer to her sister's questioning frown. 'Does a lot of pinnies.'

'Christmas stocking,' said Jane hurrying her into the kitchen and thrusting a cold bottle of wine at her. 'Be an angel and take that up to the others. David got home late in a foul mood, and now I've got so far behind we may *never* eat.' She pushed her sister in the direction of the stairs. 'Go on upstairs and rescue me. The whole thing's a disaster. Nobody knows anybody else. I could tell straight away that they all loathe each other and now David, who's usually so good at smoothing things over, has done a bunk. The mousse hasn't moussed and the meat's almost raw and the tart – well the tart doesn't bear thinking about, let alone looking at.' She sighed. 'Mother was right. She always said it never does to mix one's friends.'

'Mother doesn't have any friends,' Martha said drily.

'Oh, don't *start*. Of course she does. Now go on. Go *on*.' Jane shooed Martha up the stairs but, just as Martha had reached the top, called after her. Her face appeared below. 'By the way,' she said awkwardly, 'you look really smashing.'

Martha pulled a face. 'I bet the mousse does mousse,' she said with a small smile.

The sitting room, which was on the first floor of the

house, was an elegant, high-ceilinged room with tall windows draped in pale blue silk taffeta caught with striped blue and lemon bows. The walls were painted in cream and pale yellow, divided by a picture rail picked out in blue from which hung, suspended on extravagant blue moiré bows, watercolour portraits of the family.

Five people sat in it, engaged in animated conversation. A couple of them looked up and smiled vaguely at Martha who busied herself opening the bottle of wine. Pouring herself a glass, she went and sat on the sofa, distracting herself by trying to work out who belonged to whom. A woman with fine mousey hair and pale, thin lips said urgently, 'We've wrestled with our consciences day after day but in the end we felt we just had to face the inevitable.' She bent forward to pick up her drink; the front of her blue silk blouse gaped, revealing the blurred contours of small, sagging breasts. 'I mean, it is their *future* we're talking about.'

'Quite,' said a man with smooth-shaven, plump, prosperous cheeks and a self-satisfied expression; her husband, Martha assumed. 'State schools no longer attract the right calibre of teacher. Simple as that, really.'

The group nodded thoughtfully in assent except for a thin woman with close-cropped dark hair who shifted uncomfortably in her seat. 'Not all of them,' she said shyly. 'There are some that are really very good.'

'Very good?' echoed the man who had just dismissed state education, staring at her incredulously. 'Name me one.'

'Anthony,' his wife said in a low, warning voice, glancing nervously at the tumbler of whisky he held carelessly in his hand; his second. Anthony appeared not to hear her although Martha, whose attention was fully on him, noticed an almost imperceptible flicker of his eyes as he took a large, deliberate swallow of his drink and fixed his stare challengingly on the dark woman. Flushing slightly under the full gaze of the group, she named a large local comprehensive which both her children happened to attend.

'You may well be right,' said Anthony, smiling pleasantly at her then turning to the rest of the group as his smile expanded to include them all, 'that is, if you think house breaking should be included on the school syllabus.' Somebody laughed loudly, drowning the woman's retort. The flush deepened, crept up her neck and suffused her thin cheeks as she cast a nervous, appealing glance at her husband, a thin, bespectacled man who wore his few strands of sandy hair drawn across the pale shining dome of his head.

'As a matter of fact,' he said tightly, once the laughter had died down, 'I think Helen's right. In my experience the teaching in state schools is much more...committed. One just gets the feeling that the staff still believe in the old principle of every child's right to an *education*,' he stressed the last word, 'instead of the private sector attitude which is, to my mind –' a slight, humourless laugh – 'more akin to force-feeding knowledge in order to gain exam results...rather like geese being fattened to produce expensive foie gras.'

'I say, old man,' Anthony protested, 'that's a bit strong.'

'Well, perhaps, a bit,' admitted the thin man, with a wry smile, 'but I don't think everything in the private sector's nearly as rosy as it's usually painted.'

There was a fake gas log fire burning in the grate despite it being April and the weather unseasonably warm. For effect, Martha supposed, stifling a yawn. A dark-haired man who was sitting directly opposite her caught the gesture and smiled sympathetically. She returned the smile then blushed, wondering if he was her date for the evening. When he turned back to join the conversation, she cast covert glances at him.

He was good-looking, she supposed, although there was a blandness to his looks. His dark navy suit was impeccably cut and the heavy cream silk shirt, no tie, looked expensive and foreign. The suit in particular had a lightness to its structure that one never found in England. Was it his clothes which Jane thought might appeal, or his legs – they were certainly long – or the way his blonde hair fell over his eyes? Martha was so busy trying to work out what it was about him that Jane thought she might find appealing that she didn't realise she was staring until she looked up to his face and saw his smile, both intimate and challenging. Blushing, she looked away.

Anthony, who had been watching Martha secretly since she arrived, although not so secretly that his wife had not noticed, saw her gaze move in his direction and smiled. 'I hope we're not boring you?'

Martha stared at him for a moment in bewilderment before she realised that he must have noticed her yawning. 'No,' she said. 'Not at all. I'm sorry, I had rather a late night last night. Is it very stuffy in here?' she asked, looking around self-consciously as the conversation faltered and people began to turn and stare.

'Yes, it is rather,' Anthony said, jumping to his feet and wrestling with a sash window while his wife looked on sourly.

'I was just thinking that the weather was beginning to turn,' she said, just as he had succeeded in heaving the window open. She appealed to the group. 'There's rather a nip in the air, wouldn't you say?'

Her husband looked at her wearily, his face purple from the exertion. 'So I'll shut it again, shall I?' he said, with an air of resignation.

'Oh, don't mind me,' she said, 'it was everybody else I was thinking of.' She cast a sly sideways look at

Martha. The others in the room, obviously relieved at a diversion from the conversation, gazed at Martha expectantly.

'Perhaps you're right,' she said, with a little apologetic smile. 'I always have been rather warm-blooded.'

The woman's eyes flicked over Martha's sleeveless, short black dress and fragile satin shoes. 'So I see,' she said with a dismissive lift of an eyebrow, and turned to her neighbour with a loud remark about the crippling cost of keeping three children at boarding school. 'One simply can't waste one's money on absurd evening dresses,' she said, 'when there are so many important things to worry about.' Anthony rolled his eyes then gave Martha a broad wink and levered the window open a few more inches. She smiled conspiratorially but, just as he was about to move over to the sofa to talk to her, a woman walked into the room. There was a flurry of introductions and loud, affectionate greetings, she was obviously an old friend of Anthony and his wife, so Martha made a grateful escape, going in search of her sister.

Jane was in the kitchen, carefully dragging a sharp metal instrument across a block of butter and dropping curls of it on to crystal bowls shaped like shells and filled with chips of melting ice. Martha stood in the doorway, smiling slightly as she watched her. Nobody but Jane would bother with butter curls in this day and age. 'Shall I do that?' she said.

Jane shot her a quick, distracted smile. 'Oh, would you? That would be marvellous. I've just lost another fifteen minutes fussing over David who's convinced he's coming down with 'flu or something, but you know what a –' she glanced over her shoulder and dropped her voice – 'what a terrible hypochondriac he is, so what with that and everything else I seem to have got a bit behind. Are they all right up there?' she asked, casting a quick, worried glance at the direction of the ceiling.

'They're fine,' said Martha, 'well stuck into the wine and having a heated discussion about private versus state education.'

'Oh God,' Jane exclaimed, 'that means Anthony will be on his high horse about state education and Susan, his wife, will be tense because he's inclined to belt down the whisky when he's giving a lecture. Then Paul will be feeling sensitive and Helen – Paul's wife,' she explained in a breathless aside, 'will be in a quiet fury but won't dare say anything for fear of upsetting Paul who'd much rather send his kids privately but can't afford to so goes quite the other way and insists that there's nothing better than state education.' She sighed heavily, grabbed some salad leaves out of the sink and threw them into a salad spinner. 'Are they getting very agitated?' she said, shaking it furiously.

'Slightly.'

'That's really all I need. Christ, where *is* David?'

'Maybe he's gone to look after his French man. After all, the party is in his honour, isn't it?'

'I suppose so,' said Jane vaguely, her attention now concentrated on cutting tomatoes into heart-shaped pieces with which to decorate the smoked salmon mousses. 'Yes, that must be where he is. I think Joe got here some time ago but what with all the panic, I scarcely noticed. Was he upstairs with you? Maybe David *has* gone to find him, he said they had some business to discuss.' She put the last piece of tomato on a plate and shot Martha a quick, amused glance. 'Poor Martha, how dull all this talk of children's education must be for you. Is that why you're down here?'

Martha shrugged. 'I just thought you might need some help.'

Jane gave her a quick hug. 'How nice to have a sister!'

she exclaimed. 'And I'm fine now. You go on upstairs and I'll join you in a sec. Oh, grab another bottle and take it up, would you? Go on,' she insisted as Martha hesitated, 'I really am coming. There's just one more little thing I must do.'

When Martha went back into the sitting room, she discovered that David had joined the party. 'Hello,' she murmured, kissing his freshly shaved cheek. 'Are you feeling better now?' He frowned at her, nonplussed. 'Jane said you weren't feeling too good. A touch of 'flu or something?'

'Oh, *that*. Nothing serious,' he said, his smile brave. 'Bit of a headache, so I went and put my feet up. I thought that – Well, my glands *were* up a bit but it was probably all the fuss going on in the office.' He took the bottle from her. 'But really, I'm fine. Couldn't be better.' He busied himself with a corkscrew. 'Not that I need to ask how *you* are,' he added under his breath. 'You look wonderful. Not a new lover, I hope,' he whispered teasingly, 'because Jane will be very disappointed. She's got some match-making scheme up her sleeve for you.'

'Yes,' Martha said, 'I know.' Her eyes slid over to the man who she assumed was her date for the evening.

'Well go on, go and talk to him,' he said, still busy with the cork, which appeared to have stuck.

'Think I'll just get a refill first.'

'OK. Won't be a second. At *last*. There we are, get that down you. Tell you what, I'll come over and introduce you, then I can give everyone a refill. Actually, why don't you take a bottle with you as well, then we can get them all done at once.'

Again, Martha's eyes slid across to the man sitting on the far side of the room. She took a deep breath and was just about to walk over to him when David grabbed her by the arm and led her in the opposite direction. Martha, stumbling after him, was startled to find herself face to face with a man she had never seen before. Well, where did he suddenly spring from, she wondered vaguely. She only had time to form the haziest impression – thick, dark hair, white teeth, blue eyes – before David was saying, with a hearty laugh, 'Found you a beautiful woman, Joe.'

Joe looked up, smiling lazily. 'That's nice,' he said. He assessed Martha quickly then his questioning stare softened to a smile which, as his gaze flicked briefly to David beside her, broadened to a grin. Martha thought there was something curiously intimate about the exchange but, when she glanced sideways at David, he had turned his head away and was smiling and saying something she did not catch, to Anthony. He laughed loudly then looked back at Martha, affecting suprise. 'You still here? Go on,' he urged gently, patting her lightly on the bottom, 'sit yourself down and amuse this man. He's one of my most *valuable* clients.' Laughing, he turned away.

Joe smiled at her again. Martha smiled back uncomfortably. The jumble of first impressions had sorted themselves into a pair of blue eyes, a strong, thrusting nose with a bump to its centre, and a greedy, red-lipped mouth. His hair was dark, almost black, and so thick it seemed to crackle with vitality. He was beautiful. There was no other word for it. 'I was hoping David was going to send you in my direction,' he said in a soft, American accent. 'I was just beginning to feel completely out of my depth with this country's education system.'

'I know nothing about it,' she said, sitting down stiffly in the far corner of the sofa. Heat seemed to be coming off him in waves; she felt a slow blush flood her face. 'Would you like some of this?' She offered the bottle of wine as a distraction. His eyes flicked lazily over her then he smiled a slow smile and shrugged. 'Sure, why not? I've been dreading this evening. Perhaps this'll give me some Dutch courage.'

'Dreading it?' Martha said quickly. 'Why?'

Joe grimaced, his eyes wandering over to David then, quickly, switching away. 'Oh, reasons... I guess I'm just not good at dinner parties.'

'Well, I promise not to talk about education or property,' she said, smiling.

'Thank Christ,' he exclaimed, then in an undertone, jerking his head in the direction of the rest of the party, 'but can you stop *them*?'

'I'm so sorry,' exclaimed the woman who had come in earlier and who was now sitting in the chair next to Martha. 'I've had my back turned to you all this time. How rude you must think me.' She leaned past Martha, directing her remarks to Joe. 'I'm Elaine, and this –' a slight wave of her hand – 'is Helen. We're talking about playgroups,' she explained, directing a twinkling smile at him. 'Or rather, the lack of them in the area. Of marginal interest, I suppose, unless you happen to have children?' She stared at him avidly.

'Not guilty.' Joe laughed, leaning forward so that Martha felt his body press against her bare shoulder. She felt her breasts tighten and the warmth rise up from them in waves, flooding her neck and creeping up to her cheeks. Elaine smiled, her eyes crinkling with merriment. 'Oh, dear. Then I suppose we've been boring you rigid for the past ten minutes?'

Joe gave her his slow, beautiful smile. 'Yes,' he said. To Martha's amazement, Elaine laughed. 'Then I shall stop,' she said, delivering one last, twinkling look, 'for now anyway. But only if you promise to talk to me later.'

He grinned. 'I promise.' Martha, looking at his mouth, at the way the full lips drew back from strong, square white teeth revealing the tender pink of his gums, wondered suddenly what it would be like to kissed by him.

As he turned to whisper in her ear, she felt the warmth

of his breath against her skin and shivered slightly. 'I'm going to break that promise I just made,' he murmured, 'and devote the whole of this long, wonderful evening to you. Why didn't David tell me about you before? Think of all the time we've wasted.'

Martha felt the heat coming off him in slow, surging waves and pulled abruptly away. 'Perhaps you didn't ask,' she said, looking away.

He smiled, delighted. 'You're blushing.'

She scrabbled around in her bag to disguise her confusion and, finding a pack of cigarettes, offered him one. 'Do you smoke?'

He studied her in silence for a few moments. 'How adorable. I've not met a girl who blushed for years.' Martha, blushing furiously now, shook the pack of cigarettes at him in mute appeal. 'OK, I promise not to embarrass you any more.' He looked down at the pack. 'A cigarette!' he said, seizing one and inhaling appreciatively as she bent to light it for him. 'Honey, you just saved my life.' He blew out a long thin stream of blue smoke. 'I thought this was one of those no-smoking houses.'

'It is,' Martha said, lighting up.

'But you don't care?'

'She's my sister.'

He looked at her carefully for a moment then groaned softly and closed his eyes. 'So you're the sister…' he said slowly, opening them again to stare at her. 'I'm sorry, I should have realised. I kind of had the sister down differently. It's Martha, right?'

She smiled at him, confused. 'The one and only. Were you expecting something else? What's Jane been saying about me?'

'Oh, only that you're great and we should meet,' he assured her. He leaned forward and, picking up his glass of wine, sipped at it, eyeing her speculatively over the rim of the glass. 'The one thing she didn't tell me was that you were beautiful.'

She blushed furiously. 'Do stop it. I'm supposed to be on my best behaviour this evening.'

He paused, watching her carefully. 'Why?' he asked, a slight smile dimpling his smooth, brown cheek.

'Jane's got me set up on a blind date with a man from Paris,' Martha said, watching the dent in his cheek and longing suddenly to put her finger against it. Her eyes slid over to the man sitting on the far side of the room. 'He sells beauty products,' she whispered scornfully, 'and he's an ex-model. He's probably a total creep, too.'

Joe looked at her speculatively for a moment and then his mouth drew back in a wide, lazy smile. 'Is he the one, over there?' he asked, following her gaze. Martha nodded. 'Are you quite sure?' he whispered, his grin broadening.

'Do be quiet,' Martha implored. 'He might hear you.'

'No chance. I guess he's too interested in himself. He's the type of guy who uses moisturiser and has a manicure once a week. And showers before *and* after sex. What do you bet, he's never had a cigarette in his life.' He nudged her suddenly in the ribs. 'Look, look. He's pushing back his cuticles.'

'Stop it,' said Martha, laughing, 'I'm the one who's got to sit next to him at dinner.'

Joe leaned back against the sofa and smiled, revealing strong, white teeth. Martha stared at him, feeling a quick fluttering in the pit of her stomach. 'I'll swap the place names around.' He traced an idle finger slowly down her bare arm. 'I promise you'll be sitting next to me.'

Martha shivered and looked quickly away. Around them, people began to pick up their glasses and get slowly to their feet.

'Looks like we're on our way,' Joe said, unfolding long legs. He stood up and stretched slowly. Martha could see a small patch of brown skin on his stomach, where his shirt had come untucked from his jeans. Blushing, she looked quickly away. He bent down so that his lips were on a level with her ear. 'Make your way down, real slow now,' he said, making the suggestion sound curiously intimate. 'By the time you get there, I'll have got something organised.' He leaned forward and kissed her, his lips warm and lingering on her cheek. 'See you downstairs.'

When Martha eventually appeared in the dining room, Jane was busily organising her guests to their seats. 'Martha,' she called, 'I've put you over here between Joe and Anthony.' Martha walked over to take her seat, Joe following closely behind her. 'You did it!' she whispered, exultant.

He smiled his slow smile. 'I told you you'd be sitting next to me.'

They sat with their heads bent close together, Martha giggling as he whispered a running commentary on all the people around the table. Jane appeared suddenly, bending over to talk to them. 'Oh, good,' she exclaimed, 'I'm glad to see the two of you getting on so well.'

Martha looked up guiltily. 'You don't mind?'

A slight, questioning frown appeared, hovered above Jane's bright little eyes. 'Mind?' she exclaimed. 'Of course I don't mind. I told you you'd like...' She hesitated, broke off, her eyes flicking to Joe. 'Why, Joe Lorusso, you are the most difficult man to pin down,' she scolded playfully. 'I must have called Paris every day for three weeks before your secretary could give me a date for this evening. But I can see I didn't waste my time,' she added, her glance taking in Martha's flushed face. 'I'd better sit down. I'm sure everybody's starving.'

'Paris,' Martha said slowly, turning to look at him.

'Paris,' he repeated, grinning. 'And what was that other word you used? Creep, or something, wasn't it?'

Martha put her hands to her face. 'If you don't mind,' she said, looking at him over the protective fence of her fingers, 'I think I'll kill myself now rather than later.'

He took a hand from her face and lifted it to his lips but at the last minute turned it deftly so she felt his tongue slide, warm, against the palm of her hand. 'Later,' he murmured.

Martha, blushing, pulled her hand away. 'I feel like such a fool. I hate you,' she whispered, her voice drowned by Jane's brisk entreaty to start and forks being scraped against plates.

Joe turned to look at her, his eyes sliding over her bare arms and across the thin silk which outlined her breasts. 'No you don't,' he said eventually, deftly shaking out her napkin, which was pleated into the shape of a swan, and smoothing it on her lap. She felt the warmth of his hands against her thighs, the strong fingers massaging their outline through silk and linen, and blushed even more furiously.

'Please don't do that,' she whispered.

He gave a long, deliberate smile. 'Do what?'

'That. With your – oh, nothing.' She blushed again.

13

'Martha, I don't believe you've heard I word I've said. And you haven't eaten a thing.'

Martha, looking up with a guilty start, picked up her fork and began to jab at her food with elaborate care.

'Oh, put that down,' Phil said. 'I didn't say you had to eat. In fact, I only mentioned it because it's so unlike you not to.' She looked at Martha thoughtfully. 'Your eyes are suspiciously bright, that idiotic smile hasn't left your face all morning and you're remarkably well dressed considering it's only me you're seeing for lunch. Is there something you'd like to tell me?'

Martha blushed. 'Tell you?' she repeated slowly.

Phil looked at her gravely, her eyes flicking down to Martha's untouched plate of food. 'I feel sure there must be a name attached to this condition and I don't think it's anorexia.'

'Who?' Martha said, her expression innocent.

'Martha!'

Martha grinned. 'It's not anorexia, I promise. We've never got along.'

'Funny ha ha.'

'Yes.'

Phil sighed. 'Martha, do stop being so exasperating. What's his name?'

'Joe.' Scarcely was his name out of her mouth than a faint pink blossomed in her cheeks.

Phil examined her with interest. 'My God,' she

marvelled, 'I'd forgotten how rejuvenating desire is. You look perfectly lovely.'

Martha smiled a small, secret smile but said nothing. 'I see,' Phil sighed. 'Struck dumb with love?' Martha's blush deepened and her smile unfolded until it consumed her entire face. 'In that case, nod your head once for yes and twice for no. First of all, I suppose he's handsome?' Martha nodded once, vehemently. 'Very good,' Phil said. 'And, let me think... Is he English?' Martha nodded twice. 'Not English? How interesting,' Phil said speculatively. She thought for a moment and then the frown indenting her smooth, pale brow relaxed and she exclaimed, 'It's the French man, isn't it? The blind date? The bum creams?' Martha nodded furiously. 'Hang on,' Phil said, watching her carefully, 'I'm confused here. Two nods for the French man which means no but one nod for the bum creams which means yes...'

'He's American,' Martha said.

Phil looked confused. 'Who is?'

'The French man. Joe. He's American but he lives in Paris and he doesn't really sell bum creams...I mean, he does but he just does that to earn some money because he's so broke all the time. He set up this deal for David in Paris but he's only the fixer; he doesn't really work for them, well, only part-time. He's a sculptor really and terribly clever and funny and charming and he made me laugh so much all evening during the ghastly dinner party...it really was unspeakably awful...that I didn't even care when they started on about mortgages...oh, God, Phil, he's marvellous and gorgeous and handsome and...well, he's quite extraordinarily *nice*, I suppose,' she finished, pausing to catch breath.

'Just your average kind of a guy, then?' Phil said drily.

Martha's eyes shone a clear, limpid blue. 'The most perfect bunch of tulips arrived this morning,' she exclaimed, 'masses and masses of them in that wonderful peachy cream you only ever seem to find in Paris. I couldn't find enough vases to hold them all. Then, just as I'd finished arranging them,' she exhaled, let out a long sigh of delight, 'he telephoned from the airport – he's gone back to Paris for a few days – to ask me if he could take me out for dinner next week.'

Watching her shining, animated face, Phil felt unease prickle at her scalp. Martha's excitement seemed to her too fantastic, too *immoderate* somehow; she had the sudden, giddy sensation of standing on a cliff high above a shining sea. A part of her wanted to take Martha by the arm and pull her away, exclaiming, 'Be careful, be careful. See what a long drop it is.'

Martha, noticing her silence, said, 'Phil, I *know* I sound like an idiotic teenager. If I was you I'd think I was absurd too. We only met last night and not even a kiss, well, a chaste peck on the cheek and here I am writing his surname over mine, like a kid in a school book. But I *feel* like a teenager, I feel like I've wanted to feel for years. Oh God, Phil, you can't imagine how unbelievably exciting that is. It'll probably come to nothing but I don't *care*,' she flung out, 'because I want to go on feeling like this; shining and excited and almost unbearably *alive*.'

Phil laughed, infected by Martha's excitement. Ever since they were children, Martha had been able to inspire in her a fearless exuberance that she knew she herself lacked. Sometimes, but not always. Sometimes she let Martha down. A sudden image flashed into her mind, of the two of them playing on some waste ground near Martha's house and Martha finding a rusty old car abandoned in some bushes. She remembered Martha tugging furiously at her arm, her voice high and thin with excitement, 'Come on, let's go and play on it. Come *on*, Phil.' She had pulled back, protesting that it might be dangerous, and then eventually she had turned and walked away, feigning indifference, when really she felt no such thing. Martha, who would do nothing without her, begged and pleaded but even when her pleas dissolved to tears Phil would not relent. Phil remembered the hateful, hot, dusty walk home with Martha trailing after her, her round face crumpled with tears and disappointment and later, scrambled eggs for tea and a cold, hard lump in her throat and not being able to eat because she had spoiled all Martha's innocent pleasure.

Now, as she watched the excitement shining in Martha's eyes, she realised, with a sudden shock of recognition, that she had not seen it there for years. Cursing her own fearful nature, she went and hugged her fiercely. 'Then I hope you go on feeling like this for ever, and that nothing your boring old friend has said has in any way spoiled it.' She pulled away and gave Martha a small, regretful smile. 'You know how cautious I am.'

Martha wrinkled her nose. 'I know,' she said. 'But I promise you Phil, I absolutely *promise* that there's nothing dangerous about Joe. He'll be nothing but good for me.'

Phil kissed her shining head. 'I hope you're right.'

'Of course I'm right. How can happiness like this be wrong?' Martha threw her head back and laughed, stretching her arms to embrace the world. 'I'm so happy. So absurdly, ridiculously *happy*. I never thought I'd feel like this again.'

Phil watched her thoughtfully. 'Do you ever think about him?'

'Him?'

'Him. Harry, I mean.'

Martha dropped her arms and looked at her oddly for a moment then shrugged. 'Not really. I don't have to.

He's always somehow…there,' she explained, pointing to the back of her head.

'Like a conscience?'

Martha frowned, pondering. 'No,' she said slowly. 'It's just a presence, a sort of Harry-ness.' She flushed, glanced away. 'I know, it sounds absurd.'

Phil looked at her thoughtfully. 'No. No, it doesn't sound absurd at all. Actually, I saw him,' she said abruptly. 'A couple of weeks ago.'

Martha, her concentration momentarily distracted by some private recollection, looked up and smiled vaguely. 'Sorry, Phil. I'm not with you. Who did you see?'

'Harry. We bumped into each other at a party, at Mike and Emma's. You were supposed to be there too.' Martha frowned slightly but whether it was a frown of abstraction or disapproval Phil did not know, was conscious only that a sudden nervousness was making her speak very fast. 'Don't you remember? We talked about going together but you decided not to because you thought Harry would probably be there and might feel uncomfortable, after all they were originally his friends. Actually, it was a good thing you didn't go. It was ghastly, full of people talking very loudly and not listening. Then Mike had invited this perfectly awful man called, oh, I forget his name, but he trapped me in a corner… you know how hopeless I am at parties…anyway, he had me pinned up against the coat rack while he droned on about something or other, I forget what exactly. I'd just started to feel desperate, you know how you do, when Harry appeared out of nowhere and rescued me and…'

'Phil,' Martha said gently, 'you're rambling.'

'Oh. Was I? Sorry.'

Martha gave her a curious look then smiled slightly. 'It's all right, you know,' she said gently. 'You don't have to feel nervous because we're talking about Harry.'

Phil gave a bright, artificial laugh. 'Was I sounding nervous? Sorry, I didn't mean to. It's just –' It was just, she realised with a sudden start, that she didn't want to talk about Harry to Martha of all people. *Of all people*. This is absurd, she thought, with rising panic. I must stop this at once. Harry is just a friend. Harry is Martha, Martha is Harry. She began silently to repeat the words, like a mantra, trying to calm herself, trying to put *her* Harry, the Harry she went for walks with every Sunday, the Harry who held her hand and teased her until she blushed, *that* Harry, she tried to put back into the old Martha Harry. It was too late. She couldn't do it. I'm in love, she thought with quiet desperation. I'm in love with Harry. How could I have let that happen? How *could* I? She gave Martha a quick, anxious glance.

'Oh, do stop looking so worried,' Martha said, laughing. 'It'll all work out fine. Harry will meet somebody else and fall in love. You'll see.'

'You wouldn't mind, then?' Phil asked, trying to make the question sound casual.

'Of course not. Well, maybe a bit,' Martha said with a small, discomfited laugh, 'at least until I got used to the idea. Odd, isn't it, how you can still feel jealous even after everything's well and truly finished.' She watched Phil carefully. 'I suppose it would all depend on who it was.'

'I suppose it would,' Phil murmured.

Martha looked at her slyly. 'Why? Is he in love with somebody?'

'Oh, no, I don't think so,' Phil said quickly.

Martha yawned and stretched. 'Then there's no point in talking about it, is there?'

'I do think that you could at least ask how he was,' Phil said, guilt making her tone sharper than she intended. 'You did ask me to find out for you.'

'Did I?' Martha looked surprised. 'Well, how was he?'

'Lousy.'

Martha shrugged. 'Well, that's rather why I didn't ask. I was afraid you might say that.'

'Well, you were right.'

Martha watched her helplessly, a puzzled frown tugging at her forehead. 'Phil, has something upset you?'

Flushing, Phil shook her head and looked away.

'Is it Harry?'

Phil shrugged, keeping her face averted.

Watching her, Martha sighed. 'Look, I'm sorry Harry's upset and that he's dragged you into this. I know how you hate it when people get messy and emotional.' Phil could not speak, wanted only to blot out Martha's gentle, insistent voice. 'He wouldn't mean to upset you. He certainly wouldn't intend to use you in that way.'

To use you... Phil felt jealousy rise like bile. This, she thought, is insupportable. She swallowed hard, felt the sourness coat her mouth. 'I know,' she said thickly, forcing a smile to her face. 'Of course he didn't.' To her intense relief she realised that she sounded perfectly normal. 'I'm sure I'm exaggerating. He was a bit upset at first but by the end of the party he was quite all right. Laughing and joking, and when we parted he asked me, quite naturally, to send his love to you.'

Martha looked at her curiously. 'But it still upset you?' she insisted.

Phil shrugged. 'You know how fond I am of him,' she said, quite truthfully. More truthfully than she could ever have imagined. 'Oh, don't mind me,' she went on quickly, 'I'm being a sentimental idiot. I'm probably just feeling a bit blue because it's Saturday and I know I can't see Peter until tomorrow night.'

'Of course,' Martha said, with a quick, curious glance. They both knew that Phil enjoyed her solitary weekends;

had often said what a relief it was to be in love with a married man. Oh well, she thought vaguely, she'll tell me when she feels like it. 'Of course you're right. I'm sure that's it.'

Phil's smile sat badly on her pale, serious face. 'Of course it is. Shouldn't you be going now? Didn't you say you were meeting Paul for tea?'

Martha laughed. 'I can see you want to get rid of me,' she said affectionately. Phil, reproaching her treacherous heart, smiled weakly.

Martha rose slowly to her feet, yawned and stretched and then, looking down at herself, exclaimed and began ineffectually to smooth away the creases in the cream linen man's jacket and blue and cream rose-patterned loose silk trousers she wore. 'I *promised* Paul I'd try to look halfway decent,' she said crossly. 'He's taking me to the Savoy. According to him there's nowhere like it for a proper appreciation of elegance which, of course, *nobody* has any time for these days.' She drawled the last few words, laughing as she mimicked Paul's fury with the carelessness of modern style.

Phil smiled. 'You look lovely.' She got up and kissed her. 'I'm glad about Joe,' she said, 'really I am. It's…enchanting, I suppose that's the right word; yes, I'm sure it is; it's *enchanting* to see you looking so happy again.'

A shy smile suffused Martha's face with colour. 'Yes,' she said delightedly, 'it is, isn't it?'

Phil smiled. 'Yes.'

'You mustn't worry about Harry,' Martha said quickly. 'He'll be OK. He'll find somebody else and forget he ever felt badly about me. And if there's *anything* bothering you, anything at all,' she added, her tone suddenly fierce, 'then you must promise to tell me. You know you can tell me everything, don't you?' She bent forward to kiss her, still with a little frown on her face so that Phil laughed and put up her hand as if to brush it away. 'I'm perfectly fine,' she said brightly, 'really I am.'

'Good.' Martha sounded relieved. 'Have a good weekend. I'll call you Monday.'

When Martha had left, Phil sat on her aunt's enormous old sofa for a long time. She sat perfectly still, as she had trained herself to do as a child, making neither sound nor movement but seemingly quite composed, her hands carefully folded in her lap, her short legs sticking out in front of her. Only the slight puckering of her smooth white forehead indicated the turbulence of her thoughts. Eventually she sighed and with a sudden, decisive movement slid from the sofa and walked into the hall and, picking up the telephone, dialled a number.

'Hello, Harry?' she said. 'It's Phil. No, no I'm perfectly all right. It's just that it's such a lovely afternoon. I wondered if you felt like going for a walk on the Heath. You would? Good. I'll meet you at the car park in half an hour.' She paused, smiling into the telephone. 'Yes, me too.'

14

'Personally, I thought it went rather well.' Jane paused in the act of spooning marmalade on to her toast from a little round orange ceramic pot, its tubby shape puckered with tiny dotted indents, and looked across the table at her husband. 'Don't you, darling. Don't you think it went rather well?'

'Mmmmm,' David's voice came from behind a newspaper.

'Well, it was a bit shaky, right at the beginning,' she admitted, cutting the piece of toast into four neat little squares and arranging them carefully on her plate. She picked one up and looked at it contemplatively. 'I must say I thought the mousse was a *triumph*. Every woman there asked me for the recipe.' She frowned slightly, and bit into the toast with a delicate crunching sound. 'Well, not Martha, but then I doubt Martha can even boil an egg; she seems to live in restaurants. Either that, or she sort of picnics. She told me she'd had cauliflower cheese for supper the other night; turned out what she meant was she ate a lump of cheese and some raw cauliflower. Imagine,' she continued with something close to awe in her voice, 'caring so little about things.'

David sighed and snapped the pages of the newspaper irritably.

'Well, of course,' Jane said, with a lift of her eyebrow, 'she thinks we're terribly suburban. I keep telling her we can't be because Barnes is as much a part of central

126

London as that slum of a street she lives in. Ladbroke Grove, central? I ask you.'

'I don't think that's what she means,' said David's muffled but irritated voice.

'Well, no, she never actually *says* as much,' said Jane thoughtfully, 'but you can see it in her face when she comes round to see us. That way she has of standing on the doorstep, staring around with that look on her face, slightly *contemptuous*, if you know what I mean. I sometimes feel like telling her that rubbish on the streets and dog shit and half-dead trees are hardly glamorous or…' She thought for a minute. 'What's the word she uses all the time? I know, *urban*. She's always saying that cities should be urban, that if you're going to live in London then you should live in it and not spend your whole time pretending to be in the country, driving Range Rovers and wearing green wellies. David? David, are you listening.'

'Yes,' he said, without moving the newspaper.

Jane smiled complacently 'She liked Joe, though. I knew she would. Although I could see from her face when I first mentioned it that she didn't believe she would. I don't suppose I'll get any credit for it,' she mused with a little sigh. 'She'll forget it was me who got them together. Did you see them at dinner? Could hardly keep their hands off each other. Really, I felt quite embarrassed, although I was pleased for her at the same time. She's been looking a bit peaky since Harry left. Well, she claims *she* left him, but I don't believe her.' She gave a bright little laugh. 'Well, Joe certainly put the roses back into her cheeks. And the way he looked at her; it was almost indecent.' She lowered her voice to a breathy, girlish whisper. 'Can't imagine what they got up to when they left.' She looked across at the newspaper. 'Can you, darling?' she said, brightly.

The newspaper rustled irritably. 'No.'

She sighed longingly. 'They've probably spent the whole weekend in bed together. Right now, they'll be sitting in that great big double bed of hers, surrounded by crumpled newspapers and toast crumbs.' She smiled to herself. 'Just like we did that first weekend. It was blissful, I'll never forget it. Will you, darling?'

He lowered the newspaper and glared at her over the top of it, his face white and set. 'Will you just *shut* up.'

'David!'

'Can't you hear yourself?' he said, through gritted teeth. 'Blathering on like some mindless fool.' He pitched his voice to a cruel, high falsetto. 'Martha and Joe, Joe and Martha, why, aren't they adorable, aren't they just itsy-bitsy little lovebirds?' He stared at her contemptuously, his voice dropping to its normal register. 'Christ knows what they're saying about you. Probably having a good laugh.'

Two spots of colour flared in Jane's thin face. 'I was only trying to make conversation.' Her voice was tight, offended. 'You used to like talking about parties afterwards, having a giggle about who got drunk and who said what to whom.' She got up, busied herself stacking plates and cups. 'I couldn't get a word out of you yesterday.' She looked across at him, eyes bright with tears. 'You didn't even thank me for a successful dinner party.'

'You were the one who wanted to have a dinner party,' he said with barely concealed distaste, 'so you could pimp for that sister of yours.'

'Don't be revolting,' she said quietly, carefully covering up the butter in its crystal dish with a silver lid, 'I wasn't pimping as you so disgustingly put it. I simply thought a dinner party might cheer her up.'

'Call it what you like.' His face suffused an ugly shade of red. 'The end result's the same.'

'*And* I arranged for Simon to be away,' she went on,

her eyes flickering away from his, 'so that we could have a quiet weekend together.'

He stared at her, his eyes narrowing to contemptuous slits. 'Why bother?' he said. 'Go on. Do tell me, because I for one can't think of a single reason.'

She looked at him imploringly. 'David, do stop this.' She tried unsuccessfully to smile. 'So that we could have some time together, to…well, you know.'

'To what?' His voice was dangerously quiet.

Jane looked at him, then dropped her eyes, discomfited. 'Well, you know…' She flushed slightly. 'So that we could go to bed.'

He looked back at her with disgust. 'Christ, Jane, why don't you just say it?' He leaned across the table, shoving his face at her, his smooth cheeks mottled with angry dull red patches. 'So that we could *fuck*, you mean?' He stood up, and threw the newspaper down on the table. 'Fuck!' he shouted, 'fuck, fuck, fuck, fuck!'

She bent her head and quickly began to clear away the rest of the things on the table with trembling hands. 'Stop it, David,' she said in a low voice. 'Stop it. You know I hate that word.'

He watched her thoughtfully. 'Your sister's right,' he said, 'you are bloody suburban.' He mimicked her voice, lifting his own to a squeaky falsetto. 'Don't you think it all went *rather* well, darling? Did you see how much they all *adored* the mousse? Christ!' he shouted. 'Christ, don't you ever *listen* to yourself? You sound like the worst kind of prissy middle-class bitch, you with your *nice* house and your *nice* kids and your *nice* little decorating hobby, let's not dignify it by calling it a job, and your *nice* little dinner parties and your *nice* sex life. Of course Martha means you, you silly cow. She's seen you stomping off to the Common wearing those ridiculous boots with a sodding stupid head scarf knotted at your chin.' He stared at her, his breath coming in heavy gasps, his eyes narrowed to ugly slits in his mottled face. 'Have you also told your precious little sister that you don't like sex? Have you? You're so fucking suburban that you only like doing it on a Saturday night, flat on your back with the lights off. And don't think I'm fooled by those breathy little noises you make.'

'That's unfair,' Jane whispered. 'I love sex.'

'You!' David laughed. 'Love sex! Come on, Janie, it's me you're talking to. Your husband, remember? What you like, my sweet little wife,' he sneered, 'is fucking bed-time stories, not sex. Snuggling up to Big Bear and letting him lick your honey pot. We even have to call it your honey pot so you don't think it's dirty.' He looked at her, exasperated. 'You even keep your eyes closed so you don't have to see anything nasty like my prick. Well, that's what men have, you silly bitch. They have pricks. At least your sister knows that. In the Seventies she must have gone down on every bloody prick in London.'

'I'm not listening to this any longer.' Jane gazed at him, white faced. 'You've been like this for weeks. I don't know what's wrong but I do know that it has nothing to do with me.' Tears seeped out of her eyes and poured down her face but she ignored them, staring at him defiantly. 'Whatever you say, I know that you like your life, that you love me and love your kids and that you're only like this...' she hesitated, took a deep, shuddering breath... 'you're only like this when...'

'When what?' he said quietly, his eyes widened by a curious mixture of fear and elation. 'When *what*?'

'When you're...' She dropped her eyes suddenly and gave a broken little sigh, quiet as a whisper. 'Oh, it doesn't matter,' she said exhaustedly. 'It really doesn't matter.' He opened his mouth to reply but she caught the slight movement and glanced sharply at him. 'Don't say it.' Her voice was harsh. 'Don't go and spoil everything now by saying something stupid.'

David looked at her and suddenly his shoulders sagged, breath hissing from his mouth like a slow puncture.

She took a long, deep breath, walked over and stood squarely in front of him. She was so small against his height and bulk that she had to tilt her head back to look at his face. He stood with his head bowed, his arms dangling limply at his sides. 'Are you listening to me?' she asked softly. He nodded. 'Good, because I'm not going to say this again. I'm *never* going to say this again. I want you to get into your car and go and do whatever you have to do and when you come back I want you to be my husband again.' Her glittering eyes stared out of a white, and pinched face, the skin stretched taut across sharp cheekbones. 'I want you to be my sweet, loving husband,' she said slowly, as if she was talking to a child. 'Do you understand me?'

He nodded dumbly, his eyes squeezed tightly shut.

'Good,' she said and, turning her back on him, began quietly to do the washing up.

'Jane,' he pleaded, reaching out an imploring hand.

'Not another word,' she said, without turning around.

15

Martha was so anxious not to be late that she arrived at the restaurant twenty minutes too early. After she had paid off the taxi she hovered uncertainly outside, undecided whether to go in and wait at the table or to linger in the street. She glanced anxiously at the reflecting glass of a shop window. Well, she looked all right, although she was beginning to regret the dress she wore; the other creased so much less easily.

As she hesitated, a couple, heavily perfumed and expensively clothed, swept past her and moved, amid much loud talk and laughter, through the heavy polished wooden door with its discreet brass plaque. Martha, shrinking from their confident passage, turned away and made a great show of looking at the window of the shop next door. It took her a while to realise that there was nothing in it save a small sign directing customers to new premises. Blushing, she turned on her heel and looked up and down the street. There were few people in it and even they seemed to have a clear purpose, no doubt made yet more purposeful by the light rain that fell. Nobody dawdled as she did, uncertainly on the street. Just as she had decided that she must go into the restaurant, which did not look, at least from the outside, like the sort of place which welcomed early arrivals, her attention was caught by a small shopping arcade. It looked inviting enough with its brightly lit windows and would keep her out of the rain. She glanced anxiously down at the silk dress she wore, as she had done a hundred times since she put it on, and stepped into the arcade.

Phil, as it happened, was also dining out that evening, at a restaurant a few streets away. Just as Martha stepped into the arcade, Phil's slight figure, neatly packaged in a navy jacket, trousers and white silk T-shirt, rounded the corner of Jermyn Street. She strode with brisk purpose, only slowing her pace as she passed a news vendor, a few yards from the arcade where Martha was standing. Knowing that Peter was compulsively punctual, she decided against buying an evening paper and walked quickly on. Nor did she slow her pace as she approached the restaurant, but went quickly up its few steps and was immediately shown to her and Peter's customary table. She was surprised not to find him waiting for her and, realising that she was a few minutes early, regretted not having bought a newspaper. Once the glass of wine she had ordered appeared, she sipped at it idly and began to enjoy the unexpected few minutes of peace.

Martha, who had by this time decided to brave the interior of the restaurant, was also regretting not having bought a newspaper, but for quite a different reason. Had she had one with her she would not have been able to concentrate on reading it, but nonetheless would have preferred Joe to find her absorbed and indifferent and not staring, as she knew she was doing, with rapt concentration at the door. She decided eventually to order a drink, hoping that the alcohol would calm her, picturing him finding her there, relaxed and enjoying a glass of wine.

Realising suddenly that it was Friday, she looked at her watch to see that it was exactly eight o'clock, the time at which she and Harry always met. Harry had never, in all the years they had known each other, been late for their Friday evening meeting. The thought caused her a slight twinge of guilt, but the guilt was quickly replaced by panic as she realised that she had not, during the past seven years at least, sat in a restaurant on her own waiting for a man to appear. What if he didn't turn up? She looked at her watch again. Two minutes had elapsed.

You're being absurd, she told herself. He's only two minutes late, which isn't really late at all. But still she could not shake herself of the sudden conviction that she would be left waiting, like the woman she had once seen in Le Tour Eiffel, who had sat looking nervously at her watch every thirty seconds and staring with appalled fascination at the door.

Martha remembered vividly her pity and shame on the woman's behalf and, when it was evident that the man she was to meet (Martha was convinced by the woman's nervous demeanour that it must be a man, and one she did not know very well but wished to know better) was at least half an hour late, she began to long for the woman to pay for her drink and leave instead of subjecting herself to the humiliation of being stood up. The woman did leave eventually, at nine-thirty, by which time Martha was herself in such a state of pity and vicarious humiliation that she was unable to eat. The woman, she remembered, had not had a newspaper with her or a book or anything with which she could have distracted herself or the other diners' attention from her, and her agitation was such that nor could she manage a passable pretence of having decided to go out for a solitary dinner.

By eight-fifteen Phil had ceased to be irritated by Peter's lateness and had instead begun to worry over it. It was so unlike him to be late that she decided something dreadful must have happened to him. It did not occur to her to consider, as it might a less indifferent woman, that he might have decided to signal the end of their affair by not turning up; for while she had reason to be suspicious in that he had cancelled at least four of their dinners in the past few months on very little notice, she knew he was a punctiliously polite man and, while she privately thought him occasionally pompous and often self-interested, she knew he was neither thoughtless nor brutal.

Another five minutes elapsed. Really, something terrible must have happened; an accident, a slight stumble as he walked along a pavement and lurched suddenly, unexpectedly in front of an oncoming car which had no chance of avoiding him. Or perhaps a bomb on the Underground, Peter even now being carted off to hospital unconscious, blood streaming from his head. Or, perhaps, a heart attack. Yes, that was more likely. He worked so hard. All barristers worked hard but Peter took it to an extreme, insisting on being briefed on even the tiniest detail of a case and relying on nobody's judgement other than his own. He had, she knew, been preparing a large and complex case for the past few months, the details of which he could not, of course, divulge.

This was to be their first dinner in three months, although they had met, briefly, in the intervening weeks. She did not resent his work taking precedence over her, even though that and the time he spent with his family meant that they had seen little of each other of late. I don't resent it nearly enough, she thought, with a sudden spasm of guilt. The guilt made her feel so uncomfortable that when she looked up to see him standing over her, she said, too sharply, 'You're late.'

He frowned, taken aback. 'I'm sorry,' he said, sliding in to the seat opposite her. 'A telephone call came through just as I was leaving. A piece of new evidence which, it seems, might have a bearing on the case.' He waved his hand vaguely in the air. 'I could hardly…'

'No. No, of course you couldn't,' Phil said quickly, ashamed of her previous abruptness. 'I was worried, that's all. It's so unlike you to be late.'

He relaxed and smiled at her. 'Worried?' he echoed. 'How nice that you should still worry about me after all this time.'

The smile made his face appear more youthful, smoothed out the habitual lines of worry and fatigue which were scored in deep grooves in the thin, papery skin on either side of his mouth. She could see, suddenly, the eager, serious boy he must once have been, and returned the smile.

'Ten years,' she said, with pretended horror. 'It makes you wonder where the time goes.'

He looked at her intently. 'You don't regret it?'

'Oh Peter,' she protested, her laugh ringing with a shameful artificiality in her ears. 'What is there to regret?'

He looked at her then glanced away, his expression discomfited. She noticed how sparse his fine, sandy hair had become, clinging to his bony skull and revealing glimpses of the pink, shiny scalp beneath. 'A woman like you,' he murmured, and then shook his head. 'You deserve more. I think, sometimes, that I should have…'

She cut him off. 'They've been ten perfect years,' she said firmly. 'Happy, peaceful. It's more than most people have in a lifetime.'

Her tone was too bright. He looked at her, his gaze enquiring, and she saw apprehension and concern flicker briefly in his watery blue eyes. As she noticed the faded red at their rims and a faint caking of yellow on his sparse, stiff eyelashes, she felt a quickening distaste and, dropping her gaze, studied the menu carefully. 'I'm starving,' she exclaimed in a high, strained voice. 'Let's order quickly and then we can talk.' She was conscious of his eyes on her and, looking up, forced a bright smile. 'You know how hopeless I am when I'm hungry. I shan't be able to concentrate on anything until I've got some food inside me.'

He nodded, smiled briefly and looked down at the menu. Phil made a show of reading it with elaborate care, to give herself time to compose her thoughts.

Peter, after a brief, thoughtful glance at her bowed head, summoned the wine waiter and ordered a bottle of champagne.

She looked up in surprise. 'Champagne? Are we celebrating?'

He gave a strained smile. 'That's entirely up to you,' he replied.

She frowned, but seeing his hurt, puzzled expression, forced herself to laugh and say, 'Well, if it's entirely up to me then of course we're celebrating. This is our first dinner together in three months. What better reason is there?'

The anxious expression left his face, he relaxed perceptibly. 'Lobster, then, and perhaps some oysters to start. Let's make an evening of it.'

They ordered their food and, once the champagne arrived, sipped at it as they began to catch up on all their news.

Martha, meanwhile, sat nursing a drink. It was eight thirty-five and she had begun to abandon any hopes of Joe appearing. She was halfway through her second glass of wine which she was drinking in tiny, desperate sips, making it last as long as she could, although she longed to tilt the entire contents into her mouth.

Her mind raced feverishly. She did not dwell on her disappointment and humiliation; the thought of it was so unendurable that she knew she must save it for the privacy of her own bed. She was more concerned as to how she could leave the restaurant with as much of her dignity, tattered as it now was, intact, but found that she could not sort her thoughts into any coherence. She thought, at first, that she should go to the pay phone, call the restaurant in which she was sitting and have herself summoned to the phone; until she realised, her stomach lurching with despair, that of course the waiter would go to the table to fetch her and she would not be there but in the phone booth. Nor would it work to leave the phone off the hook and race back to her table; she would never get there in time.

She decided that she could call the restaurant, pretending to be his secretary and ask for a message to be delivered to the lady waiting for him, to say that Mr Lorusso had been taken ill and would consequently be unable to join her for dinner. Even so, she would not be able to get back to her table in time to receive the message. But if *before* she went to the telephone she asked the waiter to direct her to the Ladies and then went off and made the telephone call, perhaps they might believe that she was making her way back to her table where she would be given the message and so could pay her bill with a show of regretful, but worried, concern and leave quietly.

She sat, frowning slightly, as she worked out this elaborate strategy; was so lost in her thoughts that she did not, at first, register the bunch of long-stemmed red roses which had been laid gently on the table in front of her. She was so convinced that Joe was not going to turn up that when, eventually, she noticed the flowers it was with miserable bewilderment, an expression which stayed on her face as she turned it up to the person standing over her.

'Martha?' Joe dropped to his knees so that his face was on a level with hers. 'What an expression,' he murmured between kisses. 'Did you think I wasn't coming? The plane was delayed, some mess up with traffic control at Charles de Gaulle, and when I finally got to Heathrow I ran to the phone booths in the airport but they were all busy so I thought it was better to find a cab and rush to you.' The words tumbled out of his beautiful, agitated mouth in a breathless rush so that Martha could hardly keep pace with them. 'I was hoping that the cab might have a phone but, of course, it didn't and then I thought of making the driver stop so that I could find one and call you but then I thought I'd be even later so I made him drive like a madman. Oh God,' he exclaimed, feverishly kissing her mouth, which was now tilted in a smile, 'Will you ever forgive me? I thought I was going to *die* of impatience. I allowed an extra two hours for the journey so I couldn't possibly be late because this is the most important night of our lives. You do believe me?' he added, stroking her face with clumsy, urgent hands.

'Yes,' she protested, laughing in delight and embarrassment.

'You're an angel,' he exclaimed, still crouched on his knees by the table as he grabbed her hands and covered those in kisses too. 'A sweet, patient, tolerant angel. But say you believe me, that this is the most important night of our lives?'

'Everybody's looking at us,' she whispered.

He did not move. 'Say it.'

She stared at him, a smile playing uncertainly around her mouth. She hesitated. Could she believe him? Would this face, now strange yet so dear, one day be as familiar to her as her own? Eventually, she spoke. 'I believe you.' She knew that she had just uttered something momentous, even in her confusion and delight; confusion that he should kneel in front of all those people, making a spectacle of their intimacy, and delight at the warmth of his hands, strange yet thrilling, holding hers. She let go reluctantly. 'Now do go and sit down,' she pleaded.

'All the way over there?' he said, staring across the table at the empty chair.

'All the way over there,' Martha whispered, conscious of the waiter standing by the table, a look of pained indulgence on his face.

'Would sir care for a drink?' the waiter asked, drawing out the chair as Joe rose to his feet, his heavy cream silk jacket settling in graceful folds around his muscular body. Watching him walk the few, brief steps to his side of the table, Martha felt her stomach twist with desire; she stared longingly at the silken brown skin above his white T-shirt, imagining the feel of that smooth, yielding warmth against her lips.

'Sir most certainly would,' said Joe, sinking gratefully into the proffered chair. Looking up at the waiter, he grinned broadly. 'Men make plans and the gods laugh,' he said.

'Quite so, sir,' said the waiter carefully. 'And what plans does sir have for the wine this evening?'

'A bottle of Cristal champagne. Vintage.'

'That should make the gods smile, if I might say so.'

Joe laughed, revealing strong white teeth. 'You may. You most definitely may,' he said, looking over at Martha.

'I haven't told you my best bit of news,' Peter said, an expression both proud and shy illuminating his thin face.

Phil looked up at him in surprise. 'What?'

'Jamie's won a scholarship to Oxford. To Christchurch.'

Phil, knowing that Christchurch was Peter's old college and how much the news must mean to him, said, 'Oh, Peter, that's marvellous! No wonder we're drinking champagne. You must be terribly proud of him.'

He nodded modestly. 'We knew he was bright, but we never dared hope for as much. Mary's over the moon, of course.'

It was the first time he had mentioned his wife that evening. He did not usually talk about her much, other than to give Phil the practical details of her various comings and goings because they affected Phil as much as they did him, but she noticed that he had not even done that this evening.

'Is she well?' she asked brightly.

Peter looked down at his plate and then, as if steeling himself, looked directly at Phil. 'As well as can be expected,' he said quietly.

'Expected?' Phil was alarmed. 'She's not ill, is she?' Peter smiled suddenly, pale, thin lips drawing back to reveal sharp, discoloured teeth. 'Really, sometimes I think that you're the most extraordinary woman,' he said. 'Have you no idea what I mean?'

Phil, who had a very good idea but did not want to hear it, said quickly, 'When does Jamie go up? Next October I suppose? You never said what he was to read? Will it be law? Following in the family tradition?'

'Actually, it's history,' Peter answered, a quizzical, wounded expression on his face. He leaned across the table, taking Phil's hand, and she felt the papery dryness of his skin. 'Phil, my dear, you seem to be avoiding me. You know very well that there is something I want to say to you yet you've spent the entire evening trying to ensure that I don't say it.'

Phil feigned surprise. 'Have I?' Her hand lay limply in his.

Peter frowned and withdrew his hand. 'I had thought,' he murmured, 'that you would want it as much as I do. After all, it's been ten years now. The children are almost grown and Mary...well, Mary has made her own life without me, a life that I daresay–' he hesitated, looked away– 'that I daresay,' he continued, with an expression of resignation in which pain faintly glimmered, 'she prefers to one that includes me.'

'I doubt that's true,' Phil said, although her concern was as much for herself as it was for him. She did not want him to leave his wife; had never wanted it. Somehow, she thought he knew that. In their taciturn way, she had imagined that they had reached an unspoken agreement whereby they would continue to be lovers and good companions but that the real part of his life, which was how she saw it, or perhaps, she thought guiltily, what I actually mean is not the real but the emotionally complex part of his life, was conducted at weekends. She was happy with their life together, did not want it to change. I passionately do not want it to change, she thought, and then the word, passionate evoked an unbidden memory of Harry's face and, blushing, she dipped her head and fumbled in her bag for a handkerchief to disguise her confusion. This is hopeless, she thought, with despair. I'm behaving like an adolescent, yearning after a man who doesn't return my feelings and would be horrified, even disgusted, if he knew them. And, to make it worse, I'm sitting with my lover of ten years, a man I like and respect, who is even now offering to share his life with me.

Yet as she looked at Peter, she knew that he repulsed her; knew that his face and hands which even only a few months ago had roused in her, if not passion, then at least a tender affection, had become distasteful to her. How did I let this happen, she wondered in a panic of loathing.

Peter was watching her intently. Flushing, she managed a tight smile. 'Perhaps Mary's terribly upset and puts up a front in order to protect herself.'

Peter shrugged. 'It's kind of you to say so but I'm afraid it's not the truth. Mary has said, quite distinctly, that she's perfectly happy.' His eyes, their blue faded with age and fatigue, flickered uneasily. 'You see,' he persevered, clearing his throat loudly, 'I told her last weekend that I was intending to leave her.'

Phil was silent. It was entirely her fault, of course, for letting him believe that this was what she wanted. She felt a sudden surge of panic and dropped her eyes lest he should see and understand her distaste.

Peter studied her averted face and punctuated the silence with a small, dry cough of embarrassment. 'I had thought,' he said eventually, 'that I would be leaving her in order to be with you, but I'm beginning to see that, perhaps, that's not what you want. In which case –' he leaned across the table, took her hand again, 'in which case I'll be terribly saddened but I want you to know that I haven't made the decision to leave Mary simply in order to be with you. As far as we're both concerned, our marriage is over and so it seems kindest to admit that now and allow ourselves the possibility of establishing new lives, in whatever form they might take.' He relinquished Phil's cold, lifeless hand, and she felt in that slight gesture the depth of his anger. 'We've always been good friends and both felt that latterly, our friendship was endangered by not telling each other the truth.'

Phil looked up sharply and frowned. 'But I thought you'd never told her about us?'

Peter's smile was curiously tinged with triumph. 'Mary's known about you for many years. I didn't tell you because you seemed to prefer to maintain the fiction that she didn't know.'

'How dreadful you make me sound,' said Phil irritably. 'I'm not sure I like to be thought of as a woman who is happier deceiving another woman than one who is prepared to face the consequences of her own actions.'

Peter looked at her with pained resignation. 'Then I, and not you, am at fault for having believed that,' he said slowly. 'Please don't let's quarrel. I had imagined this would be a happy night for us both.' A trace of bitterness crept into his voice which he attempted to soften with a dry, humourless smile. 'I was obviously wrong and I'm sorry, not for myself, but because I believe I'm causing you some distress.'

Phil saw that he was playing a part, acting the measured, rational adult against what he saw as her wilful childishness. A slight tic jumped angrily at the corner of his pale lips.

'And I'm sorry that I seem so…so reluctant.' She shrugged, turning her face away from him. 'It's not entirely true to say that it's unexpected, but it's still a shock.'

'Yes,' he said quickly, 'a shock. Of course. I can see that it might take a little time to get used to.' He raised his hands apologetically. 'I was so excited and pleased at the prospect of our future together that I hadn't thought how my sudden announcement might affect you. We must take it gently, then,' he continued, almost as if he were speaking to himself. 'One step at a time, as they say. We needn't live together immediately. I have the flat in London and I'll be perfectly comfortable there.' He shrugged. 'Anyway, with this case coming up, it's probably better that we're not living together. I'm afraid there won't be much time to concentrate on us in the next few months.'

'Yes, of course. I can see that you'll be very busy,' Phil said quickly. Living together! The thought appalled her. She knew in her heart that she should tell him at once that it was over, make the break as clean and painless as possible. But then she looked at his face and could not summon the courage or the cruelty to hurt him. Perhaps, she thought, this is just a momentary mood, and I'll wake up tomorrow and feel happy that he's left Mary and that everything's resolved.

She managed to summon a smile, a small and pitiful thing. 'To the future,' she said, raising her glass.

Peter, in his triumph, did not notice the bleakness of her smile. 'To the future,' he echoed eagerly. 'To our future.'

16

Joe surprised her in the early afternoon, shouting up from the street, his arms filled with roses, a bottle of cold champagne stuffed in his coat pocket. Martha flung open the window, laughing with delight, then rounded up all the people who were lying around her flat leisurely drinking tea and eating cake and shooed them impatiently down the rickety metal staircase, clattering after them into the street and his waiting arms. He scooped her up, crushing her against the roses, her head filled with their fragrance and his maddening, intoxicating scent.

'I thought you'd gone back to Paris,' she cried, covering his face with kisses, oblivious to her friends who still loitered, looking vaguely affronted. They were not used to this Martha, this indifferent stranger with her flushed face and wide, abandoned eyes.

'Come up,' she said, and they all moved to follow but taking Joe's arm possessively, she turned her back on them, throwing over her shoulder a casual, indifferent, 'Goodbye.'

'There goes any hope of her being a great painter,' said one of them, who claimed to be in love with her, watching Joe's muscular body with narrow, envious eyes. 'She'll be cooking his dinner next.' They slouched off moodily in search of other entertainment. They knew they would not find it. 'It won't last long,' one of them said comfortingly. 'They never do.' 'Harry did.'

'Harry?' said another, 'Harry's a painter. Harry's different.' 'Yeah,' giggled a small, dumpy blonde in a tight cheesecloth blouse, 'Harry's jeans never fitted like that.'

'Have you been crying?' Phil said, peering anxiously at Martha's face.

Martha sighed voluptuously. 'Yes. I think I'm in love.'

'Oh, *please*.' Phil threw herself on to the tangle of sheets on the bed. 'Not that.'

'What do you mean, not *that*? I thought you'd be pleased.' Martha's pale eyes, enlivened by happiness, darkened to a flat stormy grey. Frowning, she sat down heavily on the bed.

Phil sighed, stretched out a hand and patted her gently on the shoulder. 'Of course I'm pleased, you idiot. I'm thrilled. It's just... isn't it a bit soon to talk about love?' Her smooth, pale face crumpled anxiously. 'Lust, OK. But love? Love's such a different thing. It's so complicated. So anxious and difficult. So *painful*,' she murmured, almost to herself. So absorbed was she that she did not notice the slow, painful flush spreading up Martha's neck or the irritated tightening of her mouth.

Nor did it occur to Martha that Phil might be talking about herself. The memory of the afternoon still hovered, warm and golden, in her mind. Phil was spoiling it, dulling its lustre to a tarnished, tacky gleam. She felt suddenly abandoned, as if the afternoon had been no more than a casual coupling, and she glanced with distaste at the stained sheets, still bearing the damp imprint of their bodies. 'Thanks,' she said irritably. 'That's really what I wanted to hear.'

Phil, adrift in some reverie, looked up in surprise. 'What did I say?' She looked closely at Martha's face and saw resentment shutter it to a dull blankness. 'Oh, Martha, I'm sorry. I wasn't thinking. I didn't mean it like that.'

Martha gave an irritable, impatient shrug. 'Well, how *did* you mean it? When I first told you I was in love with Harry, you didn't say then –' she affected a bored, pained voice–, 'love's so complicated and difficult. Well, that's how you make it sound,' she cried, seeing Phil's startled face. 'You make it sound tiresome, boring even.'

Phil looked at her then sighed deeply and rolled over, burying her face in the pillows. 'That's not what I meant and you know it. Anyway, Harry's different,' she said, her voice muffled. 'He's so gentle and uncomplicated. Being in love with Harry must be like being in a lovely deep warm bath.'

'Who wants to feel as if they're in a warm bath? Why do you think I left Harry? Because being in love with him is boring. Good, old, *boring*, dependable Harry.'

'Martha!' Phil said, sitting up abruptly in astonishment. 'Don't be unkind. Harry's not in the least bit boring.'

Martha's mouth quivered petulantly. She was still smarting from Phil's earlier words, had been lying there feeling so warm and happy, so pleased with life and then Phil... 'Why this sudden defence of Harry?' She cast a sly, sulky glance at Phil. 'You sound almost as if you were in love with him yourself.'

Phil looked at her, appalled. 'Don't be absurd,' she cried. 'What a thing to say.'

Martha held her gaze, her expression defiant, her face flushed a hectic pink. Seeing Phil's pale, stricken face, she dropped her eyes, looked away. 'Well, you do,' she complained petulantly.

Phil stared at her bowed head, her mind racing. Surely Martha didn't think that. She was just saying it because she was upset. It was her own fault for being so – so *unwelcoming* about the news about Joe. She hadn't intended to be. She felt so confused, about Peter, about these sudden, new, uncomfortable feelings about Harry. But still, what if Martha really thought..? She plucked fretfully at a stray thread on the counterpane while the silence hung over them, the last of the evening sun gilding their bowed heads. Phil could hear the bedside clock ticking. Will it always be like this, she thought in sudden despair. Will I always long for Harry and have to lie and lie to Martha? The thought was so terrible that she resolved to stop these absurd, childish fantasies and, dismissing Harry from her mind, turned to Martha and hugged her hard.

'Let's start again,' she said. 'Pretend I just walked into the room.'

Martha did not return the embrace but nor did she shrug Phil off. 'You could at least be pleased,' she said in a low voice.

'But I am,' Phil exclaimed, sensing her anger soften. 'Martha, I'm sorry. You caught me off guard. I've been in a foul mood all day. It's got nothing to do with you, or with Joe.'

Martha looked at her uncertainly. 'Sure?'

Phil smiled. 'Really sure.' She shook her head in disbelief. 'I can't believe we almost quarrelled.'

A bright sharpness still lingered in Martha's face. Phil sighed. 'Martha, I really *am* sorry. It's been a bitch of a day; Peter's suddenly announced that he wants to move in with me after promising that we'd take it slowly. Within weeks of leaving her, he's insisting we live together.' She gave a weak, wry smile. 'I should be happy, really. Most women are thrilled when their lover finally leaves his wife. But I –' Her voice tailed off. 'Oh dear,' she sighed, 'what a mess.'

Martha nodded slightly but still she looked subdued, all her happiness evaporated. Phil watched her anxiously. 'I feel such a bitch, messing up your evening just because I was feeling lousy myself.'

Martha smiled faintly. 'Now you're being silly,' she protested. 'It's not that bad. I was just a bit taken aback by all that stuff about Harry.' She sighed. 'Poor Harry.'

'Harry's no longer your concern,' Phil said quickly. 'What matters is that everything works out with Joe.' She hesitated. 'Is he in love with you too?'

Martha shrugged but a small smile crept on to her face. 'It was the last thing he said before he left for Paris. He's had to go back for the weekend. A meeting or something.' She looked at Phil, hectic colour rising to her cheeks. 'Oh, Phil, he's so wonderful. I wish you could meet him. You couldn't take the afternoon off next week could you? No, I suppose not. It's just that I've arranged to have tea with Paul, so he can meet Joe. Never mind. Anyway, look.' She scrabbled frantically under a pillow and extracted a photograph which she proffered shyly. 'This is him. Isn't he gorgeous?'

Phil studied the photograph. It was no ordinary snapshot of the sort usually exchanged by lovers, but a black and white study obviously taken in a professional studio, so intense was the contrast of light and shadow. The face which stared out at her was undoubtedly handsome, the glacial paleness of the eyes set in the shadow of a dark fringe of lashes and thick eyebrows so perfect in shape that Phil couldn't help but wonder if they were plucked. The nose was straight and fine but with a bump to its centre, perhaps the result of a childhood fight, and a fraction too big to be thought anything but masculine. But there was something about the smile which made her uneasy. It was disarmingly candid, so wide and bright was its compass, yet there was something about it she did not quite believe; as if the owner could turn it on and off at will, shut it down with a snap of those strong white teeth. She had the sensation that she wasn't looking at a photograph of a real person at all but at an air-brushed, celluloid version of a man, and glanced down instinctively to the bottom right-hand corner as if expecting to find it imprinted with a scrawled autograph.

'He's very beautiful.' She handed the photograph back to Martha who examined it tenderly, her face foolish with happiness. Phil looked at her for a minute then got to her feet. 'Shall we have some champagne to celebrate? I'll go downstairs and see if they've got any. We're going to drink a toast to you and Joe. To love,' she said, with a slight, high laugh.

'Phil, you don't have to,' Martha protested. 'There's plenty of wine in the fridge.'

'Wine?' Phil exclaimed, her voice too bright. 'Wine won't do at all. We must have champagne.' She bent down and kissed Martha on the cheek. 'Please let me buy you some. I want to make up for being such a bitch. I won't be long.'

Martha looked after her retreating back regretfully. The last thing she wanted was champagne but she hadn't the heart to tell Phil. Sighing, she fell back against the pillows. A tangle of sheets formed an uncomfortable lump beneath her back and tugging at them she smoothed them out then wrapped herself in them, curling her body up in contentment. Pressing her face into the pillow she breathed in Joe's faint, lingering scent, remembering his dazed, dazzled face. 'I love you, Martha. I love you.' That kind of feeling can't be wrong, she thought, feeling the imprint of his skin, the muscles quivering rapturously as she traced her fingers across them, the urgent movement of his mouth against her lips. Sighing greedily, she turned her face to the pillow and slept.

'There's only the Lanson that's cold,' the man in the off-licence said, his small, reddened eyes sharpening as he took in the evident urgency of her request. '£19.99.'

'You're ripping me off,' Phil said mildly, handing him

two ten-pound notes and retrieving the bottle before he could wrap it in tissue. As he scrabbled in the till she turned and threw over her shoulder, 'Keep the change.'

'Funny lady,' he said without humour, sinking back on to his stool behind the counter, his sharp eyes pricing her clothes and bag. Phil snapped the door shut with an irritated click and hurried up the metal staircase to Martha's flat, her heels clattering noisily in rhythm with the jangle of her thoughts. How could she have allowed her feelings for Harry to interfere with her relationship with Martha? How *could* she? She wondered if it was her subconscious playing tricks, willing her to confront Martha, or perhaps it was because, in some dark, unacknowledged part of her mind, she was angry with Martha for leaving Harry, not because she believed she should have stayed, but because by leaving him she made her vulnerable.

Grabbing some glasses and rearranging her face into a smile, she went into the bedroom to find Martha asleep on the bed. Phil watched her enviously for a moment, gazing at her flushed face. Laying the bottle of champagne on the pillow and extracting a little gold pen and leather notepad from her bag, she wrote a quick note which she tucked beneath the bottle. 'Sweet dreams. Enjoy the champagne. I really am happy that you're in love.' She looked at the note thoughtfully then scored emphatic lines under the word happy.

Martha called her the next morning sounding cheerful. Phil, relieved that she could detect no sharpness from the previous day's argument, nonetheless felt slightly uneasy when Martha said that she was sorry but she would have to cancel lunch. She was worried about Paul, hadn't seen or heard from him for two weeks and thought she ought to go round to his flat and check that he was OK. There was, she added, something strange going on. When she'd last seen him he'd seemed very subdued; she thought that perhaps Stevie's illness had been getting him down. 'So, if you don't mind,' she said, 'I think I'll take them out for a gossipy, expensive lunch to cheer them up.'

Phil said that she didn't mind at all. In fact, as she put the phone down, she realised that she felt only a quick, lightening sense of relief.

She had woken that morning, her arms and legs aching and heavy, her head clotted with a dull, dragging depression. She had not slept well, her dreams disturbed by Harry and Peter. In one of them the two men were running a three-legged race in her old school playground, laughing and struggling towards the winning tape which, as they approached, had begun to quiver and pulsate, transforming itself into a writhing snake, while she dodged around it, screaming at them to go back. Hearing her cries they stumbled, turning around and around, colliding in a tangle of arms and legs until she saw, to her horror, that they had grown together like Siamese twins.

The dream kept breaking into her waking mind, splintering her peaceful Saturday morning. She could not shake it from her head and, needing comfort, unconsciously picked up the telephone receiver, dialled half of Peter's number and then, with a slight start, put it down again. Her hand hovered momentarily over it again as she, briefly, considered calling Harry. She had promised she would telephone him that morning to make an arrangement to meet for a walk the following afternoon but, deciding she was in no state to face him, she turned away from the telephone. Walking quickly to the coat stand, she grabbed a light macintosh – it looked as if it might rain– and went resolutely out of the flat.

It was only when she found herself standing in front of the ticket machine in the Underground that she realised she had no idea where she was going. She stared vaguely at the names then punched the one marked Waterloo, fed the coins into the machine and, taking her ticket, made her way down the escalator. I'll go to the National Film Theatre café, she thought, and have a peaceful, solitary lunch, then go to the Hayward and see that exhibition I've been promising myself for weeks.

The decision made, she felt more cheerful. The afternoon dawned promisingly before her and she realised how much she missed her solitary weekends now that Peter lived in London. How much worse will it be, she wondered, when he has moved in with me? 'Where are you going, darling?' he'll say, as I wander, forgetting, towards the door on my solitary way to the dry cleaners to drop off my clothes and then to wind my way up through St John's Wood to Blooms. And I, astonished to be asked, will think why, if he's known me for all these years, doesn't he know that this is what I always do on Saturday? But why should he know that, she thought, with sudden despair. He knows so little about me. We've pretended to love each other for ten years and yet we know nothing of each other's lives; none of the clutter and detail which make up the real business of living. Or of loving. And how much will I resent it if he does move in with me, she wondered as the stations flashed by. She realised with a sudden, terrible sense of loss, that she would resent it very much.

As the train shuddered to a halt at Oxford Circus she looked bleakly out to the platform, at the mothers with prams and bulging shopping bags, at the couples with arms entwined, at other people's busy lives. Our life will never be like that, she thought. Our life these past ten years has had as little to do with that reality as our love has had to do with real, messy, everyday love. We have shared nothing but our selfishness. What basis is that for a life together?

As she stepped out of the cover of Waterloo station and on to the wide walkway which led across to the stained, concrete bunkers of the South Bank complex, a pale sun split the clouds and a ribbon of blue sky hovered shyly over the Thames. By the time she had walked to the café, stood in the queue and ordered herself a slice of quiche, a plate of tired salad and a watery, insipid cup of coffee, she felt more cheerful. She loved the sensation, found only in cities, of complete anonymity. The place was full and she hesitated, clutching her tray as she stared around, looking for a table at which she could eat her solitary lunch. Seeing that the sun was shining quite strongly, she decided it might be warm enough to sit outside.

There were only two tables occupied. Looking around she glimpsed a perfect spot, slightly hidden behind a pillar and thus enjoying some shelter from the wind. Installing herself at a table, she settled down to eat her lunch. She had brought the newspapers with her but the wind kept snatching at the pages and so, eventually, she gave up trying to read and sat eating her quiche and watching the river.

A few people strolled by; two elderly women, well bundled in misty tweeds and clutching walking sticks in knotted hands, inched their way along, heads bowed, suspicious eyes glued to the treacherous ground. Their querulous voices floated over to Phil, borne on a stray gust of wind. 'Wicked, I call it,' one said. 'Twenty years her daughter nursed her. She was so excited after the stroke, thought she might have a bit of life left.' 'Not much to ask, is it?' grumbled the other. 'Bit of time to kick up your heels? Now she's back home, they say she could last another five and her daughter, well, she's seventy, if she's a day. Trouble with those young doctors, they don't know the difference between life and living.'

And nor do I, thought Phil bleakly, watching their crabbed progress. Nor do I know the difference between life and living. Martha does; Martha always has. She remembered her exasperation with her when they were kids, Martha running ahead, shouting over her shoulder, 'Come on, Phil! Come *on* or we'll miss it.' And she, hanging back, hesitating even as she willed herself to follow, crying, 'Wait for me, Martha, wait for me.' I do that still, she thought, except that now it's life that runs ahead and I'm always at the back shouting, 'Wait for me.' Or perhaps I just let it go, sitting quietly as it races away from me.

Harry's like that, too, she realised suddenly. He always says that Martha reminds him of a child in that excitement she always has about her, that yearning curiosity and hunger for life. 'I feel as if she's always having to stop and wait for me,' he had said one Sunday as they strolled quietly by the Ponds in Hampstead. 'As if she's always looking impatiently over her shoulder, her body quivering to move on, and she's calling, "Come on, Harry, do come *on*." ' They had laughed about it, shaking their heads over Martha as if she were indeed a child.

We would be hopeless together, Harry and I, reflected Phil. We'd fumble our way through the days, hesitating at each new thing without Martha to call to us to hurry. She'd leave us, of course, she thought resignedly. She might say it was OK, the two of us together. She might even say she didn't love Harry any more and that she had somebody else to love so why shouldn't Harry and I be together? But, little by little, she'd stop seeing us. She'd come for lunch with me, occasionally, but there'd always be Harry between us, like one of those too-tall vases crammed with flowers which they put on tables at posh dinners so that everyone has to peer around them to see each other. That would be us, peering around Harry.

155

Her phone calls would come less and less and Harry and I would pretend not to notice, make excuses for her. 'Oh, you know Martha!' we'd say, avoiding each other's eyes. 'You know how busy she always is.' We'd go to her exhibitions, of course, and stand around with bright smiles on our faces and warm drinks in our hands, talking too loudly to hide our desperate eyes, secretly watching her with an intense, covetous yearning. We might even, on the sly, buy the greetings cards she paints, slip them between the pages of a book, slide them silently into our underwear drawers. And soon enough, we'd hate each other, marooned as we'd be without her in our cautious lives.

I couldn't bear it, Phil thought, and then realised, with an unpleasant shock of surprise, that she had let it go so far in her imaginings as to consider it possible that she and Harry might be together. She had, all her life, been dismissive of people who say that they have no choice about the people with whom they fall in love; had never had sympathy for women who said that they just couldn't help being in love with a married man because we cannot help whom we love. Fall in love with, rather, she thought; there is, after all, a difference. And now here she was, behaving like one of those women she despised.

What she knew was that she had arrived at a certainty. Whether it was hers by choice or right or simply fate, she did not know. 'I love Harry,' she murmured aloud. There, it was said. It made her feel a little better. Once we know something, she thought, then it cannot be unknown. But it can be forgotten, eventually. I know that I'm in love with Harry and now I must forget I ever was.

As she sat, deliberating, she noticed two men strolling by the river, their heads bowed in conversation. Had they not stopped directly in front of her she might not have paid them any more attention. She gave them only a glancing look but in that glimpse her attention was caught by something unusual about the hunch of the older man's shoulders. Surely he couldn't be cold, yet his body was framed defensively, as if to ward off a blow or perhaps to nurse some distress; whether it was physical or emotional she could not see. The younger man stepped in front of him, his hand on the other man's shoulder, and she could see from the eloquent movements of his free hand that he was trying to convince his friend of something. Idly wondering what it was that should provoke such urgency on a fine Saturday afternoon, she watched them more closely.

They were now standing a little to the left of her so that while she could still see them, they could not see her, at least not without craning their heads. As the older man stepped forward to the railing she sensed something familiar about him and leaned forward to take a closer look. As she did so, he turned his head and looked directly at the café, saying something to the younger man, perhaps about going to get a cup of coffee. It was with a jolting shock of familiarity that Phil realised it was David, Jane's husband. She'd met him only twice before, once at Martha's flat and also at his wedding to which she had been invited, to please Martha. She had never much liked him, was suspicious of the softness of his mouth, the lips marred by a petulant droop which threatened self-absorption and conceit. She did not want to greet him and sensed that he would not welcome her appearance; there was something curiously intimate about the two men's absorption in each other. She knew she should move away but felt compelled to go on watching them, wondering what David was doing out walking by the river on a Saturday afternoon instead of spending time with his family. Perhaps this was a business meeting of some sort; Martha said that

157

Jane frequently complained of how often he worked at weekends. It seemed a curious choice of place to talk business, but it was turning out to be a lovely afternoon and perhaps the man he was meeting was a foreigner, keen to see London. There was no reason why they shouldn't talk business and sight-see at the same time. Pleasing people was, after all, David's business. But why the urgency? Perhaps a business deal gone wrong, bankruptcy looming, a ruinous legal case?

As she watched, David said something to the younger man and moved around so that his body was pressed against the man's back. At first Phil thought that the other man must be ill, the manner in which he leaned over the railings suggested that he might be going to be sick. Still, it was such an odd position to comfort somebody who was ill that she could not help but look again, more closely. As she stared, David began thrusting his body against the other man's bottom, laughing as he did so. It was such a flagrantly explicit sexual movement that Phil gasped slightly, instinctively turning her head to see that nobody else had noticed, then leaned back in her chair, her heart beating uncomfortably.

She could not stay there, must make her escape before they saw her, and she stared wildly about her, seeking another way out. In order to leave, she would have to get up from her table and walk around it, which would bring her to the outer perimeter of the tables from where they could not help but see her. Even if she got up and walked back into the café, the slight movement might attract their attention, and so she stayed in her chair, hoping that they would soon go. She picked up a newspaper and held it in front of her face, trying to hide behind it, but a sudden gust of wind snatched the pages from her grasp. She ducked her head quickly as she bent down to retrieve them and saw, out of the corner of her eye, David begin to walk away from the café, the younger man following him some distance behind.

She leaned back in her chair, panting slightly with relief. As she did so, the younger man turned to gaze in her direction. She could see his face quite clearly. In her confusion she thought at first that he was staring at her; it took her some time to realise that he wasn't, was peering in at the café, trying to make out the interior. Finally he shouted at David that he wanted to go in and have a cup of coffee. David turned slowly, walking back in the direction of the café, giving Phil time to grab the newspaper and hide her face behind it.

No sooner had the two men passed than she rose to her feet and, grabbing for her bag, hurried away from the café to dodge around the side of the building. She had still a long run of windows to negotiate before she could break into a run, taking the flight of steps which led to the upper walkways two at a time. She stood for a moment at the top, panting and swaying slightly as she clutched the railing for support.

I must have imagined it, she thought, as she hurried towards the Underground. It's just that he looks like somebody else. It couldn't possibly be him. What would he be doing with David? He doesn't know David and anyway, he's not even in London this weekend, she said when I saw her yesterday evening that he'd just left, gone rushing off to catch his plane. And then she remembered that he did know David, that it was David who had introduced them and she wondered what to do with the knowledge, how to unknow or to forget that the man she had just seen with David looked exactly like a photograph she had stared at yesterday afternoon. He looked exactly like Joe.

17

'Well, hello stranger.' Jane gave her sister a brief, affectionate hug. 'I thought you'd given up on me. Oh, I don't mind,' she added laughing, 'I know it's because you're in love. And what better reason is there?' she asked, tucking Martha's arm comfortably under hers as she led her into the house. 'I feel so *proud* that it was me who got you and Joe together.' Her voice dropped to a confidential note. 'I said to David just the other day how adorable you two looked…' Her voice trailed off as she recalled David's reaction and a furtive, embarrassed look sharpened her pointed face. Tightening her grip slightly, she hurried her sister quickly through the narrow, cluttered passageway and into the kitchen. 'You just sit there and make yourself comfortable,' she said, leading Martha to the kitchen table and depositing her as tenderly as she might an invalid.

Martha sat down obediently, watching her sister in silence as she scurried around the kitchen, busying herself making coffee.

'You do realise,' Jane said with a little laugh, 'that I haven't seen you for *weeks*, not since the famous dinner party.' She finished spooning coffee into the filter machine and sat down opposite Martha, her sharp elbows on the table, her little eyes shining expectantly. 'Now I've got you to myself, I want to hear *all* about it.'

Martha smiled foolishly. 'There's really not much to tell.'

'Not much to tell! Martha, only you could meet a divinely handsome man, fall madly in love and then say that there's not much to tell.' She leaned forward eagerly. 'Do tell me what he's really like. He was so entranced with you at the party that the rest of us could scarcely get a word out of him.' She grinned, her thin upper lip curling back to reveal sharp yellow teeth. Martha thought how unfortunate it was that her sister always reminded her of small rodents. 'And there were quite a few women there who would have liked a bit more than a word with him.' She giggled. 'Do tell. What's he like apart from being *divinely* handsome?'

'He's…he's wonderful,' said Martha, struggling valiantly to match Jane's enthusiasm. 'Really, he's perfectly wonderful.'

'Is it serious? Do you see each other *every night*?' Jane asked, clasping her hands together and gazing over them, her bright eyes round with excitement.

Martha flushed. 'Every night we can. He has to work with David quite often in the evenings.' Her voice was carefully light; David's insistence on evening meetings had already been the cause of some friction between her and Joe. 'Maybe you could persuade David not to work quite so hard?' she said with a deliberate smile.

Jane's plucked eyebrows quivered slightly. 'He has meetings with Joe in the evenings?' she said with a slight, high laugh, reddening under Martha's curious gaze. 'I never ask David who he's seeing after work. I'd have a list as long as my arm if he told me everyone he saw. As to my asking him to reschedule work…' She paused, fiddled with one of her pearl earrings and stood up abruptly. 'Not my department, I'm afraid. Isn't that coffee ready yet?' Hurrying across the kitchen, she removed two cups from a cupboard. 'I hope you don't mind these old cups, but the bone china's gone for repair.' She frowned, remembering David throwing one

161

of the cups across the kitchen in a temper the week before. A phone call from Joe about some meeting which had to be cancelled and David flying into a fury because he said that the project was never going to get off the ground if *certain* people, meaning Joe, she assumed, didn't get their act together.

Turning back to Martha, she arranged her face carefully into a cheerful expression, determined not to let her know that Joe had been the cause of any trouble. 'Where did I put those mats?' she exclaimed, turning her back and rummaging through a drawer. She put them on the table together with a little cut glass bowl containing sugar, her efficient heels tapping smartly on the terracotta floor as she went to collect two brimming coffee cups.

'David says it's potentially the most lucrative deal he's ever put together,' she said importantly, allowing herself a small, indulgent smile. 'He spends *so* much time on it. That's why he's in Paris at the moment.' Martha, who was only half listening, nodded vaguely. 'Not every deal the company puts together gets the managing director's personal attention in this way. I'm always telling him that he needn't do *everything* himself but he says…'

'He's in Paris?' Martha interrupted, her attention immediately engaged by the mention of that city. 'Well, I suppose he would be. Joe's there, too, of course.'

'Joe's there? Funny, David didn't mention it. Well, maybe he did,' she added quickly, with a little apologetic laugh. 'David says I never listen to a thing he says. Trouble is, half the time I've no idea what he's going on about so I just blank out.'

Martha shrugged. 'Easily done.' She found David's constant, carping criticism of Jane embarrassing. 'This is delicious coffee.'

Jane smiled, pleased. 'Yes, isn't it? We've got this

marvellous little Italian shop just up the road. As good as anything you'll find in Soho. People tend to think Barnes is a bit of a backwater but I can honestly say that we've got everything here to rival the West End.' She went on to list all the shops within easy distance of the house and then explained, at length, the ease of parking compared to trying to take a car into central London. And then she moved on to the disgraceful state of the Underground system and continued in that vein while Martha, soothed by the undemanding chatter and the warm, sunny kitchen, slipped into a smiling reverie about Joe.

The noise of the front door slamming made both of them jump. 'Who could that be?' Jane said, her eyes beady with alarm. She called out, fear sharpening her voice, 'David? David, is that you?'

'Who else do you think it is? Father Christmas? Of course it's bloody well me.'

Jane jumped up, an anxious expression on her face, and ran into the hallway. Martha could hear her exclamation of concern. 'What is it, darling? Are you ill? I wasn't expecting you back so early,' and David's brief, irritated reply about a dinner being cancelled.

'Well, it's lovely to have you back so unexpectedly, darling.'

'Is it? Oh, do stop fussing. Leave that where it is. I said *leave* it. I'll take it up to my study later. All I want right now is a strong gin and tonic and a nice quiet afternoon reading the newspapers.'

Martha could hear Jane's anxious, 'But you're all right, darling? Not ill or anything?' and David's voice growing louder as he walked down the passageway to the kitchen. 'Well, I must say that I don't feel a hundred per cent but I expect I'm just tired. Bit of a headache, to tell you the truth, and my throat feels sore. You know how exhausting those meetings are, being cheerful all the time and then having to eat that interminable...' His voice trailed off as he walked in to the kitchen. 'What are you doing here?'

'Hello, David,' Martha said. 'Oh, it's all right, Jane, I don't mind.' She looked at him. 'You look like you need a drink.'

For a brief second she thought she saw hatred in his eyes but then he smiled, and the look was gone. 'Sorry. I didn't mean to snap. It's been a rotten day. Pay no attention to me.' He began to sort through the pile of letters which he held in his hand. 'Bills –' he said, 'bills, bills and more bills. Harvey Nichols,' he read out slowly and then, as his eyes scanned the bill, his face reddened with anger. 'Christ! We're not made of bloody money, Jane.'

'The boys needed some weekend clothes,' she said in a tight, pained voice.

'Well why can't they have them from Marks & Spencer like everyone else?'

'They're so...' Jane shrugged. 'Sorry, darling. I'll get them there in future.' She watched him anxiously. 'Are you quite sure you're feeling all right? Why don't you go up to bed and have a nice lie-down? I could bring you up a cup of tea.'

'I don't want any bloody tea. I told you, I want a large gin.' He turned on her. 'Oh, for Christ's sake, leave me alone. It's bad enough finding the kitchen full of women without you fussing over me like a demented hen as well.'

Jane rolled her eyes apologetically in Martha's direction and laid a conciliatory hand on his arm. 'Sorry, darling. Actually, we were just going to go and sit in the garden. The day's turned out nice all of a sudden.' She made frantic gestures at Martha behind his back.

David was clattering the ice tray, banging it down hard to release the cubes which stuck steadfastly to its metal base. Martha could see Jane standing behind his back, her hands fluttering in little ineffectual movements as she sought, perhaps by mime, to help him. He caught the movement out of the corner of his eye and with an infuriated movement turned to face her. 'For God's sake stop flapping,' he shouted. 'Can't a man get a bit of peace in his own home?'

Jane stared at him, her eyes glistening with tears. He looked at her for a moment then shrugged and turned his back.

'Was Paris lovely?' Martha asked brightly, into the silence. 'How was Joe?'

David looked at her, his smooth, boyish face reddening. 'Joe?' he said sharply. 'Why the hell would I see Joe?'

'Because he's the man you do business with, remember, darling?' Jane prompted him gently.

David looked at her uncomprehendingly and then his face cleared and he laughed awkwardly. 'Oh, that Joe! Sorry, there are two Joes working for the same company. I thought you meant the other one. Yes, of course I saw him. He was fine.' He turned away to a cupboard, stretching up to get a bottle of gin. 'Must we really keep this up here?' he complained. 'It's so inconvenient.'

'Well, it takes temptation out of Mrs March's way, if you know what I mean,' said Jane with a quick, wary glance at Martha. 'And you know I had to move it since I caught Charles with the top off the bottle having a good sniff.'

Martha smiled slightly at the idea of stolid, serious Charles having a go at his father's gin.

David, his drink finally poured and in his hand, looked up and caught the smile. 'You look very pleased with yourself.'

Martha's smile broadened. 'I feel very pleased with

myself today.' He'll be home soon, she thought, in a sudden, wild rapture of delight. And then she remembered something David had said. 'Did you say that the meeting tonight was cancelled?' she asked sharply.

He looked at her in surprise. 'Yes. Why?'

'Because that means Joe will be back sooner than he said,' she exclaimed, hurrying around the room collecting her belongings. David watched her as she struggled into her jacket and scooped her cigarettes and lighter into her bag. 'No, he won't,' he said, when at last she was ready. 'He's staying on for a few days.'

Martha frowned, bewildered. 'Staying on? He didn't mention that on the phone last night.'

'I know he didn't,' David said, then flushed and added awkwardly, 'I mean I'm sure he wouldn't have mentioned it. He didn't know himself until this morning. That's why the dinner tonight was cancelled. Something to do with a marketing problem. He'll have to stay and sort things out.'

'Are you sure? I mean, he might come back this afternoon and then fly back tomorrow to sort things out.'

'Quite sure,' David said, good humour restored. He smiled, suddenly expansive. 'God, this gin and tonic's good. Why don't you stay and have one, Martha? Nothing to rush back for now.'

'No,' she said, feeling suddenly tired. 'No, thank you, I don't think I will.' She saw David's quick, triumphant smile and wondered briefly why he should enjoy her disappointment, but then the misery of not seeing Joe that evening swept all other thoughts from her head. 'I think I'll be off anyway.' She went to embrace her sister. 'You don't mind, do you? I know I said I'd stay for lunch but suddenly I feel like getting home.'

'No, of course I don't mind,' Jane said, kissing her. 'You go and have a lovely relaxing afternoon. There'll probably be a message from Joe on the answering machine, explaining everything. Oh, look, you've left your car keys on the table. No, don't worry, I'll get them.' She hurried across the room.

'He won't have time to leave stupid lovey-dovey messages,' David said when Jane was out of earshot. 'He's in meetings all afternoon.' A cruel, taunting smile lit his face and Martha shivered, caught by a sudden, terrible premonition. She glanced uneasily at him and he flushed with spiteful pleasure.

Jane, returning with the keys, caught the end of the exchange. 'David, are you all right? You looked so odd for a second, I thought you might be ill.' She glanced at her sister. 'And Martha, you've gone terribly pale.' Neither of them spoke and she shook her head worriedly, 'Oh well, I suppose it must be the heat. It's terribly oppressive all of a sudden, isn't it? I think we may be in for a thunderstorm.'

'Yes,' Martha murmured, her eyes sliding back to David's face. 'I think we may.'

He glanced down at Jane, the smooth curves of his face sleek with good humour, and she thought, again, that she must have imagined it. A trick of the light, perhaps.

Jane moved to accompany her to the front door but David said, 'Don't I get a kiss goodbye from my little sister?'

Martha looked at him and saw how beneath the plump, boyish cheeks, a habitual, spiteful petulance marred the surface, like the fading eddies of a stone dropped into still water. She did not want to kiss him but, knowing it would seem childish not to do so, she reached up and brushed her lips lightly across his fragrant cheek. As she did so she caught a faint, disturbing scent, spicy yet tender, and frowned, trying to remember what it reminded her of.

'Christ, what a face,' he said. 'I don't smell that awful, do I?'

'No,' she said quickly. 'It's just –' she shrugged. 'Your cologne reminds me of something which I can't quite place.'

'Me, I expect,' he said laughing genially, 'I've worn the same stuff for years. Janie buys it for me, don't you, darling?' He put his arm possessively around Jane's thin shoulders and smiled down at her. 'Let's go and see Martha off together, shall we, darling?'

They accompanied her to the front door and stood there waving as she got into the car. Martha gunned the motor and accelerated hard, anxious to be away, but still she could not help smiling as she caught one last glimpse of the picture they made, standing against the roses, arms linked and smiling. Makes a perfect frame for playing happy families, she thought, knowing how carefully Jane had planned the roses and the pale blue of the front door.

As the car drew away, Jane turned to David. 'You weren't very welcoming to Martha, darling.' She kept her voice carefully neutral. 'She looked quite upset.'

'Yes, she was, wasn't she?' he said distantly, looking after the car with a small, self-satisfied smile. Then, seeming to collect himself, he looked down at her and, seeing her slight, puzzled frown, said, 'Oh, I'm sorry, darling. Was I awful?' He sighed heavily. 'I was just so bloody irritated with the meeting being cancelled and all the plans being changed. It means I'll have to go back to Paris soon, of course. Maybe next weekend.'

'Oh, David,' Jane exclaimed, gazing sorrowfully at him.

'I know, darling,' he said, putting his arm around her and leading her gently back into the house. 'But business is business. That's why I was so irritated seeing Martha sitting in the kitchen. I know I shouldn't have been rude but I'd spent the entire taxi ride home looking forward to a quiet afternoon with just the two of us.' He hugged her briefly. 'Come on, let's go and laze in the garden with a drink and you can tell me all your news. We haven't had much time together in the past few weeks.'

She smiled up at him. 'I'd never have invited her over if I'd thought there was a chance you might be home early.' Then she sighed, her pointed face sharpening. 'Poor Martha. She looked so disappointed that Joe had to stay in Paris. Still,' she added, hugging him, 'it's good news for us, isn't it?'

'Very good news,' he said, turning away to hide a smile.

It was only when Martha was driving across Putney Bridge that she remembered what David's scent reminded her of, and why it had disturbed her. It was slightly different, of course, mingled with the smell of David and the interminable cigars he smoked, but there had lingered in the fragrance the afternote of a very distinctive scent. It was the smell of the cologne which Joe wore and which he had custom made for him by a small scent house in Paris.

She steered the car through heavy traffic, frowning in concentration as she negotiated the dual carriageway over the bridge. Why would David be wearing the same scent as Joe, a scent that she knew he had individually blended for him?

She still had not found an explanation by the time she drew up in front of her flat, and she sat for a while in her car, pondering the possibilities. She did not see the man who lounged against the entrance of the passage to her front door, did not see him shift his pose, splay his long jean-clad legs provocatively or arrange the bunch of deep, velvety red roses which filled his arms. He waited for her, his head of thick, dark hair artfully tilted to catch the afternoon sun, shooting its thick depths with light. Nor did she see him as she climbed wearily out of her car and locked the door, turning sharply as she heard a long, low wolf whistle, irritation snagging at her face. 'Well, that's some homecoming,' he drawled, greeting her with a mocking smile. She stared at him for a second, bemused, and then her face cleared and she ran into his arms.

It was only later, when she climbed out of bed to make some tea, that she remembered. 'The most extraordinary thing happened this morning,' she said telling Joe the story as she riffled though the cupboard in search of a dressing gown. Turning, she caught his expression, his dark eyebrows knitted in a thunderous frown.

'I know,' she said sympathetically, 'it's weird, isn't it? You don't suppose he's got a crush on you, do you?' Joe looked so startled that she laughed, saying she didn't see why he should look so shocked; she bet that hundreds of people, men and women, had a crush on him. 'Well, you know how stuffy David is,' she teased. 'Maybe he thinks that by wearing the same cologne some of that glamour will rub off on him.' She could see the beginnings of a smile dawning on Joe's face and started to laugh. 'Silly idiot,' she said. 'He probably wants to know what brand of toothpaste you use, too.'

Joe, lying in bed, the smooth polished brown of his young, muscular arms and chest contrasting wonderfully with the whiteness of the sheets, smiled his beautiful, lazy smile.

'Poor old David,' Martha murmured, clambering across the bed into his arms, 'I bet he's jealous as hell of you.'

Joe said thoughtfully that he thought that probably he was.

18

She didn't recognise him, would have walked straight past him if he hadn't called out to her. Even when she turned and saw his face quite clearly, he wasn't as she remembered. The light had gone from him; his face had the remote, still quality of a photograph. She fumbled with her door keys, frowning in concentration. 'Paul?' she said finally.

'You've forgotten me.' His tone was accusing.

She shrugged, smiling apologetically. 'I didn't recognise you. It's been a while and I wasn't expecting to find you standing on my doorstep. But I remember you. You're not easy to forget.'

A smile quivered briefly on his lips and was gone, leaving in its place that same chilling remoteness she had noticed when first he turned to her. He was shivering, despite the warm brilliance of the afternoon. He wore bundled layers of clothing; he, who was so fastidious in his tastes, had dressed with no regard for colour or fabric, as if he had rushed out of the house in a hurry. She saw that he was very distressed but, not knowing him well, did not like to ask him directly so said, instead, 'You're cold. Come in and have a cup of tea.'

'No,' he said, so abruptly that she thought she must have offended him. He stared at her, frowning, but the frown was neither of anger nor displeasure, but rather of concentration, as if he could not remember what it was he had come to say to her. 'I won't take any tea, thank you,' he amended, in a distant, formal voice, turning to stare up the street, hunching his body inside his big coat and fumbling at the collar, turning it up to hide his face. She followed his gaze, saw nothing out of the ordinary other than an elderly man walking slowly down the street, stopping occasionally to peer up at the sky and utter a brief exclamation of delight before shambling on another few more yards.

'He's old,' Paul said, with a sharp sigh of regret. 'And sick.'

'Sick?' Phil glanced anxiously at him. He kept his eyes fixed on the street and so she looked again at the old man. She saw only his shy smile, lifted to the sky.

'Of course,' Paul said impatiently. 'Look at the way he greets the sun, as if he thought he'd lost it for ever. He's old and sick and thought he would die. Now he's a little better, he sees the world with young eyes.'

'Yes,' Phil said, remembering that Martha had said Stevie had been ill. She wondered if he was sick again but it seemed too intrusive a question, seeing as she'd never even met him. So she said instead, in an oblique attempt at sympathy, 'Yes. Yes, it must feel like that.'

Paul ignored her, staring after the man until he had shuffled his painful way around the corner out of sight. 'I shall follow the sun,' he said distantly.

Phil looked at him uncertainly. 'Are you going on holiday?'

'Holiday?' he repeated, turning to stare at her, his mouth curving in a mocking smile. 'How enchanting you are. Why would you think that I was going on holiday?'

She frowned slightly. 'You said – the sun.'

His smile faded. 'Ah, yes, the sun. Well, I am always cold.' He held out his hands, spreading long, bony fingers; their colour, Phil noticed, was a sickly yellow. They shook slightly.

172

She felt a vague sense of alarm and asked, with forced brightness, 'Are you going for long?'

'Perhaps.' He smiled and she saw, in the harsh sunlight, how he had aged. His face, always thin, had contracted to a relief of bone and shadow; his beak of a nose painfully prominent and the fine skin around his limpid, mournful eyes the texture of crêpe paper and faintly mottled. 'And perhaps not,' he shrugged, suddenly diffident. He lapsed into silence, shivering occasionally while Phil stood, irresolute, wondering what had happened to him and whether she should insist that he come in and warm himself with some tea.

He sensed her impatience. 'I won't keep you long,' he said curtly. 'I've only come about Martha.'

'About Martha?' It was weeks since Phil had seen her. She felt an instant, terrible sense of fear. 'What's wrong with her? Has something happened?'

His abrupt manner fell away. 'I'm sorry, I didn't mean to alarm you. There's nothing wrong with Martha –' he paused and shrugged slightly – 'other than love.' Phil nodded, frowning. 'I simply came to ask you if you would tell her that I've gone away.'

She looked at him in astonishment. 'Me?'

He shrugged. 'Yes. Why not?'

'It's just – surely she'll be upset that you've not told her yourself? Especially if you're going away for a long time. For a while,' she amended.

'But how can I tell her?' he said, irritable now. 'I don't know where she's staying in Paris.'

'In Paris? She didn't say anything.'

He looked at her sadly and shrugged. 'She's happy. She forgets.'

Phil considered this for a while and said eventually, 'She doesn't mean to.' He shrugged again carelessly and the indifference of the gesture annoyed her suddenly. 'Surely you could tell her yourself? I'm sure she won't

173

be away for long. A weekend, perhaps. It doesn't seem so long to wait.' He cast her a look in which impatience and contempt were mingled and she thought it was because he knew her to be dull, incapable of the large, spontaneous gesture, of the fine romance of packing up and leaving on the whim of the moment. She stiffened slightly, affronted. 'She'll be upset,' she warned in a small, cool voice.

He shook his head, his eyes sliding down the street to the place where the old man had performed his lyrical dance to the day. 'I can't help that.'

She watched him in exasperation and then said, with a slight sigh, 'Very well, I'll tell her.' He kept his head averted, his gaze still fixed on the empty street. 'Is Stevie going with you?'

'Stevie is always with me,' he said distantly.

'And where will you go, how long will you be away?'

He looked at her with surprise, smiling slightly. 'How careful you are, Sarah. All these questions.' She recoiled, stung, and thought again how he must think her a dull creature, forever checking timetables and destinations.

He reached out a hand and laid it gently on her arm. 'It's such a pretty name, Sarah. So much better than that absurd name Martha calls you.' He looked at her consideringly, the thick fringe of his eyelashes startling against the crêpey whiteness of his skin. 'She worries about you,' he said gently.

'She worries about *me*?' Phil repeated, startled.

Paul smiled slightly, the peculiar sweetness of his smile softening his face. She saw suddenly how his habitual haughty demeanour disguised an essential kindness. 'She thinks you're worried about something and you won't tell her.'

She shook her head rapidly. 'It's nothing.'

He looked at her curiously for a minute, then shrugged. 'You keep your secrets, Sarah. Caution is a good quality, like a brake on a car that's driven too fast.' He sighed. 'It's what Martha needs. She's sometimes too reckless. Like with this Joe person.' He looked at her with mournful eyes, but she shook her head slightly, looking away so that he wouldn't see her expression.

'I wouldn't know,' she murmured. 'I haven't met him.'

'It's no great loss.' She looked up, surprised at the sharpness in his voice. He shrugged. 'Men like that…'

She watched him, alarmed. 'What do you mean, men like that? Do you know something?'

He looked uncomfortable. 'Just a feeling.'

She hesitated, unsure what he meant, and then the memory of the man she had seen with David by the river that day prompted her and she faltered. 'That he might be gay, you mean?'

'That he might like men sometimes, yes.'

'Shouldn't we tell Martha? Warn her, or something?'

He looked at her sadly. 'Warn her of what? She's blinded by love. Lust, I should say. And anyway, what can I say? That there's something about him that worries me, that isn't quite right?' He smiled ruefully. 'It's not much to tell, is it?'

Her shoulders sagged. 'No, I suppose you're right. It's not much to tell.' And what, she thought, do *I* have to tell? That I thought I saw a man who looked like her lover, a man I had seen only once and in a photograph, fooling around on a river bank with her sister's husband? She would think me mad, or foolish, or simply vindictive.

'Don't look so worried. At least she has somebody to love.'

She looked up at him in surprise, curious at the bitterness in his voice. He had become deathly pale and she noticed that the trembling had started again. 'You must look after her,' he said, pulling his coat tight around himself with shaking hands. He smiled briefly. 'I leave her in your careful hands.'

'Won't you stay? She may need you.'

His eyes were sad. 'It's not possible.'

She noticed suddenly how tired he looked and reaching out a hesitant hand, put it to his pale face. 'Are you all right?'

He frowned slightly. 'So far,' he said obliquely. He glanced at her sharply. 'Do *you* think I'm all right?'

'Yes,' she said, bewildered. 'Of course I do. It's just that you're not…you're not as I remember.'

'We are none of us as we are remembered,' he said, bending down and kissing her lightly on both cheeks. 'Nor as we are seen. Not even you.' She felt the brush of his hair against her cheek and smelled the faint, clinging scent of tea rose. Reaching up, she put her arms around his neck and hugged him fiercely, as if by holding him she could make him stay. But even as she held him she saw that his face was turned to the street and his whole body strained to be free.

She dropped her arms and reluctantly let him go. His step was quick and graceful, even under the heavy bulk of clothes. She watched him until he reached the end of the street. Just as he was about to turn the corner and walk out of sight she called to him, her voice high and anxious. 'Paul?'

He stopped and turned to look at her, his pale face glimmering in the strong sun, anxious to be gone. 'Yes?'

'You will come back?'

'I promise you,' he called, and with a quick wave of his hand was gone.

19

She found Martha unpacking, carefully shaking creases out of pale silk dresses and arranging them lovingly on hangers. Phil sat on the bed watching them unfurl like crumpled flowers from the depths of a large, unfamiliar leather suitcase.

'Those are new,' she said, eyeing them curiously. Could these really belong to Martha? These pale, cautious dresses with their neat bodices and fluttering skirts?

Martha looked at them fondly. 'Pretty, aren't they?' she murmured, smoothing their crumpled skirts tenderly. 'Joe bought them for me in Paris.'

'Very nice,' Phil said, looking at the elegant, fragile dresses with distaste. She looked around wondering where were the satins and velvets, the men's shirts and old 40s jackets, the exuberant rose prints that Martha used to wear; found them discarded in a heap on the floor, shed like a second skin. She scarcely recognised this new, pale, shining creature who had emerged from their folds, gleaming with silk and scent. Martha seemed to her diminished, her vitality dimmed, as if a veil had been drawn across her features. Even her bright hair was tamed, the wild tangle of curls drawn tight in a smooth, sleek chignon. From her ears hung small, discreet gold hoops. She looked beautiful but remote.

'Martha,' Phil said quietly, 'there's something I have to...'

Martha, absorbed in unpacking, did not hear her. She moved, Phil thought, like a sleepwalker; her bare arms, gilded a light brown by the sun, rose and fell in slow curves as she methodically unpacked, sliding the limp silk dresses on to plump satin hangers. 'We bought them in this extraordinary place Joe knows,' she murmured dreamily, 'just off the Place Victoire. We went into a courtyard and then up a staircase to a big scarred mahogany door and pulled on an old brass bell. When the door opened, I felt like I'd stepped into a garden; there were so many colours and the silks and satins seemed to be perfumed with roses and lavender.' She smiled contemplatively. 'I suppose they must have come from Provence.'

'Martha,' Phil said gently, 'Paul's gone away for a while.'

Martha looked up. 'Gone away?' she said, a slight frown marring the smooth contentment of her face. 'Where?'

Phil shrugged. 'I'm not sure exactly. He couldn't get hold of you so he came round to the flat on Saturday to ask me to tell you. He said something about following the sun.'

Martha's face cleared. 'Oh, that.' She bent her bright head over a tangle of delicate lace. 'Was he all right?' she asked vaguely.

'Quite all right.' What, after all, was the point in saying that he was not? She could not be sure that the remoteness she had seen in him that day was anything out of the ordinary. Perhaps he was prone to fits of depression. Even if he was not, there was nothing Martha could do about it now.

Martha unravelled the last garment from the tangle and looked at it contemplatively. 'We had a silly quarrel, about two weeks ago,' she murmured. Phil frowned, bemused, but Martha shrugged lightly. 'Oh, it was absurd, about nothing really, but it upset me at the time. He told me to go back to Harry. As if I could now,' she added, half to herself.

'What do you mean, *now*?' said Phil, her voice sharp.

Martha looked up in surprise. 'What?' Her mouth curved in a small, secret smile. 'Oh, I'm not pregnant, if that's what you mean, although Joe says he'd love to have a child. Our child,' she said, subsiding dreamily on to the bed, a slip of silk clutched in her hands.

'Are you serious?'

Her voice seemed to jolt Martha out of her reverie. 'You don't like him, do you?' she said, colour rising in her cheeks.

'I've never met him.'

Martha shrugged. 'No, I suppose you haven't. Paul has, though. He doesn't like him. I think he's just jealous.'

'Jealous? Martha, Paul's gay, remember? He's hardly going to be jealous.'

Martha turned her head away affronted by Phil's tone. 'Joe says it's not Paul's fault, it's because we go back so far and he's used to having me all to himself. It's nice of him to understand, but he's generous in that way.'

Phil stared at her, wondering how she could delude herself so entirely.

Martha caught her look. 'Well, it is. The trouble with Paul is that he's not used to competition,' she said spitefully. She flushed again, casting a proud, possessive look at Phil. 'Joe says he sees him as a threat.'

Phil nodded mutely, wondering how far Joe had gone in turning Martha against Paul. He wouldn't enjoy their closeness; if anyone felt threatened it was likely to be Joe. She realised suddenly how he had insinuated himself, like a barrier, between Martha and her friends; the unanswered telephone messages, the last-minute excuses. Now, perhaps, he was separating them with words; a casual phrase dropped here, a gentle reproof there. She felt a sudden prickle of alarm. Was it her turn next?

Martha looked at her and sighed. 'Can I confide in you?' she said. Phil nodded again, frowning slightly as she watched a delicate flush flood Martha's neck. Martha looked away and said nervously, 'Joe's had affairs with men. A long time ago,' she added quickly. 'So of course, I think that's why Paul...' Her voice trailed off and she turned and looked at Phil beseechingly. 'It was when he was very young. He must have been impossibly beautiful when he was eighteen, lived in Hollywood... All those rich, old men... His head must have been turned... You can see how it might happen.' She shrugged lightly. 'Well, all that's the past now. He says...well, he says he's never felt like this before.'

Phil felt a terrible, inarticulate sense of foreboding; her whole body prickled with alarm and she heard Martha's voice, as if from a long way away. 'Phil? Phil, you do understand, don't you?'

With an effort she roused herself, managed a faint smile. 'Yes,' she murmured, 'yes, of course I understand.'

Martha laughed with relief. 'For a moment I thought you were shocked. I don't know why but I've been incredibly nervous about telling you.' She threw herself on the bed, sprawling inelegantly. 'I can't tell you what a relief it is to be able to talk about it. Especially after that dreadful tea with Paul.'

'Did you tell him?'

'No, because I know what he'd have said. Like most gay men he believes that once a man's had sex with another man then he's always going to seek out men for sex, however hard he tries to go straight. Then,' she continued with a deep sigh, 'there's AIDS. He would have lectured me for hours.'

It had not occurred to Phil to think about AIDS, let alone to worry about it. In 1983 there had been so few cases in England, the newspapers, if they wrote about it at all, treated it as an American phenomenon. Still, if a man was gay, had slept with other men, even a couple… She looked at Martha in alarm. 'You will be careful, won't you?'

Martha sat up in one quick, angry movement. 'Oh, for God's sake, not you as well!' she exclaimed. 'I told you, Joe hasn't had sex with a man for *years*. The first AIDS victims were diagnosed in the States three years ago. Joe's been in Paris for at least the past five.'

'Still,' said Phil uneasily, 'be careful.'

'Phil, get real, will you? The guys who got it were fucking their brains out at the Baths every night and shoving poppers under every orifice they could find. Joe's not like that, all he did was to sleep with a couple of men when he was a kid. He's clean. He's never touched drugs.'

'I'm sorry, I didn't mean…'

Martha shook her head wearily. 'I know you didn't.' She held up her hands, the palms flat. 'So he's done it with men. Big deal. End of story.' She dropped her hands and looked challengingly at Phil. 'I mean it. OK?'

Phil shrugged. 'Sure.' Still she could not shake off a lingering feeling of unease and longed for somebody to talk to. If only Paul hadn't gone away.

'Has Paul just taken off like that before?'

Martha, who had sunk into thoughtful silence, looked up, frowning. 'What? Oh, yes. A couple of times. He and Stevie go to the States, Venice Beach or Long Island, somewhere like that. Of course Stevie's still got a lot of friends over there so they can borrow a room and just hang out on the beach for a few months.' She laughed, shaking her head indulgently. 'They always come back looking fabulous and complaining bitterly of boredom.'

'I suppose he must be tired after all those months of nursing Stevie,' Phil said thoughtfully.

'You're quite sure Stevie's gone with him?' Martha asked, her voice suddenly sharp.

Phil shrugged. 'So he said.'

'Oh well,' Martha said carelessly, 'he'll be back.'

'Of course he will,' said Phil, comforted yet alarmed by her indifference.

20

'It's almost as if she's become a stranger,' Phil complained. 'Nothing about her is familiar any more, even down to the clothes she wears. She seems so distant and so...indifferent, I suppose. It's been weeks since Paul left and not a word, not even a postcard. Yet she seems not to care.'

Peter looked at her oddly. 'She's in love. Perhaps you've forgotten how consuming that can be.' An edge of bitterness sharpened his voice.

'Surely, not so consuming that she can forget her friends?' Phil said in exasperation.

'To *some* people, a lover is more important than a friend. But I know that you're not of that opinion.' She said nothing and after a brief, irritable sigh, he carefully picked up a newspaper which he had earlier placed, neatly folded, on the low table beside him. Opening it with a slow, deliberate movement, he lowered his eyes and began to read.

Phil watched him regretfully. She knew he was not reading, was instead brooding on some small injustice he thought had been done him. What could it be now, she thought in exasperation. Was it because she had mentioned Martha? He resented, she knew, the positions which Martha and Harry occupied in her affections. 'Martha and Harry; Harry and Martha,' he'd said, one day, in exasperation. 'What about me?'

She looked at him, bewildered. 'Well, what about you?' she had finally asked.

'Precisely!' he exclaimed, in the small tight voice he used when he was upset. 'What about me indeed?' retreating, as he so often seemed to these days, behind the protective cover of a newspaper.

Phil glanced at him again, only to find him watching her circumspectly. She looked away, embarrassed. It was odd, she thought, how displays of emotion from Peter had always embarrassed her; she even disliked his rare, murmured words of endearment. He offered them sparingly enough these days and for that she was grateful, for rather than soothing her they made her feel awkward and graceless. He seemed to give them in a spirit of challenge, as if to say, 'See here, I say I love you and you must love me back.' She knew she did not love him; that much had become apparent to her in the months since he had left Mary, and she wondered now whether she ever really had. She heard the rustle of a page being opened and folded with a discreet but irritable snap. Peter would never do anything so vulgar as to openly express his irritation.

His fastidiousness, which once she had admired, she had come to find irritating. She understood, seeing him more clearly now that they spent so much time together, that what she had previously mistaken for confidence, an ease with the world, was in fact a coldness and a slight tendency towards pomposity. Why had she never noticed how many of his sentences began with the words, 'In my opinion'? How could anyone love a man, she thought in exasperation, who cared so much for his own opinions and so little for those of others?

She knew that she didn't please him either. He had begun to criticise her about little things, her weekly lunches with Martha, her solitary Sunday afternoon walks on the Heath (she did not mention that she sometimes walked with Harry), her preference for staying in on Saturday night with supper on a tray while watching a video. When he said that he didn't like watching videos but preferred to read a book, she'd said mildly enough that she wasn't stopping him. He'd glared at her with reddened, watery eyes and said, in a tight voice, that it was impossible to concentrate with all that racket going on in the background; and anyway he preferred to listen to classical music. She'd even offered to move the stereo for him, the flat was certainly big enough, but that hadn't been good enough. Bewildered, she had asked him what he would like to do instead but he complained even more then, saying that he thought it only natural that she should want to be with him, adding in a tight voice that if the thought didn't at first occur to her then who was he to interfere with her 'little habits'?

The bewilderment turned gradually to resentment, then faded altogether as she came to understand that he needled her only because he was hurt by her refusal to live with him and by what he perceived as her indifference. She knew that he thought she didn't pay him enough attention and therefore could not really love him, and while this was true he couldn't be entirely sure, for she was careful never to let her irritation show. His idea of love seemed to her to be more to do with a defined etiquette of behaviour than with any real feeling, his distress more to do with damaged pride than love. He resented her failure to put him first in all things; a position he had evidently occupied with his wife.

He liked, she saw, to get his own way in everything and she began to notice how, when he came back from work, he always made mention of some small victory he'd had over a colleague that day, couching it in carefully considered language that seemed to say he'd made a modest suggestion which, to his surprise and delight, had been proved correct. 'In my humble opinion,' he'd say modestly, shaking his head, 'I think I was right to bring it to James's attention. He'll be glad of it later.' She saw how he hugged his small victory to himself in smug delight, as small boys do whenever they triumph.

She glanced at him, absorbed in reading the newspaper, and turned to look out of the window. 'It's a beautiful evening,' she murmured. 'Perhaps we should go for a walk? It seems such a shame to waste it.'

'Isn't it a little late to go out walking?' he said irritably, without looking up from the newspaper.

'Is it?' She looked down at her watch. 'It's only seven o'clock.' He raised an eyebrow. He liked, she knew, to eat at eight sharp but suddenly she couldn't bear the prospect of the two of them trapped together in that cool, quiet flat when outside there was light and life and air. And, she thought resentfully, freedom. It was the end of a week during which she'd felt a stifling sense of claustrophobia, closeted away in a small, airless office during the day, only to be released in the evening to Peter's dark, brooding presence.

It seemed to her unendurable to stay in that flat for another minute. 'Do come for a walk, Peter,' she pleaded. 'It's so rarely that we get these fine summer evenings. And,' she added, to placate him, 'it's so nice for me to have you back from work so early. It gives us more time to do things.' She could not bring herself to add, 'together.' 'We could go for a walk,' she pressed on eagerly, 'and then maybe try out that nice little restaurant you admired in Hampstead.'

'But you've already bought supper,' he protested. 'You said you'd picked up something on your way back from work.'

'It'll keep,' she said briefly and glanced again out of the window. 'And the same can't be said for the English weather.'

186

He sighed slightly, folded the newspaper carefully. 'Very well, if that's what you'd like.'

Phil smiled at a group of teenagers sprawled lazily in the long grass, surrounded by beer cans, chattering excitedly, deaf to the music which blared from a luridly painted cassette player. Watching them, she realised with regret that she had never sprawled carelessly in the long grass on a summer's evening, her head pillowed in a lover's lap, had never enjoyed that fine, brief abandon before the cares of the world closed in, and she longed to tell them to savour every moment. She turned again to look at them, thowing a quick, wide smile of encouragement over her shoulder. One of them waved cheerily back, raising his beer can in a silent salute to the evening.

'Did you see the mess they're making?' Peter exclaimed. 'Not to mention the noise.'

'Oh, they're all right. They're having a good time, that's all.'

'I don't know what you're being so complacent about,' he complained. 'You'll be the first to complain if they destroy your beloved Heath.' He was, Phil knew, determined to pick a fight; intent on finding a reason for voicing all the slights and injustices he felt himself to have suffered over the past few weeks.

She looked up at him and smiled. He was, she saw, affronted by her smile but at the same time, disarmed. 'Yes,' she agreed, 'I'm sure you're right.'

He glanced at her suspiciously but she said nothing and they walked on in silence for a while.

'Isn't that Harry?' Peter exclaimed abruptly. 'Over there?'

Phil glanced in the direction of the Ponds and quickly away again. It was Harry; she saw the dear, familiar slope of his shoulders, the way his shirt always became untucked from his trousers and flapped hopelessly beneath the hem of his old faded green corduroy jacket. 'No,' she said decisively, 'No, I'm certain that it's not.'

'Are you sure?' Peter said doubtfully. 'It looks very much like him to me. Harry! Harry, over here.'

'Don't,' Phil exclaimed sharply, pulling at his up-raised arm. Peter glanced down at her in confusion. 'He may want to be alone,' she said, muttering an explanation.

He gave a quick, exasperated sigh and pulled his arm away, frowning. 'Don't be absurd. I'm sure he'll be delighted to see us. Anyway, it's too late now. He's coming over. Phil! Phil, where are you going? Christ, I don't know what's got into you recently. Oh Phil, do come back!'

Phil felt foolish hurrying away but it had been her first instinct and, having felt it, she knew it must be obeyed. She thought she could not bear to compare the two men, for any comparison would reveal to her too clearly her true feelings. But having once moved away she knew, equally, that she must go back. How childish and absurd Peter would think her for walking off like that. Although, being Peter, he would imagine it had something to do with him and that silly quarrel they'd had earlier. And then, of course, he would be irritated with her for embarrassing him in front of Harry. But what would Harry think? His concern, she knew, would be for her and not for himself.

She turned, intending to walk back, but seeing the two men approach each other she stopped a little way away to watch them. It made her smile a little to see them; Peter, so stiff and formal, standing with his hand held out before him and Harry, hurrying forward with that long, loping stride, taking Peter's hand and pulling the other man to him in a brief, affectionate hug. Peter always claimed that Harry's physical exuberance em-barrassed him although Phil suspected, when she saw his flushed, animated face, that it pleased him in some way too. He longed, she knew, to be more demonstrative but found it impossible to express his affections physically.

The only time he ever touched her in public was to put his arm around her and steer her across a busy street; in the early days of their relationship she had once taken his hand when they were out walking and had immediately felt him tense as he exerted all his will not to snatch it away. Eventually she had relinquished it, handing it back with a playful, 'There! That wasn't so bad, was it?' but even then he could not relax and laugh, but had to maintain his dignity by pretending confusion as to her meaning. Eventually, she saw that her teasing attempts to cajole him into showing her some physical affection caused him genuine pain and embarrassment and so she had stopped. These days they scarcely touched at all, except in bed.

She saw them turn to look at her, saw Harry's bewildered smile and Peter's stiff, embarrassed shrug as he made some excuse for her. She knew she couldn't linger any further and hurried towards them saying, a little breathlessly, 'I'm sorry, but I thought I heard a child cry out.' The two men looked at her curiously. 'But as it happened it was just...' Her voice trailed off and she grinned foolishly at Harry. He smiled back, his eyes almost disappearing in the welter of wrinkles which appeared around them. She thought it was that she loved most about him; the way he smiled with his whole face. He enveloped her in a strong, welcoming hug. 'Good old Phil,' he said, laughing, 'always looking for somebody to look after.'

She felt the soft pile of his jacket against her cheek and smelled the warm, familiar smell of turpentine and cheroots. Stepping quickly away, she put a careful distance between them and stood blinking foolishly in the sunlight. The two men smiled down at her; Harry with a look of amused affection and Peter with a small, cold smile of dislike. 'Yes,' he said tightly, 'that's just what I was saying to her earlier.'

She knew then that it was hopeless; that whatever she and Peter had once felt for each other was irrevocably lost. She shivered suddenly, feeling desolate, and heard Harry say, 'Well, she's been wonderful to me. I don't know what I'd have done without her.'

'I've done nothing,' she said abruptly, for she saw suddenly how that was true, too. She had been nothing more to him than a friend, had never meant anything else to him but that. And what had he been to her? What had either of them been to her? She felt, standing there under the pearly expanse of a summer sky, that she saw the two men each in their separateness; unique but insignificant. She saw them dwindle, restored to their small place in the great order of things, and wondered at her imagination, how it had magnified Harry until he became not Harry, but some fantastical being, an invention, she supposed, of her desperate longing. And her longing seemed to her then to be absurd; she knew that it was not for Peter, nor even for Harry that she yearned, but for a sense of her own being. It was not loneliness that she suffered from but rather an emptiness. It was to herself that she must look; not to Harry.

She longed suddenly to go home to her quiet, peaceful flat and her soothing, solitary rituals; something to eat, a boiled egg perhaps, and then that grateful clamber into bed, her four cats purring watchfully until she settled and they could begin the dignified jostle for the place on her lap. Looking around her, she realised with a start that they must have walked some distance around the Heath, were nearly back at the car park. Peter and Harry walked beside her, heads down, absorbed in conversation. She laid a hand on Peter's arm.

He looked at her, frowning in distraction. 'Do you mind,' she said, 'if we go now?'

'Very well,' he said, an injured expression still on his face so that she realised with surprise that he knew nothing of what had been going on in her head. He did not see the two of them, as she did, in their separateness. She said goodbye to Harry, who gave her a private, questioning smile to which she nodded and smiled absently in return, watching his familiar, jangling walk as he loped away over the long grass.

'What on earth was all that about?' Peter said as they walked to the car.

'All what?'

'With Harry.' She felt his curious eyes on her and kept her head averted. 'You were so, well, so *awkward* with him.'

'Was I?'

He sighed in exasperation. 'I would hardly say so if you weren't,' he said shortly.

Phil laid a conciliatory hand on his arm. 'I'm sorry, I don't mean to be difficult. I feel rather tired suddenly.'

'You're certainly not very forthcoming,' he said in injured tones, moving away from the touch of her hand. She said nothing and they walked on in silence for some time, Peter increasing his pace so he moved slightly ahead of her. She saw how he stiffened his back self-consciously and the abrupt, jerking movements of his steps and felt a brief wash of tenderness. She understood his bewilderment and his poor, wounded pride and felt sorry for her impatience with him. How difficult he must find her sometimes. As they reached the car park he stopped suddenly and turned to her. 'Phil, everything is all right, isn't it? I mean…' he shrugged, his eyes flicking nervously away and back, 'there's nothing you want to tell me?' She knew how much it had cost him to say those few words, and how he held his body stiff, steeling himself for rejection. He looked bewildered, forlorn almost, and she knew, seeing him like that, that she must put an end to it at once.

'Peter, it's over,' she said, conscious of the absurd melodrama of the words, scattering in the slight wind, settling quietly around them in the dusty car park. 'I'm sorry.'

He winced slightly but then, to her astonishment, she saw a small, secret smile of triumph steal across his face. 'I thought so,' he said and she saw how, even though it distressed him, it somehow also pleased him to be proved right. 'I knew it wasn't just tiredness.' He looked at her abruptly. 'Is that it, then?'

'Yes,' she said wearily, 'that's it.'

The decision came almost as a relief to both of them and they smiled then, like old friends parting, and hugged each other, feeling the warm press of each other's body, once so familiar and now, within the space of just a few words, so strange. With that sudden alienation came regret. Not much, but enough to make them treat each other with a careful tenderness as they climbed in to the car and prepared to make the short journey home.

Peter drove as Phil sat in silence beside him. Although he said nothing, she could feel his mood shift from the tenderness of regret to the cold anger of rejection. As his fury mounted, so he drove more and more slowly and with exaggerated concentration, until they virtually crawled the last few hundred yards to her flat. As the car finally shuddered to a halt outside her front door he said quietly, his face averted, 'I must say I think you've behaved rather badly.'

'I'm sorry,' she said regretfully.

'Is there somebody else?'

'No.' She knew as she said it that it was true. The feelings she had for Harry were under control. It was finished.

She leaned forward to kiss him. 'There has never been anybody else.' He jerked his head back to avoid the embrace and stared stonily at the windscreen. She watched him in silence for a minute and then touched her hand to his cold, resisting cheek. 'Goodbye,' she said.

21

Phil thought later that it was that particular Friday when it all started to change. Even as she stepped out of the car into the fading light of that July evening and saw Peter's set white face flicker and finally dim behind the refracted light on the windscreen, she knew that something had irrevocably altered. Not simply between her and Peter; that, of course, had changed, but something greater had happened, something that would in later years affect all of their lives. To say that she understood it then was to confuse hindsight with instinct; at the time she felt only relief.

It was later, when looking back at that evening, that she understood how knotted and tangled the threads of their lives, hers, Martha's and Harry's, had become. How, even though they fought against it, ineluctably they would always be drawn back together again.

That evening, she felt only a quiet but profound liberation; sensing that, by freeing herself from Peter, she had similarly severed her attachment to Harry. She knew that nothing could break that entirely, he was the thread which bound her again to Martha and from that she could never really be free; nor did she want to be. But on that summer evening, joyous, heady liberation surged through her and she ran, laughing, to her front door, unlocking it with a sense of purpose and excitement. Walking into her flat she saw it with fresh eyes, its emptiness not a reproach but a blessing; a first, faltering step towards independence.

As she stood there, light-headed with excitement, she felt that she understood how she had subjugated herself to Martha; in a sense led her life through her, even seeking out a lover who occupied her time without capturing her emotions, leaving them free for Martha, and through Martha for Harry. By breaking with Peter she had somehow freed herself from both Martha and Harry; she felt that she was, if not leading, then at least no longer following. She no longer envied Martha, had ceased, she realised, to compare herself to her. She felt, for the first time, like her own person.

She thought too that now she was finally free to help Martha and saw clearly how much in need Martha was of her help. Martha was also trying to escape, fiercely resisting the line that pulled her back and back again to Harry and Phil. The pale silks and polished hair were the tangible symbols of that struggle; by changing even her outward appearance she hoped to regain her sense of self.

She knew how feverish were Martha's attempts to capture happiness, how the faster she chased after it, the more it eluded her, understood Martha's bitterness at discovering her own insignificance. She did not mean that unkindly; she appreciated only too well Martha's worth but knew that Martha did not count it, for she valued herself only in relation to her talent which flickered erratically, sometimes burning with brilliance but then wavering into mediocrity. What Martha could not live with was the slow steady glow of competence, she longed always for the purifying flame of brilliance.

In Harry she had found the comfort and support that maintained that steady glow. But what Martha wanted was genius; the colour and excitement of pure inspiration.

Phil knew that she thought she had found it in Joe; remembered her exclaiming, her cheeks hectic with elation, 'Oh, Phil. He's what I need. He makes me feel alive like I've never felt before. He makes me paint again. Can you understand that? Can you?'

Phil had shaken her head sadly, knowing that she could never understand, could recognise only the ephemeral nature of Martha's happiness and saw in her intense, feverish blue gaze the capricious nature of her passion. While she doubted, from all the accounts that Martha had given her, that Joe could give her the support she craved, and resented him for it, she pitied him too. She understood how consuming Martha could be, how her bright light could eclipse the dark side of her soul and just as suddenly be extinguished. What would Joe do then? With that frail, anxious and diminished creature who lurked at Martha's centre? Could he succour her, as Harry had, as Phil still did? 'Joe says,' Martha announced, laughing and triumphant, 'that a life spent without passion is a life wasted.' And Phil had nodded uneasily and wondered whether there is anything so unsatisfying as a life led in only one dimension, anything so bitter as to be forced always to seek excitement in others because we find none in ourselves.

Phil remembered Martha in her teens and then in her twenties always chasing after happiness, finding it first with this person and then that; remembered her rapt, fevered protestations of joy and then the dull dragging days of self-recrimination and hopelessness until there came another man and a few more fine, careless days of rapture. Then along came Harry, at first sight an unpromising candidate for happiness, but happiness there was in that slow, painful climb to contentment. Phil thought then that she understood Harry's tender, anxious expression when he spoke about Martha. His unhappiness was not for himself but for Martha, for fear that he was not up to the fight, had failed her and in failing her had lost himself.

And then she thought that perhaps she did still envy Martha, she envied her Harry's eternally tender regard. She longed suddenly to find that for herself, that loving, focused gaze that sees and yet forgives. Love is not blind, she thought. Love is the clear eye of compassion.

It was with those thoughts that Phil decided to build her own life part by part, to tend to Martha and care for Harry, but never again to see herself through them. What she had not bargained for was the conspiracy of circumstance which renders all our fine resolutions hopeless.

Fate, if you like.

22

The rest of that summer passed uneventfully; too un-eventfully, Phil thought. It was as though time had slowed, was reduced to a trickle behind a dam which threatened at any moment to burst. The sense of libera-tion she had felt when Peter left passed; she was con-scious only of a fractured, brooding calm. She felt, every day, as if something momentous was about to happen and woke with a start each morning, filled with a charged, nervous expectancy. The feeling caused her to hurry with her bath and dressing and to run to the hallway, her spirits lifting, as she heard the thud of the post hitting the mat. She did not know what she was expecting or even what it would have delighted her to see, but it was not those familiar buff envelopes; domes-tic bills, letters from her bank, credit card reminders and circulars.

One day there was a postcard from Paul announcing sternly, 'Having a good time', signed with a scrawled P slashed through with a kiss. The stamp was American, the date smudged and illegible. She turned it over and over, examining it as if it might contain some secret code, but even the image on the front, a serene black and white Horst photograph, offered up no message. She put it in her bag and carried it with her every day. She did not know why.

The weather had turned, July's brilliant promise dis-solving to a steady trickle of humid, wet days. It was warm, but still the lowering grey skies dawned one upon another and the rain fell in a constant fine drizzle so that people began to complain that nothing was ever dry and there lingered in the air the faint, musty smell of damp. Even the roses drooped in front gardens, their heavy heads bruised and dispirited by the constant rain.

Phil thought how well it mirrored her mood, that curious dragging expectancy as people waited for summer eventually to happen; one minute nervously optimistic as a ray of sun peeped from behind a cloud and the next numbed by an apathetic, fatalistic resignation to months of leaden grey skies.

Her morning optimism diminished similarly as the hours moved slowly on. With its passing came weary resignation; it was as much as she could do to muster the effort to get through the rest of the day. She found herself watching the hands of the clock which sometimes seemed to hang upon the minute, grudgingly relinquishing every hour until six o'clock when she was delivered to the hot, damp streets and the slow ride home on a Tube full of people whose mood seemed to match her own as they drooped dispiritedly in their seats. Either that or her mood swung wildly to one of nervous anxiety when even the slightest noise alarmed her and her body seemed subject to constant, minor electric shocks. She felt as if she was driving a car with one foot on the brake and the other on the accelerator.

During those weeks she saw little of Martha, who spent most of her time in Paris with Joe. The few days each week she stayed in London were spent hidden away in her flat, trying to paint.

One evening, when she was filled with a pricking, restlessness anxiety and felt she could not bear the prospect of her dim, empty flat, Phil dropped in unexpectedly on Martha. She found her hunched over a painting, working with tiny, cramped strokes, layering colour on colour with a nervous intensity that was so unlike her usual style of bold, splashy washes of colour streaking across the canvas that Phil watched her in quiet alarm.

'It just won't come right,' Martha cried, throwing down her brush in despair. She cast a wild eye at her surroundings. 'Nothing will come right. Look at this place. It's such a mess.'

Phil glanced at her in surprise. The flat was not merely neat, it was obsessively tidy. Even the atmosphere had changed, so unnaturally quiet and calm was it compared with the disorderly, colourful place it had once been. Everything was put carefully away, the people included, sent away by Martha who said she no longer had time for them and their languid afternoons. The dead roses and dried fruits were gone, the shelves swept free of their bunches of dried, fragrant herbs and sticky jars of bottled and preserved fruits that Martha had once so languorously consumed. The old fridge with the blue sticking plaster on its door had been replaced with a new machine, monstrously efficient and gleaming with water chillers and ice makers. The dusty floor was polished to a fine patina, and all Martha's old quilts had been retired to the charity shops, replaced with plain but expensive covers and cushions. It looked like a place in which people spent their time merely waiting, had about it an air of restless expectancy. Even the faint hum of the driers from the launderette below no longer comforted, sounded instead alien and mechanical, a harsh reminder of the unnatural calm.

Watching Martha's quick, brittle gestures as she rushed to clear away her paints, stacking them carefully in a cupboard and anxiously watching for the kettle to boil as she laid a tray with new, matching china for tea, Phil felt a mounting sense of unease. 'Are you all right?' she asked gently.

Martha, intent on pouring the tea, looked up in surprise.

'All right?' she asked sharply. 'Of course I'm all right. Don't I look it?'

'You look beautiful,' Phil said truthfully and then gestured vaguely at her surroundings. 'It's just that it's so tidy in here. It feels so...so unlike you.' Her voice trailed away.

Martha looked around and, flushing, gave a short, brittle laugh. 'Oh, that! Joe likes things to be tidy.'

'Obviously.'

'*Obviously*?' Martha exclaimed defensively. 'What's that supposed to mean? It's about time this place was cleared up. Joe's quite right, it looked like a pit before. Anyway, I'd have thought that you, of all people, would be pleased. You're always telling me how hopeless I am at keeping the place tidy and Paul was always going on about...' She paused and sighed irritably. 'Oh, just going on,' she said shortly.

'Have you heard from him?'

'No.' Martha shrugged, indifferent. 'Well, a postcard, but it didn't say much. Just, "Having a good time", or something unhelpful. I expect he'll write when he's stopped sulking.'

'Sulking?'

Martha grimaced. 'Oh, you know. Sulking about Joe. He disapproves.'

'He worries,' Phil corrected.

Martha looked at her with sudden fury. 'About *what*? Christ, you two, you're so bloody *constipated* about everything. I'd have thought that the two people closest to me might show a bit more enthusiasm, be pleased that I've finally found happiness.'

'We'll be ecstatic,' Phil said quietly, 'if you have.'

Martha looked at her oddly. The anger seemed to leave her and she subsided, as if exhausted, into a chair.

'Oh, what would you know?' she muttered in defeated tones, closing her eyes.

Phil watched her anxiously, noticing how thin and tired she looked. 'Martha,' she said gently, 'I'm sorry if I annoyed you. But please don't let's quarrel.'

'No,' Martha said. 'No, let's not.' She sighed. 'I have enough of that with…Oh, never mind.' She opened her eyes and looking at Phil, smiled faintly. 'I'm so pleased you came. I thought that perhaps you were angry with me.'

'Angry?' Phil exclaimed. 'Why should I be angry?'

Martha shrugged. 'We don't seem to see each other as much as we used to.'

'Well, you're not here very much these days,' Phil reminded her.

'No.' Martha said quietly, 'I suppose I'm not.' Closing her eyes again, she leaned back against the chair and fell silent.

Phil sat and drank her tea, looking around her occasionally at the strangeness of her surroundings. 'Is Joe here with you?' she asked hesitantly. Martha said nothing so Phil stared around, searching for some sign of his presence. She could see nothing, no coat or jacket, no discarded cufflink or any evidence of his ever having been there.

Martha sighed again then opened her eyes and sat up, blinking slightly. 'He doesn't stay here,' she said, with a small, embarrassed shrug. 'Says he hates the mess. You know how Americans are about things being clean.' She smiled faintly. 'He has about four showers a day and won't wear a shirt if he's had it on once, even for five minutes. I sometimes think he's got a phobia about dirt but then I remember how *scrubbed* Americans always look, so wholesome and shiny, like those perfect red apples you see in supermarkets in the States.'

Phil did not remind her that those perfect red apples

tasted of nothing. Martha glanced around nervously. 'Well, he comes here a bit more since I've cleaned the place up but really he prefers to stay in a hotel; that fearfully smart one in Soho which only has eight rooms. God knows how he stands it, there's no room service and they're wildly inefficient about taking telephone messages; they never seem to know whether he's there or not.' She smiled suddenly. 'I think he thinks it's quaint; you know how Americans sometimes mistake our inefficiency for charm. Talking of which,' she looked at her watch, 'I'm going to be terribly late if I don't get a move on and get ready. I'm meeting Joe. That kind of inefficiency,' she said, with a grimace, 'he doesn't find in the least bit charming.'

Phil picked up her bag. 'I'd better be off, then.' She paused by the door, frowning slightly. 'Martha, if there's anything wrong, you would tell me, wouldn't you?'

'Why on earth should there be anything wrong?' Martha said, with a sudden flash of irritation.

Phil shrugged. 'No reason.'

Martha flushed, then looked away so Phil leaned forward and kissed her gently. 'But if there ever is...' Patting her gently on the shoulder, she turned and walked down the narrow corridor which had been cleared of its debris of old books and newspapers. Just as she reached the bottom of the metal staircase she heard the clatter of heels and, looking up, saw Martha hanging over the rusty banister, her face flushed and worried. 'Phil,' she said breathlessly, 'look, I'm sorry if we don't see each other very much at the moment, but it's only because...' She gestured vaguely. 'Well, you know why. And I haven't even *asked* you how things are with you. To tell you the truth, my dear,' she said, mimicking Paul at his most petulant, 'I'm feeling rather *distrait* at the moment.'

She sounded so comical that Phil laughed. Martha's face relaxed in a smile but as quickly began to crumple again with anxiety. 'Promise me we'll see each other again very soon,' she said urgently. 'You won't go and disappear on me, will you? I couldn't...' Her voice trailed off and Phil saw suddenly how upset she was by Paul's leaving.

'Of course we'll see each other. Soon as you like. Now go and get ready.'

Martha smiled faintly. 'Yes, I must. I'll call you next week then, as soon as I get back from Paris.' She hovered anxiously on the staircase. 'You are all right? And Peter too?'

'Peter and I –' Phil began but, seeing Martha's tired, strained face gazing down at her, said, 'He's fine. Couldn't be better. Now you *must* go or you really will be late.'

23

Jane sighed and peered in at the oven for the fifth time in as many minutes. Really, it was too bad of David to be late when he'd promised that for once he'd be home at a reasonable hour. He was an hour late already; if he wasn't back by eight-thirty dinner would be spoiled. It was his favourite too; chicken roasted with whole cloves of garlic and she'd even made a dish of *pommes dauphinoise*, labouring for hours over the potatoes, slicing them to exactly the right wafer-thinness. She grimaced slightly, remembering the first time she'd made it, for a dinner party last year. She'd been in a tearing hurry, late back from a meeting about curtains for a house she'd been doing up in Belgravia. Well, it hadn't actually been her fault that she was late, the woman, Mary Somebody or other, had been late herself and then simply would not stop talking. She'd been feeling guilty enough already because David didn't like her to work, although he let her so long as it didn't affect the family. By which, she thought wryly, he meant him.

When he'd said that morning that he was bringing home a potential client for dinner, she'd tried to re-arrange things, really she had, but the woman had been so insistent that she'd eventually agreed even though she knew she hadn't left enough time to get home and get the dinner on. It would have been all right if everything had gone according to plan.

She sighed. Why was it that, no matter how hard she

tried, things never did go right? Sure enough, she'd been late and, ignoring the recipe's stern admonishment to slice the potatoes very finely, had thrown the dish together in two minutes and rushed off to do something about her face. The man they were entertaining, Len or Ken or something, had a fat, jovial red face, a thin, scratchy ego and a chip the size of one of the chunks of potatoes she'd just cut up on his shoulder. He'd arrived half an hour early and then announced bluntly that he liked to eat at a reasonable hour because of his ulcer.

She begged David not to announce dinner until at least eight o'clock and he'd been magnificent, keeping up an endless stream of drinks and conversation until, at eight sharp, he'd led the way into the dining room. She knew she hadn't made the dish quite according to the recipe but nothing prepared her for the sight of it when she opened the oven. She'd considered dropping the whole lot on the floor but at the last minute had lost her nerve, somehow convincing herself that it would taste all right. She'd placed it carefully on the table where it sat like a reproach, the pale chunks of raw potato winking balefully from their glistening sea of curdled cream.

Len or Ken, who prided himself on being direct, 'Didn't get where I am today by pussy-footing around,' had taken one mouthful and announced, 'Well, you've made a right mess of that, girl,' and then spent the rest of the meal extolling the virtues of good, honest plain food. 'None of that fancy stuff for me,' he said, complacently. Not that it had stopped him from demolishing the Beef Wellington which she'd been sure would stretch to a cold lunch the following day.

David turned the whole incident into a marvellous joke. At her expense, but still. But when she'd got up to clear the dishes he'd followed her into the kitchen. She shuddered, remembering his cold, hard voice. Even that hadn't been as bad as the weeks following when it turned out that his company hadn't got the account after all and he'd blamed her, not directly of course, but with endless silly jokes about one raw potato costing him a thousand pounds. 'And there must have been, what, twenty in there, Janie?' he'd say indulgently, in front of friends. She remembered being surprised it was so much.

She sighed fretfully. Maybe *pommes dauphinoise* weren't such a good idea after all, even though she knew he loved them and she wanted terribly to please him. She was determined that they were going to have a proper sit-down dinner tonight; none of those silly snatched meals hunched over trays in front of the television that David often insisted on. They couldn't talk properly with that racket blaring but he said it was important for him to keep up with current affairs; he hardly had time to read a paper properly these days. She wondered uncomfortably if he found her boring and that's why he preferred to sit in front of the television but it couldn't be that, because he'd looked quite pleased this morning when she'd suggested they have a proper dinner, with candles and everything.

He'd been so sweet to her recently, even apologising for having to work so hard in the evenings and be away such a lot in Paris at the weekends, although really it wasn't his fault. He'd promised finally to take her with him, was coming home that evening with the air tickets. She'd been so excited she'd sent Simon off to stay with a friend for the night and had gone out to that nice little shop in the high street and bought herself a new dress. She glanced down at it nervously. Perhaps it *was* a bit young? And was the neck-line too low? He hated it when she wore sexy clothes, 'tart's tatters', he called them. Not that she had much to show; her breasts had almost disappeared since she'd lost those extra few pounds. Still, it had been worth it. He liked her thin, said it suited her so much better. When he was in a good mood he'd come up behind her, cupping a breast in each hand. 'My perfect little handfuls,' he'd call them, flattening them to her chest. Until she'd met him, she'd always hated her small breasts; had been horribly nervous the first time they'd gone to bed together, but he'd been so gratifyingly pleased about them, saying he hated large breasts. She didn't believe him, she'd seen the way he looked at women who were really, well, quite *big*, but it was nice of him to say so.

She knew he was highly sexed while she enjoyed sex *sometimes*, but really would rather lie warm and quiet in his arms, feeling close to him. It frustrated him sometimes, she knew that, which was why she turned a blind eye when he got in one of his funny moods. She knew he went to see somebody when he was like that. She suspected it was one of those places in Soho and felt quite pleased with herself for being so *mature* about it.

After all, she reasoned, a marriage wasn't just sex, it was a union based on mutual understanding and, if she couldn't sympathise with his frustration and allow him to resolve it his own way without asking too many questions, then what kind of partnership did they have? Anyway, it had only happened perhaps four times in all the years of their marriage, which wasn't a lot if you thought about it. Which she did, sometimes. Not very often because it made her feel a bit funny. Well, it wasn't as if he hit her, like Maureen's husband, or drank too much like Rosie's; he gave her as much money as she needed and was, in many ways, the most generous and considerate of men.

She peered anxiously at the oven. Perhaps if she turned the temperature down and left the potatoes in – they could take any amount of gentle heat – she could rescue the chicken by taking it out now and putting it back in on a high heat for ten minutes when David got home? She was just reaching for the thermostat when she remembered all the stories she'd read in the newspapers about food poisoning caused by heating and reheating food.

The last thing she wanted was to be the cause of David being ill; these days he complained so often about feeling unwell and, while she knew that he was a terrible hypochondriac, really dreadful, even the boys teased him about it, he did seem awfully tired all the time and then there were those strange hot flushes he'd been getting at night. She'd tried to make a little joke of it, teasing him about going through the Change. She ought to have known, by his face, that he didn't think it was funny but she so rarely thought of a joke that, having once discovered one, she found it almost impossible to let it go.

Frowning, she walked into the dining room to check that she had put everything on the table. It wasn't that bad a joke, she thought vaguely. People were always laughing about women's hormones. Surely men must have them too? Anyway he'd been absolutely furious, didn't see the funny side at all so then she'd tried to get him to go and see a doctor but he'd become irritable and told her to stop fussing at him.

It was odd really; any excuse usually and he'd be down that surgery in a flash. Mind you, he hadn't had any of those night sweats in over a week now so perhaps it had just been a mild flu or some virus or other, you never knew with viruses. As she idly polished an already gleaming silver fork, she wondered vaguely what a virus actually was. What did it look like? She thought of bacteria as tiny brown buzzing specks with busy little wings, rushing here and there infecting things. A bit like flies which you could swat or kill with a squirt of chemicals. But viruses were much more sinister;

shadowy amoebas slithering around the place and seemingly immune to being swatted or squirted.

Whenever either of the boys had a virus, the doctor always said, with a hopeless sort of a look on his face, that it was no good giving them any medicine because nothing, not even antibiotics, were effective. 'Colds are viruses,' he'd say, spreading his hands in a vague, impotent gesture. 'And you know how little we can do about them. It'll pass. Just give it time.' She liked the doctor, his pink cheeks, thin, fair hair and long, clean white hands. He was so kind whenever she took the boys to see him, which was quite often. But as David said, when he looked at their monthly medical bills, he could afford to be at those hourly rates. Not that he minded. He was very keen on good health, worried about the slightest twinge or sniffle. Not so much about the boys; he always dismissed everything they had with a casual remark about kids getting everything, but he was very particular about himself.

One always does feel a bit run-down after those things, she thought, staring worriedly at the claret, wondering if it was the right sort. She was sure he said that the good bottles were kept on the left in the cellar and the not so good on the right. She'd hesitated about which to take but had eventually decided, after three trips up and down to the cellar, that she ought to open a good bottle tonight.

After all, it was some sort of celebration, wasn't it, their going to Paris, the first weekend they'd had together since – since she couldn't remember. She stared worriedly at the wine. Perhaps it was *too* good; she knew he liked to keep the best bottles for his really important clients. Then again, perhaps it wasn't good enough. He hated indifferent wine although he kept a stock downstairs to take to other people's dinner parties, said there was no point taking a decent bottle because it always got put on the side and somehow never reappeared. He said he'd been caught that way more than once before.

She looked at the wine doubtfully. It was a pretty label. Oh well, it would have to do. He could always open another bottle if it was no good, although he'd grumble that it hadn't had time to breathe. To breathe! she stared in horror at the uncorked bottle, then ran through the still, empty house back to the kitchen and scrabbled around frantically in a drawer, trying to find the corkscrew. As she searched she registered a slight but unmistakable smell of burning. Just as she was reaching for the oven cloth, she heard the front door slam.

She was struggling with the chicken, trying to scrape off the worst of the burned bits, her face flushed with guilt and exertion, when David walked in holding the most enormous bunch of flowers. She felt close to tears; it was typical, really it was, for him to walk in at that moment when she'd had everything so well planned. She peered down anxiously at the neck-line of her dress and gave it a quick, discreet tug.

'Some flowers for my flower,' David said, smiling broadly and dropping a kiss on her forehead. He looked very pleased with himself.

'How lovely!' Jane exclaimed, quickly shoving the burned chicken behind a pan to hide it. 'But you shouldn't have. I mean, you really shouldn't have, although I adore them,' she added quickly. 'They'll fade over the weekend, while we're in Paris.'

He looked discomfited. 'Ah, yes. Paris.'

'You haven't forgotten,' Jane exclaimed anxiously, 'not about this weekend?'

He laid the flowers down on the table and, putting an arm around her thin shoulders, hugged her. 'I haven't exactly *forgotten*, darling,' he said. 'Just a small change of plan.'

'Change?' she said tremulously.

He looked down at her in surprise then laid a gentle, warning finger against her parted lips. 'What's all this?' he said, smiling sternly. 'You're not upset, are you?' He pulled her to him so that his chin rested on the top of her head. 'You're not to get yourself in a state about this. It's not the end of the world. All it means is that we'll have to put it off for a week. Turns out that we've got to see the big cheese this weekend so I'll have to do all sorts of last-minute paper work and won't have time to concentrate properly on my lovely little wife.' He looked down at her, smiling. 'And we wouldn't want that, now, would we?'

She smiled up at him though tears of disappointment welled in her eyes and threatened, at any minute to spill. 'No, I suppose not,' she whispered.

He gave her a brief hug. 'I knew you'd understand,' he said genially, turning away from her. 'I say, what's that delicious smell?'

'Chicken with roasted garlic,' she said, sniffing slightly. 'And *pommes dauphinoise*.'

He went whistling to the cupboard in search of the whisky bottle. 'Lovely,' he said absently, glancing at his watch. 'We'll have to hurry it a bit though, if I'm to catch that plane.'

'Plane?' she asked, bewildered. 'What plane?'

He flushed slightly, looked at her in surprise. 'The plane to Paris, of course.' His tone sharpened. 'Where did you think I was going? Timbuctoo?'

'But I thought you said the last flight out was at eight-thirty,' she said, bewildered.

He cast her a quick, hard look, then frowned. 'Did I?' he said with elaborate indifference. 'Oh well, I suppose I must have been talking about a weekday. There's an eleven-thirty on a Friday night. They lay an extra service on for the weekend.'

'Are you quite sure?' Jane faltered.

'Of course I'm bloody sure!' A dull, mottled flush spread across his face. 'What exactly are you accusing me of?'

Jane picked up a dish cloth, absently began to twist it round and round in her hands. 'Nothing, darling!' she protested. 'Really. I'm not accusing you of anything.'

'Would you like to call the airline and check?' he asked, through clenched teeth. He grabbed at the phone, pulled it roughly across the kitchen and slammed it down on the table. 'Go on, ring them.' She made a brief, helpless flapping gesture with the dish cloth then turned away to hide her tears.

'Well, you obviously don't trust me.'

She shook her head. 'I'm sorry. I didn't mean –'

Her bowed head seemed to inflame him still further. 'Christ, Jane, it's bad enough being under incredible pressure at work without coming home to be accused by my wife of lying to her.' He picked up his glass, and slugged the contents back. 'I mean I'd understand all this fuss if I'd cancelled the trip altogether, but it's only a question of a week.' He gestured at the flowers lying entombed in their cellophane wrapper on the table. 'I feel rotten enough about it already, without you going on. Do you know how difficult it is to find decent flowers at this time of night? I drove halfway round London and ended up having to blackmail some poor woman to open her shop for me. It cost me a fortune. *And* it made me late when I'd made a particular effort to leave the office on time because I knew you were cooking something special.'

Jane stared at him beseechingly. 'Darling, I'm sorry. I was just a bit disappointed, that's all, so it came out all wrong. I love the flowers and I know how hard you work, really I do. Everything's ready. All I've got to do is get it out of the oven.' She looked around frantically

213

in search of the oven cloth. 'Look, why don't you just go through to the dining room and sit down? I'll have this all on the table in a matter of minutes and then you can have a lovely meal and a bit of a rest and we'll order a taxi so you don't have to rush.'

He smiled, mollified. 'Well, that does sound good,' he admitted, 'although you don't need to worry about calling a cab. I've got one ordered for ten-thirty.' He hovered in the doorway. 'Sure I can't help, darling?' he said, smiling boyishly.

'No, darling,' she said, relief at seeing him smile making her voice slightly shrill. 'You just go and relax. Can't have you tired for the great day, now, can we?'

He smiled, good humour restored. 'By the way, you look very nice tonight, Janie.' She flushed with pleasure. 'I've always loved that dress on you.'

24

'Are you sure you don't know anything about it?' Phil said as they hurried up steep steps at Charing Cross Underground station. 'I promise you,' Martha said breathlessly. 'I haven't spoken to him since he got back. In fact, I didn't even know he *was* back, which really pissed me off, especially when the invitation arrived. It was so cold and formal, there was no note in with it or anything. He could at least... Oh! Damn, hold on a minute. The strap on my shoe's come undone.' She bent down to fix it and, as she stood up, swayed slightly and stumbled. Phil put out a hand to steady her. 'Are you all right?' she asked anxiously.

Martha shook her head as if to clear it. 'Just a bit dizzy, that's all. I must have just stood up too quickly or something. Phil, do stop looking so worried. I'm perfectly all right.'

Phil hovered irresolutely. 'Are you quite sure? You look very pale. Do you want to sit down? We could go to the café in the main station and get you a glass of water. We don't have to rush to get to the party. There's plenty of time.'

'Really, Phil, I'm fine. Do stop looking flapping and let's get on. I want to get there early so I get Paul to myself for a bit. You know how impossible it is to talk to anybody at parties.'

'Well, if you say so,' Phil said, reluctantly relinquishing her arm.

They hurried along the brightly lit Strand in the cool, crisp night air, a relief after the unseasonable damp warmth of September. As they walked, Phil cast worried glances at Martha, anxious lest she should slip on the dark pavements, slicked to a shine after a light fall of rain. The small side street which turned up into the forecourt of the Savoy was cluttered with taxis depositing their fragrant cargoes of over-dressed people, chattering excitedly as they anticipated the evening's pleasure. Dodging around them, they hurried towards the big swing doors and, pushing through them, were ejected into the perfumed warmth of the foyer.

Martha, blinking slightly in the sudden brightness, shivered and drew her arms around herself. 'Are you all right?' Phil asked, but her tone was less urgent for she could see that the colour had returned to Martha's cheeks.

Martha shook her head. 'I'm fine,' she said. 'It's Paul I'm worried about. I just had this sudden, weird feeling.'

'That he's unhappy or something?'

Martha frowned. 'Yes, something like that,' she said absently. She turned to look at Phil. 'Do you think he's all right?' Her frown deepened. 'I know this sounds stupid, and he's only giving a party, but I can't get it out of my head that there's something not quite right.' She fished a piece of white card bordered in black out of her bag. 'I suppose it is *him*,' she said doubtfully, staring at the invitation.

'Of course it's him,' said Phil, peering at it over Martha's shoulder. 'What confuses me is, why.'

Martha looked up sharply. 'What do you mean, *why*?'

'Well, that bit there.' She pointed at the invitation. 'About the exhibition. What on earth does that mean? An exhibition of what? I thought he'd gone away to have a rest, not to paint.'

'What really bothers me is where he got the money,'

216

Martha said as they walked slowly across the foyer to the lift. 'A river suite at the Savoy doesn't exactly come cheap.'

'Oh well,' Phil said vaguely, 'we'll know soon enough.'

An irate American voice issued forth from behind the closed door of suite number 123. 'Goddamn it,' it bellowed, 'how many times do I have to say this? You've got the wrong room.' Martha and Phil stared at each other in consternation. 'I told you it was a joke,' Martha whispered loudly. The door opened and the owner of the voice stuck his head into the corridor. His short, stout body was wrapped in a white towelling dressing gown and his hair, obviously still damp from a bath, stuck up in a little halo of spikes around his bullet-like head. 'Is everyone on reception in this goddamn hotel dumb as well as deaf?' he yelled, then grinned ruefully as he caught sight of Martha and Phil. 'Sorry, ladies,' he said, 'but I thought you were the concierge.' He frowned in annoyance. 'I guess you've come to the party. Didn't they tell you downstairs that they changed the suite? It's in 323 now.'

Phil and Martha looked at each other then stared back at him. 'At least it's not a joke, then,' Martha murmured. He looked at her quizzically. 'We were just wondering whether the whole thing was...' she said. 'Oh, never mind. I'm so sorry we bothered you. It never occurred to us to stop and check with reception. We just came straight up to the room number printed on this.' She waved the invitation vaguely in the air.

The American grinned suddenly. 'That's OK,' he said, eyeing Martha speculatively. 'And if your crazy boyfriend's party doesn't materialise, you're sure welcome to come see me.' His grin broadened. 'We could have ourselves our own little party down here.'

'You're too kind,' Phil said politely.

'He's gone mad,' Martha muttered as they made their way down the long cream and gilt corridor, their heels sinking in the deep pile carpet. 'It's some sort of elaborate hoax. He won't be there at all.'

Phil gave her a pained look. 'Do calm down,' she murmured as they stepped through the open door of the suite. 'I'm sure there's a perfectly reasonable explanation.'

A waiter stood in the doorway holding a silver tray on which were arranged a collection of glasses brimming with champagne, orange juice and Perrier water. They helped themselves to a glass of champagne and, not seeing Paul, hovered uncertainly on the fringe of a crowd of people, all of whom were dressed in black. 'Looks like a bloody funeral,' Martha said, sipping at her drinking and eyeing the crowd speculatively.

'Do you recognise anybody?' Phil asked doubtfully.

'Not really. Yes, that woman over there, the one in the black dress.'

'That's most unhelpful. Everybody's in a black dress.'

'No, look. The pale skinny woman wearing the thing that looks like a shroud with bits hanging off it. She's something to do with *Vogue*, I think, and that man, the one with the blonde hair and red glasses? I met him at Paul's flat. He's something in advertising. Paul did some work for him once.' Phil looked over at the man Martha was pointing to. 'He doesn't look like a very Paul sort of person,' she said, noticing his tie which was made of plastic and printed like a celluloid film strip. 'I can't somehow see them getting along.'

Martha shrugged. 'It's surprising how well you can get along with somebody if they're paying,' she said absently.

'I suppose so,' Phil said, peering through the crowd, looking for Paul.

'Look, that's his work on the wall. The exhibition, I suppose. Over there.' Martha indicated a series of large framed charcoal line drawings of women in various stages of undress.

'He's good, isn't he?' said Phil, following her gaze. 'I hadn't realised he was so talented.'

'Very good,' said Martha impatiently. 'Even if it is all old stuff.'

'Are you sure?'

'Of course I'm sure. He did those at least two years ago. Oh, where the hell is he?'

They scanned the crowd until Phil uttered a brief exclamation. 'Look, he's there. Over there, next to the man who looks like he's wearing full make-up.'

Martha peered into the crowd. 'Where?'

'*There!*'

'Is that him?' Martha said doubtfully. 'What's he done to his hair? And what about his tan? He's supposed to have been on a beach. He looks as pale as the grave.'

'It's fashionable,' said Phil, examining him speculatively. 'Every time I walk through Soho I see men looking like that. As if they're…' She had been about to add 'going to a funeral' but for some reason changed her mind. 'Look, he's waving. He's seen you. Go over and say hello. I'll join you in a minute. Go *on.*'

Paul detached himself from the group of people surrounding him and walked towards Martha, his arms held wide, his long, cadaverous face illuminated by a sweet, lopsided smile. Wordlessly he gathered her in his arms, buried his face in her hair and hugged her hard. 'Dearest girl,' he said, holding her tightly. At last he let her go and gazed at her, his limpid, mournful eyes missing nothing. 'You look –' He put his head to one side and looked at her thoughtfully. 'You look as if you've been polished,' he said eventually. 'So bright and glittering.'

'You look a bit different, too,' Martha said, with a brittle, nervous laugh. She reached out a hand to stroke the top of his shaved head. 'Feels nice, though.'

His eyes drooped slightly. 'Ah, yes, that.' He shrugged, giving her a brief, sweet smile. 'I'm told it's fashionable.'

They were silent for a minute, a brief awkwardness springing up between them. 'I suppose this is all to do with the new boyfriend?' Paul broke the silence, his long, elegant fingers fluttering over her sleek chignon, her pale, fragile silk dress.

Martha flushed, her hand flying to her hair. 'His name is Joe,' she said, a slight chill entering her voice.

He watched her sadly. 'I'm sorry we quarrelled before I left. I would have done anything not...' His voice trailed away and he smiled. 'I've missed you.'

Her smile was wary. 'Not enough to write.'

'I wanted to,' he murmured. 'But it was difficult to know what to say.' He looked away, his eyes sombre.

She frowned in concern then gave a high, forced laugh. 'Oh, never mind that now. It's lovely to see you. What's the party in aid of? Have you got some secret announcement to make?' He glanced sharply at her but she did not notice his look. 'I dressed up especially, wanted you to see my new, sophisticated image.' Her voice was too shrill as she attempted a light, teasing tone. 'Don't you just love it?'

He looked at her, startled by the artificial brightness of her voice. 'I love *you*,' he said, catching her hands. 'Forgive me?'

'Forgive you?' she faltered, and then her smile crumpled and tears started to her eyes. 'Of course I forgive you. It's been hateful without you.' She hugged him fiercely. 'Don't ever go away like that again.'

His thin body stiffened and she stepped back, alarmed by the resistance she felt, but then he caught her to him and dropped a kiss on her startled face. 'Enough of all this,' he said, smiling down at her. 'Tonight, I want us to be happy. I'm sick and tired of...' His gaze flickered and he glanced away.

She gave him a curious look then smiled back, tucking her hand under his arm and leaning her head against his bony, black-jacketed shoulder. He looked down at her bright golden head. 'Will you do something for me?' he said.

'Anything,' she laughed, looking up at him. 'Anything at all.'

'Then take your hair down.'

She stepped away, her hands flying to her elegant, polished chignon. 'My hair?'

'Please,' he begged, 'just for tonight.'

She smiled nervously. 'You don't like it?'

'It's lovely, but it makes you look so different. I want our last night...' He broke off abruptly. 'I can't get used to it,' he said with a helpless shrug.

She did not catch what he had said, heard only the part about her hair and stood, blushing with confusion. 'Here?' she said. 'With all these people watching?'

'Why not?' he said, burying his hands in the mass of thick, golden hair and plucking pins from it.

'Paul, you're impossible,' she protested, laughing, but stood perfectly still in her, prim silk dress, balancing precariously on high-heeled shoes as he continued to busy his hands in her hair.

'I know,' he mumbled through a mouthful of hair pins. He freed the last pin and ran both hands through her hair, tumbling it over her shoulders. 'There,' he said, holding her at arm's length while he studied her face. It seemed to satisfy him for he smiled his lopsided, sweet smile, and pulled her to him in a fierce hug. 'There you are at last,' he murmured. 'My dear, wild, *beautiful* Martha.'

She pulled away, blushing furiously and running her hands self-consciously through her hair. 'I suppose it's all flat now,' she mumbled, her eyes averted from his intense gaze.

He smiled fondly and gently tucked a stray strand of hair behind one ear. 'It looks beautiful. Come on, let's go the bathroom and rearrange it properly. You'll adore it. It's cream marble with five mirrors. *Five* of them! You can see yourself from every angle. *Come.*'

Martha laughed, infected by his excitement. 'Crazy man. And I want to hear everything you've been up to for the past few months. Do you hear? *Everything!*'

Phil made no move to join the party but stood on the fringes of a group, quietly eavesdropping. 'God knows what this is all about,' said a thin blonde with a hard, dissatisfied mouth. Her friend, an alarmingly thin man with a pale face and huge jug ears, their stiff, translucent cartilages pierced with a row of tiny silver hoops, gave a brief high-pitched cackle. 'It's a wake, sweetie. Didn't you know?'

'Oh, shut up, Freddie, you're drunk,' she said coldly.

He looked at her sadly. 'No I'm not, duckie. I wish I was. I wish I could drown this whole, ghastly nightmare in alcohol.' He glanced across the room at Paul, who had just emerged from the bathroom with Martha, flushed and laughing, on his arm. 'Although it has its advantages. Look at that gorgeous pallor, that fierce hair,' he marvelled. 'Death becomes him, wouldn't you say?'

'Don't say that!' the blonde said fiercely. 'You don't know. Not for sure.'

Freddie shrugged, lifted a long arm and a bony white wrist shot out from the black silk of his sleeve as he plucked a glass of champagne from a passing tray. 'If you say so, duckie. But why the party then? That's what I ask myself.'

'Maybe he just wanted to give a party,' the girl said angrily.

'And maybe I like to fuck women,' Freddie said, emitting another high-pitched cackle. 'Oh, duckie, don't be a bore. You've got to laugh, haven't you? Amanda? Come back. Oh, shit.'

He turned sadly to Phil. 'Well, if you can't laugh, duckie. That's what I always say, if you can't laugh then you may as well…' He tapped the side of his big pale nose with a bony finger and blinked large, pale grey eyes, the lashes beaded with tears, like minute diamonds. 'Mustn't say that word, now must we, duckie?' he said vaguely. 'Mustn't say it.' The words trailed after him like a curl of cigarette smoke as he wandered off in search of Amanda. Phil watched him go, an elegant black crow delicately picking his skinny black legs and enormous black booted feet across the deep-pile rose pink carpet.

She did not know what he had meant, nor did she want to find out.

Martha said later that she should have known. But that evening, light-headed from the effect of too much champagne and the pleasure of seeing Paul again, she was oblivious to everything but pleasure. Her impossibly frail shoes long since discarded and her prim, silk dress rumpled and stained with champagne, her bright hair snaking down her back in tangled curls and her cheeks flushed pink with wine, she looked like some carefree nymph as she wandered happily around the room. Phil watched her from the confines of the deep, chintz-covered sofa where she had somehow ended up, Freddie's head lolling drunkenly on her shoulder. Phil didn't mind, on the contrary she found some curious comfort in the warm, heavy weight against her neck and felt content, seeing Martha's obvious happiness.

Martha, seeing Paul standing alone by the window,

staring out at the lights which danced like fireflies over the inky black Thames, flickered up to him and laughing, threw her arms around him. 'I've missed you,' she murmured, nuzzling her face against his neck. 'You don't know how I've missed you.'

Turning, he gently disengaged her arms but kept her wrists held in a tight grip. He gazed down at her, eyes glittering in his thin, pale face. 'Say you love me,' he said, staring at her intently. 'Say you'll forgive me anything.'

A foolish expression lit Martha's face, her smile pink and sweetly tender. 'Of course I love you,' she said, gazing back at him. 'I've loved you since the day I first saw you at college, lying on the floor of the painting studio because you said,' she adopted his lazy, affected voice, 'you were too unutterably bored to get up.'

He did not smile. 'Say it,' he insisted. 'Say you'll forgive me.'

'I suppose you mean Joe?' she asked, her pink smile melting away.

'Say you love me,' he repeated, 'and that you'll forgive me anything.'

She pulled away from him, laughing nervously. 'Paul, do stop it. I hate it when you're like this.'

He let her go but kept his eyes fixed intently on her. 'Like what?'

'Like... Oh, in one of your crazy moods. Do stop looking at me like that. OK, OK, I love you and, as for forgiving you, why–' she shrugged lightly and traced a gentle finger down his thin cheek 'there's really nothing to forgive.'

He smiled faintly, turning his head to kiss the hand which still lingered on his face, then plucked a bright curl which had fallen across her cheek and tucked it tenderly behind one ear. 'And if there was?'

'What are you going to do?' she asked teasingly, her eyes sparkling. 'Something really wicked?'

'Yes,' he said simply.

She looked at him with a puzzled frown, then her face cleared and she laughed. 'Yes, sure. Of course you will. You're such a deliciously wicked man. That's why I love you.'

'Say it.' His eyes burned with a strange intensity.

'Oh, very well,' she giggled. 'Paul, I forgive you anything you have done, are doing and may do in the future.' The smile died suddenly on her lips. 'Paul, you haven't...' She looked around in alarm. 'Of course! That's what's wrong. Where's Stevie?'

Paul frowned slightly. 'What are you talking about? Oh, you mean have I left Stevie? Of course not. Don't be absurd.'

'Well, where is he?'

Paul shrugged. 'He couldn't make it. But he's here with us in spirit.'

'He is all right?' Martha said anxiously. 'He's not sick again?'

As Paul opened his mouth to say something, a woman cloaked in silk like a little fat, black bat swooped down on him. 'Darling, how lovely this is and how clever of you to think of having a little soirée. It's too chic for words, but then you always did have monumental style.' As she bobbed to peck him on both cheeks he smiled ruefully at Martha over her shoulder. Martha returned the smile, mouthed something about catching him later and went in search of Phil.

She found her sitting on the sofa, gently stroking Freddie's thin hair. He appeared to be sleeping peacefully although Martha could see the tracks of fresh tears glittering on his pale, bony face. She looked down at Phil, mouthing across Freddie's sleeping head, 'Is he all right?' Phil smiled briefly and, gently lifting his head, plumped a cushion and slid it beneath it. Grimacing slightly, she rose slowly to her feet. 'My leg's gone to

225

sleep,' she muttered. Martha helped her hobble over to Paul who was standing patiently by the door, saying goodbye to his guests.

'Hello, Sarah,' he said, his smile tender as he enfolded her in a warm, rose-scented embrace. 'See, I told you I'd come back to say goodbye.'

'Surely not goodbye?' Phil said, with a puzzled smile.

He shrugged. 'Au revoir then. Until we meet again.'

'Is he showing off his French again?' Martha interrupted, reaching up to wrap her arms around him in a fierce embrace. 'Bye, sweet, don't do anything I wouldn't.'

He gave her a startled look and then his mournful eyes drooped with disdain. 'That's a little limiting, cherie,' he said in a lazy, teasing drawl.

'Show off,' she murmured affectionately, leaning her bright head against his shoulder. As he stroked her hair a look of unutterable sadness flickered across his face. 'Take good care,' he whispered. She straightened up and gazed directly into his face. 'Why, Paul,' she exclaimed, 'you look so sad.'

He smiled tenderly and tucked away a stray strand of her bright hair. 'Nothing serious.'

'Call me tomorrow?'

A shadow flickered across his face and was gone. 'I love you.'

'Me too,' she said, kissing him goodbye.

Martha and Phil walked down the Strand arm in arm, Martha teetering in her thin, spindly heels and giggling slightly, her cheeks flushed with champagne and the cold of the night air.

'Who was that man you were locked in an embrace with on the sofa?' she teased. 'Honestly, Phil, I can't take you anywhere.'

'His name's Freddie,' Phil said, her voice growing suddenly quiet. 'He said he was –' She gave a quick,

226

wary glance at Martha who tripped suddenly. 'Whoops,' she exclaimed, an expression of comic disbelief crossing her face as she began to laugh, 'somebody keeps moving the pavement.' She stood, laughing helplessly, until eventually her laughter subsided to a weak giggle, punctuated by gentle hiccups. 'Oh dear. Sorry, Phil, you were saying?'

'He said he was –' She looked at Martha's flushed, happy face, unwilling to spoil her mood by telling her what Freddie had said, that he was dying. She shrugged. 'He said he was a bit drunk.'

Martha laughed. 'Aren't we all?' she said and started to dance along the Strand, skittering crazily across the shining black pavement in her absurd shoes. 'There's a taxi,' she yelled, waving her arms wildly above her head. The cab screeched to a halt, narrowly avoiding her. 'She drunk?' the driver said, jerking his head in Martha's direction. Phil assured him that she was, but perfectly harmless. 'All right,' he grumbled, 'Get in.' Martha kept up a bright, inconsequential stream of chatter all the way back to Notting Hill while Phil sat in silence, content to let it wash over her. They drew up outside Martha's flat and, kissing Phil affectionately, she climbed out, still teetering slightly. Phil had just settled back in the seat when Martha's face appeared at the taxi window. 'He was all right, wasn't he?' she demanded abruptly.

'Of course he was,' Phil said, although the feeling of unease still persisted. 'But why don't you drop in at the flat tomorrow morning, just to be sure?'

Martha, her anxious frown fading, said that yes, she thought she would and, laughing gaily, blew an extravagant kiss and turned away.

'Are we having lunch tomorrow?' Phil called out of the taxi window.

Martha turned a flushed, smiling face to her. 'Of course we are. It's Saturday, isn't it?'

25

The persistent ring of the doorbell roused Phil from a deep, dreamless sleep. She glanced, befuddled, at her watch and saw that it was four in the afternoon. One of the cats gave a brief, sleepy growl of protest as she shifted his warm weight off her lap and sat up, staring around in bemusement. She must have fallen asleep on the sofa waiting for Martha. 'That's late, even for Martha,' she said reproachfully. The cat opened a sleepy, curious eye and yawned luxuriously while the bell continued its harsh, jangling ring. 'All right, all right, I'm coming,' Phil grumbled, still disoriented from sleep, stumbling through to the hallway and pressing the intercom. No answering voice was heard; the bell shrilled on and on. She shouted, trying to be heard above the noise, but still the bell continued its persistent, piercing ringing. 'Who is it?' she shouted again but still there was no reply. Cursing furiously, she scrabbled around in the little Chinese pot to find her keys and cast her eyes around for some means of protection. Seeing an umbrella she grabbed it, brandishing it as a weapon as she advanced nervously down the hallway and opened the big outer door a crack.

'Martha,' she exclaimed, laughing and shaking the umbrella ruefully. 'You gave me such a fright. I thought you must be a nutter or something. Only last week, one of the old ladies in the building was mugged. You're so late, even for you,' she added with a slight laugh, 'that

I fell asleep... Martha? Martha, are you all right?' she said urgently, suddenly noticing Martha's deathly white skin and pale, bloodless lips. Martha said nothing but her knees seemed to give way and she lurched forward. Dropping the umbrella, Phil stepped towards her to take her arm as she swayed slightly. 'What is it? What's happened?'

Martha looked at her, her eyes coming suddenly into focus. 'Paul,' she said distinctly, then lapsed once more into silence.

'What's happened to him? Have you just come from his flat?' Martha shook her head helplessly, an expression of dumb anguish contorting her bloodless face. She seemed incapable of movement so Phil put both arms around her shoulders and helped her across the hallway and into the flat. She allowed herself to be led, walking with small jerking steps until they reached the kitchen where she sat down slowly on a chair, her back straight, her hands placed flat on the table, like an obedient child waiting for its tea.

'Martha,' Phil said gently, 'please tell me what's happened.' Martha, hearing her name, turned her head slowly and gazed unseeingly in the direction from which the sound came. She thrust her face blindly at the air like an animal catching an unfamiliar scent but then, with a vague, puzzled frown, bent her head and stared down at her hands. Phil, watching her thoughtfully, moved across the kitchen and filled a kettle. 'I'm going to make us some nice hot, sweet tea,' she said in loud, deliberate tones. 'And when I've made it, you're going to drink it up and tell me exactly what's been going on.'

'I don't want any tea.' Martha's hands began to tremble violently and she watched her fingers dance on the table's edge with dispassionate calm. 'I don't want any tea,' she repeated.

'Well, I want some,' Phil said brightly, casting a

worried eye at Martha's trembling which had extended up her arms until her entire body shook as if in some helpless dance. 'Just hang on a minute. Won't be long.' She hurried into one of the spare rooms and pulled a quilt off the bed, running with it back to the kitchen where she wrapped it around Martha, rubbing at her shoulders and back to warm her. 'There. Keep that round you.' Although Martha gave no sign that she had heard, Phil was grateful to see her hands creep up to the edges of the quilt and pull it tightly around herself. 'Paul used to tease me about drinking tea,' she said in a remote voice. 'Do you remember? How he used to say I thought a cup of tea could solve any problem?'

'Yes, I remember,' Phil said carefully. 'Martha, where is Paul?'

Martha dragged an arm out of the confines of the quilt and looked at her watch. 'He's at the Savoy. No, he must be gone by now. I don't know where he is,' she said fretfully. She looked up, her eyes bright with alarm. 'I never thought to ask them where they were taking him.'

'The tea's nearly ready,' Phil said slowly and loudly, as if she was speaking to a child. 'When we've had a cup, you can tell me what happened. And then, if you like, we could telephone and find out where Paul's gone.'

Martha gave a brief, mirthless laugh. 'Gone,' she said. 'All gone.'

Phil put two mugs on the table and, sitting down, took Martha's hands in hers. They were as stiff and white as pieces of frozen fish. Phil rubbed them hard, trying to get the circulation back into them. Eventually, when some warmth had returned, she placed them round the steaming mug. 'Now, drink your tea and tell me all about it.'

Martha picked up the mug and sipped at it obligingly. When she had drunk half of it and a faint flush of pink began to rise in her face, Phil said, 'What do you mean about Paul being taken away? Has he done something wrong?'

Martha stared at her, frowning slightly. 'Wrong? Yes, I suppose it is wrong.'

'I see. Then it's the police who have taken him somewhere?'

Martha smiled. 'He was very nice, the policeman. Said if there was anything they could do, I had only to ask. I had to ring his parents myself, of course,' she added thoughtfully. 'Wouldn't have done to have the police telephone them. I didn't give them any details. Just said...' She looked at Phil, her face crumpling in an anxious frown. 'Do you think that's awful? Not to have told them face to face, I mean. There's the letter, too. I'll have to take it round there later.' She dragged the quilt around her shoulders, retreating into its comforting depths so that just the triangle of her white face was visible. 'I couldn't have faced them this morning, to be perfectly honest,' she said through chattering teeth.

'Tell them what?'

An expression of comic disbelief crossed Martha's face. 'That Paul's dead, of course.'

Phil's body jolted violently under the impact of her words. What does she mean, she thought wildly, opening her mouth to speak, but her lips would not form words and so she sat in foolish, open-mouthed silence.

'It must have been about lunch time when they found him,' Martha explained in a distant, almost conversational tone. 'I suppose he hadn't checked out at twelve, you know how strict they are. He left a note, just inside the door, so the chambermaid would find it and not have to be confronted by his dead body. Apparently it said not to go into the bedroom but to call the police, and me of course.' She pulled the quilt tighter around her shoulders, her voice so quiet that Phil had to lean forward to hear. 'He must have been planning it for months. The room reeked of Floris's rose geranium bath essence so I expect he'd had a bath after everyone left. He always was very particular. He'd put on his navy silk suit with his diamond pin in the lapel, and a cream silk shirt. The neck of the shirt was a bit stained,' she said sadly, 'because he'd vomited. He'd have hated that. Everything else was perfect,' she added quickly, as if anxious that Paul should not be reproached for carelessness. 'He'd arranged the letters, one to me and one to his parents, and put them with his will on the table next to the bed. There was an empty champagne glass and a bottle of pills, anti-depressants of some sort. The prescription was American. I suppose he must have got them when he was over there.'

'Why?' Phil said, her voice emerging on a cracked whisper.

Martha cast her an anxious, reassuring glance. 'He looked very beautiful,' she said, as if it might be that which was distressing Phil, 'and quite peaceful.'

'But why?' Phil said again, her voice unnaturally loud.

Martha gave her a little, puzzled frown. 'He'd have wanted to look his best,' she said obliquely, looking absently around the kitchen as if surprised to find herself there. The grandfather clock in the hallway chimed, ringing the hour in a deep, mournful peal. The noise roused Martha and she started violently, exclaiming, 'Oh God, is that the time? I must go.'

'Where?' Phil cried in alarm.

'To see Paul's parents, of course,' Martha said reproachfully.

'I'll drive you there and wait in the car.'

'I suppose they're expecting me,' Martha said vaguely, ignoring her. 'I'm not sure how much they took in when I telephoned them earlier.'

'Do you know them?'

'I've met them once. Paul and I went round for tea.' Martha smiled fondly. 'Paul said his mother had probably spent the entire week cleaning and polishing. She'd even put those white lace things, what are they called?... antimacassars, I think, on all the chairs. They were stiff with starch, not a crease in them. Paul smiled when he saw them, whispered to me that his father would have been banned from sitting down all that morning in case he smudged his hair oil on them. Apparently she makes them all herself, even the lace. After we'd had tea she showed me how she did it, on a little velvet cushion with pins. Terribly painstaking work.' She laughed suddenly. 'Honestly, the tea she'd laid on. It was like a five-course banquet, with all these incredible little pastry things, savoury and sweet and light as air. She wouldn't eat a thing herself, just sat there in silence watching us with big, dark anxious eyes as we tried each different thing. Every time we ate a mouthful she looked so pleased and proud it was as if we were babies and had just done something remarkable. We had to eat it all, of course.' Martha's eyes glittered, washed by a sudden fall of tears. 'It was only later, when Paul said that he'd never taken a girl home before, that I understood why it mattered so much to her. I think they thought that we were... Those poor, sweet people. It breaks my heart to think of it.' She gazed at Phil beseechingly, the corners of her mouth jerking insistently as tears spilled unheeded out of her eyes. 'Doesn't it break your heart?'

'Yes,' Phil whispered.

Martha dragged her knuckles savagely across her eyes. 'Silly boy. Why didn't he tell me he was dying? Maybe I could have done something. At least I could have shared it with him.' Her face crumpled, the skin pale and fragile as tissue. 'He must have felt so lonely, with Stevie gone.' She buried her face in her hands and sobbed noiselessly.

Phil watched her helplessly, then patted her shaking shoulders. 'What do you mean, Stevie gone?' she said gently. 'Had he left him?'

Martha nodded, her head still bent, and scrabbled around in her bag. 'He... It's all in here,' she said in a low, strained voice, handing Phil a letter. 'It explains everything.' She closed her eyes and, with a great hiccuping sigh, leaned forward on the table, pillowing her head in her arms. 'As much as can be explained,' she said wearily.

Phil took the letter. 'Can I have a cigarette?' she asked. Martha lifted an arm and scrabbled blindly about on the table until she found the pack and pushed it across to Phil. 'You don't smoke,' she said accusingly.

'I know,' Phil said, lighting a cigarette. The letter was long, four pages of heavy cream vellum inscribed in black ink in a beautiful, flowing hand. As she bent her eyes to the first page she felt profoundly shocked to see Paul's beautiful, unfamiliar handwriting and wondered absently how many drafts he had rejected before arriving at this final, perfect one. She imagined his anxiety, knowing that it was the last letter he would ever write, saw his beautiful hands, the long, tapering fingers gently cradling the fountain pen as he wrote, imagined him putting the pen down and with one last regretful glance folding the heavy paper, placing it in the tissue lined envelope. She stared at the handsome, bold script with disbelief. It did not seem possible that he was dead for, as she read, she heard his voice and he seemed to her then to be more alive than he had ever been.

Stevie, he said, had recovered well from the pneumonia but by then his weakened body had succumbed to Kaposi's Sarcoma which spread, from that first red mark on his back, to his entire body, finally disfiguring his face. 'It was hard, even for me,' he wrote, 'to look into that beloved face, the beautiful eyes blackened and

234

half closed, his handsome nose swollen to a monstrous carbuncle and his fine white skin coarsened by raised, angry purple lumps.' As the disease progressed Stevie refused to leave the flat, even had he been well enough to, and made Paul promise never to allow anyone in or to tell anybody that he was ill. He had been forced to leave the flat on two occasions, when he was admitted to hospital for emergency treatment, but otherwise Paul had kept his word, nursing him at home until he died. The illness claimed him quickly; 'that, at least, was a blessing,' Paul wrote, 'for the pain, both physical and emotional, was intolerable.' He made no mention of his own pain and Phil winced as she read the letter, imagining the tearing grief he must have felt, and no doubt had to hide, as he watched his lover die.

The result of his own test arrived the day after Stevie died. It was positive. 'I wasn't surprised,' he wrote. 'I'd seen the stigmata of AIDS on my arm, watched it swell and grow for weeks.' He buried Stevie alone; Stevie's family refused to attend the funeral, refused even to acknowledge Paul when they came to the flat to collect his possessions. 'His mother didn't come,' Paul wrote, 'only his father and the poor man was so consumed with disgust and guilt, he couldn't speak.'

The day after Stevie's funeral Paul had finished packing up the flat and had gone to find Martha, to tell her that he was leaving the country that night. Discovering that she was in Paris, he had gone, instead, to Phil. She remembered his dazed expression, his strange, remote manner, and felt sickened with guilt and grief when she remembered that she had let him go without even a question.

He had gone to San Francisco, he explained, 'in search of a dream'. He knew that there was no cure but thought that maybe, as there were so many more cases of the disease in America, that the understanding of it might be more advanced. 'It was so advanced,' he wrote, 'and what I saw there was so horrible that I knew I wanted a quick death, not the slow, hideous destruction that I daily witnessed. Suicide might seem the coward's way out and I'm sorry, but I know I couldn't bear to die in the way that Stevie did.'

His final wish, he said, was that his funeral should be a happy affair. 'Not too happy,' he wrote, 'I want *some* tears.' A separate enclosed document included the guest list for the funeral, the music to be played, the flowers and type of candles (and where they should be ordered from) and a budget sheet, carefully costed out right down to the cost of the hire of glasses and the brand of champagne to be served at the party afterwards. Stapled to it was a cheque made out to Martha for the correct amount.

As Phil finished reading, Martha raised her head and picked up the list of funeral arrangements. 'I must have gardenias,' she read out loud, 'and tell them I want all the leaves left on but only if they are that dark, shiny green. Then I want stephanotis and cream roses, *not* white unless they haven't any in which case very pale pink.' She looked at Phil and smiled shakily. 'Typical, isn't it? Bloody, bloody typical.' She bent her head and wept.

26

Martha took a sip of camomile tea and wrinkled her nose with distaste. She'd been drinking it for the past few days, since Paul died, hoping it would calm her. She supposed it was better for her than the interminable cups of black coffee she was used to drinking and at least it seemed to soothe the nausea which was increasingly bothering her.

Even the thought of Joe, who was due back at the end of the month, failed to cheer her. She had begged him to come over for the funeral but he had refused, his voice strangely cold and remote, saying he had business to attend to. As the day of the funeral grew closer she felt oddly grateful that he wouldn't be there. The thought of his burning vitality exhausted her, she hadn't the energy for it and she knew how he hated to have depressed people around him.

'All that negative energy,' he'd said, 'it's so bad for you. Who needs it? Life should be fun.' When she'd tried haltingly to explain that sometimes even negative emotions can be good, giving time for reflection, he shrugged. 'I don't go with any of that stuff,' he said, and a furtive, closed look crept over his face. She'd watched him with alarm, understanding that she was included in his frantic search for pleasure. If she was not bright or light and indifferent, then he would abandon her to her own darkness for there was no gentleness in him, no dim and quiet resting place. When once she tried to express something of that to him, she found herself sharply rebuked. 'Don't get heavy on me,' he complained, his beautiful face distorted by a petulant frown. She stiffened slightly and when he felt her withdrawal, his expression changed to a disarming smile. 'You like fun, too,' he said, pulling her down on to the bed, covering her face in brief, urgent kisses. 'This kind of fun.' His tongue flickered over the sensitive skin of her neck, tickling her until she laughed. 'That's why I love you. You're so alive. You're like a pink neon sign in a dark street. You light everything up. And you're mine. All mine.' And she, seduced by this vision of herself and the kisses which rained down relentlessly on her neck and breasts, had abandoned thought entirely and given herself up to sensation.

Sighing, she walked heavily over to her dressing table, grimacing as she caught sight of her white face and pale, bloodless lips in the mirror. She arranged her little battery of brushes and pots of colour and began to paint her face as Paul had taught her, carefully blotting out her features with a pale foundation and powder, drawing in a pair of crimson red lips, dusting her cheeks with rose and outlining her eyes with a smudgy black pencil. Finally she brushed her hair back severely, pinning it to her head and twisting the weight of it into a smooth bun which she secured at the nape of her neck. Reaching over, she picked up the hat and placed it carefully on her head.

She stared at her reflection for a while, wondering at this woman with her pale, hollow cheeks and feverish, glittering eyes. It did not look like her, but just lately she had come to wonder who she was; this polished, perfumed creature with her shining hair and subdued, elegant clothes. She saw then that she was wearing one of her old dresses; she must have put it on without thinking. It was plain black silk lavished with lace and unsuitable sequins and she smiled, remembering that Paul had bought it for her in a junk shop in Camden Passage. With a quick, defiant gesture, she tore off her hat and pulled all the pins out of her hair so it fell down her back in a disordered tangle of curls. She heard Paul's voice. '*Much* better, my dear. I never liked that constipated look.' Scooping up her bag, she went quickly out of the door.

She was late arriving at the church, there had been some problem with the lid of the coffin. As she stepped out of the gleaming black hearse she looked around in amazement, thinking for a moment that she had come to the wrong place. The tiny churchyard was thronged with people, laughing and talking, smoking cigarettes. One man, resplendent in a silver brocade waistcoat, stiff white-collared shirt and impeccably cut black suit, passed around a bottle of champagne. His diamond earring winked cheerfully in the sunshine. Pushing her way in to the crowd, Martha stood on tip-toe, peering over the heads and extravagant hats, looking for Phil. There seemed to be hundreds of people there, although she knew that there couldn't be more than eighty. A woman in a short black silk dress pushed past her, waving frantically at somebody she had just spotted in the crowd. She wore a wide black lacquered straw hat which she clutched on to, laughing merrily, as she attempted to kiss her friend who wore a similar hat. 'Darling,' Martha heard her say, 'isn't it a perfect day for it? You look absolutely marvellous. Love that dress. Whose is it?'

The other woman looked down at herself dubiously. 'Jasper,' she murmured, staring slowly around as if startled to find herself there. 'Well, I was told to dress up.' She looked at her friend doubtfully. 'You don't think it's a bit *much*?'

'No, sweet,' shrieked her friend above the babble of the crowd, 'I think sequins for a funeral are just exactly right. Paul would have adored it and the invitation –' She looked around doubtfully. 'Is one *invited* to a funeral? I must say this one seems more like a jolly party. Anyway, it did say to dress up. I just wish I'd had the courage to wear sequins myself. It's just, at nine o'clock this morning, they seemed a little… outré. Have you got a ciggie? I'm absolutely gasping.'

Martha made her way slowly to the front of the crowd, sliding between the crush of bodies, rustling with silk and starched white cotton, the air between them heavy with perfume and cigarette smoke, until she found herself standing in a small, open space just in front of the church.

Looking around she noticed a small, forlorn couple dressed in immaculate stiff black clothes, staring around in bewilderment. The scene seemed to her so unreal that for a moment she could not place them, wondered vaguely if they had stumbled into the wrong church, but something about the woman, her large, dark eyes glancing fearfully at the dim entrance to the church, jolted her memory and she realised that they were Paul's parents, Rosa and Carlos.

She hurried over and they stared up at her, towering over them in sequins and high heels, fearful but curious expressions on their faces. 'It's Martha,' she said gently, 'Paul's friend.' They frowned, momentarily confused, blinking in the crisp autumn sunshine at Martha's twinkling black dress and glossy red mouth, then Carlos's face cleared and he smiled apologetically. 'Of course it is you,' he murmured in halting English, indicating with a little wave of his hand the crowd of people. 'We're sorry, we didn't recognise you. The dress…and so many people. We did not know that Paulo knew such people.'

Martha glanced around worriedly at the glittering,

perfumed people, wondering if she should have ignored Paul's wishes and organised a small, quiet gathering instead of this frantic cocktail party. 'It is what he wished,' she said, frowning slightly in her distress. 'He said in his letter that he wanted it to be like a party –' Her voice trailed off. They looked up at her, their kind, gentle faces expectant. 'They've dressed up to pay their respects.'

'They're his friends,' said Rosa with a little quelling look at her husband, 'and we're proud he had such friends.'

'Of course,' he said gently, with a little cough of distress, 'I did not mean…' He glanced worriedly at his wife but she smiled at him and the smile seemed to give him courage for he took Martha's hand and said, 'Paulo spoke about you very often. He loved you very much.' He frowned a little, his large, expressive eyes misting. 'He said that when he got married, you would be the one.'

Martha stared at him uncomprehendingly for a moment, and then her frown cleared and she smiled. 'Yes,' she said formally, 'it was agreed.'

Rosa smiled and stretched out a trembling hand to finger the beaded and embroidered lace of Martha's dress. 'Such fine workmanship,' she murmured.

Martha smiled. 'Paul bought it for me,' she said.

'Ah, yes.' Across Rosa's small, tired face there stretched a smile, as sweet and illuminating as her son's. 'He liked beautiful things.'

Martha took her hand and gently tucked it under her arm. 'Shall we go in?' she said, her voice unsteady.

The church was decorated with garlands of lilies and stephanotis woven with ivy and heavy white satin ribbon. Tubs of cream rose trees were placed all down the aisle and at the end of each pew burned fat white candles. In front of the altar lay Paul's coffin, smothered

241

in lilies, roses and honeysuckle, its fragrance filling the small church. Martha heard Rosa's sharp intake of breath and she glanced down worriedly, concerned that she thought it too frivolous, for the church indeed looked as if it was prepared for a wedding rather than a funeral.

A man with a shaved head wearing full evening dress knelt in one of the pews, sobbing quietly into white-gloved hands. Next to him, sprawled against the polished wood bench, was another man, dressed in black leather and chains, one heavy boot thrust out into the aisle, his handsome, fleshy face swollen and blurred with tears. Martha felt Rosa's hand slip out from under her arm and she darted across the church to lay a small hand on the heavy leather jacket, bending her head to murmur something. As she straightened up, Martha saw the man's face lift to her with a look of startled gratitude, then his face crumpled like a child's and he leaned against her black silk bosom while Rosa gently patted his shaven head.

After the service had ended, Rosa and Carlos stood in the cool, dim porch of the church as the congregation, in black dinner suits, heavy studded leathers, silk cocktail dresses and frivolous hats shuffled up to pay their respects. Martha smiled as she watched Rosa occasionally lift her crisp white lace handkerchief to pat away a tear or move her black-gloved hand to stroke a head as it was laid heavily on her small, padded silk shoulder. As she watched she was enveloped suddenly by the sweet, suffocating smell of tuberose and turned to find a heavily built man towering over her, his fleshy cheeks smeared with mascara. 'Darling,' he said, blinking small, swollen blue eyes alarmingly rimmed in red and the remains of black make-up, 'I haven't cried so much in years. That was perfectly fabulous. You made it look like a tart's boudoir in there.' He sighed extravagantly.

'Paul would have been in heaven,' he said and then giggled stupidly. 'I suppose that's the idea really, isn't it? Well, sweetie, you must do mine when the time comes. Do you take forward bookings? If this AIDS thing goes on the demand's going to be crazy quite soon.' He laughed, a hysterical high pitched sound, and, waggling his fingers, disappeared into the crowd.

'He's right, of course,' said a calm, quiet voice, 'it was perfectly lovely. Paul would have adored it.'

'Phil! I thought you hadn't come. Where were you?'

'I sat at the back,' Phil said, nodding at Paul's parents. 'I didn't feel that I should intrude. Anyway, I thought…' She looked around. 'Is Joe not here?'

Martha flushed. 'He doesn't like death,' she said in a cold, flat voice. 'He says it depresses him. I think he's…' She shook her head abruptly. 'Well, never mind what I think. He didn't come. Let's leave it at that.'

Phil nodded. 'Harry's over there. We came together.'

'Harry?' Martha exclaimed, and a bright, joyous look flashed across her face. 'Harry came to Paul's funeral? Oh, the kind, dear man. Where is he?' She stood on tip-toe, eagerly peering across the forest of heads, and as Phil watched her searching face it occurred to her that it was not, as she had once thought, finished between them.

'Oh, I can't see him,' said Martha disappointedly. 'And I must go in the car with Rosa and Carlos, take them to the party. You will come, won't you? And Harry? No, I suppose not. Well, when you see him, will you tell him that I…' She paused, sighed suddenly. 'Will you tell him – thank you?'

27

When Phil got home from work that evening, she found a note pushed under the door. Recognising Martha's handwriting she stooped, frowning, to pick it up. It said simply, 'Please come. I need you.'

Shivering with impatience she listened to the interminable ringing of Martha's telephone then slammed it down. Hopping agitatedly across the cats who, having found her, were determined not to release her, she ran out of the door and back into the street. Seeing a man paying off a taxi, she pushed past him and clambered in, growing frantic with impatience as the driver slowly counted out change and laboriously wrote a receipt. He had, Phil noticed, tufts of hair growing out of his ears.

The short ride to Martha's flat seemed to take hours. 'Might never happen, love,' the taxi driver said cheerily when he finally drew up outside. 'I think it already has,' she said, flinging some money at his startled face. She ran up the narrow passageway leading into Martha's flat and clattered up the metal staircase in the pitch dark to arrive, breathless, outside her door. She could hear no noise and, after ringing the doorbell persistently, scrabbled blindly on the ledge above the door, praying that Martha had not moved the key in her obsessive tidying-up. She swore as her fingers met only dusty emptiness but suddenly she felt the key's cold, shiny weight and in her impatience dislodged it so it fell with a tinny clatter to the floor. By this time, she was panicking and close to tears, but she got down on her hands and knees, forcing herself to work carefully across the dark, splintery floorboards until eventually she found it.

She unlocked the door and stood panting with anxiety in the silent, threatening gloom. A sudden movement made her start and she looked up fearfully to see a vague shape fluttering above her. Shrinking against the door, feeling its solid, reassuring bulk against her back, she raised reluctant eyes to the ceiling. There, in the flickering shadows which danced through the silent kitchen, illuminated by the yellow light of the street lamps, were hundreds of streamers of pale silk, fluttering idly in the breeze from the open window. As her eyes became accustomed to the dim light she saw that the silk streamers, coloured apricot and peach, lemon and pink, pale turquoise and sky blue, were hung not simply from the ceiling but tied in bows on the wall lights, and each had at its centre a pair of knickers or a bra, tied artfully to form a mad, frothy explosion of lace. The telephone was tied up like a present, its receiver strapped down to the cradle with long ribbons of silk, its coiled wires threaded like a maypole with coloured silks.

It was very quiet save for the distant roar of the launderette. Phil longed suddenly to be down there, in the bustling, soapily fragrant warmth, among the crying, restless babies and silent, dazed young men.

She called out in the stillness but, hearing no answering cry, stepped fearfully into the darkened bedroom and flicked on the light. The room was filled suddenly with a yellow glow, the brightness of the light diffused by a piece of apricot silk tied around the chandelier, giving it the effect of a monstrous inverted mushroom.

Martha lay on the bed, her eyes closed. Her pale face had a curious shuttered blankness and her hands were folded carefully on her chest, her long, white feet poking out from beneath a faded quilt. Phil tip-toed fearfully across to the bed and reached out a fumbling hand to touch Martha's cold white cheek. Martha opened her eyes and looked up, blinking. 'Odd, isn't it,' she said in a conversational tone, 'how you can't cry when you most need to?'

Phil let out a low moan of relief, her legs buckling as she sank on to the bed. 'Christ, Martha, I thought you were dead.'

Martha shrugged and a small smile crept slowly across her face. 'Sorry, did I frighten you?' she said in a remote voice. She stared at Phil thoughtfully. 'I used to think it might kill me if, or rather *when* it happened, but curiously I feel only a great sense of relief.'

'When what happened?'

Martha turned her head away and stared up at the ceiling. 'Joe's gone,' she said. 'He left a note. I found it on the staircase this morning when I went out to get some cigarettes.'

'Gone where?'

'Away.'

'That's most unhelpful,' Phil said fiercely.

Martha smiled slightly. 'Of him or me?'

'Him, of course. What did the note say?'

'That he loved me and was sorry.'

'Sorry?'

'For leaving, I suppose.'

Phil lay down on the bed next to her. 'Shove up, will you?' Martha rolled over obligingly. 'Did he give a reason?'

'No. He simply said that he's sorry for *everything*. God knows what that means. I've spent the best part of the day trying to figure it out and I'm still not sure whether it means he's sorry for ever having got involved or sorry for leaving me.'

'Leaving, I expect,' said Phil absently. 'But is that *all* he said? He gave no reason?'

'No.'

'Bastard.'

'Not really. He's… Well, he's confused, I suppose. There's a part of him that wants to love and be loved, *really* loved, I mean, and then there's the greater part which is terrified of what that means.'

'Stop being so bloody charitable.'

Martha sighed heavily. 'OK, so he's a little shit.'

They lay in silence for a while, Martha with her eyes closed, Phil staring at the silk streamers fluttering from the ceiling. She jumped at Martha's voice, sounding unnaturally loud in the still room. 'There's something else,' she said, and laughed sharply. 'Or perhaps I should say, *somebody* else.'

Phil raised herself on one elbow and stared into Martha's face, her dark, protuberant eyes blinking in owlish alarm. 'You mean he's found another lover?' she said slowly, fighting to keep her voice steady.

Martha stared at her then smiled faintly. 'No, it's nothing like that. I'm pregnant. He doesn't know,' she added quickly.

'Oh.'

'Yes. Oh.'

'You're certain?'

Martha nodded. 'Eleven weeks. I've been feeling a bit odd for a while but I thought it was just Paul's…' Her voice caught and she struggled for a moment to regain her composure. 'I eventually went to the doctor.'

Phil's smooth face crumpled anxiously. 'Oh dear. Will you try and find Joe and let him know?'

'No. Things weren't… Well, they haven't been great between us in the past few weeks.'

'But I thought –,'

'Oh, I know. You all thought it was the great romance. Even Paul believed that. In a way, I suppose it was.' She laughed humourlessly. 'I wanted passion and, my God,

I found it. But in the end it became a sort of sickness.' She stared thoughtfully at the streamers of pale silk fluttering from the walls and ceiling. 'They look good hanging up there, don't they?'

Phil shrugged.

'Oh, it's all right, I know they look better there than they did on me. But that's the way he liked me, dressed up like a doll.' She laughed. 'It's even what he called me; his doll. At first I thought it was a game, it seemed wonderful to have a man care about me so much that he was even interested in stupid things like what clothes I wore and how I did my hair. I did everything to please him but, eventually, I understood that he wanted me to become somebody else, someone quite different, and it began to frighten me.'

'Why didn't you leave?'

Martha turned her head on the pillow and stared at Phil, her pale face thoughtful. 'Because I couldn't. I suppose you think that's absurd.'

Phil shrugged again. Martha smiled at her fondly. 'Wise, clever Phil, always got your head screwed on. You'd never do anything so foolish as let your emotions get the better of you.' Phil looked at her uneasily, thinking of Harry. 'Oh, I don't mean you're not capable of love,' Martha said quickly. 'You're more capable than anyone I've ever met. It's just that you're so careful with it. So proper. Everything in its right place.'

An image of Harry's face leapt suddenly into Phil's mind and she felt her stomach lurch sickeningly with longing. 'Yes,' she said bleakly, 'everything in its right place.'

Martha sat up abruptly, the colour rising in her face, her eyes a painful, burning blue. 'You won't leave me, will you?' she whispered, plucking fretfully at the counterpane. 'Everyone keeps leaving. First Harry, then Paul and now Joe. You won't go, will you?' she pleaded.

248

'No,' Phil said, hugging her, 'but if you remember, it was you who left Harry.'

Martha bowed her head. 'Yes,' she said with a broken sigh, smiling lopsidedly as she dragged a hand roughly across her face, wiping away a stray tear. 'Sometimes, I can't believe how stupid I am.'

'In that way, we're all stupid,' Phil said quietly. She saw then that it was inevitable, Martha and Harry, and wondered why she had ever thought otherwise. How absurd she had been to believe that she was free of him. Even the mention of his name made her heart quicken with yearning and her body grow heavy with despair. Yet she didn't resent Martha's claim; some part of her was even gladdened that Harry would be happy again. 'Will you keep the baby?' she asked in a low, strained voice.

Martha looked up in surprise. 'Of course. It's not the way I would have wished it but...' Her voice trailed off. 'Well, we'll manage. We'll have to.'

'I'll help.'

Martha nodded vaguely, staring down at her stomach in disbelief. Her hands, already gentle with the promise of the child, patted at its flatness tenderly. 'Oh God, Phil, I don't know if I'm ready for this. I've thought about it, of course, but it always seemed to be – well, tomorrow, I suppose. I know I'm going to be a hopeless mother, leave it on the bus or let it drink turpentine or eat my paints or something.'

'Have you ever heard a mother claim to be anything but hopeless?' Phil said briskly, getting to her feet. 'Now, have you eaten today?'

Martha stared at her, mystified. 'Have I what?'

'Have you eaten?'

'No, as a matter of fact I haven't. What's that got to do with anything?'

'I thought not. You're very pale and much too thin.

I'm going to go and scramble us some eggs and you are going to eat them, all of them. The last thing you need is to become anaemic.'

Martha laughed. 'Phil, you're priceless. Here I am, broken hearted and sobbing over my errant lover, and you're trying to feed me scrambled eggs.'

'Somebody's got to,' Phil said briskly. 'And while I'm cooking, don't moon around. Tear up some more dresses or something.'

Martha grinned. 'Yes, I might.' As Phil hurried towards the door she watched her retreating back thoughtfully. 'Phil, will you tell me something, honestly?'

Phil turned, her expression wary. 'If I really must,' she said eventually.

'You didn't like him, did you?'

'I didn't know him.'

'But you know me, better than anybody. You saw how I was when I was with him.'

Phil looked at her regretfully. 'Then I'm afraid to say that I didn't like him.'

Martha gazed at her reflectively then with a small, weary sigh got to her feet and walked across the room to the rocking chair. On it lay a silk chiffon evening dress, its stiff boned corset slumped in the likeness of a broken doll. She stared at it for a while, eyes glittering, then gave a brief, sharp exclamation of despair and began methodically to tear it into little pieces.

28

They met, as usual, in the car park. Phil, who was early, sat waiting on the bonnet of her car, enjoying the pale sunshine. It was crisp and cold but there was no wind save a gentle breeze which made her cheeks glow agreeably. It was, she thought, a perfect afternoon for a walk. Perfect, that is, had it not been for the news she had to break to Harry. They had not seen each other for months. When Harry telephoned, she always found some excuse not to meet.

She looked at her watch, two minutes to two. Harry was bound to be on time, he always was. Martha was always late. Eventually, after missing the opening acts of two plays in a row, he had forced her to set her watch half an hour too fast, which she did with laughing compliance although she said it would make little difference or, worse, would make her even later because she would always assume that she was early. Phil smiled slightly, remembering, then seeing that it was two o'clock precisely lifted her gaze from her watch to see Harry's car turn into the car park. His familiar head bobbed behind the windscreen as he looked round, searching for her. When finally he saw her, he accelerated, turning into the space beside her car with a protesting squeal of brakes and a splash of muddy water.

'Thanks,' Phil said, laughing.

Harry climbed out of the car grinning. 'Sorry, I couldn't resist it. How are you? You look well.'

'Pretty good.' They stood for a moment, smiling at each other awkwardly. Phil's smile faded as she remembered what it was she had to say to him and, turning away, she said abruptly, 'Shall we walk?'

He looked at her curiously then took her hand, tucking it comfortably under his arm. 'Sure. You're not in any hurry, are you? I thought we might take the long way round. I haven't seen you in such a long time, I want you to myself for a bit.' He glanced at her averted profile. 'I've really missed you, you know.'

She smiled faintly but said nothing and they walked on in silence for a while. From time to time Harry cast curious looks in her direction and she, conscious of his glance, eventually looked up with a faint, reassuring smile. He returned the smile but when she said nothing he caught her hand, forcing her to stop.

'Look,' he said, with a perplexed frown, 'we may as well get this over with now. Are you pissed off with me about something?'

She looked fully at him, her expression startled.

'You seem to have been avoiding me for a while,' he said gently.

'But it's nothing to do with you,' she blurted out, then shook her head. 'I'm sorry, I know I seem a bit odd today. It's all a bit complicated. I'll explain it to you sometime.'

'But not now?'

She gave a small, helpless shrug. 'No, not now.'

Something in her solemn face seemed to reassure him for he smiled and said, 'OK as long as you promise it's nothing I've done.'

She smiled awkwardly. 'I promise.' Nothing other than be yourself, she thought wretchedly. She had thought she was over him, was not prepared for the emotion which crashed through her at the sight of his dear, familiar face, but as he took her arm and they

252

walked quietly through the fading winter light she gave herself up to the physical sensation of his arm through hers, turning her head occasionally to laugh up at him as he told her stories of the latest political in-fighting at the polytechnic where he taught. Gradually, lulled into a contented stupor by the warm, reassuring sound of his voice and the deserted pathways, she came to believe that there were only her and Harry in the world. If only it could always be like this, she thought, and sighed softly. It was only when Harry stopped abruptly and she looked up to see his puzzled frown that she realised he had asked her a question. 'Sorry,' she said, 'I was miles away.'

'God, I'm not that boring, am I?' He smiled but then the smile faded, to be replaced by a perplexed frown. 'Phil,' he said hesitantly, 'are you sure you're OK?'

'Quite sure,' she said, her reverie abruptly broken. She stumbled slightly in confusion. 'I'm sorry, I'm not very good company at the moment.'

He caught her arm to prevent her falling. 'It's not that. I just can't help feeling that something's wrong.'

'If there is, it's nothing to do with you,' she said shortly.

He gave her a puzzled, hurt smile and Phil, immediately regretting her abruptness, sighed and smiled back at him. 'I'm sorry, Harry. I didn't mean it to sound like that. It's just that I've been a bit pre-occupied lately.'

He nodded. 'Paul, you mean?'

'That, and other things.'

He hesitated. 'Is it Peter? Has something happened?'

'We separated,' Phil said roughly, 'about five months ago.'

'Why didn't you say?' he asked, startled. She glanced quickly at him but said nothing, simply shrugged as if to say it wasn't that big a deal. He watched her in silence for a time then said quietly, 'Poor Phil. I am sorry. Has it made you very unhappy?'

She winced inwardly at that. *Poor Phil*. Was that really all she was to him? 'Not really,' she said, turning away from his expression of concern. 'I'm sorry to say that it's made very little difference to me. I suppose that sounds dreadful.'

He smiled. 'Not really. Sometimes you just grow out of people.' He looked away from her, gazing thoughtfully over the skyline of London. 'I suppose,' he said, 'that you begin to understand that they're no longer important to you, and any residual emotion is based almost entirely on sentiment and habit.' He turned to her and smiled again. 'But then I expect you know that.'

'I'm not sure I do.' Phil avoided his gaze, wondering if he was referring to Martha. Was it possible that he no longer cared for her? Her heart leaped at the idea, did a crazy double flip in her chest leaving her momentarily gasping with happiness, while at the same time her mind told her coldly to stop being absurd. But just as our hearts betray our minds so that we behave in the most foolish of ways, so Phil abandoned herself, however briefly, to the possibility of happiness. Harry, who heard only her breath coming in quick, short gasps, turned to her, frowning. 'Are you all right? It's a bit steep, this hill. Perhaps we should sit down for a bit.' He took her by the hand and led her gently away from the path. 'Come on, there's a bench over there.'

She stopped, pulled him back away from the bench, but kept her hand firmly in his. 'No, I'm fine. Really, I'd rather keep walking if you don't mind.'

'OK, but only if you promise to go slowly. I'd like a gentle meander rather than your usual brisk style of hill walking.'

She smiled up at him and his hand moved over hers, gripping it tightly. She walked, conscious only of the

254

burning heat of it and the delicious unfamiliar feel of his skin against hers. It was extraordinary, she thought, how the mere touch of a hand can make your whole body sing. She ignored the cold, hard, nagging voice of reason, felt only the contentment which his physical presence brought her, her body softening and her mind growing idiotic with happiness so that she forgot Martha and the baby, knew only the pleasure of that moment and his hand on hers. The usual muscles which maintained her pale, serious face in its habitually solemn expression seemed not to be functioning and she felt a foolish smile breaking uncontrollably over it, as a wave does on the shore. He glanced at her from time to time and then, unable to contain himself, burst out laughing. 'Have you just taken some magic drug? Whatever it is, I'd like some.'

'You can have any amount,' she said laughing back at him, 'it's free.'

The smile faded abruptly from his face. 'Are you in love?' he said, his voice hard, cold and unfamiliar.

In her confusion she smiled, the corners of her mouth dancing uncertainly, her expression flitting from doubt to happiness and back. 'Yes, I suppose I am.'

He turned his head away and his voice, caught by the wind, seemed to rush away from her so that she heard it from a great distance. 'Is it anybody I know?'

She stared at his averted profile, her heart pounding loudly in her ears. Eventually he turned to look at her and she realised that she was holding her breath. 'I said, is it anybody I know?'

'I –' The word emerged on a gasp, a quick sigh of breath, and then she found that she couldn't speak so she shrugged miserably and turned away from him.

'It's just that I thought – Oh, never mind. It's not important.'

'But *what*?' she cried, turning back to him, her face

foolish with hope and longing. 'What did you think?'

He did not see her face, had bent his head and was kicking angrily at a clump of wiry grass. 'I thought you might feel –' He hesitated, kicked again at the clump, dislodged it so it was caught by the wind and bounced in a crazy dance across the grass. They watched it in silence. 'I thought you might feel something for me,' he said quietly. She said nothing and he jerked his head abruptly then began to walk away from her, down the hill in the direction of the car. 'I'm sorry,' he threw over his shoulder, 'just forget I ever mentioned it. Come on, let's get going. It seems to have got rather cold all of a sudden.'

As she watched him walk away from her, Phil felt a terrible sense of loss. I have this one chance, she thought, this one try at happiness, and forgetting Martha, forgetting what she had come there to tell him, she called, 'Harry. Harry, please listen. I do – I do feel something.'

He stopped and turned slowly to look at her, his face sombre. 'But not enough?'

'There's Martha…' she said quickly.

He walked towards her. 'Let's forget Martha,' he said. 'Martha's not here. We are, you and me.'

As she walked into his waiting arms and felt his mouth on hers, all memory seemed to leave her, all thought of the past or the future, until there was only her and Harry and the feel of his skin against hers, so strange and yet so startlingly familiar. She closed her eyes, breathing in the smell of him, of cigars and turpentine and his own indefinable scent. She pressed her face against the harsh wool of his coat, felt a button jab painfully at her cheek, and was content.

He hugged her to him, stroking her hair with a trembling, clumsy hand. 'Come on,' he said, looking down at her with an awkward smile. 'Let's go home. I want to make love to you.'

'Harry, we can't –,'

'Yes, we can,' he said, leading her down the hillside, one arm wrapped around her neck so she caught at his hand, rubbed her lips against the skin, roughened with paint and turpentine. He laughed joyfully, the sound triumphant in the still, cold afternoon air. 'We can do anything we like.'

Hearing his laugh, sensing his clumsy grab for happiness, she knew that she had to tell him, for both their sakes. She was not Martha and never would be, would be simply a poor substitute. She supposed that if Martha had not wanted him back then perhaps it might have been different, he might have learned to forget and, eventually, to love her in return. But she knew, hearing his laugh, that when she did tell him it would destroy all the flimsy defences he had built up against Martha and in his impotence he would hate her for allowing him to go on when three words would drag him back to the brink again. 'Harry –,' she said.

'No,' he murmured, turning to her, stopping her mouth with kisses. 'Don't say anything.'

She pulled her mouth away, stepping back regretfully from the sweet, encircling warmth of his arms. As she gazed at his puzzled face she felt the bitterness rise in her throat and flood into her mouth. She looked away from him. Her brief, glorious moment of happiness was over. 'Martha's pregnant.'

His head jerked sharply under the blow of the words and then his expression settled to a look of dazed stupefaction and he let out a great sigh. 'I see,' he said eventually.

Phil watched him for a moment, torn with pity, although she did not know if it was for him or for herself that she felt the greatest compassion. She took a step towards him but he held up a warning hand and, turning, blundered clumsily in the direction of a solitary

257

copse of trees. She let him go, huddling into her coat to protect herself from the cold which seeped through the thin wool. Shivering, she thrust her hands into her pockets and walked back up the hill, going to sit on the bench where he had just tried to persuade her to rest. She wondered, in a detached way, if she would ever feel warm again. Some way in the distance a man was throwing a ball for his dog. It was, she noticed, a red ball and a yellow dog.

She didn't know how long she sat there; time seemed to freeze, hanging around her in clouds, like the breath which emerged from her warm body, clotting in the cold, still air. It could have been an hour or maybe only a few minutes before she sensed a movement behind her and, turning her head, saw Harry standing silently behind her. 'I'm sorry to walk out on you like that,' he said, his voice rough with embarrassment. 'You caught me off-balance.'

She looked at him directly. 'I should have told you about the baby straight away.'

'No, it's just that I...' He sat down next to her, dropping his head to his hands. They sat in silence for a while. 'I've always wanted children,' he said eventually. 'Martha knew that, she even said she wanted them too but somehow, the time was never right.' He looked up, stared bleakly into the distance. 'She said she wanted to paint, needed the freedom to be selfish with her time. Anyway, there was always a reason not to.'

'Yes,' Phil said, 'there usually is.'

He stared at her, surprised by the anger in her voice. 'Don't think harshly of her.'

She turned her head away from his intense gaze. 'I don't,' she said quietly.

He put out a hand, stroked a finger gently down one cold cheek. 'Phil, back there...' He hesitated. 'That wasn't compassion or pity I felt just then. I...I love you and I believe we might have been happy together. It's just that I'd forgotten, or perhaps I was kidding myself that I'd forgotten what Martha…'

'It's all right. I know.'

He let out a sigh. 'I'm sorry, Phil.'

She looked away. 'Yes. Me too,' she said distantly.

'Is she going to have the baby?'

'Yes.'

Harry's face distorted as he struggled to form words but in the end the effort seemed too great and he fell once more into silence. After a while, he rose abruptly to his feet. 'Come on. I need to do something.' They walked for a while, each sunk in their own private thoughts. Once Harry stumbled and bumped into her, pulling his body away sharply, as if the touch of her body might burn him. 'I'm sorry,' he muttered. She watched him sadly, knowing that all along she had believed it would end like this, that it should never have begun.

He heard her sigh and turned towards her. 'I'm sorry, this is difficult for you.'

'Just as it is for you,' she reminded him.

'Yes,' he said absently, and she knew then that she was as far from his thoughts as if she had never been in them. 'May I ask you one more question?'

She nodded curtly. 'Yes.'

'Is he…is Joe happy about it?'

Phil looked at him, aghast. In her misery and confusion, she had forgotten the most important detail. 'Harry, I'm sorry, I thought I'd told you. Joe's gone. He left last week.'

She saw the hope flare in his eyes and then the slow realisation dawn in his face and she stood, powerless, as she watched Martha creep slowly back into his mind and inhabit his soul.

'Gone?' he said slowly. 'Gone where?'

Phil shrugged. 'Nobody knows. He left a note which said simply that he was sorry and had gone away.'

'For good?'

'It looks that way.'

He stared into the distance for a while then let out a great, broken sigh. 'I expect you know what I'm going to do?'

She watched him sadly. 'Yes.'

He gave a small, rueful smile. 'That's why you came to tell me yourself.'

She nodded abruptly. 'Yes.'

He leaned forward to kiss her and she saw in his face how gratitude and pity replaced the passion which, briefly, had illuminated it. She jerked her head away. 'Don't do that,' she snapped. 'I'm sorry, Harry, but I can't bear it. Good old Phil,' she mocked, '*good old Phil*. Well, I want to be bad old Phil, just once.' She felt tears on her face and angrily dashed her sleeve across them. 'It's not much to ask, is it? *Is it*?'

He watched her, his face expressionless. She raised both hands in a gesture of surrender. 'I'm sorry, I know it's not your fault. None of this is anyone's fault. Just give me a week and it'll be as if it never happened. But don't talk to me now. Don't touch me. Don't... Just *don't*.'

She turned and walked quickly away from him, a small, solitary figure wrapped in a neat navy coat.

29

Phil had never seen Martha so happy. That spring, before Georgia Sarah Randolph was born (named after Martha's father, George, and Sarah, after Phil) she fairly blazed with it. A halo of tranquillity settled over her, misting her natural colouring until she shimmered gold, pink and blue. She seemed dazed, her blue eyes unfocused and her pink mouth slightly parted in an expression of constant surprise as she hugged her growing belly in silent delight.

It was as if the past six months had never happened. And if, on occasion, Phil found Martha's benign absorption tiresome, then she found it soothing also. Harry too was content, his long, lugubrious face settled in an expression of happy stupefaction. If Phil had expected awkwardness, she found none. The Harry she had come to know, *her* Harry, was gone as completely as if he had been a stranger who had slipped out of their lives. They slid seamlessly back into the relationship they had always known; pale stars, satellites around Martha's sun.

Martha said afterwards that those six months had changed her life; before the separation it had been as if she and Harry were a jigsaw puzzle in which the pieces weren't quite true so they were jammed uncomfortably together. Then, afterwards, it was as if some unseen hand had smoothed all their edges so they slid easily into place. Bountiful with happiness, she did not notice Phil's tight, uncomfortable smile when she told her how

Harry had appeared, as if from nowhere, that Sunday afternoon, his hair a little windswept.

'I was sitting in the chair, the one by the fire, drinking a cup of tea and feeling a bit low, worrying about the future, I suppose. I heard a key in the door and thought it must be you so I called out something like, "I'm in here." When I looked up, there he was. He didn't say anything at first, just went and made us both a cup of tea and came and sat down next to me. Then he asked me what *we* were going to do, just as if we had never been apart. Not what was I going to do, but what were we going to do. It was extraordinary, but then he is, isn't he?'

Phil agreed that he was.

Now that Martha's flat was tidier, not exactly tidy but neither the chaos it had been in the old Harry days nor the sterile, soulless place of Joe's brief tenure, Harry was content to live there with her. He had even suggested that they turn his flat into a painting studio, which suited them both perfectly for it kept Martha free from distraction while he, inspired by Martha's prolific output, began to paint again himself.

Martha became a commuter, the charm of novelty lending her discovery intense delight, setting off on the bus every morning to go to Harry's flat in Hammersmith, while he went to the polytechnic to teach. He would arrive to pick her up in the late afternoon, put in a couple of hours work himself and then they would travel back to Martha's place for a quiet supper before retiring early to bed. Enough of the old Martha remained to cause her to grimace ruefully as she described the routine to Phil, protesting that she knew it sounded boring but it made her happier than she would ever have believed possible. She was earning more than she ever had before; the regular hours meant that she could easily keep up with her commissions if she worked on them two days a week, and the other three days she dedicated to her own work. There was even talk of an exhibition in the autumn. Quite a major one, she said, pleased.

The weeks and months tumbled one into the other and the previous year grew ever more dim and distant until it came to seem to all three of them to have no more substance or terror than a dream, vaguely recalled, easily forgotten. On occasion Phil looked up to find Harry's heavy-lidded grey eyes resting thoughtfully on her but as time passed she learned to smile and in that secret, silent exchange began to discover that her memories held more pleasure than pain. When Georgia was born and they sat, all three of them, cross-legged on Martha's hospital bed gazing in bemused adoration at the baby who lay, a tiny, beached frog at their centre, their union seemed complete.

Georgia's birth was an easy one and she was an easy baby; content to lie quietly in her wicker Moses basket in a corner of the studio, her dark, smudgy blue eyes focused in rapt attention on her starfish hands or softly cooing like a small, plump dove as she gazed at the mobiles, lovingly painted by Martha, revolving slowly above her basket.

Martha spent hours gazing dreamily at her daughter's downy head as it bobbed frantically in her vigorous search for the breast. 'She had the most comic expression on her face when she was born,' she said. 'Harry says that when her head emerged she looked completely startled, like somebody who's turned up at a party only to discover that everyone else is in fancy dress. She took one look at us, gave a big sigh, and went straight back to sleep.' Martha looked at Phil anxiously. 'I do hope we're not going to be a disappointment to her.'

Phil smiled. 'You're bound to be,' she said. 'Parents

always are, at least at some time. But you've a few years yet of mindless adoration.'

As for Phil, she was hopelessly, passionately in love. She knew, when she first gazed into Georgia's startled, unfocused eyes, saw the tender pink curl of her upper lip, the pale, translucent shell of her tiny ear, that she had never known such helpless desire. The baby seemed to sense in her some safe, familiar presence, for if Phil ever came into the room and did not immediately go to her and pick her up, she would bleat pathetically, her cries eventually building to such a pitch of fury that Phil hastened to hold her.

One evening, when Martha and Harry had gone out to the opening of an exhibition, Phil sat with Georgia in the old rocking chair, the two of them gazing in be-mused contentment at the flickering television screen. Georgia, grown bored or sleepy, had wriggled her little body, curling and uncurling like a shrimp until she arranged herself to her satisfaction, her face pressed into Phil's neck and her hands up to her face. With a tiny sigh of pleasure, she fell fast asleep. As Phil felt her plump, damp, silken face against her neck, a small hand stuck warmly to her cheek, she felt such happiness she scarcely dared breathe and sat for the rest of the eve-ning, rocking gently, as tears trickling helplessly down her cheeks.

'We're going to have lots more kids, of course,' Martha said, her cheeks pink, 'or at least as many as we can fit in, being late starters. And we thought that one day we might buy a house in the country. London's so dreadful for children. Harry's already put his flat on the market as a matter of fact. Then we could have a studio each and of course we'll buy a place with a big garden so the kids can run around barefoot and be quite safe. And,' she added, with a quick, assessing glance at Phil, 'we thought you might come and live there too.'

'What,' Phil said, 'have a sort of spinster flat attached?'

'Don't make it sound like that,' Martha protested, flushing. 'We simply thought you might prefer to be self-contained.'

'Martha,' Phil said, exasperation sharpening her voice, 'just because you've become a mother doesn't mean that we're all children around you. Had you thought that perhaps I might like to organise my own life? I do work, you know. What would I do in the country?'

'But you don't really like it, your job, I mean.'

Phil looked at her oddly. 'I do it, don't I?'

Martha shrugged, blushing violently. 'But you could do the same thing somewhere else,' she said stubbornly. 'A small country practice… You might like it.'

'Martha,' Phil said patiently, 'just because I don't talk about my job endlessly, it doesn't mean I don't like doing it. It's something I do, not something I talk about.'

Martha frowned. 'Oh dear,' she murmured, 'this is coming out all wrong. I hadn't meant it to sound like some sort of benevolent patronage.'

'It doesn't. It sounds like bullying.'

The colour, which had just begun to subside in Martha's cheeks, flamed again violently. 'Oh, God, does it? I suppose it must. I'm sorry, Phil. It's just –' She gave her a beseeching look. 'Well, it's just that I'd feel so odd without you. We've been together all our lives. I'd be lost without you. And Harry would miss you terribly,' she added quickly, for Harry had become strangely quiet when she proposed the idea. Phil smiled reluctantly but Martha, her eyes gleaming, still had her ace to play. 'And then, of course,' she went on, unable to keep the triumph from her voice, 'there's Georgia.'

It did not occur to Martha, as Phil knew it wouldn't, to think that she might yearn for her own share of happiness; a love of her own perhaps, maybe even a child. Then again, why should it? There had never been anyone in Phil's life important enough to threaten Martha's position. Unless, of course, you counted Harry which Phil, these days, didn't. It was not, after all, any selfishness on Martha's part which had cast her in that position, but rather Phil's own diffidence in matters of the heart. She was right, they had never been parted. The separation would be painful, for both of them. Then, of course, there was Georgia.

'I'll think about it,' she said.

Martha's exhibition was a great success. Everyone agreed that the work was that of a mature talent; *The Times* called it 'a radical step forward'. Nobody, it seemed, had a bad word to say. Even the most waspish of critics marvelled at how Martha Randolph, who had shown an early promise which seemed to have fizzled out, had been reborn as an artist of real stature.

'It's how I feel,' Martha said, her smile as pink and sweet as strawberry ice cream. 'I feel reborn.'

30

'You're early,' Martha called, laughing as she flung open the door. 'I'm not ready...' Her laughter evaporated. 'Jane! What a surprise. I'm sorry, I must look quite crazed.'

Jane stared at her in astonishment. 'Slightly.'

Tinsel was wound through Martha's hair and tied in big bows at her wrists and ankles, she wore frothy net skirts spangled with silver tin foil stars, her eyes were fringed with black pencilled eyelashes and her cheeks painted with pink lipstick circles. She began to giggle. 'I was expecting Georgia. Harry's taken her off to the playground at Paddington Rec so I thought I'd dress up as a fairy and surprise her when she got back. It's her second Christmas so she might be a bit more aware of things than last year. Or do you think she's still a bit young?'

Jane looked at her in bewilderment.

Martha grinned. 'I know, who'd have thought it? Come in. I'll make some tea.'

Jane walked unsteadily into the kitchen and stood looking around her as if she didn't quite know why she was there. 'This is a surprise,' Martha said again, frowning slightly at her sister's bemused expression.

'What?' Jane said absently. 'Oh, yes, I see, I suppose it is. I brought Georgia's Christmas present. It's just a small thing.' She handed Martha the brightly wrapped parcel and looked around, her expression vaguely startled. 'I was in the area so I thought I'd drop in.'

Martha, who knew that her sister loathed spontaneity of any kind, looked at her curiously. Why, anyway, would she be in Notting Hill? Jane had always gone to extreme lengths to avoid ever being in the area; she had once read an article in *The Times* about the drug dealers of All Saints Road and was convinced that heroin addiction was somehow contagious. 'You have to buy drugs,' Martha had said laconically, 'they don't give them away, you know.' Subsequently, every time Jane saw a Rasta on the street she lowered her eyes, convinced that he was attempting to sell her drugs. In Barnes this did not pose too great a problem but, as Martha's flat was a stone's throw from All Saints Road, even the short walk from her car was hazardous.

'Do you think the car will be all right outside?' she asked suddenly, her eyes darting nervously to the window, as if she could see through solid brick and down to the street below.

'It'll be fine,' Martha said cheerfully, 'although the tyres and engine will probably be gone by the time you get back downstairs.'

'Oh, God.' Jane rushed to the window. 'If anything happens to that car David will die...' The words tailed off and she shrugged helplessly. 'He'll be terribly angry,' she amended, glancing back anxiously out of the window.

Martha watched her. Jane looked more rodent-like than usual as she chewed anxiously on her lower lip, her hands scampering nervously up and down the curtains. 'Do come and sit down,' she said. 'I'll make some tea. Jane? Jane, I said I'll make us some tea.'

Jane looked up distractedly from the window. 'What? Oh, yes, coffee would be fine.'

'Well, actually, I'm afraid I don't have any coffee. Neither of us drink it these days. I stopped when I was pregnant and just never seemed to get back into the habit.' Jane said nothing, just stared restlessly around her then scurried over to a chair and sat down. Martha frowned. 'Would you like me to go and get some? I'll run downstairs to the shop. Won't take me a minute.'

'No,' Jane said quickly, starting in alarm. 'Please don't leave me... I mean, don't go to any trouble on my account. I'll have whatever you're having.'

'Tea, then. I'll go and put the kettle on.'

Jane half rose from her chair. 'Shall I come and help?'

'I'm only putting a kettle on,' Martha said in exasperation, but her sister's white, anxious face caused her to soften her tone, and she added, 'Look, why don't you just sit there and relax? I'll be two seconds.'

When she came back into the room Jane had retreated into the chair and was sitting fearfully still.

'Are you all right?' Martha asked, beginning to wonder whether Jane's extreme agitation was entirely to do with being on unfamiliar teritory. She had been so astounded to see her sister on her doorstep that she hadn't at first noticed that her usually immaculately manicured nails were bitten to the quick and that the cuffs of her white shirt were faintly rimmed with dirt.

'What? Oh, yes, I'm fine. It's just that Christmas gets a bit much...I haven't done half the things I was going to and Charles will be home from school next week and there are all the presents to get. Well, I've got a few but the list still looks endless. I was just saying to David this morning...' The mention of David's name seemed to agitate her still further and she leaped forward from the comforting confines of her chair and sat perched on the edge, clasping and unclasping her hands. She seemed at a loss for anything more to say, her eyes darting anxiously around the room as if she was a stranger in unfamiliar surroundings, searching for neutral, pleasing topics for discussion. 'It looks, well, very *homely* in here,' she said eventually.

'That's probably because it is our home,' Martha said, with mild irritation.

Jane's bright little eyes went on raking the room, as if she was taking an inventory. 'A home,' she said quickly, 'yes, of course it's your home. You're very happy here, then, the three of you?'

'Yes,' Martha said with exasperation, 'we're very happy here. Well, we have got vague plans to move to the country. Did I mention it? Not for a while yet, but if the next exhibition does as well as the last...' She broke off, realising that Jane was not listening. 'Jane, what's all this about? Has Mum sent you to check up on me or something?'

Jane looked startled. 'Mother? Why should she send me? Oh, I see. No, it's nothing like that.' She gazed at her sister appealingly. 'Look, I think you'd better sit down.'

'I don't want to sit down.'

Jane looked at her anxiously. 'Well, if you'd rather not.' Her agitation increased and she stared desperately around the flat as if it might offer up some answer. 'It looks so different,' she murmured. 'The last time I was here –'

'The *only* time you were here,' Martha corrected, remembering an uncomfortable evening when, in a rush of sisterly affection which she'd regretted immediately she put the telephone down, she had invited Jane and David over for a meal.

'The only time I was here,' Jane agreed, 'it looked... Well, it looked so bohemian, like a student's flat. It gave me the impression that, I suppose, that it wouldn't matter.'

'That what wouldn't matter?' Martha said, stung.

'Well, that you would take everything in your stride,' Jane said, half to herself. 'I had somehow thought... Well, I suppose I thought that nothing would shock

270

you,' she said reflectively. 'But now it seems like such a home, well, it's different somehow.'

'Don't be so bloody rude,' Martha exclaimed. 'It was nice of you to bring Georgia a present but if you've only come round here to pick holes then I'd really much rather –'

'To pick holes?' Jane said, looking bewildered. 'What do you mean? Oh, Martha, I'm sorry, that wasn't what I meant at all. I just didn't expect it all to be so cosy here, like a family.'

'This is too much,' Martha snapped, snatching up the present Jane had brought and handing it back to her. 'I know you think I'm a slob but to come round here and infer that I'm incapable of giving my child a decent home...' She took a deep breath. 'Jane, I'm sorry, but I think you'd better go now.'

Jane stared at her, appalled. 'But Martha, I can't go. Not till I've told you. It's taken me all week to find the courage.'

'Courage?' Martha stared at her sister and then something in Jane's face seemed to calm her, her shoulders relaxed and she said slowly, 'Look, why don't we start all over again? I'll go and make us both some tea and then maybe you can tell me whatever it is that you're making such a mystery of.'

Jane gave her a wan smile and settled back obediently in the chair, her hands clasped in her lap. Martha glanced at her, frowning, then went off to make tea. When she returned, Jane seemed more composed.

'I'm sorry,' she said, but Martha waved an irritated, dismissive hand and, picking up her cup, went and stood by the window, looking down on to the busy street while she sipped at the hot tea. Jane watched her anxiously for a time, casting quick, nervous glances at her averted profile. 'It would be better if you sat down,' she said eventually.

Martha looked at her in exasperation. 'I've already told you that I don't want to sit down.' She looked down at the bright pink net skirts spangled with tinsel and stars. 'Anyway, I'd crush these before Georgia gets home. They're only stuck together with glue.'

Jane looked at her in alarm, her small, bright eyes blinking. 'Oh God, Georgia,' she whispered, tears springing to her eyes.

'What do you mean?' Martha said sharply.

Jane looked at her beseechingly. 'That's what I'm trying to tell you.'

'Well, hurry up,' Martha said urgently, her face suddenly pale under the brilliant pink of the lipstick circles painted clownishly on her cheeks.

Jane clasped and unclasped her hands. 'I hardly know how to begin.'

'Oh, for God's sake! Try the beginning.'

Jane frowned, examining her bitten nails. 'Yes, the beginning,' she repeated, in a low, strained voice. Her face was deathly white, the lines around her mouth etched deeply in the fine skin. She looked up abruptly, gazing at Martha with mute appeal.

'What did you mean?' Martha said, her voice sharp with anxiety. 'What does all this have to do with Georgia?'

Jane shook her head. 'It's David,' she whispered. Her hands were shaking violently; she clasped them together, forcing them down to her lap to control their trembling.

Martha frowned. 'David? I thought you said...'

'He's sick,' Jane whispered.

'Sick?' Martha said in alarm. 'What sort of sick?'

'He's got–' Jane's voice caught in her throat, she gave a short strangled gasp and swayed slightly in her chair, her face ashen and beaded with sweat. Martha took a step towards her. 'Are you all right? Take some deep breaths. There, that's it.' Jane took a deep, shuddering breath and waved Martha away. 'No, I'm perfectly all right,' she said in a high, strained voice. 'David's got cancer.'

'Cancer?' Martha said, staring at her sister in horror. 'Oh Jane, I'm sorry. I'm so sorry.' She moved back across the room towards Jane, her pink net skirts rustling, but Jane shooed her away with a quick, agitated gesture and clasped her arms around her thin body to stop her violent trembling. 'It's a very rare form of cancer. It's called Kaposi's Sarcoma.'

Martha frowned. 'Kaposi's?' she said in bewilderment. 'But that's one of the symptoms of –'

Jane's head jerked slightly. 'Of AIDS,' she said, her voice shrill.

Martha stood in the middle of the room, her body, stiff with shock, emerging sharply from the froth of pink and silver net skirts. 'AIDS?' she repeated in a puzzled voice. 'David's got AIDS?'

'Yes,' Jane whispered. 'It's quite advanced.'

Martha stared at her, horrified realisation slowly dawning on her face. 'But that means –' Jane returned her look, her small face a white triangle in which the little eyes burned brightly. 'It's all right,' she said quickly, 'I'm negative.'

Martha walked slowly over to the table by the window and slumped into one of the chairs. 'Oh, Jane,' she murmured in a broken voice, 'I'm so terribly sorry. I don't know what to –'

'There's more,' Jane said roughly.

'More?'

Jane looked away. 'You haven't asked how he got it,' she said, her voice low.

Martha frowned. 'A blood transfusion?'

Jane kept her face averted and shook her head sharply.

273

'He's not –'

Jane turned to stare at her. 'Not what?'

'He's not a haemophiliac, is he?' Martha said in bewilderment. 'I mean, you never said anything but some people don't like to talk about…'

Jane dropped her eyes. 'He's not a haemophiliac.' She fell silent and the tension seemed to build around her until Martha felt the bright, crackling static catch at her throat so she could hardly breathe. 'He's a homosexual,' she said at last.

Martha stared at her sister with disbelief. 'David? A homosexual? I don't believe it.' Jane put up a hand, covered her eyes, but kept her head turned away. 'Oh, Jane, I'm so sorry. I didn't mean I don't believe *you*, I meant I can't believe it. Are you completely sure?'

'He showed me a mark on his arm,' Jane said, in a small remote voice. 'I'd noticed it before, of course. He had one on his neck too. I thought it was a bruise or something, or a weal from his collar chafing. He'd been complaining of feeling unwell for some time,' she gave a short, high laugh, 'but you know what a hypochondriac David is. Well, you probably don't, but he is. He even started saying, whenever it was mentioned on the news, that he thought he probably had AIDS. I just laughed.' Her face crumpled. 'God forgive me, but I just laughed.' She turned to Martha with a pleading expression. 'You see, I thought it was the same as when he saw reports about cancer. He'd always say he had that, too. When he had a headache, he was convinced it was a brain tumour. So when he said he had AIDS I just thought he was…' She began to laugh hysterically. 'I thought nice middle class people like us who lived in Barnes couldn't possibly get it,' she stuttered, between fits of laughter.

'Oh my God,' Martha said quietly, absently picking up one of Georgia's teddy bears and hugging it for comfort. Jane caught the movement out of the corner of her eye and the laughter died in her throat. 'Martha, I'm so sorry,' she said, her eyes wide with fear. Martha frowned, perplexed but Jane closed her eyes and collapsed back into her chair. 'I'm so sorry,' she whispered brokenly.

Martha stared at her in confusion. 'Well, so am I if David... Oh look, Jane, if there's anything I can do... What's the prognosis. Have they said?'

'He'll die,' Jane said, her voice remote, 'but that's not what concerns you.'

'Not what concerns me? What do you mean?' Martha's voice rose sharply. 'Jane, what do you mean?'

'David and Joe were lovers,' Jane said, staring into the fire, her back stiff and her hands clasped in her lap.

Martha stared at her in disbelief. 'For a moment I thought you said...'

'David and Joe were lovers,' Jane repeated.

Martha shook her head, frowning. 'It's not possible.'

'They were lovers,' Jane said emphatically. 'David told me everything.' She dropped her head, stared down at her hands. 'I can't forgive myself,' she whispered, 'for introducing you to Joe.'

'But Joe's all right,' Martha said, her voice rising. 'Joe doesn't have AIDS.'

Jane looked at Martha, her face bleak. 'How do you know?' she said simply. 'Did you take precautions?'

Martha's face was ashen and she began to shake violently. 'Take precautions?' she said. 'No, of course not. We were in love with one another. We wanted to have a baby together.' She stared at Jane, gave a sudden, sharp cry. 'A baby!' She looked unseeingly round the room, her eyes blank with horror. 'Oh, my God, Georgia.'

Jane winced. 'I'm almost certain that Joe didn't give it to David,' she said quickly. 'So Georgia might be fine.'

Martha stared at her in appalled fascination. 'Might?' she said unsteadily. '*Might?*'

Jane looked away. 'David received a letter from one of his…' she paused, took a deep breath… 'from one of his lovers. In it he explained that he was HIV positive and that David must go immediately and be tested. He went for the tests.'

Martha gazed at her in disbelief. 'How long ago was this?'

'About eighteen months,' Jane whispered.

'And it was positive?'

'He never went back for the results. And he gave…he gave a false name.'

'A false name,' Martha whispered hopelessly.

'They were very careful.'

'Careful!' Martha exclaimed, starting to her feet and walking agitatedly around the room, her hands clasping and unclasping. She looked at Jane who gave a silent, helpless shrug which provoked Martha to run at her, grabbing her by the shoulders and shaking her furiously. 'Careful! Do you know what you've just said? Your precious husband knew he had AIDS even when he was fucking Joe who he *knew* was fucking me.' She began to laugh hysterically. 'It was you who set me up, to take the heat off David.'

Jane gazed at her in horror. 'I never knew,' she whispered. 'It was my idea but he was so pleased when I suggested…'

'Of course he was pleased!' Martha shouted, shaking her savagely. 'He didn't want you to know he was a homosexual, you stupid cow!'

Jane closed her eyes, let her body go limp in Martha's hands. 'He doesn't believe he's a homosexual,' she said brokenly.

'He doesn't *what?*'

Jane said nothing but on her face there was an

expression of such profound despair that Martha, after staring at her in disbelief, let out a great sigh then gently removed her hands from her shoulders. She walked quietly over to the window and stared down at the street, at the Christmas shoppers coming back from the market, their arms filled with bright, bulging parcels. Two men dragged a Christmas tree down the road, laughing and shouting as they swept people off the pavement with its feathery branches. A small child ran after them, screaming with excitement and clapping her hands in joy.

Martha watched the child, her face pressed against the window until her warm breath misted the cold glass and she could no longer see. She turned away, smoothing her pink and silver net skirts tenderly, carefully readjusting the tinsel wound at her wrists. 'Now my make-up's ruined,' she said brokenly. 'And I was going to be such a lovely fairy for Georgia.' She turned to look at Jane, her pale eyes glittering in her smudged, comic clown's face. 'I hate David,' she said quietly. 'If anything happens to Georgia, I'll never… I hope he dies. God forgive me, but I want him to die.'

Jane flinched slightly and bowed her head. 'Don't worry,' she said. 'He will.'

31

Phil was hurrying back to the office with her lunch, tuna mayonnaise on brown, cappuccino no sugar, and an apple, when she was struck by a fierce premonition that something was wrong with Martha. The force of her instinct was so strong that she felt as if she had been struck a physical blow. As she stood hesitating on the pavement, a taxi drew up beside her and within minutes, feeling slightly foolish, she was sitting in a traffic jam on Oxford Street.

A poinsettia, pathetically festive, its rain-spattered scarlet leaves bleeding into a wrapper of white tissue, stood on the landing outside Martha's door. Phil picked it up and rang the bell. When there was no reply she was not much surprised; after all, it was a weekday and Martha would be at the studio working. She stared down in bewilderment at her arms, filled with the poinsettia, the now damp sandwich, its pink innards oozing into the white paper bag in which it was wrapped and the leaking polystyrene cup of coffee. Unused to obeying her instincts, she was convinced that they were foolish and was just bending to replace the poinsettia on the step when she heard a slight scuffle behind the door. Georgia's high voice pierced the silence, announcing importantly, 'Knock door, knock door.'

'Georgia?' she called. The scuffling stopped abruptly. Phil could not repress a smile as she imagined the child's small, sturdy body poised behind the door, her

278

head cocked as she listened intently. 'Georgia, darling, it's Phil,' she said loudly. 'Go and tell Mummy I'm here.' Still there was silence and Phil began to grow alarmed, imagining all manner of things, that Martha had fallen and was lying unconscious in the flat, that she had been burgled, perhaps raped and left for dead while Georgia... She looked quickly at the door to check for signs of forced entry. Seeing none, she relaxed slightly but could not keep the shrill agitation from her voice as she called again to the child.

Suddenly, there was the sound of more excited scuffling and Georgia's high treble diminishing as she scuttled away from the door calling, 'Mummy, pill, pill,' and then Martha's low, murmured protest that no, it couldn't possibly be Phil. Phil was at the office, but if they must go and look then she supposed that they would have to, all this growing louder until finally the door was inched open and Martha peered out at her, her pale eyes slightly unfocused, as if she had just been roused from a deep sleep. 'Phil,' she said, smiling vaguely.

'Were you asleep?' Martha shook her head and, turning, moved with small, fumbling steps back into the flat, Georgia tottering unsteadily after her, her scarlet stockinged feet scrabbling to find purchase on the polished wooden floor. Phil followed them slowly. 'I found this outside,' she said, her voice loud and forced, as she looked around for somewhere to deposit the plant, its leaves like a red feather duster, startling against her navy coat. Seeing a space on the table amid a pile of wrapping paper and ribbons, she made her way purposefully towards it. Martha sank into a rocking chair and watched her distantly.

Phil laughed; a high, strained sound. 'I know it sounds silly,' she said, 'but I had the strangest feeling that something was wrong.'

Martha gave a dim smile then laid her head against the chair and closed her eyes. The chair squeaked in protest as she set it to a slow rhythmic rocking. Glancing at her worriedly, Phil ducked down to kiss Georgia who had retired to her favourite place under the table and was busily stuffing scarlet tissue paper into her mouth. 'So I just thought I'd pop in and see my favourite girl,' she said brightly. She carefully unpeeled a strip of scarlet tissue which had become stuck to Georgia's plump cheek. 'Don't, darling,' she murmured, 'you'll get covered in dye. Look, you've gone and got lipstick and rouge on you.' She kissed her downy head, gently rubbing her lips over the flaxen wisps, then tried to extricate the tissue paper from her insistent grasp, gently uncurling the plump fingers which as quickly clamped tight shut to a chorus of protesting squeals. Phil glanced at Martha doubtfully. 'Well, if your mother says it's OK then I suppose it is,' she said, to Georgia's evident triumph.

Martha squinted down at Georgia. 'She'll be fine,' she said vaguely.

Phil went and sat in a chair, her large protuberant eyes darting anxiously across Martha's face, noticing how pale and drawn she was. 'But you're not?' she asked quietly. 'Have you been overdoing it? I know how exhausting Christmas can be with a small...'

'It's nothing to do with her,' Martha said, waving a hand in Georgia's direction. 'Well, it is, but not like that.' She stared at Georgia, blinking slightly as she opened her mouth as if to say something, then closed it abruptly.

Phil felt a sharp prickle of alarm. 'What's happened?' she asked.

Martha opened her mouth again to speak but then her lips crumpled to a broken pink line and she stared at Phil, shaking her head helplessly, her eyes bright with fear.

'It's all right,' Phil said quickly. 'Tell me when you can. There's no hurry. Shall I make us both some tea?'

Martha smiled faintly. 'That would be nice,' she said in a passable semblance of her normal voice. Phil hugged her briefly then bent down to check on Georgia, now absorbed by a pink and gold plastic angel whose blue plastic blobs of eyes she was busily trying to gouge out. The angel stared up at her, unmoved. When Phil returned with the tea, Martha seemed more composed. 'Sorry,' she said, as Phil handed her a mug.

'Don't be,' Phil said, and they sank into silence, sipping tea and watching Georgia experiment with the angel, skimming it across the floor or flying it high above her head making vague aeroplane noises.

'I think Joe disappeared because he has AIDS,' Martha said suddenly, in a gentle, apologetic voice.

Phil felt the floor tilt and teeter crazily and then right itself again but when she looked around the room everything seemed slightly, yet perceptibly, off balance. Her eyes caught a slight movement, a flash of scarlet, and she glanced fearfully at Georgia who had found the tissue paper she had earlier abandoned and was shredding it, sprinkling it all around her so it lay like bright drops of blood on the polished wooden floor.

'I'm sorry,' Martha said eventually.

Phil frowned fiercely, struggling to remain composed. 'How do you know?' she managed finally, in a strained, unfamiliar voice.

Martha explained how Jane had come to see her. 'I was dressed as a fairy,' she said inconsequentially.

Phil shook her head in bewilderment. 'David?'

Martha laughed sharply. 'Yes, he's a fairy, too,' she said without humour.

'Don't,' Phil said fiercely. 'Please don't.'

Martha was quiet for a bit. 'We went for tests,' she said eventually, her voice distant. 'It was almost surreal because the clinic was so normal. You know, that same dirty cream gloss they always use on hospital walls and half-dead potted plants and even the woman at reception, fat and bored and cross because she hadn't got her Christmas shopping done. It made it all right somehow,' she added vaguely, 'her being bored.' What she didn't say was that the nurse had made her cry, her young, round face flushed with pity as she'd gently pushed the needle into Georgia's plump thigh. 'There's a good, brave girl,' she said, deftly stopping Georgia's protesting mouth with a jelly baby and silently handing Martha a white tissue across the baby's wispy curls.

'Christ,' Phil said, and fell silent. Then the room tilted suddenly again and Harry's face, set in the expression of quiet, fierce joy he had worn since Georgia was born, spun before her eyes. 'Harry?' she whispered, her voice seeming to come from some distant place.

'I'm pretty sure he's fine,' Martha said, starting at Phil's low moan of relief. 'Are you all right?' Phil nodded, unable to speak. Martha glanced away, flushing slightly. 'We didn't make love, at least not until after Georgia was born. I couldn't, you see, it felt so odd when I was carrying another man's child. And I wanted to be sure that we were back together because... well, just because it was *right*, I suppose. I thought perhaps he had come back out of pity. And then later when we...' She hesitated. 'Well, after Georgia was born we didn't want another child, at least not until we can afford one, so we've always used condoms.'

'Why didn't you tell me before? I would have come to the hospital with you.'

'I didn't *want* you to come with us,' Martha said bitterly, her face white and set.

Phil looked at her, startled. 'Why not?'

Martha shook her head helplessly. 'I thought you might blame me,' she said in a low, strained voice. 'I couldn't bear to tell you that I might have killed…' She broke off and stared blankly at Georgia who, alerted by the change in her mother's voice, looked up from the plastic angel whose candid blue gaze she had adjusted to a leering squint, her plump face crumpled in a worried frown. Martha managed a watery, reassuring smile. 'It's all right, darling,' she said. 'Do you want some ice?'

Georgia flapped her hands excitedly. 'Ith, ith,' she chanted.

'Her new thing is sucking ice,' Martha explained, smiling faintly in answer to Phil's bemused expression. She got heavily to her feet. 'I'll just go and get her some. It'll keep her quiet for hours. Or at least until it melts.' She came back with a plastic beaker filled with crushed ice which Georgia grabbed eagerly, her face crumpling in concentration as she picked up pieces between a delicate finger and thumb and dropped them gingerly into her small pink mouth.

Martha sank back down into her chair. 'If I am HIV positive,' she said, watching her, 'there's only a thirty per cent chance that she will be too.'

'Oh,' said Phil, both startled and relieved.

Martha smiled faintly. 'Yes, it's better than you think.'

'And you?' Phil faltered.

'They reckon it's about the same. It depends on the virulence of that particular strain of the virus and also on my susceptibility.' She grimaced. 'We just have to hope I've got a strong immune system. Jane's negative. At least, so far.'

'But wouldn't you know?' Phil said urgently. 'Surely there'd be symptoms?'

Martha looked at her sadly. 'Once there are it means you've…' She took a deep, shaky gulp of air. 'There are people who are thought to have been positive for six years, since the virus was first isolated. And then there are people who die within a year of contracting it.' She looked away. 'Nobody knows.'

'And Georgia?'

'Good news and bad. The good news is that she's old enough for us to be definitely sure, either way. And the bad news is that if she's positive...' She broke off, blinking, and looked down at Georgia, scowling fiercely. 'A lot of them die.'

Phil watched Georgia sucking unconcernedly on the ice, her little bud of a mouth stung bright pink with the cold, her gaze blue and serene as she watched the two women talk.

'How's Harry taking it?'

Martha frowned. 'I haven't told him. Oh, I can't,' she protested, seeing Phil's startled face. 'He's so happy. He adores Georgia. If anything happened to her I don't think he'd...' She uttered a sharp moan of despair. Georgia's face flushed delicately, her limpid eyes rounding in puzzlement as she stared doubtfully at her mother.

'Martha,' Phil warned quietly.

Martha glanced at Georgia, forcing a smile to her face. 'I'll be all right,' she said in a strained voice. 'Just give me a minute.'

'You're going to have to tell him.'

Martha turned to look at Phil, eyes brilliant with fear. 'Not yet. As soon as I'm sure about Georgia.'

Phil looked uneasy.

Martha shrugged, her body slumping with despair. 'I got us into this,' she said in a low voice.

'Don't punish yourself,' Phil said sharply. 'It does no good.'

Martha glanced at her, then looked quickly away. 'You don't hate me, do you?'

Phil stared at her. 'Why should I hate you?'

'Because if I hadn't...' Martha shook her head, buried

284

her face in her hands. 'If I hadn't gone off with Joe,' she continued in a low voice, 'then none of this would have happened. I can't forgive myself,' she cried, rocking her body to and fro. 'I can't, I can't.'

'If you hadn't met Joe, you wouldn't have Georgia,' said Phil, going to put her arms around Martha and hugging her hard. 'And I might not forgive you for that.'

'But what if I've…' She raised her head and stared at Phil, her pale eyes darkening with horror. 'Oh, God, Phil, I can't stop thinking I might have killed her.'

'Well you must stop. It won't help any of you, torturing yourself like this. Anyway, you don't *know* yet. It'll be better when the results come through.'

'You mean then I'll know I've killed her,' Martha said bitterly.

'No. I mean that fear is worse than certainty.'

'But what if I have? What will I do then?' Her whole body shuddered. 'I really don't think I can bear this.'

Georgia, hearing the shrill fear threading through her mother's voice, looked up, her wide, placid brow creased in a frown. 'Mummy?' she said doubtfully. 'Mummy?' Martha stared at her, her eyes wide and unseeing. Georgia's face began to redden and crumple uncertainly. 'Mummy?' she pleaded, stumbling to her feet and tottering unsteadily across to Martha's chair. She began desperately to pluck at her mother's limp, cold hands. Martha looked at her helplessly, tears coursing unchecked down her face; from deep within her throat came a low, inhuman wail of despair.

'Come and look at this lovely book,' Phil said, quickly scooping Georgia into her arms. She hurried with her to the far side of the room. Georgia whimpered, struggling to see around Phil's body. 'Mummy.' Her voice was shrill with fear. 'Mummy.'

'Look at the lovely pictures,' Phil persisted, flicking through the brightly coloured pages of a book about farmyard animals and finding a picture of a duck, Georgia's favourite creature. Georgia stared down at the page, her attention momentarily captured, but as Phil looked at it with her, seeing the duck's round beachball of a body, its comic, stubby wings and its round, startled eye, its pathetic innocence seemed to her unbearable and she felt her mind go dark with horror. 'Duck!' Georgia announced loudly in her ear so that Phil started and said unsteadily, 'Yes, darling, a lovely yellow duck. And look, here's a cow. What does a cow say?' An uncertain smile flickered briefly on Georgia's face but then she remembered Martha and began to squirm and struggle in a desperate, pathetic effort to see her mother's face. Phil was astounded by the strength and resilience of her pliant little body. She cannot die, she thought fiercely, feeling the silken smoothness of the chubby arms tangling around her neck. She *will* not die. They heard a faint noise from the other side of the room and turned to see Martha smiling at them.

'Moooo,' Martha said, holding out her arms. 'That's what a cow says, isn't it, darling?' She hugged Georgia fiercely. 'See, darling? It's all right. Mummy was just being silly, making that funny noise.'

32

There was a note, hurriedly scrawled in a child's pink wax crayon. 'Can't wait. Sorry. Georgia's in a tearing hurry to get to the swings. Come and join us. Love.' Phil smiled faintly, seeing the familiar signature, the rolling lines of the initial encased in a lopsided heart.

Next to the note, propped up carefully against a tubby blue vase of orange roses, was a brown envelope, not very big. So it's finally arrived, Phil thought, feeling vaguely affronted by its ordinariness. What had she expected? Not this small brown rectangle with its window of milky cellophane, the letter shoved back carelessly so it showed only half an address and above it, three neat lines printed in blood red ink; St Mary's Hospital, Praed Street, London W2 1NY.

She stood motionless, staring at the red letters until they began to waver and run, leaking their ink one into the other. A tear trickled down her cheek and splashed on to the table top. Smudging it absently with her thumb she saw a dark stain bleed into the pale wood. Is there anything more pathetic, she thought, than a death sentence sent by second-class post?

Eventually she let out a tiny, broken sigh and picking up the envelope, cradled it tenderly in her small, elegant hands. This is the future, she thought with mild astonishment. I hold the future in my hands. She didn't open it, knowing that it wasn't hers to read, but stood with it pressed against her heart as she stared out of the dusty window across to the pub on the opposite corner of the street. Across the windows somebody had scrawled a Christmas message in artificial snow. The white powder was dried and flaked, falling like dandruff on the shoulders of the window ledge, leaving only the word Happy, faded and scratchy but not yet lost.

She placed the envelope back on the table, propping it carefully against the flowers. As she turned to walk away, her foot caught one of Georgia's yellow plastic ducks, sending it spinning across the polished floorboards. The noise startled her and she hurried to pick it up, closing her eyes as she pressed her lips tenderly against the cold, unyielding plastic of the duck's orange beak. Opening her eyes, she stared at it in bemusement for a second then, with a quick movement, thrust it into the bottom of her bag.

It was not far to walk, yet it seemed to her the longest journey she had ever taken. In fifteen minutes, she thought, my life might change irrevocably, shattered by a smear of blood and a neatly typed slip of paper. As she trudged slowly down Elgin Avenue she wondered, with a faint, injured sense of propriety, how tragedy could appear in such little, unremarkable guises. She saw herself, a cautious, ordinary woman in her neat navy coat carefully buttoned over a paisley silk scarf, brown leather boots gleaming with polish, plain, knitted wool gloves, a leather bag swinging carelessly from one shoulder.

She wondered what people thought as they saw her walking down the street. Do they say, when they look at me, see that woman? Yes, that one, over there, the one in the navy coat and brown boots. She is going to meet her destiny.

No, of course not, she thought. They'd never imagine that, would think, if they thought about me at all, that I was on my way to do some shopping, pay a visit to the bank, perhaps to drop in on a friend for lunch. All around me are people dressed as I am, ordinary people in unremarkable clothes going about their daily business. Over there a woman in a brown suede jacket, an expensive silk blouse, grey trousers flapping idly at her nylon ankles, a man hurrying past, plunging into the dark, litter-blown mouth of the Tube, his suit wrinkled, his tie slightly awry, and there, shuffling her way across the zebra crossing, a woman in a pink cardigan and dirty yellow slippers, once fluffy but now bald with age. She wondered what tragedies lay behind those normal, everyday faces. Perhaps chance had touched them too, bowled down their dreams like nine-pins.

There is no such thing, she thought, as an ordinary life.

She heard the shout before she saw her, heard her joyful cry echo, piercingly sweet, across the bleak, windswept park. 'She's negative, she's negative.' Phil stopped, frozen in her tracks, and then she saw her, a tiny figure in the middle of an empty playground, jumping up and down, arms raised in a crazy victory dance as Georgia, a bundle of pink with a dot of flaxen hair, yelled with laughter on the swing behind her. 'She's the most positive negative baby in the history of testing,' Martha shouted, using her hands cupped around her mouth to form a megaphone. 'She's brilliant, a genius, the most wonderful, gorgeous baby ever born. Dance, Phil, dance,' she yelled, capering madly around the frame of the swings. 'Come and dance with me.'

Phil danced, the wind and happiness tearing at her eyes as she skipped and scrambled across the frozen ground, her silk scarf streaming behind her, the buttons of her coat tearing loose. 'I'm coming,' she shouted, her cry snatched by the wind and hurled back in her face as she ran, as fast as her legs would carry her, fumbling to undo the catch on the playground gate, laughing as she slipped and skidded across the chipped bark surface, falling into Martha's arms, and the two of them spinning in a wild waltz around the swings while Georgia threw back her head and laughed, clapping her hands with joy to see them.

'Champagne,' Martha panted, running to her bag from which she pulled a half bottle, uncorking it with a frothy gush, while Phil went to Georgia and covered her plump, dimpled face with kisses. 'Pill, Pill,' Georgia crowed triumphantly, patting clumsily at Phil's cold cheeks with warm, urgent hands. 'Here,' Martha said, thrusting the freezing bottle into her hand. 'Let's drink to life.' Phil tilted her head and closed her eyes, felt the cold champagne pour into her mouth and explode like stars in her throat and she thought that never in her dreams had she tasted anything like that sweet, foaming pleasure.

'Drunk in charge of an angel,' Martha laughed, bending to form her mouth to a kiss as Georgia swung towards her and Georgia puckered her mouth too so they kissed in the air, screaming again with laughter as the swing bore her away, pushed her in the air and sent her swinging back again to her mother and another kiss. 'Smart stuff, hey?' Martha laughed, glancing at Phil proudly.

'Brilliant,' Phil agreed, dancing around the swings, the champagne bottle held aloft. 'You're brilliant, both of you. Brilliant, brilliant, brill...' As she spun past them, she caught sight of Martha's fading smile and the words caught in her throat. She stopped abruptly, felt the world tilt and then collide in a blur of heaven and earth; sky and ground both rushed to meet her as she teetered crazily on one leg, caught in mid-pirouette. Martha's face, pale and anxious, her pink mouth trembling in an uncertain smile, hovered dimly behind Georgia's plump, rosy cheeks, appearing and disappearing as the swing curved slowly through the air. Phil felt happiness evaporate like a mist and she took a few, shuffling uncertain steps, clutched on to the railing for support, feeling the cold metal bite into her bare hands. 'You are *both* negative?' she whispered, her voice hoarse.

'Not me, I'm afraid,' Martha said. 'Oh, Phil, don't look like that. *Don't.* It'll be all right. I might be one of the lucky ones.' She laughed suddenly, her voice lifting triumphantly. 'I *am* one of the lucky ones. Don't you see? If Georgia had been positive then what meaning would my life have had anyway? I would rather die, knowing that I'd killed my only child. Be glad for us, Phil. Phil?'

Phil's head filled with noise and she wondered if this was how the future would be, drowned in the remnants of a half-remembered life, all sense and colour lost save for Martha's dear, familiar face forever imprinted on her mind, the fading pinks and golds and blue of distant happiness. She opened her mouth to speak but no sound came out.

Martha's voice rang through the still, frozen air like a warning. 'Be happy, Phil.'

Phil's mouth trembled. 'I'll be happy,' she whispered.

Martha watched her for a moment and then nodded. 'Good. Then let's go and get a cup of tea.'

They walked slowly across the hard, frozen ground to a scattering of wooden benches and trestle tables.

Martha looked dubiously at the low, dismal cafe. 'Doesn't look very cheerful in there,' she said. 'Let's have it out here. Georgia would prefer it anyway.'

'You won't be too cold?' Phil asked anxiously.

A glimmer of exasperation flashed dimly in Martha's face but she said nothing, only raised a laconic eyebrow.

'OK, I'll get the tea then,' Phil said quickly, and plunged into the damp warmth of the cafe, the air sour and heavy with rancid chip fat and stale cigarette smoke. 'Yeah?' said a bored girl, emerging reluctantly from the kitchen and slouching to the counter. 'Two teas? Righty-ho.' She slopped stewed tea into two poly-styrene cups and slammed a jug of milk down next to them. 'Nice day for it,' she said, jerking her head at the grey sky which lowered dimly beyond the condensa-tion spattered windows.

Phil agreed politely that it was and went back outside. Martha smiled briefly when she gave her the cup of tea but said nothing and the two of them sat in silence, watching Georgia rushing busily to and fro between the warped wooden benches, cheeks pink with cold and the pleasure of some intricate, private game involving an old crisp packet, her mother's door keys and a few wisps of grass. Eventually she grew bored and went to her mother, in search of entertainment. Spying Phil's entic-ing, familiar handbag, she dragged it over to the grass and delved her arm into it, emerging, with squeals of triumph, clutching a yellow plastic duck. 'Duck!' she yelled, 'duck! duck!' scampering away with it across the lawn.

'Is that yours?' Martha asked, staring after Georgia in astonishment.

Phil flushed painfully. 'I stole it from the flat,' she said. 'I'm sorry.'

Martha frowned in confusion then, noticing Phil's flushed, miserable face, said, in a teasing voice, 'If I'd known about you and plastic ducks, I'd have bought you your very own.'

Phil tried to laugh, her mouth twitching in a nervous grin, the corners jerking spasmodically as she fought to keep it turned to a smile but eventually the effort proved too much and her face crumpled, her mouth hanging open in helpless grief as she began silently to cry. 'I th-, th-, thought that if Georgia died...' she sobbed, pluck-ing frantically at a buttonhole on her coat as the tears streamed down her face and splashed on to the dark wool. 'It sounds so stupid,' she wailed, her words scarcely audible, 'but I found it on the floor of the sitting room, looking so forlorn all by itself that I wanted to keep it, look after it. You know how she loves ducks.' She looked up, her face contorted in anguish. 'Sorry,' she said, tears strangling her as she gasped for breath, 'I know I should be brave for you but I can't bear it. I just can't bear it.' She grabbed Martha by both arms, felt her warm flesh through the velvet of her coat, shook her frantically then fumbled at her face with urgent hands. 'Please don't leave me,' she sobbed, tears streaming into her helpless, open mouth, 'Please, please, *please*...'

Martha gathered her up in her arms, stroked the neat, shining head, rocking her as gently as she would Georgia. 'There, there,' she murmured, 'it'll be all right. It's the finding out that's the worst. It'll be easier from here, you'll see.'

Phil sat up and blew her nose furiously. 'I'm sorry,' she said sullenly, 'I'm behaving appallingly badly.'

Martha smiled faintly. 'Makes a change.' She hesitated, and said quietly, 'Phil, would you do something for me?'

Phil sniffed, wiping angrily at her pale, swollen face. 'Anything,' she mumbled.

'Will you pretend that there's nothing wrong with me? I feel fine at the moment but I know I won't if you all go round behaving as if I'm dying. Promise me, no pitying glances, no family conferences, no special treatment, and especially, no chicken soup.'

Phil hesitated, uncertainty glimmering on the pale oval of her face. Then she looked at Martha and saw how the strain of the past few weeks had taken its toll in the fine lines drawn around her eyes, the faint, bruised smudges beneath her eyes, and from somewhere she found a voice, loud and bright and cheerful. 'Have you ever tasted my chicken soup?' she said, grinning.

'Yes. That's why I mention it. It nearly killed me last time.'

They glanced at each other uncertainly and then they began to laugh, the laughter building until they were helpless with it, clutching on to each other as tears ran down their faces.

'Funny Mummy,' Georgia said, beaming. 'Silly Pilly,' as she plucked wildly at tufts of grass with fat little hands. Every time she succeeded in picking one, she crowed triumphantly and stuffed it into her mouth. 'Georgia,' Martha called, her voice light with laughter, 'don't eat the grass.' Georgia smiled and popped a green strand into her mouth. Walking over to her, Martha squatted down next to her and began softly to sing. 'Picking up the daisies, picking up the daisies, atishoo, atishoo, we all jump up!' Georgia made a final desperate grab at the grass and jumped up on cue, applauding herself furiously. Martha scooped her up in her arms and looked down at Phil while Georgia, scowling with concentration, tried to stuff a piece of old crisp packet into her mother's ear. 'Look after her for me,' Martha said, ducking her head to avoid being deafened.

Phil nodded mutely.

'Promise,' Martha said fiercely.

'I promise.'

'And Harry too.'

Phil nodded again.

Georgia peered down at Phil from her vantage point in Martha's arms. 'All fall down,' she crowed, clapping wildly.

Martha, smiling radiantly, kissed her plump cheek. 'Very good, my angel.' She looked down at Phil, still smiling. 'You never know,' she said. 'I might be around for years yet.'

33

Martha died two years later. She was my mother.

It's not a happy ending but in a funny way, it makes me happy. I suppose it was the not knowing that made me imagine all sorts of crazy things, like she'd murdered somebody or had gone insane; was so mad or bad they wouldn't let me see her. In my lighter moments I thought she'd committed suicide but I didn't see why they'd make such a big deal about that.

Because I didn't know she was dead, not dead *dead*, even though they told me she was, I kept expecting her to turn up. I suppose I've been looking for her ever since I remember. That's the trouble with secrets, isn't it? They're black holes, a sort of freefall for the imagination.

I think Phil and Harry are surprised that I'm taking it so well, but then they don't know what's been going on in my head for fifteen years. What upsets me more is that they didn't tell me the truth in the first place, made such a big thing about it for all these years, as if an illness could be good or bad. Weird. I mean, would they have tip-toed around me, bursting like ripe plums with the truth, if she'd died of cancer? Would her cold-eyed friends still poke at me with their hard fingers if she'd died of multiple sclerosis? No chance.

When Martha died we moved into the flat with Phil. Me and Harry, that is. I was four at the time, or perhaps I was three because I left Martha when she got too sick to look after me. Phil says she kept me with her for as long as she could; I used to sleep in the big bed next to her, sometimes I'd be there all day, playing. She bought me a box of paints and one day Phil arrived to see her and found her shrieking with laughter, lying in white sheets splashed with cobalt and viridian and lemon and scarlet. I don't remember it, although sometimes the scent of freshly ironed sheets gives me a funny feeling and the smell of roses always mades me feel sort of weird and sad. Phil thinks it's because of the perfume Martha used to wear when she was very ill because she said she couldn't stand the smell of death, some precious essence of roses she got in Paris.

They seem happy enough, Phil and Harry. When Phil was telling me all that stuff about being in love with Harry, I asked her if she still was. She didn't say anything, just gave me this small, shy smile. I guess that means that she is, although she won't admit it. She's so fierce, Phil, in a really tender way.

Harry has his moods, of course. His Martha moods, Phil calls them. He still misses her and sometimes when he looks at me his face gets this look of unbearable yearning. When it gets really bad, he goes and sits in the rocking chair, swinging back and forth, like he's in some kind of torment. Phil's very gentle with him when he's like that, sort of shoos and shushes me round the flat.

He sometimes calls me by her name. He did it the other morning, when we were all standing in the kitchen. When he said it there was this awful silence, as if we were waiting for the word to land, standing round a deep well and straining to hear the splash. When it came it rippled through us like a shudder and then we all turned away as if we hadn't heard.

David died. I tried to hate him but I couldn't. Well, it's nice to have somebody to blame, isn't it? I thought about it very hard and in the end I decided that it wasn't his fault, because if we weren't all so dumb about sex then maybe he could have talked about it and been properly gay instead of sneaking around having affairs.

I don't think that's being – what's the word? Magnanimous. I think it's just what Phil calls Life. When she says that word it's always accompanied by a hopeless little shrug.

Harry still doesn't like me talking about Martha but it's taken me so long to find her that I'm not going to stop now. I guess this is going to sound dumb because, really, I never knew her. But I miss her, I miss her so *badly*. Mummy, mum, mother. I never had anybody to say that to so I try the words out all ways, roll them round my mouth like wine.

Martha is mine.

A Selected List of Fiction Available from Mandarin

While every effort is made to keep prices low, it is sometimes necessary to increase prices at short notice. Mandarin Paperbacks reserves the right to show new retail prices on covers which may differ from those previously advertised in the text or elsewhere.

The prices shown below were correct at the time of going to press.

☐	7493 0780 3	**The Hanging Tree**	Allan Massie	£5.99
☐	7493 1224 6	**How I Met My Wife**	Nicholas Coleridge	£5.99
☐	7493 1064 2	**Of Love and Asthma**	Ferdinand Mount	£5.99
☐	7493 1368 4	**Persistent Rumours**	Lee Langley	£4.99
☐	7493 1068 5	**Goodness**	Tim Parks	£4.99
☐	7493 1492 3	**Making the Angels Weep**	Helen Flint	£5.99
☐	7493 1364 1	**High on the Hog**	Fraser Harrison	£4.99
☐	7493 1216 5	**The Fringe Orphan**	Rachel Morris	£4.99
☐	7493 1510 5	**Evenings at Mongini's**	Rusell Lucas	£5.99
☐	7493 1509 1	**Fair Sex**	Sarah Foot	£5.99
☐	7493 1558 X	**Sunday Lunch**	Nora Naish	£5.99
☐	7493 1831 7	**Landing on Clouds**	Olivia Fane	£5.99
☐	7493 1518 0	**The Ex-Wives**	Deborah Moggach	£4.99
☐	7493 1747 7	**Fluffy Butch**	Eda Zahl	£4.99
☐	7493 1599 7	**Friends and Lovers**	Mary Bernard	£5.99
☐	7493 1319 6	**Air and Angels**	Susan Hill	£5.99

All these books are available at your bookshop or newsagent, or can be ordered direct from the address below. Just tick the titles you want and fill in the form below.

Cash Sales Department, PO Box 5, Rushden, Northants NN10 6YX.
Fax: 0933 410321 : Phone 0933 410511.

Please send cheque, payable to 'Reed Book Services Ltd.', or postal order for purchase price quoted and allow the following for postage and packing:

£1.00 for the first book, 50p for the second; **FREE POSTAGE AND PACKING FOR THREE BOOKS OR MORE PER ORDER.**

NAME (Block letters) ....

ADDRESS ....

....

☐ I enclose my remittance for ....

☐ I wish to pay by Access/Visa Card Number

☐☐☐☐☐☐☐☐☐☐☐☐☐☐☐☐☐☐

Expiry Date ☐☐☐☐

Signature ....

Please quote our reference: MAND